THE
FORERUNNER
FACTOR

WITHDRAWN

Baen Books
by Andre Norton

Time Traders

Time Traders II

Star Soldiers

Warlock

Janus

Darkness & Dawn

Gods & Androids

Dark Companion

Masks of the Outcasts

Moonsinger

Crosstime

From the Sea to the Stars

Star Flight

Search for the Star Stones

The Game of Stars and Comets

Deadly Dreams

Moonsinger's Quest

The Forerunner Factor

THE
FORERUNNER
FACTOR

Andre Norton

THE FORERUNNER FACTOR

A Baen Books Original

Baen Publishing Enterprises
P.O. Box 1403
Riverdale, NY 10471
www.baen.com

ISBN: 978-1-4516-3808-0

Cover art by Tom Kidd

First Baen paperback printing, March 2012

Distributed by Simon & Schuster
1230 Avenue of the Americas
New York, NY 10020

Library of Congress Cataloging-in-Publication Data

Norton, Andre.
  [Forerunner]
  The forerunner factor / by Andre Norton.
     p. cm.
  "A Baen Books original"--T.p. verso
  ISBN 978-1-4516-3808-0 (trade pb)
  I. Title.
  PS3527.O632F6 2012
  813'.54--dc23
                                        2011045755

Printed in the United States of America

10 9 8 7 6 5 4 3 2 1

 CONTENTS

FORERUNNER

1

Kuxortal had always been—any trader would have sworn by his guild oath to that. No one had the need to dig deep into the mouldering wet-season, dry-season records (many layers of which had long since become dust, and dust of dust) to know that. The sprawling city stood on its own past, now well above the sea wharves and river landings, raised high on the mount of its own beginnings as men had tirelessly built on the ruins of other men's warehouses and dwellings, adding to the height of that mountain as the past leveled the holdings of their forebears.

The city had already been immeasurably old when the first needle ships of the space farers, those merchants of the stars who sewed together world upon world with their own trading ventures, had set down upon the plain beyond.

Kuxortal was old, but it did not die. Its citizens had become an incredible mixture of races—sometimes of species—or mutations and new beginnings of life forms springing out of old. Kuxortal had been favored ages ago by the fact that it had come to birth at the meeting of the river Kux, which drew upon the trade of a full continent, wafting boats and rafts to the western sea, with that same sea. The harbor was a safe one even during the worst of the wet-season gales. Its natural protections added to by the ingenuity of generations of men who knew all the perils of sea and wind, of gale and raider attack.

Once more, it was favored when the starmen came seeking not

only trade, but an open port where those who dealt in commodities which they dared not be subject to strict legal inspection might buy and sell in complete freedom—once the proper dues had been paid to the Guilds of the city. Now it had been well over tens of double seasons that rocket fire had scorched the plain beyond the town, and no one any longer marveled at the sight of an alien on the crooked streets which sometimes formed a deadly maze for the unwary.

For where there are traders and their riches, there are also predators. They also had their Guild, their standing in the hierarchy of Kuxortal, it being an old belief that if a man did not guard his own possessions, then he well deserved to lose them. Thus, wily thieves and private guardsmen fought small secret battles, and the peacemen of the Guild kept safe by the rigor of their instant and bloody justice only those streets, those courtyard homes, those trading depots which paid peace tax.

Just as there were thieves to prey upon the riches of Kuxortal, so were there also the small traders, those who lived like ver-rats in a grainery where there was no winged and clawed zorsal to go a-hunting, aided by dark-piercing eyesight. These, too, bought and sold, and perhaps some of them dreamed of making the big sale, the big find in the drift of strange merchandise, which would give them a chance to rise to greater profits.

Simsa was Burrow-wise enough not to dream big dreams—at least not enough to cloud the here and now.

She understood her very lowly place in the general scheme of life where she was near as small as a gamlin and certainly as agile as those furred creatures who were used by the Lovers-of-the-dark in their own raiding parties. She had no people as kin—being, as she had known as far back as any child learns of the world about, one of those strange mixtures of blood and breed which added to the general difference of Kuxortal. Also knowing that her very strangeness made her vulnerable, and so disguising that strangeness as best she could.

She had been fetcher and errand runner for Ferwar—until the mists of the riverside burrow bit so far into Old One's crippled bones that her body at last gave up its spirit essence. Simsa it had been who dragged that light, twisted body down to the under holes and heaped over it there the cover stones. Ferwar had had no kin, and was somewhat shunned even by the Burrow dwellers, for she was learned in strange ways—some of which might be profitable, others hinting of danger.

That Simsa was blood kin to herself Ferwar had denied. However, it was true that she never beat the child with her staff, much as she lashed out with an acid and biting tongue; also, she passed on to Simsa much which would have surprised even a Guild Lord had one known where or what lived in the Burrows beneath his own palace-of-plenty.

The Burrowers were perhaps the least and lowliest of Kuxortal dwellers. They scooped out their dwellings from the mass of former buildings, sometimes being lucky enough to break into a cellar or a passage which could have been a long forgotten street, roofed over by buildings fallen during some raider assault before the dawn of time. Things could be found in Burrows, things worth trading, especially to the Starmen, who seemed to take a perverse interest in broken bits which meant nothing to any denizen of Kuxortal. So such finds were close-held secrets and even among the Burrowers there were strongly defended treasure houses.

Simsa had her talents. Her agility had served her many times. Over and over, she practiced ever with her lean body the twists, turns, and certain grips which Ferwar's hands, cramped even as they were by the painful crippling, had patiently shown her. As a Burrower, she was small, though two seasons after the death of Ferwar, she had suddenly shot up like a well-watered thrum vine. It was in that same season that she had changed her style of drab clothing, for Ferwar had been emphatic with certain warnings for the future. The loose smock she had always worn over breeches, which had left her legs free for running and dodging, was not laid aside. However, under it she had wound a strip of stout chir cloth tightly about her body from waist up, constraining her breasts to give her still a childish flatness. That was a precaution she need only take with strangers—to those who know her, her own natural weapons made her untouchable.

Simsa's skin was black, a deep bluish-black; in night darkness she could pad through any street which had no large number of lamps with a spirit's invisibility. On the other hand, her hair, which she now wore confined and covered with another length of cloth, was pure silver light, as were her brows and lashes. Those, she disguised with sooty fingers rubbed on a fire pot before she ventured out as she did, reveling in her ability to conceal herself.

She had her own form of steady livelihood, one begun when she had found a broken-winged zorsal fluttering out its life on a waterside rubbish heap—those mounds often provided unexpected finds for Ferwar. The zorsal had tried to bite—its sharp-edged jaws were strong enough to take a finger off a full-grown man. Simsa had not stretched forth any hand at first, had only squatted down beside the injured creature, crooning to it in a small guttural sound which came from far down in her throat and which she had never made before; at that moment, it had just come to her naturally as fit and right.

As the zorsal's first hissing and snapping subsided, and it settled down to watch her with huge, round, night-seeing eyes, the girl had perceived that it was a female, its furred body heavy with young. Perhaps it had broken out of some warehouse cage, striving to find a place in freedom in which to nest and bear its coming brood.

Though Simsa had had no reason in her short life to trust or show any liking for another living creature (her bond with Ferwar being one of respect, awe and more than a little straight wariness), she sensed now within her a reaching out for another living thing which was perhaps as lost as she from any kin-tie. As she crooned, she at last advanced a hand, was able to touch fingertips to the soft down which covered the zorsal's back, felt even there the fast pound of the flyer's heart. After long moments, the girl had been able to pick up the hurt creature, which nestled against her, giving Simsa a feeling such as she had never experienced before.

Zorsals were prized for ridding dwellings and storage places of larger vermin. She had seen them sold for solid sums in the markets and realized that she could now seek out the owner of this stray and perhaps claim a reward. Instead, she took it back to the Burrow, where Ferwar looked at it but said nothing at all. Simsa, prepared to defend her actions, had been left oddly at a loss.

The zorsal littered within a night of her discovery of it.

She had bound up its injured wing as best she could, but feared that her tending was so awkward it might remain a cripple. Ferwar had drawn her aching body away from the mat place to watch the girl's struggle, finally grunting as she brought out of her jealously guarded supplies some salve which smelled oddly fresh and clean in a cave-room never touched by light of day.

There were two young males. Simsa had been right in her fear concerning the complete recovery of the mother. On the other hand, the adult creature was surprisingly intelligent, in its own fashion, and after its cubs were weaned, it became Simsa's companion in her own night prowlings. Its eyesight was far keener than that of any human—even one trained as Simsa was, and it could communicate with a series of soft clicks which followed a pattern her own lips and throat could echo, so Simsa learned from it a small vocabulary of sounds which meant danger, hunger, others on the prowl, and the like.

In turn, the zorsal trained its own young. Then Simsa, after a careful study of the market rented—did *not* sell—the two to Gathar, a warehouse commander who had dealings with the Burrower people from time to time, and was rated by them as never taking more than half of any profit. She paid her charges visits at regular intervals, not only checking on their care, but also continuing to impress upon them her own personality. When she went forth on most nights, the parent (whom she named Zass from a sound which it uttered when striving to attract her attention) rode on her shoulder, she having fitted a pad there as protection between the strong talons of the hunter and her own flesh.

Not only did Gathar pay her for the use of the zorsals (which, he admitted once in an unusual burst of good nature after a very successful bit of trading, were very well suited to their job), but also her regular trips to his establishment gave her a familiarity with another section of Kuxortal into which she could not normally have ventured while those on duty there grew used to seeing her come and go; after a season, no one questioned her.

There were several among the Burrowers who had seen in Ferwar's death a chance to not only move into a snug and well situated lodging, but also marked Simsa down for bedmate . . . or profit. Traders from up-river—even some of the Guild Lords—liked curiosities in women now and then. There were certain suggestions which she brushed brusquely aside. Then one day, Basher of the Hook decided to play no more with the whims of a female and strode up to establish ownership in a way he had twice before. A small crowd gathered to watch the fun. Simsa, standing straight before the entrance of her Burrow, heard the calling of small wagers back and forth.

She was so much the smaller and slighter, a child in their eyes, that the bettors found very few who would take their offered rates in her favor. Baslter drank heavily from one of the pots his followers handed him, swiped the back of his hair-furred hand across his blubber lips, and advanced as might one of the fabled Tall Ones from the inner mountains.

He was still out of reaching distance of the girl when she went into action so fleetly and with such driving force that her body appeared raised by a whirlwind, rather than through any action of her own.

As her feet lifted from the ground, her bare toes unsheathed to strike full against the man's protruding belly, raking deeply through even the leather of his jerkin. At the same time, her body arched so that her hands struck the ground and, still raking upward with those claws, she somersaulted, rolled, and came lightly to her feet without more than a heavy intake of breath.

Baslter squalled. His hand going to the tatters of his jerkin came away red and wet. With the hook that gave him his second name he flailed out, prepared now to bury the metal in her flesh and jerk her close enough to crush the life from her with a single closing of his left fist upon her throat.

She was no longer there. As a zorsal might bait a pruhound, Simsa moved about the lumbering man. Not only did her toes unsheathe those claws which few of the Burrowers had ever seen, but her outspread fingers carried equally grim and punishing armament. She sprang, tore, was gone, before Baslter, now bellowing his rage, could even turn to face the direction in which some agile bound had taken her.

At last, streaming blood, having yielded an eye to the punishment, the man was caught by several of his fellows and towed back and away, frothing in a fury which had no sanity left in it. Simsa did not even watch his retreat, but went back into the home she had so defended, there to sit down, shaking a little and fighting within her to control, first her rage, and then the deeper-seated fear from which that rage had sprung. Zass fluttered her good wing, made small movements with the crooked one as, at last, the girl conquered herself enough to take up a cloth, wipe her claws thoroughly; then, with a wrinkled nose, toss the rag into the basket which must be taken to the dump place.

Her victory over Baslter did not inflict her with overconfidence. She was well aware that there were many ways she could be entrapped by a man subtle enough of thought, and she did not underrate her neighbors on that score. It was then that Simsa realized the true worth of Zass and began to make very sure she was with her on every night foray, and installed a perch above the door of her Burrow where the zorsal could keep sentry duty when Simsa was within.

That the creature was also wary enough to protect herself the girl became aware on the day when Zass fluttered and hopped to her with a piece of meat, red, raw, of a nature to tempt the appetite. Simsa accepted the strip, examined it closely, discovering within a bluish mark which, she had no doubt, meant poison. It was from that hour that she began to think more constructively of her own future, of what she might do to climb out of the Burrows where she must now be ever on constant alert, not only for her own safety but for that of the creature she had come to value very highly.

Life in Kuxortal was layered in castes as well as by the mound of the city itself. A Burrower might lurk on the fringe of one of the least of the markets with his or her collection of salvaged bits and pieces, but such a meager trader could not even aspire to the smallest and most primitive of stalls. Thus, most of their trading must be done either through the outlets of the Thieves' market, where they fared very badly indeed, or by trying to sell to a stall holder.

Since the coming of the skymen, there had been a second market established down by the edges of the fire-pocked field where their ships planted. But that was far too chancy to depend upon for any settled trading, since no one ever knew when one of the ships might arrive. Also, when it did, the rush was so great that few—only the very lucky—were able to get near enough to one of the crewmen to even show his wares. They might not hope to trade for the cargoes of such ships, those were haggled over by the Guilds, but crewmen often could be coaxed into buying strange odds and ends, carrying out small ventures of their own.

Simsa had made a habit of hanging about and watching such transactions, and thus she knew that what the starmen wanted most were curious things: old finds or objects which were particular to this world, and small enough to be easily stowed in what must be very crowded and limited space on board those ships, which had never been planned for the comfort of their crews, but rather to handle cargo valuable enough to make the long star flights profitable.

The cargoes they unloaded were varied also. Sometimes, such simply rested in some warehouse to be picked up again by another starship; in fact, that was most often the case. Simsa, from what she had overheard, was very sure that much of it was Thieves' loot from a score of worlds—to be sold where it could not be traced.

On the hour Zass had brought her the poisoned meat and she knew that perhaps she would not even last over the few days left of the season unless she made plans which could outscheme Baslter and others of his ilk (who now held her presence among them to be a personal affront), the girl turned out Ferwar's hidden treasures to examine them closely.

The old woman had had her own hiding places and most of those she had kept secret from Simsa also. But over the months since her death, with the aid of the zorsal's keen sight, the girl had managed to uncover a number of them.

Their burrow was one of those which had originally been a

portion of a house, long buried by debris from above. Simsa had often marveled at patches of painting which still clung to the walls in one corner and had wondered what it must have been like to have lived here when Kuxortal was lower and this house might have been even a portion of a High Lord's palace. The wall itself was of sturdy stones, set in careful pattern, yet not as solid as they looked.

Now, she pressed at points here and there and then slid out what appeared to be intact stones, but were in truth shells of such, behind which were hollows from which she garnered all the contents, to spread these gleanings out on the floor and survey them critically to judge their market values.

Some that she knew or guessed might be of great value, though only to special buyers, she had to regretfully push aside, for Ferwar had collected old writings, pieces of stone on which were carvings of broken length, a few pieces of rotting leather scrolls which she had protected as best she could. Simsa could spell out some of those words, having been lectured on their value when Ferwar was in a good mood. Only none of them made sense. Now she bundled all those together and packed them carefully into a sack. Valuable to no one else, such just might be of interest to some starman, but she knew she had little chance of finding such a buyer. However, this was her day to check on her charges. If Gathar was in a good mood, she could perhaps sell these to him at a price which might make her inwardly rage but would be more than she could raise by any effort of her own.

Placing the bag carefully to one side, she concentrated on the rest of the plunder she had uncovered. There was more hope of bargaining over this on her own.

These were the best of Ferwar's treasures and the Old One had never told where she found them, but Simsa remembered seeing them from her earliest days, thus they had been a long time in the old woman's possession. The girl had often wondered why the Old One had not made some bargain—perhaps directly with Zack who was known to be a runner for the Thieves' Guild and who was as honest as any such would be (especially if first he were blood sworn as Ferwar could insist, and had in the past).

There were two pieces of jewelry, a broken chain of thick links of silver—bearing at one end a long, narrow plaque set with pale stones. The other was a thick cufflike armlet certainly forged for the wearing of some man, also silver. It had a ragged break across it which destroyed part of an intricate pattern consisting of heads of outlandish monsters, most of which gaped wide to show fangs, those being insets of a crystalline, glittering stuff.

Both pieces came, Simsa was sure, from the far past. If she sold them to the wrong hands, they would go for the metal alone to be fed into some melting pot and so be forever lost. Something within her resisted the thought of that. She draped the necklet across her knee, and as she turned the armlet around in her hands, she thought.

There was one more thing—but that was her own find and she did not want to get rid of it. Also, it had come to her almost as a gift from Ferwar, though she was not silly enough to believe in such things. When she had gathered the rocks to pile over that thin and wasted body, she had seen a glint in the earth and scooped up what seemed to be a bit of metal, sticking it hurriedly in her belt pouch to be examined later.

Now, she brought this out, laying the armlet aside. It was a ring—but not a broad band, gem set, such as she had seen commonly worn in the upper city. In its way, it was cumbersomely made and awkward to wear. Still, as she slipped it now over her thumb (for that was the only finger it would fit), she eyed it with a fond feeling of possession. The band was fashioned of a silver metal, which apparently neither age nor exposure could darken or erode. Its form, jutting well up above the round of her own dark flesh, was that of a towered building wrought with minute detail—showing even a tiny stair which led to a doorway in one of the two towers. The smaller of those towers had been used to form the setting for a white-gray opaque stone as its roof. There was a vague hint in its styling of one or two of the more imposing buildings of the upper hill. Still, Simsa decided the ring was much older and of a time when there was much danger from raiders perhaps, and such structures were meant as positions of defense.

This was her own. It was not as beautiful as the other bits of jewelry, but something within her made her stare long each time she brought it forth. Sometimes, a queer idea crossed her mind that if she were able to lift the milky jewel which formed that roof on the second tower and peer within she would see—what? Strange forms of life busy about their own concerns? No, not this to be sold, she decided quickly as she rewrapped and returned it to her pouch.

Even as she put out a hand for the bag of Ferwar's fragments with the plan of going straightaway to Gathar's, there was a roar. The ground under her shook slightly, small bits of broken stone and dust shifted from over her head.

A starship had planeted.

Ferwar had spoken now and again of the luck which fate might dispose, even on those as lowly and portionless as the Burrow folk. Was this her luck arriving—so that on the very day, the moment when she had made up her mind to part with that which held the greatest worth, a ship had landed to offer her the best customers? She mumbled petitions to no gods, as some of those about her might. Ferwar had at times crouched over the fire basin, tossed a handful of larweed into the coals to puff out sweet smoke while chanting a sentence or two. However, the Old One had never explained to Simsa why she did so or what ancient power she might think would stir carelessly, if at all, to bring her an answer to such petition. Simsa had no gods, and trusted in no one—save herself, and Zass—and perhaps somewhat Zass's two offspring, who at least would answer her calls. But in herself first and most. If she were ever to achieve any rise above the Burrows, out of this constant state of having to be on guard, it would not be by the wave of any god's hand, it would be by her own determined efforts.

She slung the bag by its cord over one shoulder where the bones were sharply apparent and hissed gently at Zass, who made her crippled half-flight down to perch on the girl's other shoulder. Then, after a quick look right and left at the opening of the Burrow, Simsa went out. It was still day, but she had taken the usual precaution of covering her hair and blacking her white brows. Her ragged clothing was drably brown-grey against the darkness of her skin and, as she went down the zigzag path to where the river water washed, she passed very light-footed and as unseen as she could hope to be in daytime. Though she could not be sure that she would have no followers, the zorsal would warn her if any tried to overtake her.

One could not approach the landing field of the starships too closely. All the town Guild officials would be there to greet the newcomer, their guards quick to drive off any save the representatives of those who had paid trader's tax and so wore their proper badges about their necks. Simsa could not go there as yet, but she could visit the warehouse which was her regular place of call each fifth day. No one watching her so far might guess she was planning to leave the Burrows for good.

Already, her mind was busy with what she might do if she were able to part with the contents of the bag in the manner she wished. She would do the best bargaining possible, then go straight to the Thieves' market to dicker for clothing which did not stamp her as a Burrower. She had three bits of broken silver in her pouch, turned up on a last rake through of a side tunnel where she had been engaged in delving earlier. Those were worth something even though they were but shapeless knobs of metal, that metal was not base.

Gathar was striding down the wide aisle of his main warehouse as she flitted in, keeping prudently to shadows as she always did. She had no need to call the zorsals. Through the dusk of the large building they came planing down to encircle her and their crippled mother, uttering sharp cries, their voices so high the girl could hardly distinguish them, though she had learned long ago that her hearing was keener than that of most of the Burrow people.

Their dam lifted her undamaged wing and fanned it, the leathery surface whispering through the air. At some signal from her which Simsa, for all her familiarity with the creatures, had never been able to catch, they went silent. The girl did not try her throat talk with them, rather padded on in a noiseless, barefooted tread until she rounded a mountain of crates to confront the waremaster himself.

He was in a good mood, showing teeth in a grin which suggested more a desire to devour than to please, but Simsa knew that of old. Now she made a single slight gesture with one hand—his eyes, narrowed, were instantly drawn to the bag she shouldered. He pointed up the ramp which led to the quarters from which he could watch all the activity below. As Simsa ran lightly ahead of him, she heard his voice bellow an order or two before he followed. She was frowning, wondering just how much it would be worth to share a little of the truth with him. Their relationship had never developed any difficulties, but then she had always been the one with a necessary commodity to offer. Truth came very high in Kuxortal, sometimes beyond the power of any to buy.

As the bag thudded from her shoulder to the top of a table littered with sheets of tough grif-reed paper, all scrawled upon with untidy lines of crooked script, Simsa had her story fully in order.

"What's to do, Shadow?" Gathar asked. She saw, with satisfaction, that he closed the door behind him. So he thought that she might have something to offer worth serious notice.

"The Old One died. Some things she had worth selling to learned ones in the high towers. I have heard there are such who pore over such bits and pieces, just as mad about them as was the Old One. Look!" The girl opened her bag and dragged out several slabs of the inscribed stone.

"I don't deal in such." However, he came nearer, leaned over to peer at the markings.

"As we both know. But there is a profit in such, I have heard."

He was grinning again.

"Go to Lord Arfellen. He has taken a fancy these past two seasons to having men grub for such since that mad starman talked with him so long and then went off hunting a treasure which he never found. At least he never returned here with it."

Simsa shrugged. "Treasures are never lying easily about for one to pick up. The gateman at the High Place would never look or listen to a Burrower. I know that you shall take a goodly portion." She grinned in turn, her teeth so white in her black face as to startle one who did not know her. "But the Old One is dead—I have plans—I will give you these for fifty silver bits."

He exploded as she knew he would, but she also knew the signs—Gathar was caught. Perhaps he might use her bits and pieces to sweeten the temper of this lord he spoke of, gain some favor from him. That was the way Guild's men worked. They fell to serious bargaining then, and each was a worthy match for the other.

2

Simsa turned this way and that, studying her reflection. The slab of cracked mirror wedged up on one end in the back of the frowzy tent gave one only a crooked view, but she nodded briskly in satisfaction at what she saw. The dealer in old clothes (undoubtedly many of her wares stolen) stood to one side so she could keep an eye on both the girl and the forepart of the tent which lay beyond the half division of a much mended curtain. Simsa strove to catch a glimpse of her back over one shoulder.

She had, she was very certain, chosen well and made the string of trade tokens, plus one of her bits of broken silver go farther than most she knew who dealt in this part of the market. Now, she stooped and gathered up the smock and underpants she had discarded and rolled those into a bundle, which she tied up into a shawl of a drab and dusty grey. The shawl she had insisted on sale-gift. It had a number of holes but it was still serviceable for transport purposes.

However, the girl who turned purposefully away from the cracked mirror was quite different from the ragged Burrower who had entered a short time earlier. Now she wore a pair of quasker-skin trousers, tapered down to her slender ankles, their sturdy outer layer lined withfes-silk. They were a dark, serviceable blue and perhaps had been snapped out of the luggage of some ill-fated land-rider. She was lucky in that they were so narrow of leg—a fact she had pointed out firmly to the seller. There were few potential customers who could have drawn them on with any ease.

Her own undershirt had been the best piece of clothing she had owned and she had kept it reasonably clean even in the Burrows. Simsa had a fastidious dislike of filth and washed both her underclothing and the body beneath it whenever she had a chance, a trait which most of the Burrowers found a matter of huge amusement. So this, she had kept and beneath it, the band about her enlarging breasts; in its folds were hidden Ferwar's two jeweled treasures, plus the ring.

Over the chemise Simsa now wore the short coat of a courtyard upper servant. That was tightly sashed about her narrow waist, and she felt the weight of the long, wide sleeves which were gathered into wrist bands so that their folds also served as storage pockets. It was of the darkest color of the three Simsa had been offered, a wine, near black. There were roughened threads on one shoulder where some House badge must have been cut away, and it had no trim, except for a piping of silver gray about the high neck and wrist bands. The material was good; there was not a single mend nor fray, and the girl decided that it was enough to pass her into the lowest round of the hill city—perhaps even a round above that. Certainly, she looked respectable enough to be allowed onto the ship-verge market, which was what she wanted now.

Her hair she still kept within its tight wrapping and she had darkened her eye lashes well before she had come into the market. Not for the first time, she wished that nature had not made her so noticeable. Perhaps when she could make more free of the upper town she could discover some dye which would serve to keep her what Gathar had called her—a shadow.

"You are not the only buyer," snapped the woman by the curtain's edge. "Should you take all day to view those clothes you have stolen from me? Stolen indeed! I am too kind of heart with the young, too ready to give when I should get!"

Simsa laughed and the zorsal croaked.

"Market woman, when you are kind in any dealing the cie-wind of Kor will bring the vasarch trees into bloom. I should have bargained for a full turn of the sand glass longer, but I am in a good mood today, and you have profited by that."

The woman pursed her mouth in a gesture of spitting and made an obscene gesture. Simsa laughed again. She no longer had the bag she had left at the warehouse, but she swung the shawl bundle to her shoulder with the same practiced ease, then scooped up Zass who settled on her other shoulder. Slipping by the woman, she was out of the tent in a moment.

This section of the frowzy market was above the lines where the Burrowers were usually to be seen. For all of that the girl still kept a wary eye on what lay about her, the din of market seller cries and shouts being enough to cover the advance of an army.

By now, the starship would have landed and the authorities should have begun dealings with the officers over the main cargo. There would be little or no trading with the crew until perhaps the next day. However, that delay would give the small traders, the lesser thieves, and the scavengers time to gather and stake out their own places, to wait until the crewmen were released for planet leave and a chance to dicker. Most of the crew would, she knew from having watched a number of such landings during past seasons, head for the upper town with its better drinking places where there were rent-women and other things denied during long voyages. Always, though, there were some to come seeking what they could buy—pickings which just might make them a small fortune when offered on another world. Simsa, shuffling sandals (which were a bit too large for her narrow feet, but in her present garb she could not go bare of sole) across the pavement, wondered briefly what it would be like to spend one's life going from world to world, always greeting the new and strange. She had never been away from Kuxortal and, though she had explored all of the city save those crowning palaces at the very crest of the mound, her world was a small one indeed.

Those born in Kuxortal did not wander. They knew that there was a wide land behind them, a broad sea before. Ships came overseas, barges, smaller sailing, and slave-oared vessels down the river. Still the land immediately beyond the wide cultivated strips that provided the double croppings per year that fed the city was desert, and no man traveled on land when there was water of sea or river to carry him. There were a number of ancient and very strange tales about what might lie beyond the city gardens—tales such that no one was minded to prove the truth of them.

Simsa found a stall selling ripe fruit, some cakes of dark bread of nut-flour, and stacks of hardened packa pods hollowed out and filled with sap-sweetened water. Again, she bargained, sharp-tongued and narrow-eyed, tucking her provisions into the ever-ready sleeve pockets.

As she prowled through the market, she eyed stalls and ground boards, assessing the worth of what she could see. Most here was broken trash but several of the dealers of such called a greeting as she paused, recognizing her for one who dealt in the lesser finds of the Burrowers. She knew that each and every one would note her new clothing, would speculate on how she had raised the price of such. Rumor spread through any market even faster than the first breezes of the wet season. She would be a fool to return to the Burrows now. There would be those who would lie in wait seeking to discover what she had found—what Ferwar must have treasured through the years.

The Old One had had her own ways of handling any upstarts who might question her rights. Only a cursing from Simsa, no matter how dramatically delivered, would mean nothing to the combined forces the Burrowers could assemble at the faintest hint of loot.

She went on down the long ramp which was only one of the many cut into the mound of the city, leading to the plain where the starships planeted, twice backing against the wall to let pass trotting gangs of laborers from one warehouse or another, all of them wearing Guild badges on their grime-stiff sleeved jerkins, each group urged on by pairs of trumpet-throated bosses, one in the lead, one bringing up the rear. These would provide the transport for the off-laden goods.

There were others like herself, moving with purpose to find pitches at the ship field. A number led shaggy, hoofed beasts, horned and ugly of mood, from whose snapping teeth one kept a prudent distance, over the backs of which were hung bulging bags. These were the more important of that motley trading crew, and the majority of them went with a swagger, expecting all others, save of course the Guildsmen, to make way for them.

Simsa saw the ship clearly, looming near as high as the mound of Kuxortal itself, a gleaming arrow, finned down on still smoking earth where its landing rockets had scorched the ground, nose pointing arrogantly skyward. She had inspected a number of such during the past three trading seasons, drawn here by a curiosity she did not even try to understand. Though before she had had no chance to ever bespeak one of the starmen, nor sit in the fast crowding circles of those waiting small trades, where there were already squabbles and, once or twice, a shouting and milling about of those waiting, as if they ringed in some fight.

Then the field guard came with a rush, striking out viciously with the peace staves against any in their general path. Thus all scattered quickly for there was no general law in Kuxortal; all men knew that a guard might lash out and club to death the unwary, and his action never be questioned.

She stood a little to one side of the general mass of waiting tradesmen. There were some who had already erected their four-poled awnings and set up their boards. They were laying out their wares with the expectancy of those well accustomed to this game. Simsa could see that those flanked the way which was kept open for the passage of the cargo handlers—a passage which led directly to the side of the ship, a small section away from where there was already an open port ladder let out to touch the ground. Above was the cargo hatch, larger, also open, but nothing as far as she could see stirred within that. While on the ground at the forepart of the landing ladder gathered a knot of men wearing the uniform of star traders, conferring with several Guild masters—or else their First Men.

There was no way, she decided, that she could wedge into the already formed lines of temporary booths that walled in the alley-way right to the foot of the ramp. That was packed four and five deep with would-be merchants. Now she raised a hand and bit thoughtfully at the top of one finger, extending the claw to nibble at while she thought.

Zass shifted weight on her shoulder and uttered a very low, guttural noise. Zorsals were fond of neither the direct light of the sun nor crowded and noisy places. Simsa put up her hand to stroke her companion's furred head. The long, feathery-edged antennae, which served the creature for hearing and less understood sensing, were curled tightly against its skull, and the girl knew without glancing around that its big eyes were nearly closed. Yet it was completely alert to all which went on.

Simsa reached the end of the ramp to wedge herself back to the rise of the city mound, her shoulders against its stone shoring of the mound face, watching intently as that group of men at the foot of the ship's ladder broke apart. Two returned into the ship, three others started along the open aisle toward where she stood, the Guild officers flanking them. None of the waiting small traders raised a voice to hawk any wares. They knew better than to attract the attention of the Guild; a market which was illegal but tolerated must avoid excess.

Simsa studied the starmen as they came closer. Two of them wore what she had come to know as ship's uniform—their winged helms glittering in the sun, which also picked out the emblems appearing on the collar and breast of their jackets. But the third of their party, though he wore a close fitting one-piece garment like their suits, as well as the boots of a star rover, was different.

His one-piece garb was of a silver-grey, not unlike the piping on her new coat, and he had no distinguishing badge. Nor did he wear the winged helm, but a tight-fitting cap. His skin was not the dark brown of his companions, but much lighter in shade and he had dropped a step or two behind the rest of the party, who had completely ignored the would-be traders, his head turning from side to side as he went, as if he were fascinated by what he saw.

As he came up to the ramp, Simsa studied him very carefully. It was very plain, she decided, that this was his first visit to Kuxortal and, as a newcomer, he could be the very prey the merchants would be waiting for. It was difficult, of course, to judge ages—especially of these off-world men—but she thought he was young. If that were true, then he must also be a person of some consequence or he would not be included in the party of Guild and ship's officers. Perhaps he was not part of the crew at all—rather some traveler who had been a passenger on board. Though why he would be here if he were no trader she could not begin to guess. His lighter skin was not the only difference about him. There was an oddity in the way his eyes were set and he was taller and thinner than his companions.

Those eyes were never still, she also noted. Then they met hers—and held. She thought she saw a kind of surprise in them. He nearly stopped, as if he thought he had met her somewhere, some-time, and wanted to call a greeting. Her tongue swept over her lips as if she could taste the sweet drink which the Old One used only on state occasions. If she could but get to him now! That spark of interest he had shown in her was an opening for bargaining.

He must have rich resources or he could not be a star traveler. She shifted the sleeve in which hung the weight of those pieces she had retained, and was inwardly irritated that she dared not approach him now.

Only after having glanced so long and with such interest at her, he was now going on up the ramp. Zass gave another small cry, protesting the light, the heat, and the noise of the market. Simsa watched the stranger out of sight, her mind busy making and discarding a number of hopeful plans.

At length, she decided that she could only leave matters to chance. The starman had noticed her where she stood. If he returned to the ship with any thought of individual trade in mind, then he might come seeking her. In the meantime, there were others on board. Sooner or later, they would be given planet leave— already the cargo crane had swung out of that larger hatch and the first of the boxes was swaying down to the waiting Guild handlers.

Simsa squatted down where she was, the mound to her back, the ramp close enough that she might have touched it—if her arm was only twice its length. She untied the shawl a little and Zass dropped thankfully down into the nest the girl so devised as she arranged the top folds to shelter the creature from the direct rays of the sun.

The girl was far away from the main lines of the merchants that none would try to encroach upon the small piece of ground where she so established herself, and she had learned patience long ago. It might be many turns of the sand glass before those from the ship would be free, which gave her time to fasten upon a plan of her own for attracting the right kind of attention. It was hot, and many of the merchants had settled down now, their wares ready; those who were fortunate enough to have a strip of cloth awning keeping well within it shade. As a Burrower, she had long since learned to stifle discomfort herself.

Opening her packet of food, she ate, sharing bites with Zass who was too sleepy to eat much and only wanted to be left alone. As she drank sparingly, Simsa's other hand sought within her coat for that packet of jewelry she had stowed in the safest keeping she knew. She had prudently kept two of the best picture fragments belonging to Ferwar. Those would be her come-on. Then, if she could judge the interest of any those attracted, she could produce the cuff armlet, which to her own valuing was the least important of her other wares.

The pieces of stone she brushed off with the edge of her sleeve and set out just beyond her knee near the ramp. One was the likeness of some kind of a winged creature, time-worn so that only the general outline could be seen. The stone on which it had been engraved was a light green, veined with yellow—the veins having been cleverly used by the unknown artist to outline wings and form a crest for the figure. Simsa had never seen such stone hereabouts, or even in the city. However, it might have traveled many days from the place where men had freed it from the earth and fashioned it to their fancy.

Beside it, the other piece was in direct contrast for it was a velvety black, and it was not just a tracing upon a flat piece, but worked into the crouching form of an animal with one paw upraised, claws spread—though several of those had been broken off. Only half of the head remained also and that was time-worn so that one could see only a thick mane, the splintered stub of what must have been an ear, and a portion of face. For face it was, more than a beast's mask, having an eye, a nose, and a bit of mouth which was not too far different from her own.

The substance of the stone was somehow pleasant to the touch. Simsa discovered that rubbing fingers back and forth across it gave one the same feeling as one might have caressing finely woven material. This she had felt when she had been able to hold and finger lovingly a fragment of some rich fabric found among the rags the Old One had dealt in as long as she could still hobble about raiding the dumps and trash places of the upper town.

Now Simsa sat, rubbing her black stone, thinking and planning. Though now even her thoughts came more slowly; she had to make an effort not to drift into drowsiness. Even her long-cultivated patience was beginning to wear thin by late afternoon. The cargo had come out of the ship, been transported city-wards.

Along the way leading from ramp to ship, people were stirring, shifting their bits and pieces, hoping to catch the eye more quickly with this adjustment or that. Simsa stood up, moving about, loosening her legs from their cramped position. She could see the sky turning orange red and that worried her. If the crewmen did not come soon, dusk would fall when they came and she would have no side lamp to show her wares. This would be a race between the setting of the sun and the ways of the starmen, a race which could disappoint her after all.

Zass poked her head from out of the bundle nest. The sensitive antennae on the furred head were half uncurled, an action which surprised the girl a little, for she would have believed that the subdued roar of the alerting market would have been too much for the zorsal. Now she noted that the creature's head had swung part way around so that it faced, not the line of merchants with the ship, but rather the ramp itself as that same small head was forced up and back to allow the creature as much seeing vantage in that direction as she could achieve. On impulse, the girl swept Zass unceremoniously out of her bundle hiding place and brought the zorsal once more to perch on her shoulder.

Still the head was turned back and up towards the city, a certain intensity of that small body about which the wings were gathered like a night cloak developed as if she were about to be challenged.

Yet Simsa could see nothing but the ramp and, above its summit, the stir of guild guards.

Not for the first time, she longed for clear communication with the creature. Though during the seasons she had nursed and sheltered the zorsal, she had learned to judge much of the creature's emotions by its small actions, many times she could only guess. The zorsal now was nearly as alert as if she perched within striking distance of a ver-rat den and the den sharers were stirring, about to venture forth.

The girl clucked to the zorsal, drew the fingers of her right hand slowly and soothingly about the base of those half uncurled antennae. She could read no sign of alarm in the other's watchfulness, merely an alertness. Still, that was enough to make her divide her own attention between the ramp and the starship.

The cargo hatch was closed now. A light had snapped on to glow outward from the smaller aperture which gave upon the landing stair. Below, the merchants were growing restless, there were noisy quarrels erupting here and there as they pushed and shoved for front-line showing.

Finally, there were crewmen coming out; Simsa counted five of them. They were too far away from her own place—badly chosen she now decided, and they seemed far more eager to reach the town above than to carry on any private trading ventures. In fact, in their tightly fitted ships-clothing, they had no pouches which showed that they transported anything of value. Also, none carried a bag or bundle and they passed the calling traders on either side without so much as a glance at what they had to offer. Instead, they ignored those, chattering among themselves and quickening pace towards the city ramp and whatever pleasures they had marked down for their own during a night of planetside freedom.

Simsa fought down her disappointment. She had been very foolish to think that she might make the beginning of her fortune on the first such try. Certainly, none of these looked to be the kind of man to pore over bits of broken carvings and consider them worth a price no matter how small a price she might make it. She studied them carefully, however, as they brushed past the merchants, sometimes actually pushing some overly importunate man or woman out of their paths, talking in their sharp, clicking language which resembled at times a zorsal's grunts.

Nor did she raise her hand or voice to try to catch their attention as they strode past her chosen place to tramp up the ramp. Ruefully, she stooped, picked up her pieces, drew out bits of rag to rewrap them. Tomorrow would be another day. Men long in space could well have other things on their minds this night beside trading, though that might be their whole way of life.

Here and there, one of the disappointed merchants had already turned back to his or her pitch, set a brazier burning, getting ready a scrap meal. They would sleep curled among their wares, await the coming of sun and another contingent of starcrew, or else these who had gone on their way back, their space starved appetites of the body sated, ready to think once more of long-term gain rather than fleeting pleasure.

Simsa hesitated over her own choice. She had promised herself that this night she would sleep in a real bed place in one of the taverns on the lower reaches of the street where carveneers sheltered during their stay in Kuxortal. Weighing her one sleeve was a twist of broken silver from which she could pinch a finger's length to ensure her that much. Also, her position here by the ramp was not so choice a one that she need defend it by hunching there to sleep in the chill open.

She made her decision and started back up the ramp where the crew men, well ahead, were just entering into the town. The Guild guards glowered at her but there was no reason for any questioning. They did not police the field market, and unless she were one who wore a cheek brand of a failed, outlawed thief, or committed some act against the city peace right before their eyes, they could not cross weapons before her to take her for questioning. The neatness of her newly purchased clothes were those of one who could be a messenger for some House Merchant sent on a private errand where a house badge would be an advertisement her master was not prepared to allow.

"Gentle-homo—"

It had been one of Simsa's private employments to learn what she could of other tongues. She could speak with the same fluency that she could mouth the Burrowers' coarse speech, the tongue of an upper river-man and two distinct seafaring dialects. Now she recognized off-world words—a salutation. But that it was addressed to her was a surprise which took her a breath or two to realize. It had been she who had been seeking to contact the starmen, she did not expect any of them to come seeking her. Nor was it one of the five who had climbed the ramp ahead of her, rather this was the stranger who come up town earlier with the officers.

He was looking straight at her though and the Guild guards had taken several steps away as if to pay him deference. Now, he pointed to the zorsal and said haltingly, in the speech of the merchants of the upper town: "You are the one Waremaster Gathar spoke of—the trainer of zorsals. I thought I would have to hunt far for you—yet here you have come as if I called and you heard."

Gathar, Simsa thought swiftly—why? Zass shifted on her shoulder and grunted. The zorsal's antennae had unrolled to the farthest extent the girl had ever seen happen save when the creature was on night guard. Both of them pointed directly at the off-worlder as if the creature listened to more than Simsa heard, something other than those halting words.

"Will you give me of your time, dealer in old things—" the starman was continuing. "There are questions of import which mean very much to me—some of which you may be able to answer."

Simsa was wary. In her new clothing, she was sure she looked more boy than woman, and she did not believe that this was some ceremonious route to name a bed-price. If Gathar had mentioned her in connection with old things . . . Her fingers tightened about her swinging sleeve, weighted as it was with the two finds she had kept to tempt trade. All knew that the starmen were largely credulous about such discoveries and they could sometimes be bargained into such gains of trade as no one but the simple-witted here would strike hands over. She could not understand why Gathar had spoken of her at all. Which meant caution until she found out that much about *his* dealings. No one gave away even a smell of profit if he could help. However, if this starman had come to her because of the Old One's bits and pieces, she would make the best of what she had left. Now, she nodded abruptly. Let him believe that she knew less of any save up town speech; such small precautions could sometimes lead to profit.

Taking her nod for assent, he looked about over his shoulder and gestured towards the Street of Cull Winds leading off straightly to the left, down which the coming shadows crept out from several darkened patches between three or four welcoming door lamps of inns. It was not the best Kuxortal had to offer any traveler, still this was much better than the hostel she had thought to try. If nothing else, she would gain a full belly out of this meeting; the starman could readily be maneuvered into paying for the food that he would offer out of courtesy before he would state his true reason for seeking her out.

3

The room was low and dark. Along one wall, well-worn curtains hid a number of booths. Some flimsy lengths were drawn, and Simsa, in passing, heard the squeals of women, once the drunken brawling of a riverman's song. She stepped back to allow the starman to lead the way, her sense of caution fully aroused. On her shoulder, Zass muzzled against her neck, thrusting snout right under her chin, antennae again curled close, as if the zorsal wanted a hiding place and was making do with the best she could find.

He who had brought them here swept aside a curtain to wave Simsa in. She chose a seat placing her back to the wall from which most of the room was in view. Involuntarily, she flexed her claws a little, projecting their needle tips from her finger sheaths.

To the crop-headed boy in the stained shirt who lounged over to serve them she quickly gave her own order—making sure that she would not be fuddle-headed by any potion as strong as the traders used to bewilder those they would entangle in some ploy to bring themselves a double return. If starmen followed such practices, she would be prepared.

This stranger might appear open-faced, even eager, but a man could wear many masks and never show what lay beneath them. What still astonished her the most was that Gathar had spoken of her and that, in turn, this one had recognized her from the ware-master's description. Unless, of course, it was because of Zass. She smoothed the head fur of the zorsal now. Only, this man had looked upon her down by the ramp when the zorsal had been hidden nearly from view. So—she waited for him to speak, knowing that thus a small advantage was hers.

He opened a large bag which had swung from his shoulder and which now rested on the stained table between them. From it he took with the same caution that one would use to handle leaf gold, two of the fragments she had traded to Gathar earlier that day. Seeing the care with which he touched those now, Simsa could have snarled in frustration. It was certain that Gathar had made an excellent bargain, far beyond what she had or could hope to gain herself. Under the table, she felt again for the two things in her sleeve pocket and her hopes stirred higher. If such fragments were what this one sought, she perhaps could drive her own price well higher than she had first planned.

"These—" the starman had laid his hand flat upon the larger of the two, "where were these found?"

He believed in coming directly to the point. Simsa felt a growing contempt triggered by this display of eagerness. Now she *could* believe that Gathar must have nicked him well if he had displayed the same eagerness to that trader old in well-learned craftiness.

"If you know Kuxortal," she answered, speaking slowly and with care, using the accent of the upper town, "you would also know that such as these," a flick of the finger pointed to what his hand near covered, "are apt to be found anywhere. Though—" (should she pretend that such "treasures" were hard come by and that she alone held the secret? No, better not chance that; she had no idea what Gathar had told him already. Those she had sold were not the easily found gleanings of any dump, they were the result of seasons of delving first on Ferwar's part and then by Simsa herself.)

"You say anywhere—" he spoke slowly as she did, as one feeling his way through an alien tongue. "I do not think that is true. I have already spoken to Guild Lord Arfellen—" He was watching her narrow-eyed now, and Simsa sat very still, holding his stare with her own eyes, determined not to let him see that he made any impression on her, if he had meant that as an implied threat. He could, with fewer words that he had just mouthed, have her up into the question room of a guild and that was something to shake anyone's mind with fear.

Zass quivered until the girl could feel the shaking of the small body so closely pressed against her. The zorsal was always, she had discovered long ago, well able to pick up her emotions, translate them in turn into a reaction of the creature's own. The girl stroked the leather wings covering the upper part of the back, unable to see how she would twist and turn to answer with anything but the truth.

"Those I did not find—not all of them." Truth had a bitter taste when it was forced out of one and she seldom had used it save with Ferwar, who had always recognized a lie and could not be misled.

"The Old One died—what she had saved was then mine. She sought old things and dreamed over them, believing them true treasures."

He did not answer her at once, then the serving boy was back with their footed drinking horns, two platters of still smoking stew, tongs and spoon stuffed upward in the center holders. The starman had swept his finds off the table, into his bag, and out of sight with a swift deftness which Simsa was forced to approve. It would seem that, if he was willing to show her what he carried, he had no mind to let others inspect such wares.

Zass stirred and scrambled down from Simsa's shoulder quickly. Such a lavish display of food was not common for either of them and the zorsal could be greedy when she had gone on short rations for a day. The girl picked up the tongs, searched for a lump of meat as big as her thumb and preferred it to the creature who seized eagerly with a throaty gurgle.

"The small one," the starman observed, "seems well trained."

Simsa chewed and swallowed a fragment of crisp tac root, spicy from being broiled in the stew, before she answered:

"One does not train zorsals . . ."

Now she saw him smile and his smooth face looked even younger. "So we have been told many times over," he agreed. "Still, it would seem that this one lives content with you, gentlehomo. While Gathar admits that he has never had better hunters of vermin than those he received from your hands. Perhaps only you have the secrets of the art to make friends between man and such."

Was he trying flattery now? There was no reason for him to believe that she could be so moved to his will. He must have sensed her instant wariness, or read it somehow in her face, for he had laid aside his own tongs and spoon, making no headway with his stew, but took up his drinking horn and watched her across the rim of it, as he sat with it half way to his lips, a picture of a man caught up in a puzzle.

"Your Old One—she was a Burrower." He did not make that a question but a statement and Simsa knew that he must have gotten from Gathar all the waremaster knew. "Did she find many such in burrowing?"

Say 'yes' Simsa decided quickly and she might unleash on the Burrows half a force of guild men. The same would be well warmed with anger when they found that there were no such pickings left. She must be very careful.

"I do not know where first she found such." That *was* the truth. "Of late, she traded for them—"

The starman leaned forward, setting down his drink as untasted as his dinner.

"With whom did she trade?" His voice was low, but he rapped that out with a ring of authority which again hinted of the power to discover what he wished to know if he need call on such aid.

"There was—" More truth, enough to lead him away from her, point him toward the source which had dried up a good four seasons back and the uncovering of which would reveal nothing now, "one of the rivermen who was in debt to the Old One. From time to time, he brought such, then ceased to come—death is easy along the waters and he was said to be a man with a price on him—a thief who had broken faith with the Master."

Though those oddly shaped lids veiled the starman's eyes, they had not moved quickly enough, she had seen that sparking of interest there. So telling the truth was the right path here after all. Turn this one's nose up river and she was free of him.

The heavy downward swing of her sleeve was a reminder of

what she still carried. Why not make a deal with him since he was a hunter of old things? He believed her story, of that she was sure and, since he was so eager, she could get enough for them. Quickly Simsa disciplined her soaring hopes, it was never well to tempt fortune by expecting too much.

Now, she pushed aside the platter before her and moved to unfasten the tight wrist band of her sleeve. Not the jewelry; those she would hold on to until the last. But the other things.

She reached inside the inner pocket and pulled out the broken beast carving. He was looking at them now as if *they* were the plate of stew and he was a Burrower who had gone at least a day and a half without eating.

"These are the last!" She was determined to make that plain. "I would bargain for them."

He picked up the carved beast before she could stop him. Turning it about as if it were the most precious possession of a Guild Lord.

"X-Arth—It is X-Arth!" His voice was hardly above a whisper and the name meant nothing to her. But her hand shot out to cover the piece even as he tried to raise it closer to his eyes.

"First we bargain," Simsa said firmly, taking the opportunity to sweep with her other hand, bringing the second piece of stone under her palm. "First—what is X-Arth?" She might well sell these two bits if the starman met her price, which she had revised upward several times in the space of the same number of breaths. However it would be well to know *why* these, or at least the one piece, was so important. All such knowledge which could be filed away in one's head made one just that more able to keep life in one's body.

He put the piece down very reluctantly, releasing his hold on it so she gathered it in.

"It means 'out of arth'—from another world—a very old world on which, some believe, all our kind originated. Or at least some of us who range the stars believe it. Tell me, have you heard of an off-worlder—a man named Thorn Tseng?"

"The crazy witling who went up river and then into the desert about the Hard Hills? He went hunting treasure, but he never returned. Men do not spit in the face of luck by journeying so."

"He was my elder brother." If the starman had resented her contemptuous estimate of his close kin-blood's mentality, he gave no sign of it. "It was another kind of treasure which he sought, knowledge. And he had good reason to believe that he could find it. This—" he touched fingertip to the head of the image, "would argue that he was right. I have come to try to find him."

Simsa shrugged. "If a man puts a knife to his throat and says 'I would let out my life', why stop him? The world is over-full already of fools and turned-wits," she repeated words of the Burrows. "Some live, some die, some seek death, others flee it—it is all the same in the end."

His face was expressionless now. "Fifty mil-credits."

Simsa shook her head. "I do not deal with off-world payments," she answered decisively. Zass reached a long thin limb across her arm and clawed up a lump of stew for herself. The girl did not care. Her own hunger was not assuaged, but she was uneasy. If this off-worlder knew or guessed, he could take those two bits which he wanted so much and have her thrown out, hunted down slope, perhaps beaten into a broken-boned pulp by merely raising the cry of "Burrower" in this upper-city place.

Also, if she tried later to get rid of off-world payment in any money changer's stall, she could condemn herself as an unregistered thief. Now she was well able to see the folly of having come here at all—she was the witling!

"I will pay the credits to Gathar, he will change them for you."

Simsa bared her teeth in just such a snarl as Zass could show when she was crossed. Use the waremaster man for a cross-payer? What did this off-worlder think she was? She would be lucky to get two tens of anything he left for her by doing so.

"Pay me ten tens of loft marks, in broken silver," she returned, "and no less."

"So be it!" He held out his hand palm down above the two old pieces. The move awoke her complete amazement. For a moment, she regretted not having demanded twice as much. Still, caution advised her quickly; it is never well to be too greedy. For one ten of broken bits, she could establish herself in the lower part of the upper town, find some way to earn her living well away from the Burrows. If the starman did not know how to bargain, then she was the winner.

Simsa swept both of the pieces back into her sleeve pocket and snapped shut the wrist fastening. Then she dropped her hand across the waiting palm to seal the bargain between them, her skin looking so dark against that of the off-worlder.

"Bring me the silver and both are yours—the bargain is set and may fortune strike us both with her dark wand if we fail in it!" She recited the old marketplace formula, which even a thief would not gainsay once it passed his lips.

"Come with me to Gathar's and I'll have it in your hands now."

Simsa shook her head determinedly. To have such a piece of good fortune viewed by even a half-friend was stupid. Only what if he told Gathar why he wanted such a sum? That would be as bad for her as having it paid right under the other's eyes. How much did she dare explain to this stranger? Could she depend on any understanding from him at all?

She had thought herself so clever, her plans had appeared so smooth in anticipation—why had she not foreseen these difficulties? She surveyed that smooth face, those strange half-hidden eyes. Then she looked directly at the zorsal and with tongue against teeth made an odd, clicking noise.

Zass had finished the piece of meat she had snatched, her thin purple tongue darted into first one corner of her big mouth and then over to the other. At Simsa's signal, she raised her head with a jerk, her antennae uncurled and rose straight up, the fine feathery hairs along the edges quivered.

"Put out your finger!" the girl commanded, making a gesture to the zorsal. The off-worlder look at her for a long moment and then obeyed.

The creature's long neck stretched, her pointed snout, ringed round with fangs, two of which were hollow and filled with a poison which could make a man suffer for hours, approached that finger.

Then the antennae flicked down, the tip-ends just touching hand and finger for a second.

Zass turned her head on her hunched shoulders, made a guttural sound. Simsa drew a deep breath. This was a new thing between them and it had been used only two or three times before—each time proving that Zass was right in her estimation of the good or ill will of those so tested. There was still the fact that this was an off-worlder and so some strangeness in him might not register properly for the zorsal, but as far as Simsa could now see, she had very little choice anyway. She could only protect herself in so much.

"Do not tell Gathar of me, or of why you want the silver. Get large pieces, not broken bits from him, and say that you could not find me. Exchange then the takals for bits. Then bring them to—" Not to the Burrow—she had no intention of returning there ever if she could help it. But earlier, after she had put on her new clothing, she had done some scouting of the inns in the lower regions and had marked down one she had thought might serve her purpose— The Spindwaker. It sheltered river traders, but this was not the season when it would be crowded and it had a reputation for not encouraging brawling. Also, the Wifekeeper there paid her dues regularly to the Thieves' Guild and those within its walls were safe from pilfering. Swiftly Simsa told the off-worlder of the place and how to find it.

"What do you fear?" he asked quietly when she had done.

"Fear? Enough of everyone and everything to make as sure as possible I keep breath in my body," she told him sharply. "This world teaches one sharp lessons: learn or die. I shall expect you before the dawn gong—will that be so?"

"As close to that as I can make it," he agreed.

Simsa slid out of the booth, scooping the zorsal up as she went. The sooner she was undercover in her proposed shelter for the night the better. Though in the streets, now dusk filled, she could depend upon the zorsal to give alarm of any who might follow either to spy or to rob.

When she leaned against the half-opened shutter of the cubby in the inn, she was torn between walking, or rather stealing forth, from her present room or waiting for the dawn gong and the off-worlder. Simsa had no liking for such risks as she believed she might be running now. She could watch the street below for a goodly length in both directions while the zorsal perched on the edge of the shutter itself, its head bent at what might appear an impossible angle, gazing with the same intentness, and, the girl knew, far better night sight.

There was an over-abundance of shadows along the way. Here in the lower town, the lamps were well apart both for reasons of economy and the desires of those both dwelling and walking here after nightfall. She had marked carefully the comings and goings of a few. But she was sure that perhaps others made far less visible journeys which she was not aware, for the zorsal had picked up at least three such.

Since there was no reason for the off-worlder to come with any great stealth, she did not allow herself to do more than catch a quick breath or two at the quivering of Zass's extended antennae and try to judge, by the movements of those slender wands, who passed. She thought once she caught a shadow, but that was all.

In her room, she had blown out the lamp as soon as the frowsy maid had left. Then, with Zass's small grunts as a guide, explored it with care, assessing its dimensions by feel and an odd impression of proximity which she had learned during her working with the creature now riding on her shoulder.

Though she could not in all earnestness say why she felt so uneasy, it was like a warning of trouble to come and, against any such, Simsa prepared in her own way. She had made three circuits of the small room, the first slow and tentative, the last with the sureness of one walking a well-known path. After each, she paused for some time to watch out of the window.

The off-worlder had offered what was to her a fabulous price. His eagerness without the process of bargaining made her suspect he might have given even more. But greediness itself was a threat, and one she would not bring down upon herself. She still had the jewels, too. The Old One's treasure was a goodly inheritance indeed.

There was someone coming, walking plainly down the middle

of the narrow, cobble-paved street. He came with confidence and as
he passed beneath the light of the second lamp from the first corner,
Simsa identified the fitted body-suit of a starman.

Only—

Zass's antennae stiffened, the zorsal rumbled a low note of
warning. As the starman came on, Simsa pushed the closer to the
window, knowing well that her dark face, from which she had not
rubbed the soot that overlaid her brows and lashes, could not be
sighted by any watcher below.

Six paces such as his long legs would take, a little more, from the
outer door of the Spindwaker's and a shadow detached itself from
another doorway diagonally across the way. With a leap like that of
a throat-slashing ver-rat, the lurker was on the man she waited for,
hurling feet inward in one of those maneuvers practiced by night
runners, so that boots, especially made for the purpose with four
heavy thicknesses of hide, would strike against the back of the
intended victim's legs, sending him forward in a helpless crack
against the cobbles.

Thus, the attacker planned. Only, when he would have thudded
home to complete his skillful and long practiced attack, this victim
had moved with a matching speed slightly to the left. Only one of
those boots struck, as at the same time, the off-worlder spun about
and brought a hand chopping down.

Simsa's hand struck out into the night air in turn without her
quite realizing that she did so (unless she could not bear to so easily
lose the only fortune she had ever come even promise-close to
obtaining). Zass, though her flying skill had never been restored
since her wing had mended, was still not altogether lost in the air.
The zorsal's claws scraped the girl's arm as she ran down its length,
Simsa holding steady until the creature took off in a fluttering
downward spiral which was far from the beautiful, exact swoops of
her progeny, but which landed her near upon the struggling men
below. Simsa turned and grabbed for a weapon—the extinguished
lamp on the table. Pushing that, dripping its oil down her, into her
broad girdle, she flung the shutter wide and followed the zorsal out.

There was a narrow ledge, which she had earlier marked, running to the edge of the inn's front wall. From that. it was easy enough to swing to the pavement, land with the expertise she had learned years earlier. Once she had shaken off the jar of her meeting with the cobbles, she was on her feet and running.

There came a screech from the entanglement on the pavement. Simsa nodded to herself. As silent as any night thief, the unexpected attack of a zorsal was something which could tear worse than that cry out of him if Zass was given a fair opening to go for throat, face or eyes.

Before the girl reached the fighters they had separated.

One lay in a huddle on the ground, but the one who had risen to his feet was clearly the off-worlder. There were voices now—Simsa reached the two and the man turned, crouching, ready to attack just as she got out:

"Come, star rover!" She caught at the arm which was rising to aim at her, held on while she stooped and dropped her heavy burdened sleeve for the zorsal to catch at and climb so swiftly that its claws tore well into even that stout material.

Then with her fingers sliding down the man's arm to close about his wrist, she jerked him towards the other end of the street.

"We run!" she said and gave an extra pull to the wrist she held as a way of urging him on.

He did not stop to question her and for that she was thankful as, still hand linked, they dodged into a side street, found the wide door of the inn's ware entrance and that gave to the nudging of her shoulder. Since there were no rivermen here to leave their cargoes in the cubbies provided, she had made very sure earlier that the bar was loosened to aid in an unseen going or coming. The Burrowers' instinct that one must always have two entrances at least to every hole had brought her to make this discovery and prepare to take advantage of it.

Inside, she led her companion up the back stairs to the upper-roofed but unsided gallery and so through a hall and into the room. Even as she dropped the bar of that into place and was free to jerk the dripping lamp out and smack it down on the uncertainly legged table, she could hear movement, low voices, and a clatter in the street.

The zorsal fluttered toward the now open window where Simsa, brushing past the off-worlder, was also a moment later.

There were men below—at least three of them—gathered around one who lay groaning on the pavement. Coming with stick lamps down the street were peacemen—who never ordinarily ventured into this district at all. Simsa's eyes narrowed almost as did Zass' when the sun struck them. There was no reason for the Guild Watch to come—who had summoned them? The one cry the assailant had uttered could not have reached over five streets, up one wide avenue, to their usual patrol route. Even if it had, they would have taken no note since that sounded from the lower town. The Thieves' Guild had their own watchmen—so—

"Arfellen's men—" He spoke in a whisper which was uttered so close to her that his breath could be felt against her cheek. She started, unaware that he could move so silently as to come up beside her without her noting.

Lord Arfellen! So sure was she that the attacker had been one of the Thieves' Guild that at first the name he had uttered meant nothing to her. Then she saw in the blaze of the stick torches gathered in a knot about the man still lying on the pavement (some of those about him had managed to get away before the arrival of the watch guard, but two were having their arms twisted expertly behind their backs, nooses drooped over their heads) that these same guards wore shoulder badges not of the Guild itself but of some lord's personal following—

Arfellen! Without thought, Simsa whirled, her claws unsheathed, ready to tear to ribbons this fool who had brought down upon her such disaster. She heard her own guttural sound of sheer rage, not unlike that cry of Zass's when the zorsal was about to attack. Her claw nails caught—once—and then there was a grip of iron about her thin wrist; expert in defense as she was, she could not break that grasp. He twisted her arm about and up behind her shoulders with the same ease that the guard below made sure of their prisoners. Next he would march her down the stair, join her to that sorry company and what she could expect waited beyond!

Simsa shivered and hated herself for shivering. However,

instead of jerking her around and pushing her towards the door she had so lately barred, he instead pulled her closer to him. His other arm came up about her waist holding her a vise of bone of flesh strength such as she had never met before, once more then he whispered, his breath once more warm against her cheek.

"Be still!"

Completely bewildered, Simsa tried to understand. Was the starman not going to claim protection from one of the foremost and most powerful guild lords? Surely that squad below who had come so swiftly after the attack on him must have been sent for his benefit. It was well known that the off-worlders were not to be touched in Kuxortal—they were not to be considered natural prey by anyone, high or low.

Yet this one did not call down to his would-be deliverers. He was acting instead as might a man who had something to hide, or someone to fear. Slowly, Simsa relaxed a little, no longer tensing her whole body against his prisoning hold.

4

No one approached the inn door nor the doors of any of the other buildings though Simsa fully expected them to come searching for this off-worlder. Why else would the personal guard of one of the highest of the Guild Lords trail him to this lower level? She stood unresisting now in his grasp watching the men gather up the one lying on the street, forcing at least two of their other captives to carry him, or rather half drag his limp body between them, as the whole party started up slope the city above.

Zass had flown over to hang on the shutter, her antennae fully extending towards what was happening below. Now, as the guards went on their way, the off-worlder released the girl and reached out to swing the shutters to, leaving them in darkness.

"What do you do here?" Simsa broke the silence of that darkness first. She had to know what he was involved in in order to prepare for her own defense.

"What I promised—to bring you this!"

She heard a rustle in the dark, then a clinking from where the table must stand.

"Here is the reckoning between us."

She felt her way to the table, sought the lamp. A goodly portion of its content had gone on her when she had seized it up as a possible weapon. She stank of its thick odor. Now she clicked a fire-spark and set what was left to its work. There was indeed a pouch, a fat pouch, on the table top. On the other side of the board stood the

45

off-worlder watching her through eyes which seemed now to be the narrowest of slits.

Simsa made no move to touch the pouch. To be drawn further into this stranger's affairs, even just to the point of selling him what he wanted, was the last thing she desired. Yet—they had made trade bargain—and no one save he, she, and the Old One (in her time) knew of the two pieces Simsa carried. She was very certain that if they did trace what she had sold Gathar back to her, they could not fix on this second sale. She would leave here before dawn, using that same back way—or even the house tops if she must. Still—she had to know.

She used her oil sticky fingers to free the wrist band of her sleeve, seek out the carvings, not looking at what she did, rather keeping a wary eye on the other. He had not moved and his hands, free and empty, hung in plain sight.

As the girl pulled out the small packet which contained the carvings, something else spun free into the light of the lamp, the violence of its spin freeing it from the scrap of cloth she had thought so firmly bound around it. It was as if fate itself had begun to betray her, Simsa thought, as she snatched for that, caught only the cloth and dumped the contents fully into the shine of the lamp.

The ring did not glitter, the metal of its fashioning was too soft a sheen, it had been buried perhaps too long, and its single remaining stone was milkily opaque and not cut to blaze forth in glory. Yet, there was no mistaking, no hiding now what had so seemingly loosened itself through no will of hers.

That circlet with its tiny castle mount for the unknown stone lay revealed to both of them. Simsa hurled aside the packet of the carvings, scooped, with claw-extended fingers, for the ring. She might have parted, had there been both opportunity and need, with the two other pieces of jewelry—those from the Old One's caches, but this—no! From the first moment she had found it, something within her claimed it, knew that it must be hers alone.

Though the off-worlder had picked up the packet, shaken the carvings free of their covering and inspected them as any prudent purchaser would, he quickly turned his attention again to her hand.

For some reason, perhaps defiance, because he had handled her so easily at the window, Simsa did not thrust the ring into hiding once again. Rather she slipped it over her thumb in full sight.

He did not bend his head any closer to view it. Still, she was as certain as if he did, that he studied it with care. Then, at last, he said—as if the words were forced from him against his will:

"And from where came that?"

"This?" She tapped it with the slightly extended foreclaw of her other hand. "This was the Old One's gift—(which was truth after a fashion—had Simsa not labored to bury Ferwar, she would never have chanced on it)—I do not know from where she had it."

Now he did extend his hand. "Will you let me see it?"

She would not take it off, the longer she felt its weight on her finger the more natural that seemed. But she lifted her hand a fraction closer to him.

"X-Arth maybe," he said very softly, almost in wonder.

"The ring could be that of a Moon Sister, or High Lady. But here?" He must ask the question of himself rather than her, Simsa decided. She had a new flow of curiosity.

"What is Moon Sister? A High Lady? Yes, of them I have heard."

He shook his head and there was impatience in his voice when he answered.

"I do not speak of the Lady of one of your Guild Lords. The High Lady was of another world and time. She could summon powers my race were never able to measure, and the Moon was her crown and her strength."

Though the Burrowers gave no lip service nor bowed knees except to Fortune, Simsa thought she understood: A goddess.

The temples of the upper city served only those with precious metal to pay for sacrifices (not that Simsa had ever heard of any surprising answer to prayer muttered or full-sung in any of *those* halls). If there were gods and goddesses on this world, they busied themselves only with those who already had the warm right hand of fortune on their shoulders. Only how did the symbol of a goddess known to the off-worlder come to lie under a rock down by the burial pits?

This X-Arth he hunted—what did the Lord Arfellen have to do
with that?

"Those guards—they followed you." She flipped the ring about
so only the band was showing, the castle, as he called it, lay against
her palm in hiding. "What has Lord Arfellen to do with you—or—
what is more important—does he know of me?"

She was not sure he would tell her. He was frowning now,
wrapping the carvings in the same piece of cloth she had used,
putting them with care into his belt pouch. He did not answer, but
rather went once more, with a tread so quick and easy that in spite
of his spacer's boots he made no sound crossing the room, to peer
out a crack between the shutter and the casing.

"The lamp—" He made an impatient gesture and she guessed
what he wanted, blew out the flame, then heard the squeak of the
shutter as he must have pulled it farther open. Zass complained with
a growl and Simsa joined the off-worlder in time to take the weight
of the zorsal back on her shoulder.

There was nothing below. No one moved. They might be looking
down upon the street of a deserted city. Simsa, bred to the Burrows
and the alarms of the fringe places, understood the threat which
hung as a part of that very silence.

"Lord Arfellen—" she whispered.

He made a swift movement, held his hand hard across her
mouth. His answer came in the thinnest thread of a whisper. She
wouldn't have believed he could have spoken so softly and yet have
the words reach her with such clarity.

"Listen well—Arfellen's men followed me to spy. Is there any
way out of here? He may have loosed more than just the guard to
dog me—"

How much would her help be worth, that question flashed first
into her mind, only to be followed by the sense of her own danger.
If the Guild Lord's men hunted this off-worlder, an alien whom all
the customs of Kuxortal protected, then how much more they
would profit in taking her for whose very skin they would not have
to answer to anyone? They could crush her dry in one of their
question rooms and learn all she knew—yet try to wring more out

of her. Only if the off-worlder was safe—for now—could she also hope to have time to work out her own method of escape from his troubles.

There was only one place—the Burrows. No one of the upper city came seeking there. There were far too many runways and passages, too many hiding holes. Those from the upper city had long ago given up hope of flushing any who fled there, depending indeed on the clannishness of the Burrowers themselves, who resented any newcomers and would set up and deliver up to the authorities an upper-town fugitive.

Only if one struck a bargain with a Burrower—one of enough weight of arm to defend himself and his prey—could any fugitive hope for refuge—then only for a short time.

Simsa's thought spun back and forth in a whirl. There was one way she could take the off-worlder back to the very den she had hoped to have seen the last of. It would cause talk, yes—but she could do it openly and none would stand between her and a dubious, fleeting safety. First—the money.

She pulled out of the off-worlder's loose hold to catch up the bag of broken bits, stuff it deep into her sleeve and fasten the wrist button. Then her hands went to the tight wrapping about her head. She pulled off the many strands of that, shook free her thick mat of silver hair, then smeared the band pieces across her eyebrows and lashes to remove some of the protective coloring. She was not to be Shadow now, but play a very different role.

"There is a way," she said softly as she scrubbed away her disguise. "We have some play-women in the Burrows. None have ever brought back a ship man. Though some of the lesser river traders—when they are drunk enough—will come for their pleasure. Take this," she groped her way to the bed she had hoped to lie soft on and never had a chance to even try, and snatched up its upper cover pushing it on him where he stood—a darkened blotch between her and the open window, the lights from below giving her that much guidance now. "Put it about you as a cloak. Now—if you can stand being thought a Burrow woman's pleasure buyer!"

He was following her, though she was not sure at that moment whether she wanted that or not. Once more, they made the way through the back parts of the inn, even as they had entered a short time before.

As they came under a dim lantern, she thought she heard a faint exclamation out of him, but when she turned her head quickly he was quiet. So they passed into a side street, Simsa in the lead, he following with that soft tread on her very heels. Down they went, skirting a wall which was a division point between the city and the fringe. There were secrets there, known well to her people. She stopped beside what looked to be a regular section of that same wall, but was merely lamperwood, hard as iron even in such a small panel and skillfully overlaid with paint and dirt to appear as solid as the stone on either side.

Simsa slipped through that easily enough, her large companion found it a tighter squeeze, but he did not delay her longer. She went only a few more steps until she darted into a cellar left open to the sky and then caught his hand to lead him through a maze of passages far better known to her than the streets above their heads.

Thus she came back after a momentous day and night in a full circle to that place she had never thought to see again—Ferwar's Burrow. In the dark, she found a battered lamp which fed upon not oil from the upper city but the squeezings of certain ill-smelling ground nuts which had to be pressed for weary spaces of time to give forth their juices, so that lamp light at all was treasure in the Burrows. Still, if there were eyes for the seeing now, let them mark that she was not alone.

However, as she set spark to the battered saucer-like bowl of mud which held that oil, she was not prepared for the wonderment in the off-worlder's eyes. For a moment, she was startled at the strange look he turned upon her. Then she remembered that, for the first time in years, she had taken off that discreet covering which had made her "Shadow."

"But you are—you are a woman!" His surprise was so open and complete that she was startled a little in turn. Did her disguise then hold so well that even her sex had been undiscovered when she ventured forth? He had indeed, she remembered back now, addressed her by that queer off-planet greeting she had heard given to males. But she had merely thought that these aliens had but one form of greeting for all.

Now, hardly knowing why, she raised her hands and ran her fingers through her silvery hair. It floated a little at the touch, the electricity aroused by her treatment moving its lighter strands. It was seldom and only in private nowadays that she unwrapped her hair so. In fact, now she felt an odd kind of embarrassment which was better left hidden.

"I am Simsa—" Perhaps Gathar had already spoken her name.

She saw the look of awe change into a slight smile on the off-worlder's face.

"My House name is Thorn," he placed his two hands together, palm meeting and bowed across them. "My given-by-father name, Chan-li. My friend name—Yun."

Simsa laughed suddenly. "What a world of names! How do those you know choose among them if they would call you?" She seated herself cross-legged on the pile of mats which had been Ferwar's. With a wave of beringed hand, the girl indicated the smaller collection of woven rush squares which were of her own making and had been her bed-place.

He seated himself limberly in the same fashion. It was odd what she was finding out about this stranger. His smile was gone from his lips, but it still seemed to hold in his eyes which had opened to their widest extent when he looked at her and now remained that way.

"Those who are kin say 'Chan', my friends 'Yun'."

She gave another combing toss to her hair. To sit here in idle talk was not enough. There was that she must know and as soon as she might.

"Tell me now," she commanded, "what dealing have you with Lord Arfellen that his guards follow you and yet you would have none of them? Do you know that he has only to crook his finger joint so much as this," she stretched out her ringed thumb and made a slight curve in the air, "and he can have the life of near any one in Kuxortal, and set to tremble a few more he could not kill at once? What have you done?"

This Thorn did not seem in the least disturbed by her questions now. He sat as easily as if he were any Burrower. In fact easier than any who would now dare to enter *this* particular chamber.

"I asked questions—questions concerning my brother who went off into your world some seasons ago and of whom there had been no word since, though he was pledged to a meeting he would not have missed unless he had met with dire trouble. You spoke of him as a witling who went into the Hard Hills. I swear to you that no matter how it would seem to your people, he had good reason to go there, to hunt what he had come to discover. Now—" he hesitated for a moment and then added with the sharpness of a Guild man voicing an order, "can you tell me any other rumors concerning him? Or why anyone would wish him to come to ill?"

"There were tens of tens ways in which he could have come to ill," she returned, striving to keep her voice as cool and stern as his own. "The Hard Hills have their secrets in plenty. Most men travel by river or by sea. It used to be long ago—when I was very young, that caravans still came in from Qurux across the desert lands which front the Hard Hills. Those were from Semmele and they brought strange things from the north for the trading. Then we heard of a plague which made Semmele a place of dead men and ghosts and no caravans came. What they had ever brought was little—the Guilds could well make up the yield from the rivermen. So the way there was lost. Yes, there was talk when the off-worlder hunted out three of the old caravan men. They say he offered a fortune in broke-bits for a guide. Two of them would have none of his urging—the other got into a shuffle with one of Lord Arfellen's guards and thereafter agreed to go." She was suddenly aware of what she had said and repeated slowly, "Lord Arfellen's guard . . ." more to herself than to him.

"So and so." He used the trader's speech so easily that if she shut her eyes, she could not be sure he was not of Kuxortal. "These other two—are they still here?"

The girl shrugged. "If they are, surely Gathar will find them for you. Have you not already made such a bargain with him?"

Again he was smiling. "Your knowledge seems to stretch a long way, Gentlefem Simsa. Does it touch any more on such as this?" He patted with his hand the belt pouch into which he had put the carvings.

"All I know is that the Old One had a liking for such. What I found, what was brought to her, she kept."

"What you found—where?" He caught that up eagerly.

"In the Burrows. We dig into the back years of Kuxortal, we who live on her refuse. Some of that refuse being very old. Once this," again she gestured, "might well have been part of some Lord's palace place. There are bits of wall paint still in yonder corner. Things have been lost as houses collapsed, were built over. Kuxortal was sacked by pirates, three times attacked by armies before the rise of the River lords and their alliance. There has been much destroyed and built upon over and over again. The Burrowers live in the past and on what they can scoop from their tunnels. We are less than dust to the Guild Lords."

"Even in your place here, you must have heard things from the upper city," he seemed unable to take his eyes from her silver hair, he studied her, Simsa began to think, as if *she* were some bit or piece turned up in the underways, "what do you know of Lord Arfellen?"

Her interest was caught now. He was speaking to her as an equal, something which had never happened as far as she could remember. To the Old One, she had always been a child, to the Burrowers a stranger, though she had been born among them she was sure. Yet, none of them had ever matched her coloring of skin or hair. To Gathar, her main contact in the upper city, she was only a young one of a people his kind had long held in contempt. Though her management of the zorsals had won grudging respect in so far as it aided him. But to this off-worlder, she was a person one asked advice of, one whose knowledge and opinions were held in the same esteem as if he were speaking to one of the upper town.

"He is the richest of the Guild Lords, his line the oldest," she began. "It is he who is the first signer every third season on the trade wares brought in. He is not seen often—having many to be hands and feet for him. He is—" she moistened her lips with tongue tip—what she would say now as pure conjecture and rumor and she hesitated to add that to pad out the little she did know.

"There is something else," he broke that minute of silence.

"They tell tales about him, that he is hunted in one place and cannot be found, later he comes from there and says that he was always there. He is said to go to none of the temples on the heights as do the other lords, but he keeps in his service one who talks with the dead. And that he is a seeker—"

"A seeker!" Thorn pounced upon that as Zass would upon a ver-rat. "Is it also rumored as to what he seeks?"

"Treasure. Yet that he does not need, for much flows ever into his stronghold and little comes out again. He hires many guards and sometimes those travel up river. Their leader may come back next season but they do not. Perhaps he sells them as fighters to the River Lords—there is always quarreling there still."

"You have never heard of him sending to the Hard Hills?"

Simsa laughed. "All the treasure in the world would not send him there. No one goes in that direction, I tell you, no one."

"But one shall," he leaned a little forward, caught her gaze with his and held it steady. "For I shall, Gentlefem."

"Then you will die—as did your brother." She refused to be impressed by more than his folly.

"I think not." Now he took from his pouch the two bits of carving he had bought from her. "This I have to tell you, Gentlefem—but first answer me—how safe are you in these Burrows of yours?"

"Safe? Why do you ask that?"

Before he could answer, Zass straightened up on her perch over the low door of the Burrow. She flung back her head and gave a cry which brought Simsa upstanding, her claws expanding instantly in answer to an alarm which had reached her brain less than a second earlier. Then through the door itself came two winged creatures. As each seemed to erupt into the chamber, so swift was its emergence from the tunnel beyond, it gave a deeper cry in answer to Zass's welcome, before both planed down to stand before the girl.

There was no mistaking these—Zass's sons. That they were here meant some catastrophe at their abiding place—the warehouse. The alien caught at her hand.

"Can they be followed?"

"Not save by another of their kind. And there are none such I know of who are so trained. But—" She looked from the zorsals to the off-worlder. "I do not understand what they are doing here. They would not have left Gathar for any reason unless—unless there is trouble there! Was that the reason you asked of me concerning safety? What has happened to Gathar?" More important what might happen to her who was well known to have dealings with that waremaster even if it were only because of the zorsals? Plenty knew that she had trained them and only rented out the creature's services, refusing to sell them to him.

"I did not get your silver from him," the off-worlder returned. "When I would have gone back to his place, I saw the badges of Arfellen on men at his door. And I had already had warning that my questions had startled the lord. I do not know what he seeks—I have no reason to be connected with any trade trouble which he may have. But one of the starcrew passed me a message that much concerning me has been asked of the captain and that he has received orders that when the ship lifts, I am not to remain."

"Yet you came to me!" She spat that in pure anger and wanted nothing more so much as to claw mark that smooth, ivory skin of his so that neither friend nor foe could put rightful name to him again. Only, one ruled by anger, as the Old One had long ago taught her, made fatal mistakes.

"Because I had to, not only to get what you showed me and what is perhaps a very important pointer to that which I seek, but because you might now be my only contact to gather the knowledge I would have. At any rate," he did not drop his gaze, there was even a shadow smile at the corner of his mouth, "is it not true that any who have had dealings with Gathar in any way can now be suspected of whatever irregularity which it will be claimed he is concerned in?"

"What do you want of me?" Both zorsals had crept very close to her feet, were looking up in her face, and uttering small cries as if they would have reassurance. Whatever had driven them from their comfortable quarters had been bad enough to bring them here in open fear.

"A hiding place, whatever knowledge you can glean, and a way to reach the Hard Hills," he told her as if he were merely reciting items from some trader's list.

She wanted to screech at him in a voice as harsh as Zass's that she was no worker of powerful fortune. Judging by what she had heard, and now guessed from the arrival of the zorsals, they had been lucky in that they were still uncaptured. Simsa looked about the cavern a little wildly. She had always considered herself a cool and careful person, one who planned and thought before she tried any action. She was beginning to lose confidence in herself.

No. She bit her lip. There was enough installed by Ferwar's harsh training to hold her together now. She could think still, plan— For a start she looked to the zorsals and uttered the single short cry which was her order to search. Zass had not descended from her door perch; now she, too, urged her offspring to their duty, sending them out again to hide and spy along the Burrows.

From any of the kind who dwelt here they would have no help at all. Ferwar had been feared in her day, Simsa resented and, after her besting of Baslter, hated by more than one. They would be eager to reveal to any who came seeking where exactly the prey might have taken cover. Then she and this twice damned off-worlder would be dug out as easily as one dug a well steamed or-crab out of its shell.

There was only one choice and it was being forced upon her in too swift and too sharp a way—she wanted time to plan and she knew that she had none. With this off-worlder at her heels, she could not melt away again in a shadow role. Anywhere in Kuxortal, he would be as visible as a lighted lamp in a night-dark room.

"This way."

She had wheeled about, went to pull up the sleep mats which had formed Ferwar's bed place to reveal the secret the Old One had guarded with her own body for seasons of years, judging by the work done on it, and which Simsa herself did not know in all its parts. He joined her without asking, bundling aside the mats she pushed towards him. What lay underneath in the poor light of the Burrow was a long stone seemingly as fixed as a rooted plant. However, the girl, who had learned the secret once when she had tripped over Zass and had fallen with hands outstretched, now knelt and set the palms of her hands hard in certain very shallow indentations she could feel but not see.

The end of the stone rose as she bore down with her full strength. A musty odor puffed into their faces. Simsa clucked to Zass—knowing she need not recall the other two, for they could trace their dam to the end of this way with ease. She picked up the lamp in one hand, bundled the zorsal up against her with the other, and descended the shallow steps waiting there. The off-worlder swung down behind her. She did not turn her head as she said:

"There is a hold on the stone, fit your hand to it, close this way after us." She descended as rapidly as she could to give him the room he need to obey her orders. Then she stood in a very narrow runway which was thick dust underfoot, but which had air with a distinct smell of the river. This was a way out she believed that even Burrowers might take a lengthy time discovering. They could reach the riverside among the refuse dumps—beyond that she would not try yet to plan.

5

A smell of the sea tainted with the stench from the refuse dumps met Simsa as she wriggled through the last opening, Zass hopped ahead, grumbled gutturally to herself, the off-worlder kept to more laborious passage behind. Then they were out in the night—though Simsa believed that dawn could not be far distant. She sidled forward with no hope of avoiding all the pitfalls of water-washed trash, the pools of putrid matter, holding one hand across her mouth and nose to screen out what was possible, and regretting that so soon her hard-earned new clothing was thus being reduced to less than the rags she had discarded them for.

Once away from the worst of the heaps, on the part of sand the incoming tide washed clear by dripping rush, she turned quickly to her companion.

"Your ship lies there—" she kept her voice low. However, she had caught his arm in the dark, dragged him about to face the distant glow of light marking the landing field. "You can reach it from seaward."

"I have no ship to reach," he returned.

"You are off-world—" Simsa had yet to understand just what part the Guild Lords could play in the future of any starman. Certainly, they could not touch nor hold him.

They cared too much for the star trade to anger the off-worlders who manned those ships by making any move against a member of their company. All in Kuxortal knew only too well what might follow any interference with the ship people.

"I am on my own here," he answered.

"You said that Lord Arfellen has given word that when the ship lifts you are not to remain—" she pointed out hotly.

"I have certain duties which no ship's captain can question. I came here to hunt for a man. Nor shall I leave until I find him, or else have certain knowledge of what has happened to him—more than a general word that he has vanished in a territory which no one seems to know anything about and that no search has made for him thereafter."

"And how do you get to the Hard Hills then to do that hunting?" Simsa wanted to know. "You will not gain any aid from the men of Kuxortal, not if Lord Arfellen has declared it to be thus."

She could not see him clearly, he was only a darker blot in the night. When he answered, it was calmly and with a note in his voice which made her uneasy.

"There are always ways one can get anything one truly sets all his energy and desire upon gaining. Yes, I shall see the Hard Hills. However, what happens now to you?"

"So at last your mind turns to that?" she snapped. "Kuxortal is no place for me if Gathar is in trouble. All who had dealings with him shall suffer—for the Guildmen can nose out a trail half a year cold if they wish. Also, the Burrowers will not shield me. I was the Old One's eyes, feet, and ears—while she lived. Now I am fair game."

"Why did they fear her?"

Simsa did not know why she lingered here arguing with this alien. She owed him no explanations. Only—where might she go now? Gathar, who had been her one contact with the upper town, could no longer be depended upon. She had a bag heavy with broken bits weighing down one sleeve. But bought men and women stayed bought only so long as they were not offered more—either in silver or in freedom from danger—by another.

"They thought she had a seeing eye. That was not true. She only knew a great deal about people—she could look into their faces, listen to their voices when her eyesight dimmed the more, and tell much of what they thought or felt. She could read and she could

speak with many strangers in their own language. She was—
different—not a true Burrower. I do not know her beginnings but
they must have lain far from where she landed. Now—why do we
waste time speaking of a dead woman? You had best go to your
ship—if you would stay alive—"

"And you?" her persisted.

Did he believe he owed her something? He did not, unless she
demanded it. Any more than she was responsible for him, though
she had been forced to aid him after a fashion this night.

"I will go my own way—"

"Where?"

She felt as if he had her pinned helplessly against a Burrow wall,
held so by his questioning alone. It was not his affair that she might
find Kuxortal now too dangerous. But where *would* she go? For a
moment, the chill of panic shook her before she forced it under
control.

From overhead came a chittering. Her head moved a little as she
answered that with a click of tongue, even as Zass, squatting near
unseen at her feet, also voiced a cry. The two younger zorsals she
had loosed in the Burrows had found them. So—with them to
protect and be her eyes and ears—she had a better chance.

"If we head north," the off-worlder continued, "going along the
shore, to where will we come?"

"We—?" she questioned. "You think that I shall go with you?"

"Have you a better plan?" he countered.

She wanted so much to say "yes;" still knew that she could not.
His question had shaken her thoughts out of the whirl of uncertainty
to a point where she was trying to see ahead a little.

"If one follows the shoreline"—she would not say "we"—"there
is a little fishing village some distance on. This part of the shore is
not good—there is so much refuse spewed into the waters. Also, the
best anchorage below the city is for Guild-tied ships and they will
not permit that to be used even in the times when no fleet comes in.
Beyond the fishers there is only barren land to rim the desert. That
is the Coast of Dead Men, where there is no water to be found—only
sand and rock, and things which can live on both and do."

"For how long does this coast of Dead Men continue?"

Simsa shrugged, though she knew he could not see such a gesture. "Forever, perhaps. No man has ever in my hearing spoken of an end. There are long reefs out to sea which can claw open the hull of a boat as easily as Zass can crack a ver-rat bone between her teeth. Men do not bear north, unless the sea itself turns against them with some storm. Those who do are never seen again."

"However, if one goes far enough along the coast, one can come northward to the same general latitude as the Hard Hills. Yes, it might be done!" he suggested.

"By spirits who have conveniently left their bodies behind them!" Simsa retorted.

"North, you say—" He was moving away. Not even waiting to see if she was coming, too. Simsa seethed. He had pulled her into this black trouble and now she must agree to this new utter folly he suggested, at least a portion of it, or be left to confront too many enemies on too many levels of the city which had always been her home and given her what small security she had known.

She spat out several burning and bitter words, the vilest in her vocabulary, stooped and picked up Zass to set her on the usual shoulder perch, and then went after him with the two other zorsals taking once more to the air. At least with them for scouts, she need not fear a surprise attack.

Nor did the off-worlder wait for her to catch up. He took her so much for granted did he, that he was sure she would follow? The girl would have given anything to be able to take off in the opposite direction. She debated, as she went, whether she could just have made some kind of a case for herself by heading back to the starport and betraying him to his fellows. At least her chances of not being drawn in herself would be better with the starcrew then with any of the Lord Arfellen's men. *That* was wisdom as she had learned it in her Burrower years. Why then was she prowling along behind this stranger, half committed to his plans? Because she had no real answer to that question, Simsa was angry with herself, ready to lash out at the first chance she was given to unload this tangle of emotions she could not form into decent and regular order.

They were beyond the refuse heaps now and she breathed heavily of the cleaner sea air. The starman, she noted, in the slowly graying light rising over the sea itself was hurrying. Also, he was walking with long strides where the waves washed to erase his tracks. Simsa halted for a moment, pulled off her sandals, and followed his lead again, feeling the rise of the water about her bare feet and ankles, soaking the ends of her tight trousers where they were bound about her shins.

The fishing village showed lights ahead. Simsa, with extra-long strides, caught up with her companion, pulling his arm.

"Their boats go out before dawn," she told him. "The haverings run then. If you do not want half the world to know what you desire to do, for the present you will wait."

He slowed for a step or so and looked down at her. In this very faint light, she could see his face only as a light blur and she thought perhaps he might not be able to see her at all. Until she remembered her hair and dropped her hold on him to hastily draw out a length of head cloth, binding that into a secure head covering.

"Wait for what?" he asked. "If we want to have a boat—"

"You will not deal with the Headman," she retorted, knotting her scarf with a last twist, made so viciously tight because of her perturbation that she could have cried out in pain. "Let the men go. It is with the House mistress of the Headman that any bargain should be made. Lustita—if she is still ruling in that house—will always have the final word."

"You know her?"

"A little. She had some dealings with the Old One once or twice. She is a woman who likes a heavy purse in her sleeve, and not having it known to her man that she carries such. You wait here. I shall see—" She had taken a step or two past him and then she looked back curiously.

"How do you know that I am not going to cry up those who will hold you for Lord Arfellen?" she asked.

"That you ask me that—No, I do not fear betrayal, Lady Simsa. You have had good chances in plenty to do that several times this night and have not taken them."

"You trust too easily and too much!" The wrath she had been holding so long broke then. She could have screamed at him. "Had I been taken with you, what story could I have told which would have saved me? Me, the lowest of what Lord Arfellen would deem harbor scum? You must not trust me—nor anyone."

"Wait—" He had unsealed the front of his tightly fitting uniform. Now he tossed her a small bag which she caught without thinking. "If your Headman's woman wants pay—give it to her. Ask in return a boat—a small one, which I must see before the bargain is complete—also provisions. Sweeten her with part of this and promise her more only when all is ready."

The bag was heavy—though so small. No bits of silver in that, Simsa was sure. She said nothing but went, grim-faced as she padded along on the sand. So he thought so little of her warning that he put this in her hands? She hated him hotly for slighting her so, making it now impossible for her to do anything but her best to carry out his insane plan. She would get him his boat—if she possibly could—and what he wanted in it—but that would be the end. This village was as far away as they would continue to travel together.

The sun was well up, lighting a narrow tongue of the sea which formed a cove hardly large enough to run the small craft into shoreward. Simsa sat on her heels well shadowed by rocks with Zass on a tall, weed-draped stone near her, dividing her attention between the labors of the off worlder and the cliff above where their two other zorsals taking up sentry posts, intent, the girl trusted, on both land and sea approaches to this hideout.

She was sure after the first few moments of her trafficking with Lustita that this had not been the first such transaction which the House mistress had conducted. She had looked at the trade bar stamped with the seal of the Metal Guild, weighed it in one large red hand, then had demanded:

"For what?" Bluntly, as if Simsa merely was bargaining for a catch of spaeels.

"For a boat, foremost, a seaworthy one," the girl had answered as tersely, "later—he who sent this will ask for the rest."

The woman's small eyes had narrowed until they seemed no larger than the pits of varc fruit buried in an oversized brown pudding. Then she had nodded.

"Well enough. Go to where there are two standing rocks on the cliff. Those look like fingers raised in a scorn sign. Wait there—"

She had scooped the single bar up with a hand large enough to hold the whole of it. Though Simsa was certain that she herself had been recognized as the fetch-and-carry for the Old One, nothing in Lustita's eyes, voice, or expression revealed that. She felt a little easier in her mind, certain that she had read this woman aright.

They had gone inland, twice creeping flat on their bellies to round ends of cultivated garden fields, but had reached the appointed rendezvous well before the sun was high. Nor had they been there long before Lustita, walking easily in spite of a huge basket making a shoulder burden which could weigh as much as a small man, rounded the point of that narrow inlet. She had a rake in one hand, was methodically harvesting streamers of the dark red weed, which, when dried, could be ground into powder and sold for fertilizer on those same fields past which they had earlier crawled.

Simsa arose from behind the rocks just long enough for the fisherwoman to sight her, then ducked down again. Without missing a single strand of the weed, Lustita reached them, though Simsa had to call on patience to wait out her arrival.

Lustita gave a grunt, resting her leaking basket on a rock top, leaning back against the same support. The off-worlder stood face to face her, but did not come completely out of hiding. There was no change on the woman's stolid face.

"A boat—she said—" Lustita gave the slightest of nods towards Simsa. "What else then?"

"What all is needful to get that same boat along the coast." He spoke the straight trade language with its different inflections of speech, but Lustita had enough dealings in Kuxortal to understand. "Provisions, water—charts of the shoreline—"

Her scanty eyebrows slid up. "Why not bargain for a High Lord's own shallop?" she returned. "Boat, yes, that can be done. Frankis has been drunk once too often, his house mistress would be glad to earn a bit, and also teach him a lesson. He lies now in the watch house where he tends a smarting back for having landed too good a blow on a Guild guard, so he shall not be free for ten tens of days—maybe still longer. Provisions—yes, those can be gathered, a few here, a few there. And there will be no questions if they are brought together so. Charts—" she grinned showing gaps between big yellowed teeth, "we have none such. Our men carry their sea-lore in their heads—and beat it into their sons when the time comes. A sore back makes a lad remember very well. If you would take to the sea it will be by your own fortune and none borrowed from us."

"Very well." Simsa suspected that the off-worlder had really not expected much different an answer.

"I have one bar of trade metal," Lustita continued. "Shall we say five more?"

"Shall we say a thousand?" Simsa countered. Caution made her object. Pay the first toll mentioned and they would arouse the woman's interest in them to the point where she might consider she could perhaps deal even more profitably with others. There was only the situation of their village which linked the river traders with the sea farers, the fisherfolk were not too much in awe of the guilds. Even the laws of Kuxortal did not touch them, save when, as the unlucky Frankis, they fell into trouble within the city itself.

Lustita shrugged and her basket wavered a little. "Those who would purchase help cannot keep fast hand on the purse," she commented. "Well enough—make it four then. But less than that I shall not go. It will take time—though the boat will come first."

"How much time?" the starman wanted to know.

"A day—maybe part of the night. Things done in caution cannot be hurried. You shall have full measure. Give me half more now—"

Reluctantly, Simsa obeyed the nod of the alien and slid two more of the bars from the purse which she kept carefully concealed within her sleeve. Lustita must not be able to see the size or weight of that.

Though she had expressed not the slightest surprise upon discovering that one of those with whom she must bargain was an off-worlder, her outward indifference could mean little. Simsa did not trust her, though she believed from what she knew of the fisherwoman's dealings with the Old One that the woman was close mouthed in her own way. And she owed no service to the guild men.

The boat had arrived even as she promised, propelled by two bare-legged, bare-armed girls, who also had weed baskets with them. They had tied up the craft, scrambled out, shouldered their baskets and went on their way, carefully never raising their eyes from what they did, splashing off as if well pleased to be done with a bothersome task.

Simsa continued to sit behind her rock, watching the off-worlder carefully inspect the craft. It was not made for far sailing, though it had a single mast. She guessed it used mainly for coast traveling when the spaeels came inshore to lay their eggs and that it would not last long in storm-tossed open water. But the way the starman went about his examination impressed her in spite of herself. It was evident that he was familiar with boats not unlike this one, no matter on what strange other world he had gained such knowledge. When he at last came back to her hidden cranny, he flung himself down with a sigh as if some small part of a heavy burden had slipped from him.

"It is a stout craft," he commented, "with a shallow draw—such as can well go exploring along the coast—"

"A coast with teeth such as you have never seen—hard rock teeth!" she retorted. "And what if you do spy your Hard Hills inland? They will be well back from the coast—you will have no way of reaching them. You could not carry food and water to make such a trip and, even if you reached the Hills, you would only die there."

"Lady Simsa," he rolled over on his back, flinging one arm up to half shadow his face and screen his eyes from the sun, which had found its way into their cranny, "what legends do they tell of this Hard Hills country?"

She cupped up a handful of sand, allowed the fine grit to shift away through loose-locked fingers. "What they always say of the unknown—that there is death waiting there. Oh, they talk of treasure waiting too, but no man is mad enough to go hunting it. That is no bargain to be sought."

"Yet I have seen things which came out of those Hills—strange and wondrous things—"

Simsa stared at him. "Where? Not in Kuxortal!" She could be emphatic about that. Such tales would have filtered down the city long since—even to the Burrows.

"I have seen such on another world," he told her. "When the starships found this world, there was no landing field at Kuxortal. Ships came and went before the Guilds even knew that they had planeted here."

Which could be true, she decided, for the land was large and they had certain knowledge only of those parts the traders traveled.

"One such ship landed in the midst of what you call the Hard Hills. The cargo it brought back was such that the least man aboard her was wealthy beyond dreams—"

The girl was very still. Wealth beyond the dreams of the starmen! What could that buy one—even one out of the Burrows with no name, no kin, perhaps the Guilds sniffing at her heels?

"Your brother sought that?" No wonder Lord Arfellen was alerted if this story was true. No Guild Lord ever had enough in the way of treasure to be beyond *his* dreams!

"Yes—not the treasure for itself though—but for the knowledge which lay with it. The ship which returned had certain other finds."

"If a ship could land there once—why not again?" she demanded with instant suspicion.

"Their landing was a forced one. In getting free there was great difficulty—they were very lucky—it would not be tried a second time. But I have all the information my brother had, I know near where to look. I am not quite the fool you have been thinking me— Lady Simsa."

"You still have to cross the desert and you cannot carry enough supplies. Your brother went with one of the wandering folk and only one of those would go—he never came back."

"All true." He nodded, the sand catching in his black hair as his head moved. "However, it is not in my family to leave one of their own lost. There will be ways to fight even the desert, my lady—"

"Why do you call me that?" she suddenly demanded. "I am no kin to any of the High Lords. I am Simsa—"

"But not a Burrower, I think," he answered her.

She scowled at the rock. Before she could make answer to that, there was more splashing in the water. They huddled down behind the rock watching though the zorsals had given no warning.

The same girls who had brought the boat were coming back. Their basket thongs cut deeply into their thin shoulders near bowing them over like old women. Again, paying no attention to the upper part of the cove or the rocks behind which the two hid, they proceeded to down those baskets, scoop out armloads of weed and then dump unto the sand closely woven hampers which they left lying, as they reloaded their much lightened burdens to make off again.

There were other visitors during the afternoon, each bringing baskets, some large, some small. The last came after twilight. Lustita herself in an oared boat containing six jars near as tall as Simsa herself, but empty. These the fisherwoman told them could be filled with water at a spring a short distance to the north. She accepted the last two bars, but before she left she offered a half warning:

"There is trouble in the city—the guards have been out." She spat noisily into the heavy wash of wave. "They have not yet come beyond the north gate. But there has not been such a boiling up since the underwater spirits set the big run of the gar when I was a little maid."

Thorn looked to the girl as the woman tramped away. "I take it that we have been missed—"

"*You* have been missed!" she corrected him sharply.

"I think—"

But what he thought was never to be uttered then for both zorsals on the cliffs above took wing and came fluttering and wheeling down. Simsa did not need their hooting cries, through the deepening dusk, to know that they had sighted more than just the usual coming and going along the coast. The starman seized her hand. She had only time to catch up Zass before he pulled her towards the boat, half threw her on board, told her harshly to stay where she was.

He had brought out a long pole and braced it against the rocks. His shoulders tensed in what she could see was a great effort, he pushed them out, away from the narrow cove. They were in the open sea beyond when she caught a wink of lights on the cliff top, saw one of those on its way down, and understood that the chase had not been dropped, that somehow they had been traced.

Simsa did not like the sea. She found the pitching and rolling of the small boat terrifying, though she would not have allowed her companion to guess at her fear. Nor did she linger when they tied up again, but unbidden helped him to fill the water jars, transport them down and stow them with special care. He had already, during the day, stowed to the best advantage the rest of their small cargo of supplies, and at the time had called her attention to the fact that Lustita had included both fishing lines and a small net in their equipment.

The zorsals settled together on the edge of the small casing over the middle part of the deck which was the only protection against wind and spray. While the off-worlder stepped the small mast, set a triangle of sail to catch the night wind. He took the tiller, and swung the craft north while Simsa crouched under the shelter and wished herself back in the Burrows, ragged, hungry, but with safe and solid land under her two feet.

She had never meant to come this far. It had been her firm intention to bid the alien good fortune and hide out perhaps in the fishing village, even if it cost her most of her gains. But events had all come so suddenly, she was left with no choice—not for now.

However, she decided firmly, as the boat scudded along its way and queasiness made her hate her body, she would never go into the desert! Let this witling of an off-worlder take sight of his hills and tramp off to bake to death among them, she would stay with the boat when that hour came and somehow find a way back. She began to enlarge upon that plan. One could claim to be the survivor of a ship wreck, she thought, even if she knew so little of the sea that she might not deceive any true sailor. Yes, that was it—a traveler from over-seas—wrecked—

She would have plenty of time, maybe days of it, to plan her story. And, being Simsa, she would think up a very good one. After all, it was only zorsals that could make her true identity known. Those should be happy enough to return to a free life in the wilds, leaving her to play the role she decided upon. Settling her crossed arms upon her drawn up knees, the girl rested her chin upon them and busied herself with plans, so hoping to forget the unpleasant churning in her middle.

# 6

The sun threw a burning blight over the land. Simsa had covered as much of her skin against those rays as she could, smearing on fat she had skimmed from one of the jars of fresal soup they had eaten early during the voyage. As she drew herself up to stand beside the off-worlder on a baked rock, which radiated heat as might a cook hole, she knew how impossible were the plans this Thorn had made and added to all during that nightmare of a sea journey. Let him go out into that white hot furnace and frizzle into cinders, she would take her chance with the sea again, as horrible as that had been. Even at the thought of what she had endured the past two days while they had been tossed about by what her companion had persisted in calling a "fresh wind" made her nurse her empty and sore stomach with hands that were cracked and bleeding from the salt water and rope burns—for, as untrained as she was, she had had to lend her strength to their battle against the power of wind and wave.

Before them stretched such a forsaken land as might have been painted as a lesson to discourage any traveler. There were drifts of sand, their white surface spread under this sun to sear the eyes. When there was no sand, rock, worn and scraped by wind-driven grit for more seasons than a man could count, made reefs on land as toothed and forbidding as those reefs through which they had somehow found a way at sea. There was nothing which could live there—

Only, the off-worlder was not surveying the deadly land which stretched forth from the very foot of the cliff up which they had found their way. Instead, he had slipped from one of the loops upon his belt a set of distance glasses which had been folded into themselves, opened them and tinkered with their setting. Now, by their aid, he surveyed the country beyond where heat haze shimmered. Here and there in the middle distance, a spume of sand arose, as if by the bidding of an unseen enemy, to whirl and dance. By squinting between the fingers with which she had quickly shaded her eyes, Simsa could just make out a vague line across the far horizon. The Hard Hills perhaps. Not that she cared.

She turned her back determinedly upon the whole threat of the land and had begun to edge toward the descent from that lookout, when an exclamation from her companion stopped her. When she glanced up, she saw that he now pointed those distance glasses not toward the distant goal but rather downward toward the desert land itself.

"That is the way—"

"What way?" Even two words seemed to crack her lips.

"Our road!" He folded the glasses back, was fitting them into their loop. Simsa was too worn to argue with a madman. If he thought he had found some road, let him take it and be gone. She had been caught too long in the trap of his plans and must free herself before she lost what energy she had left.

Now she asked no questions, merely swung over and began the crawl down the cliff side to the bay where their boat, bearing the signs of its rough passage, rocked in what small waves found their way past the reefs to this pocket which was nearly as narrow and hidden as the one that Lustita had chosen for the outset of this miserable voyage.

As the girl neared the narrow strip of hard pebbles (there was no sand on this side of the cliff), which lined the shore, she averted her eyes from what had greeted her when she made the first awkward leap from boat to shingle. There lay evidence of what this dread coast could do. Still, the off-worlder had not shown the slightest dismay when he had viewed it.

Two withered, shrunken bodies, or the remains of such, had been somehow wedged between the rocks. Or had they crawled there during their last spurt of life energy to find their own tombs? A few faded, colorless rags still clung to the blackened, shrunken flesh. Simsa was glad that the heads had fallen forward so that she need not look upon what long-ago death had made of their faces; there were no birds here, no crabs or other sea spawned vermin, to clean their bones. Rather they had simply blackened under that sun to fearsome representations of what seemed to be more demons than once-living men.

Now Thorn again passed them without a glance, striding along the sliding pebbles which were quick to shift under his boots so that he balanced as he went, heading farther north. When he scrambled over the rocks guarding the other end of this small bay, she pulled herself to her feet to follow. Somehow, she could not remain where she was—along with those blackened things which she was ever aware were at her back, whether she looked in their direction or not.

Her feet slipped and slid so in the sandals that she had made patches of covering for both sandal and skin from parts of a rent sail she had found stored on the boat, twisting the thick stuff and knotting it as tightly as she could. Also, she picked her way with care, having no desire to fall. She was a fool—it would be better to crawl back under the closed part of the ship where the zorsals whimpered now and then. Though she had emptied a hamper and made them a kind of nest away from the sun, she could do nothing more to spare them the heat.

This scramble over the rocks brought her a fall which scraped a good strip of skin from the side of one hand. She could no longer suppress her misery as she had sworn to do. Forcing herself to the edge of the water to dip her hand in the harsh smart of the sea, she whimpered like the zorsals, allowing herself that small outlet for her emotions. The off-worlder was far enough ahead now that he certainly could not hear her for she had determined from the first that he would have no complaint from her.

There was another indentation of the coast beyond the rocks where she had slipped, a much wider beach in the shape of a triangle, its point running landwards between the walls of the cliff. Thorn was just disappearing into that point and, even as she squatted, nursing her smarting hand against her breast, he disappeared entirely. There must be some break or cave—

The thought of a cave and what it might mean as a refuge from the sun drew her on with a return of strength she could not have believed earlier she could summon. Thus she stumbled and wavered across the sand where Thorn's prints were formless depressions.

Only, this was not the cave she had longed for—rather a cleft leading inwards, a break in the desert floor which might, in some very long time ago, have furnished a bed for a river. If this thrice-cursed land had ever held any water at all.

There was the same sand and gravel for footing, but the rock walls on either side where sheer here, offering no holds, Simsa thought, that one might use to reach the surface of the land above. While out of the cut came a breath of fire worse than any the sun had dealt already, as if the cleft was a furnace meant to draw the worst of the heat and hold it.

Even Thorn must have found it too much, for he was returning, having gone only a short distance inland. To her surprise, he was smiling and there was a spring in his step as if he had come upon a well all ringed about with greenery, water gushing forth to run headlong. Simsa wondered for a moment or two if the off-worlder had indeed been driven mad by the heat and the barrenness of this part of the world. She had heard tales of the desert madness and how travelers were led astray there by images of that which had never existed.

"We have our road!" he told her.

"There?" He was mad. She edged away from him crab fashion, refusing to take her eyes from him lest his insanity take a murderous turn and he savage her.

"There!" he agreed, to her continued horror. Then he must have read the thought behind her expression for he added quickly:

"Not by day, no. But at night—then it will be different. I did not come here without knowledge of such travel. There is coolness at night in such a land as this. The sea wind carries moisture with it and that condenses against the rocks. We can go this way—taking water and food with us—you shall see. I have done this on other worlds."

Simsa shut her mouth. There was no use in raising any argument. If he said they could sprout wings and fly inland, then she must agree with him for this moment. He believed he spoke the truth and she wanted no part of any struggle with him. It was enough for now that he was willing to return to the boat, come into the poor shade they could find there, though he did not stretch out to lie panting, only half-conscious, as she was forced to do; her efforts had brought an end to even that wiry strength she had developed over the years of her Burrow life.

During the latter part of the day, she either slept or else lost consciousness, she was never sure just which. Only that, for a while, she had watched him ripping loose part of the ship's planking and, using ropes he wet in the sea and then knotted about these boards, pushing that knotted portion out into the sun to dry hard and stiff.

Once or twice, she wavered into enough wakefulness to want to protest his so battering a ship she fully intended to use for her own escape. Only, before she could summon either the strength or the words to do so, she lapsed once more into that daze of misery.

There came an end to the day at last. The sun crawled down the cloudless sky and a broad banner of color touched the waves far out, sending a last glare into her smarting eyes as she drew herself over to give water to the zorsals whose plaintive cries had become so faint a croaking that alarm had shaken her into action.

They lay in a forlorn heap, their mouths open, their antennae limp, their eyes closed, while breaths which were gasps for life itself lifted their furred breasts. Simsa paid no attention to the off-worlder who had now gone ashore to work at whatever had kept him busy. She forced the tight capping from one of the water jars (one of the last two which were entirely full) and held a pannikan with shaking hands as she dribbled into it the precious liquid, near counting the drops. Her body ached for a drink—she wanted to lie and just let some coolness wash over her whole sun cracked skin—

With the pannikan in hand, she crawled to the hamper nest. Zass first. The girl cradled the zorsal between her arm and her breast. With all the care she could use to keep the contents from spilling, she held the pannikan above the creature's gaping mouth, letting the moisture, which was sickly warm yet still life-giving, drip down. She could not be sure, but that body felt too hot to her, as if not only the punishing sun, but an inner fever ate at it now. At first, a bit of the liquid ran from the side of the beak-like muzzle. Then she saw Zass make a convulsive effort and swallow.

Only a little—but enough that the zorsal found voice to complain plaintively when Simsa replaced her and picked up one of the others to do likewise. Carefully, she shared the contents of the pannikan among them as equally as she could. The younger birds revived sooner, pulled themselves up with their clawed paws to the edge of the hamper and teetered back and forth there, one gathering enough voice to honk the cry with which they greeted dusk and hunting time.

The girl then took back Zass into her hold, supporting the Zorsal's head with her scraped hand. The creature's huge eyes were now open and, Simsa believed, knowing. Her plan for losing them— that she could never do here. They could not survive in a country so utterly barren and heat-blasted.

No, she must take them with her when she went—went? For the first time, Simsa looked about with more understanding. What she saw now brought such a rush of fear that, in spite of the baking her body had taken most of the day, set her shivering.

The mad off-worlder! While she had been lazing away the day he had done this!

Not only had he stripped away most of the decking on the main portion of the boat, but he had taken the sail, slit it into strips. To make what? The thing which rested on the shingle was a monstrous mixture of hide-cloth from the sail, pieces of wood ripped and then retied into what looked like a small boat—except that it was flat of bottom. To it, while she had been unconscious, he had also transferred and lashed into place the rest of their food hampers, and now he was coming for the water jars. Simsa's cracked lips were splitting sore as she snarled up at him. He had left her no way of escape now.

She could either remain where she was, to die and dry like those blackened remnants behind the rocks, or be a part of his madness.

Her claws came out of their sheaths and she growled, wanting nothing more than to make a red ruin of his smooth face, his large body. At bay, the water jars behind her, she faced him ready to fight. Better to die quickly than be baked in this furnace of a land.

He halted. At least he feared her a little. A spark of confidence awoke in Simsa at that. He had an off-world knife at his belt—port law allowed him no other weapons here. Let him use that against her claws—against the zorsals, if the creatures were recovered enough to obey her signal. She dropped Zass to the deck and heard the guttural battle cry arising in answer to her own emotion which the creature sensed. The other two lifted their wings, sidled along their perch—ready to fly, to attack—

"It is our only chance, you know," he said evenly, as if they were discussing some market bargain.

Her fingers crooked and Zass screamed. Simsa tried to throw herself forward in one of her leaps, but her weakened body did not answer. She had to put out a hand to keep herself from slamming face down upon the deck.

"You have made it so—" She raised her head a fraction to snarl at him. "Give me clean death—you have the means—" she nodded to the knife he had made no effort to draw. "I never asked, never planned—"

He did not try to come any closer. She made a weak clucking noise and the zorsals did not take flight. Kill him, she thought miserably, and she would have nothing—no hope left. Did she still hope at all? She supposed that she did. All life which had a mind to think also clung to hope, even when that seemed impossible.

Not trying yet to get to her feet, the girl drew herself away on hands and knees from the water jars and let him take them—waving him towards them when he would have come to her instead. No, she would move on her own as long as she could. When that was no longer possible—well, there must be ways of ending. She would not be beholden to this mad alien for any easement now.

She accepted the food he offered her as the last signs of the sun went, the evening banners faded from the sea. She drank—no more than her share and some of that she gave to Zass. When he returned to the thing he had made, she loosened the front of her short coat and made a place for the zorsal. The other two had already winged their way to the waiting drag thing and were perched on the lashed hampers.

Simsa followed. There was a wind now off the sea, cool. She had never believed that she would feel cool again. The touch of it reached somehow into her, clearing her thoughts—though not smothering her inner rage—giving energy to her body.

Did the alien propose to drag that thing of his? Or would he harness the both of them to it and work her as well until they both yielded to heat and exhaustion?

If that was his plan, he would discover that she was not going to beg off—she would keep with him stride by stride as long as she could—or he would drive them both to the impossible. So when she came to stand beside him she looked for the drag ropes. There was only one—a single strand which she believed could not take the weight of the thing he had built.

He asked no help of her, but faced the drag carrier front on. His hand touched his belt for a moment. Then, to her amazement, the impossible happened before her eyes. There was a trembling of the carrier. It arose from the gravel and hung in the air—actually in the air—at least the height of her own knee. Picking up the lead rope, Thorn set off along the narrow beach and the thing floated after him as if it were some huge wingless zorsal, as obedient to his will as her own birds were to hers.

For a long moment, she simply watched what she still could not believe. Then she took off in a hurry, lest he vanish from sight. What new wonders he might bring into their service she could not guess, but now she would willingly accept all the strange tales which were told of the starmen and what they could do. Even though they never, as far as she knew, had demonstrated any such powers on this world before.

Her anger lost in her need to know how such a thing might be, Simsa slipped and slid, forgetting her drained strength until she came even with Thorn who walked steadily ahead, leading his floating platform.

"What do you do?" she got out between gasps of breath as she caught up. "What makes it hang so in the air?"

She heard him actually give a chuckle and then the look he turned on her was alive with sly humor.

"If you told those at the port what you now see, they would send me back to my home world, sentenced to stay out of space forever," he told her, though he seemed only amused at being able to explain what must be a crime among his kind. "I have merely applied to this problem something common on other planets—ones more advanced than yours. And *that* is a deadly crime according to the laws by which we abide. There is a small mechanism I planted at the right spot back there—" he pointed with his thumb over his shoulder but did not turn his head, "which nullifies gravity to a small extent—"

"Nullifies gravity," she repeated, trying to give the strange words the same sound as he had. "I do not know—some people believe in ghosts and demons, but Ferwar said they are mainly what those who believe in them make for themselves by their own fears—that you can believe in any bad dream or thing if you turn your full mind to it. But this is no ghost nor demon."

"No. It is this." They were into the cut of the valley now. The sea wind behind them made the passage more bearable now than she could ever have believed it could be when she had seen it by day. Now as he halted for a moment, it was still not too dark for her to make out what he pointed to as he repeated, "It is this."

"This" was what appeared as a black box no bigger than could be covered by his hand were he to set that palm down over it. The thing rested directly in the middle of his drag carrier and now she could see that the cargo on board had been carefully stacked in such a way that the load must weigh evenly along the full length, leaving open only that one spot in the exact center vacant, the place in which sat the box.

"You toss a stone into the air and it falls," he said, "it is the attraction of the earth which pulls it down. But if that attraction could be broken sufficiently—then your stone would float. On my world, we wear belts with such attachments which give us individual flying power when they are mated with another force. We can move also much heavier things than this with little trouble. Unfortunately, I could not smuggle through the field guards as large a nullifier as I wanted. This is limited; you see how close to the ground the weight holds it.

"There is this also—the power is limited. However, it is solar powered and here the sun can renew it, at least for the space in which I think we shall have need of it."

Simsa could understand his words easily enough, but the concept they presented was so far from anything she had known that his speech was akin to a wild travel tale, such as the river traders might use to scare off the gullible from their own private ports of trade, as was well known they were apt to do. She thought of such a thing being attached to a belt so that one could share the sky with such as the zorsal and the uses one could put such skill to.

"The Thieves Guild," she spoke aloud her own train of thought. "What they would not give for such as that! No," a shiver which was not from the cooling of the wind shook her, "no, they would kill for that! Is it such as this that Lord Arfellen would hunt you for?"

She could not understand what such a thing would mean also to even a High Guild Lord.

"No," Thorn returned. "It is just what I have said; what he wanted—what I am sure he still wants—is that which we are going to find, up ahead."

That this off-world marvel gave them a better chance was what was paramount for Simsa now. Not that their way was too easy. At places the cut through which they made their way was near barricaded by fallen rocks, so that Thorn had to work his towed carrier carefully around stones which it had not power enough to lift above. Heartened by the fact that they did possess such a wonder to make easier their way, Simsa now hurried to lend a hand, steadying, or pushing, or helping to swing the thing back and forth to avoid its being caught.

Thorn did not push the pace. At intervals, he would stop to rest, more, Simsa guessed—though she did not want to admit that even to herself—on her account than from any need of his own. In the dark, the zorsals came to life, the younger two even taking wing now and then. Also, it would seem that this desert place held inhabitants after all, for one of her creatures, cruising high, gave a hunter's cry and struck down to make a kill among the rocks, his brother doing the same not too long after.

Simsa called them in with a whistle. The off-worlder had snapped another stud on that belt of marvels and a beam of pale light answered, forming a ray ahead. Into that the younger of the zorsals flew after a hunting hoot, a dangling thing, which seemed mostly armored tail, in his forefeet. Simsa set Zass down on the bobbing carrier and her son offered the old zorsal the fresh caught prey which she ate eagerly with a crunching of what could be either scales or bones.

During one of their stops, Thorn showed the girl how the cooling of the stone condensed moisture carried by the sea wind which still was pulled up the cut as if the very force of the desert would draw it in. She laid her torn hand against that damp surface and wondered if there was not some way these precious wet drops could be made to add to their store of water. Drink they did—very sparingly from one of the jars, and ate now of dried meal and fish ground together and made into cakes. The fat which bound the other ingredients together was rancid, but fishermen lived on it at sea for weeks, and this was no country for the fastidious.

Simsa had no idea how far they had gone, though her feet felt numb—where they did not ache—while the cloth she had bound about them was torn to tatters. She had been too aware of the need for watching for any obstacle which could threaten the carrier, though perhaps the off-worlder was planning to use some other amazing thing to lighten their journey tomorrow. The girl only became aware of the paling of the night sky when he paused and said:

"We cannot risk day travel. Look there ahead—see where that slide has carried down the rocks? With this," he laid hand on the side of the carrier so it swung a little under his touch, "set across the top of those we shall have a roof to give us some protection. But we must get the water jars and the food under it before sun rises."

Simsa could help with that, using care to prop each water jar stable with small stones so there might not be any chance of a spill. Zass perched first on the lightened sled, which, when all burdens were removed, shot upward until Simsa gave a cry and Thorn hauled it down, bracing it, and then taking off the box and stationing it with the same care as she had used with the water jars, not within the shadow but on a flat rock where the sun would strike it.

He then touched her shoulder, half giving her a shove towards the improvised shelter.

"I am going up—" he pointed to the cliff nearest them. "Before it gets too hot, I want to try my bearings and see how near we are to the Hills."

She was willing enough to leave that scramble to him, having no wish to expend further energy. Sitting down with her back to one of the rocks which supported the carrier, she busied herself with the windings about her sore feet. How foolish she had been not to bring with her a packet of Ferwar's healing herbs; she could well do with them now. There was no grease left. However, under the strips of rags which held them on her feet, the sandals were still stout enough so that she was not walking bare of foot—not yet.

Chirping to the zorsals, she summoned them in, selecting a flat stone, loosing her head cloth, and coiling it there for a nest. They settled down with drowsy little mutters, their antennae close coiled, far more themselves than they had been by the shore, though they had not yet had to last through the furnace of the day. She was hungry and thirsty, but she would neither eat nor drink until Thorn returned. The energy of the starman amazed her. He had worked through the heat of the past day to make the carrier; to her knowledge he had not rested. Yet, he had kept going with this easy gait all through the night and, now he had made the climb to the top of the cut.

Of what were these off-worlders made—unwearing material like their mighty starships? She did not believe that even the desert riders of the past could have done so well as Thorn had done this day or night.

There was the sound of stones falling then, very visible in the now growing light, he landed easily, apparently jumping from a point above, only a few feet away—to move in beside her. She reached for the water pannikan. There were smears of dust across his face and already those were muddied by sweat which trickled down his cheeks.

He drank slowly, though she was well certain that he would have gulped it in an instant had he not been prudent. She waited until he had swallowed the last drop before she asked:

"How far?"

"I am not sure—" At least he was not lying to her and Simsa felt pride that he would not. "It is difficult to judge distances. I would say another night's travel and we would be close—if not there."

He ate doggedly the half cake she offered him and then, without a word, curled his tall body into a position which did not overcrowd her yet still brought him full under the carrier roof, and immediately went to sleep as if that too he could do by his will alone.

7

Simsa lay gasping in the pocket of heat. Sun shining into the crevice had turned their refuge into a pot placed over the fire. She had opened her coat, pulled loose chemise and wrappings which had stiffened with the stale sweat of her body. It was too hot to move, to think. The girl wavered in a nightmare land of half-consciousness, arousing twice to tend the zorsals when she thought she could hear their gasping. If any wind blew the sand above the lip of the cut in which they rested, or sent whirling pillars of grit dancing there, it did not spill down to where they lay imprisoned.

From under swollen eyelids, she glanced at the off-worlder. The upper part of his tight-fitting suit was open, he must have pulled that so without her being aware of any movement. He had turned on his back, and she saw the rise and fall of his pale-skinned chest. Yet he seemed to be asleep, as if his efforts had thrown him so far into weariness that not even the heat could awaken him.

Time dragged on so slowly the girl felt that she had lain there forever and that there would be no end to this misery. She denied herself water—keeping what she tipped so slowly from the jar they had broached the night before to succor the zorsals.

She must have slept, for there were blurred dreams which filled much of the day. She was sure that once she had lain and watched Ferwar, wrapped in the many layers of those garments which were made patch upon patch, walk down past the rock on which the off-worlder had set his magic lifting thing. A younger Ferwar that had been, her back not yet curved into a bow, not yet leaning on the staff. She had passed their refuge and gone on with the brisk step of one bound on a certain task which must be accomplished within a given time.

Simsa shaped the name of that seeming wayfarer but did not speak aloud. Only, as if she had been hailed, the tattered figure paused by the rock on which Thorn had laid his treasure. From under the heavy, shaggy brows, she looked straight at the girl. Then, deliberately, she raised the staff which she did not need now to support herself, swinging it wide so that it swept over the off-world thing. Then its tip pointed up the cut. Her lips in turn moved with words Simsa could not hear. Having surveyed their pitiful camp for a long moment, the Old One turned and went on.

It was a dream, of course, or some vision brought by the heat and the place in which she lay. Still, Simsa dragged herself up well as she could and watched that walker until suddenly she was not there.

There was only one reason for her to appear now, Simsa decided, too far sunk in the misery of her body to know fear. Ferwar was dead, she would lead them on until they, too, joined her. The girl found she did not greatly care. She dropped back again, her hand curled up against her cheek. Smoothing cool touched her heated flesh, like a precious drop of water flung out of a fountain—

With the infinite slowness to which she was reduced, Simsa brought up her hand and looked at the ring. Days earlier, it had become too large for her shrunken flesh, but she had not put it away into safety. Instead, she had wrapped the hoop around and around with torn bits of the cloth as she had used to ease her feet, wedging it so securely as she might. Now, as she looked down into the cloudy, glowing gem which formed the roof of the keep, it was like—almost like—gazing indeed into a pool of water.

Magic—what was magic? There was the lore of growing things to cure the body—which Ferwar had known and taught her—a little. For it had been true that the old woman had been jealous of her skill and never quick to share knowledge. There were such wonders as the off-worlder seemed to know and use. But those were only things built by men, from their own learning and efforts—solid things one could hold in one's hand.

There were the tales of strange powers. Yet no one Simsa had ever known had actually seen these in action. Always such had been viewed in another place, another time, and the girl had never accepted them as anything but tales. Knowledge could be won, then lost, and won again. Those who had lived before could be wiser than the men who came after, if something happened to interrupt the flow of their wisdom from one generation to the next.

This ring and the other pieces of jewel work she carried hidden on her were finer than any she had seen in the upper-city shops when she had dared go to look upon the riches she had no hope of even laying finger on. That did not mean they were magic—merely that they were old and the fruit of labor of hands long still and dwindled into bone, even into dust.

Still, as she lay there now staring down into the pool of the grey-blue gem, she was—

Walls rose about her. There was no sun, still there was heat. Fire blazed and reached out tongues to scorch her. She heard screams, wild cries, and the roar of other sounds the like of which she had never heard before. At her feet there was a pool, bordered by shimmering blocks of blue green stone. She teetered on the very rim of that, afraid to leap, afraid to stay and face a fury which raged closer and closer.

The darkness of the sky overhead was rent by great flashes of raw fire. She saw that lick at a tower and the tower swayed, came falling down. Simsa screamed and leaped into the waiting water. But it was too hot, searing her. This was death and still it would not close its jaws well upon her—rather it played with her, using torment, as a zorsal would use its claws when, filled of stomach, it played with fresh caught prey. All the world was a fire and she was caught in the middle of its blaze—

"—wake—wake up!"

Back and forth the boiling water washed her body. She tried to fight but it had taken her, sapped from her all her strength. Still it played with her.

"Wake up!"

Simsa saw a face above her—large as the moon, round—with two dark pits for eyes, a mouth come to suck her out of the water. Still, there would be no safety in that mouth—only another kind of torment—

"Wake up!"

The huge face receded, became one she could remember dimly. She blinked, the water had made her sight hazy. She—no dream—no fire—the hands of the off-worlder were on her shoulders shaking her. She gaped at him a moment and then pulled away.

"You must have had a dream to end all dreams—on the dark side," he commented as he sat back on his heels. "Here, take this." He held out the pannikan she had last used to ease the thirst of the zorsals. "Take it," he urged again when she had not put up her hand.

This was the valley still and the heat lapped around her. But there was something curious, too. It was as if, from time to time, she saw one thing across another—the valley clear, then veiled by a toppling tower and a pool into which fear was driving her, death before her, behind her and all around.

"Drink!" He moved, was at her side, his arm firmly about her shoulders, so that she was supported against the swing of the sickening visions, one upon the other. The edge of the pannikan against her sore lips was a small pain, yet it, more than his voice, broke up that last vestige of her dream.

She did not question that the pannikan was near full. The water was warm and slightly bitter, but she drank it all thirstily, allowing him to hold the cup until the end.

He settled her shoulders back against the hamper from which she could hear the small panting gasps of the zorsals. They needed tending, but her head felt so light and queer she could not force herself to move—not yet.

Instead, not understanding what he did, she watched the off-worlder pick up a small vial from the rock by his knee, measure three drops from it into the water he poured with such care. Stoppering the vial and replacing it in his pouch, he lifted the pannikan as one who was meeting a friend in an inn, made a gesture in her direction, and sipped slowly at the portion he had allowed himself. Still over the rim of the cup, he studied her so intently that at last she moved a little, uncomfortable under so keen and searching a gaze.

"I did have a bad dream," she said, as if she must justify whatever she had done to so engage his concern. "It—it was a part of this . . . somehow."

She raised her hand and let the ring tower stand high. "Fire in the sky and a falling tower—and I jumped into a pool but the water—was boiling."

"Lady Simsa," he still kept that courteous form of speech which had so irritated her—though she would not give him the satisfaction of hearing her protest against what must be a subtle kind of mockery, "have you ever heard among your people of strange talents which some may have? Have you known, or heard, of one who can take a thing into his or her hands and read then the past through which it has come?"

For some odd reason, she was beginning to feel stronger, more alert than she had in days. She straightened up from leaning against the hamper, reached behind her to tend the zorsals. What he said— could anyone believe that such things were? No, he was not testing her by some new folly that to him *might* be the truth—on another world.

"No," she answered shortly. She did not like at all this talk of things so strange. All her life she had been burdened by her difference in color, in kind, from anyone in the Burrows, any she had seen in Kuxortal. She had done the best that she could to conceal that difference—which was of the body. Now he spoke of worse differences—for, to her, that talk appeared more dangerous than any mirror image of herself.

"Such things are known. Those who have a gift such as that are recognized among my people, trained to use it—"

"I have no such 'gift'!" Gift indeed, it would have been only one more thing which would have set her apart. "If you are through with that," she nodded to the pannikan, "the zorsals must be tended."

Unless, she thought with a sudden stab of fear, he might consider the creatures useless baggage, believe that the water she must have to keep them alive would be better used to continue their own existence.

However, he did not protest. In fact, she noted that the portion he poured out was certainly higher in the cup than that which he had taken for himself. One by one, she brought the limp and drooping creatures out of their shelter, induced them to drink, laid them carefully, their feet under them, their wings smooth against their backs, on the lid of the hamper.

She became aware as she did so that her store of new energy was growing. In spite of the heat which lingered here, she had found some reserve within herself which gave her the power to move with more strength than she had known since they left the shoreside. The cliff held shadows now and the off-worlder was settling, with extreme care, the magic lift box in the center of the carrier which arose with something close to a leap and then floated near his shoulder level until he dragged it down and had Simsa sit on the edge and hand him the hampers and the rest of the gear when he called for them, he making very certain that each was put in an exact place, though she could see no real purpose in his care.

They ate, and now the zorsals were fanning their wings, their heads raised, hooting a little back and forth.

Simsa, as Thorn tied the last cord, lifted Zass to her shoulder ready to move out. Thus, once more they began the journey along what seemed, from all Simsa could spy ahead, to remain an endless chasm, the walls, the footage no different than those they had passed the night before.

Their journey started with the coming of dusk, Thorn again in the lead, Simsa swinging from side to side behind, her attention for the carrier when its sway might bring it into contact with the rocks. It rode, she believed, a little higher above the ground than it had the first night of their journey. Perhaps the water and food they had taken, small as that quantity was, had made the difference.

It was a weary business, her own small surprise was that she found herself stepping out so briskly after the long baking of the day, able to move quickly to fend off the carrier from some obstruction at need. With the downing of the sun, the zorsals once more took to the air, Zass screaming harshly after them as if to make sure she would be entitled to some portion of any prey this achingly barren land might yield.

Once more, they halted at intervals and the second time they did, Thorn asked suddenly: "How do you feel?"

There was a note in his voice which alerted the girl. Almost as if he expected her to report some measure of difficulty—because of her dream? She shied away from such questions as he had asked her about the strange "talent," as he had named it, which some off-worlders believed in.

"I am able to go where you lead," she retorted sharply. "All have dreams they would rather not remember by retelling over and over—or are your people so different that they are not troubled by such?"

"It is not your dream." The shadows in the cut lay between them, so thick a curtain she could not see his face except as a lighter patch in the general gloom, for the light which showed them their way and which hung from his belt was now, as he sat eating, directed on the slightly swaying carrier. "I must tell you what I did, for the time may come when it is necessary that you know what to do. In this," he tapped his pouch—"the liquid you saw me add to the water before I drank—is a stimulant, a distillation of several, as you would call them, medicines which strengthen the body, clear the mind. One cannot use much, nor too often. It is meant to carry one through such trials as we have had to meet. I did not know whether it would aid you—I had to take the chance. You—you were far gone."

She chewed upon that information along with the piece of concentrated food she held and tried not to smell as she ate.

"You could have slain me so." She hoped her voice was as steady as she wanted it to be.

"Yes, I might have killed you."

Simsa considered that. He was a truth speaker, this off-worlder. At first her anger flared up, but she would not allow that to cloud her wits as badly as those half-visions she had seen upon awakening.

He had taken a chance, and it had worked. She knew she was stronger, more alert, better able to carry on. When she thought back to the heat and torment of the day behind, she wondered if she *could* have summoned the power, even if she had had the will, to start forth again on the journey unaided.

"It did not." She would not allow him to know if she cared one way or another. They were nothing to each other. Just as she had been nothing to anyone since Ferwar had died. For a moment or two, another part of her was surprised even at that fleeting thought; Simsa need not be anything to or for anyone but herself!

"Simsa,"—it was the first time he had not added "lady" to her name, but spoke it as if she were one with him, equal and a part of the same venture—"whose House gave you birth?"

"House?" She laughed scornfully and Zass gave her instant answer, querulously. "When did a Burrower have a 'House' to boast of? We may know our mothers—some our fathers also—but beyond that . . ." she shrugged, even though he might not see that gesture. "No, we count no further."

"And your mother?" he persisted past all common courtesy—though she had believed that he at least owed her that much.

She could say anything—that she was some drop child even of a Guild Woman and he could not now name her liar. Why should she? It was easier in one way to answer with the truth.

"You know as much as I do. I remember rolling in the dirt of Ferwar's Burrow—no farther back than that. But I was not any fruit of her body. She was past the age of spawning when I was born." Deliberately, she used the harsh terms of the Burrowers, stripping away all the fine talk such as he might be used to. "Perhaps I was a heap child."

"A heap child?"

"One thrown on the refuse heaps and left for the scavengers." Still deliberately, she set herself as low as this world would rate her. Taking, for a reason she could not understand, a perverse pleasure in doing so. "Perhaps Ferwar gleaned me there. She was one curious enough to bring back strange things. Do you not carry with you even now some of her finds? I am not as remarkable perhaps as your things of this—this X-Arth—but it would well be that to the Old One I had some value.

"At least I had such to her as she grew older. She was troubled with much pain in her joints and became so crippled that it was hard for her to go either burrowing or comb the rubbish. I was too small to carry large things, but she always said I had good eyes. I am lucky, too—or was—" She thought she could not claim that her present state was a fortunate one. "I found some of the Old One's good pieces. And I had Zass; no one else had ever thought of trying to tame a zorsal and then loan its services for hire."

"Yes."

She wished that she could see his expression now. He had agreed with her in a single word. Oddly enough, she would have liked him to be more astounded. But then, how could an off-worlder know what it was like to live in the Burrows? To live a life in which one existed on what all in Kuxortal threw away, or lost, or had hidden and forgotten, long before one was born?

"There were none there who were like you—with your hair— your skin?"

"None!" she did not know whether to be proud of that, but she made her answer ring proudly enough. "They called me Shadow—I need only bind up my hair, use the soot from the cooking pot on my brows and lashes and I had become part of the night itself. Also, Ferwar warned me to be careful. She said there were those who might use my strangeness for trading—making me part of what they would sell. I learned to hide much of what I am. That was useful many times over." She allowed herself a small laugh, but did not hear him equal it.

"So none saw you to remark upon your difference. And this Old One of yours believed it could be a danger—?"

Simsa could not understand why he harped so on her appearance. She was strange—but there were many in the Burrows who were the result of hasty and near forgotten coupling between strangers. She had once been envious of Lanwor who had been bought from his "father" (if Qualt was his father) because of his extraordinarily long arms. He had been taken into the Thieves'

Guild, which was an upward advance in the world. She had some-times wondered whether Ferwar had ever been approached—a small child who could fade into the dark and be a part of it should have had a price also. Was that why the Old One has so often harped upon concealment? By the time Ferwar was dead, she was too independent, too old, to be trained by their harsh and rigid under-rules.

"Not many ever saw me when I was older." Thinking back, she saw that that was true. "Not as I was. The Old One put a cap on me when I went out foraging. She did not want to shave my head, I don't know why. It was easier to go capped than to wash color out in the river. Then she began rather to send me at night and taught me how to go unseen. There were those in strange places with whom she dealt in some manner—I never understood how or why—I took things to them secretly and brought other packages in return."

It seemed that he had now run out of questions for he was busy with the water jar they had opened earlier, dealing out their shares. Having drunk down the flat tasting warmth of that, she had a question in turn:

"And what of *your* House, starman? Are you a lord's son that you have been free to flit from world to world as Zass's sons can alight on one rock and then another? How great are your courts, and how many gather to call aloud your clan name in the dawn?"

Now he did laugh. "Our customs are not quite as those of Kuxortal. No one of us sets up such a household of kin. There were my parents, but they are dead long since. My brother was the older, therefore, the head of our House, as you would name it. We have one sister. She is wed to a star captain and lives ever traveling. That life is to her liking, but I have not seen her for many years. My brother is a man respected by men of learning and, to a part, I share his teaching and his tastes. We were engaged on different projects when I heard of his disappearance here. Then I knew that I must come and seek him. So I went to my chief—the Histor-Techneer Zashion himself—and I said this I must do. He gave me leave and I came on the first ship I could find which was to make landing here. On the way, I learned from tapes what my brother was seeking and what might be before me. Hence my bringing of such as the nullifier, though that was unlawful. But I could not see why, once I arrived, the questions I asked brought such hesitations to the very people who should be the first to give me full aid.

"After all, it would be to their advantage to help a Histor-Techneer of the League. If they feared that we were such as to steal ancient treasure, they had our bonds and the assurance of the League itself that we were nothing of the kind."

"This League of yours," Simsa had given Zass a full half of her share of cake, having heard no hunting calls from the two who had taken to the sky overhead—"where is its city?"

"City? There is no one city. The League is a union of worlds, many worlds, like your union of Guild Masters in Kuxortal."

"But it has," she pointed out triumphantly, "no guild guards here has it? How think you that any Guild Lord would take seriously the word of a man whose guards he could not see every day, whose house badge was not displayed openly? Your League is far away, they are here. They will do as they please and see no reason why that should not be so."

She thought he sighed, but she could not be sure. He did not break the silence again. She had begun to lose quite a bit of her recent awe of him. He possessed such tools as the box which lightened a load until it was no real burden at all, a light which burned without consuming anything as a lamp did oil, but in the affairs of men, he was less than any child of the Burrows on his first lone seeking and shifting.

The zorsals killed and again brought a portion to their dam. Then they arose and whirled away before Simsa could lay any command upon them. It was a night without moonlight, and she had not seen in which direction they flew. She only hoped they would come home before the rise of the pitiless sun.

There was a grayness in the sky when, for the first time, Simsa became aware that the flooring of the cut was changing, deepening. Also it was smoother, here were fewer rock falls about which they must guide the carrier. At the same time, she heard an exclamation from her companion. He had halted abruptly, the carrier actually sliding a little ahead with the momentum of his steady pull, to strike against his hip. Simsa stepped to one side to see the better.

They had certainly come to the end of this valley. Before them, as forbidding as any wall set about an armed keep such as the river people spoke of in the far places, was a cliff, which went up and up. She saw Thorn detach the light giver from his belt, hold that at angle so that its beam illumined the rise. To her, it looked as if the light failed before the top, if this wall had any top at all. Certainly, it must be twice the height of the cliffs which had been on either side during their whole journey up from the sea.

"I think," Thorn said, as calmly as if he were not staring straight at what the girl saw now only as disaster, "that we have reached our goal—this must be the beginning of the Hard Hills."

Simsa dropped down. That energy which had sustained her through the night might have washed out of her in the same moment as she realized the meaning of his words.

"We cannot climb that." Oh, there were fissures and holes which she could see in the light, but they dare not attempt such a feat until day would make all clear, and with day would come the sun which would crisp them as they struggled.

"Then we shall find another way—"

She would have hurled a stone at him had there been any to hand, but this way was barren of all but gravel. He was so calm, always so very sure that there was no problem which would not yield to him.

"Your lifting box might carry Zass," she returned, refusing to let her irritation break through. "Us it could not manage."

However, it was as if he had not listened to her at all, instead he asked a question which half buried her comment: "How much communication do you have with these zorsals of yours? I know they will come to your call, and that you could set them in Gathar's warehouse to keep the vermin down. But can you impress upon them some other task?"

"What kind of task?" She was smoothing Zass's fur and felt that the antennae on the zorsal's head were not only completely uncurled, but slanting in the direction of the off-worlder, quivering slightly, which she knew meant that the creature was concentrating. Could Zass grasp the sense of what he said to the extent that she knew he was speaking of her and her two sons?

"To make it to the top of this." He let his light flicker up and down the surface of the cliff as far as the beam would reach. "We would need a rope. That we have—or will when I do a little work upon the lashings. Could your zorsals be sent to carry such aloft, put it around some outcrop there and return with the end to us or—"

His suggestion was drowned out by a scream of rage from the sky. Down into the beam of the light came one of the zorsals, and it was pursued by something else—a thing which, to Simsa, might have flown out of a dream as harrowing as that which had held her before waking last evening.

This monster was like a long thin rope in itself, and it would seem that its other end was safely rooted somehow, for they could only see the forepart of the head—that which was all gaping jaws and needle teeth, darting and striving to strike at the zorsal. Into the beam of light in which that attack was so clear to view, flew the second zorsal who flung itself, to fasten on the darting head just behind the jaws. Three long clawed paws found anchorage and held, the fourth ripped busily back and forth across the large, seemingly lidless, eyes of the monster.

Seeing its attacker so engaged, the other zorsal turned swiftly and flew back and forth while the monster apparently, so mad with rage it did not realize just which was its attacker, kept trying to snap at the second, leaving the other to inflict continued punishment.

Both eyes were bloody pits now and an outflung paw had ripped a length from the long, darting tongue. Simsa had always known that the zorsals were killers and that they took a certain enjoyment in their slaying—unless they killed quickly for food alone. But she had never guessed they would tackle so large a prey, or that they were keen-witted enough to fight it in the only way possible for them to survive.

# 8

From Simsa's shoulder, Zass set up a clamor, flexing her good wing, flapping uselessly with the other as if she fought to take to the air and be a part of that battle. The zorsal who had fastened on the head of the monster still raked that viciously. Now his brother darted in and sank both claws and teeth into the scaled throat as the embattled creature tossed its head wildly, trying to shake off its tormentor. There was a gash opened across the column of the body. From that spurted a thick, yellowish stream of blood which bespattered the stone, flew in great gouts through the air, so that the two below leaped back and away to escape the shower.

Both zorsals kept to their attack and then the great jawed head flapped in such a loose manner Simsa thought that the neck must be near bitten through. The struggles became only a jerking of the dangling length of the body, while the zorsals settled on the head, tore and feasted.

Thorn turned to Simsa. "What is this?"

She shook her head wordlessly. Though she had never thought to be squeamish (no Burrower could be that), the ferocity of the zorsals and the threat of the huge thing itself had shaken her so that she felt weak enough to put out a hand and steady herself against the carrier. Only that bobbed so under her weight that she was near thrown off balance.

Thorn went as close to the cliff side as he could. He had unfastened in some fashion the light from his belt and now he turned that up, holding its beam directly on the thing and the feeding zorsals. Simsa detached the complaining Zass from her shoulder, put the creature on the sled and, trying to avoid the smears and still falling gouts of blood, worked her way to join him. One of the hunters now dropped, with a beating of wings, a dripping piece of scaled flesh in its forefeet to present this offering to Zass, whose cries had grown louder and louder.

Simsa gasped. The light showed a length of still slightly twisting body which was far larger than her own height even added to Thorn's. Yet they could not see the end of it for, though the beam cut across the top of that wall, the body must still be longer, it fell over the edge like a rope.

They really did not need the beam to show it now. In the coming dawn, it fell very clear against the stone. A rope Simsa had first compared it to in her mind—only this thing of flesh and bone was as thick as about a handful of ropes twisted all together. Thorn switched off his off-world lamp and moved back again.

"We have found our way—" he said slowly.

The zorsals had near finished their grisly feast. The one who had attacked the monster first dropped to join Zass on the carrier to lick busily at its fur, sucking each claw in turn. While the brother tore loose another mouthful, brought that down to sample in satiated small bits. Only a near-stripped skull swung there now.

"What would you do?" Simsa watched Thorn free a coil of rope from the carrier, busy himself making a noose at one end of it.

"Our ladder aloft," He waved his hand at the dangling dead thing, "if it is well held above. We shall see."

He whirled his noose about his head, keeping careful grip on the cord of which it was a part. Three ties he made before it encircled that picked skull and he settled the rope tightly in place with a sharp jerk, as if he had often used this trick.

"Now—" pulling the rope taught, he stepped back—"let us see."

She watched his shoulders tense, could understand the steady pull he was exerting. The girl reached down and caught at the loose end of the cord, added her strength to his for this test.

The cord slipped a little in the mangled part, then caught, and though Simsa was bending all the force she could and believed that the off-worlder did also, it felt as secure as if the rope was fast tied around some spine of rock.

"I shall go—" he told her. "When I get to the top, lash the end of the cord I shall drop about your waist and follow—but bring this also with you."

He was busy once again with more rope, adding a long length to that with which he had towed the carrier. Having tested his knots, he stood over that wonder box to make some small adjustment. The carrier suddenly jumped aloft, sending Zass fluttering toward Simsa with a loud scream, the other two zorsals winging into the air. Now their transport floated at shoulder level with Thorn.

"This causes a greater drain," she did not know whether he was speaking now to her or merely thinking aloud, "but it will help."

The longer draw rope he now tossed to her while he faced the cliffside, the end of the climbing rope made fast about him, his face a mask of determination. Simsa watched him carefully. Though his hands were on the rope and his shoulders showed the strain he put upon them, he also used any toe hold on the face of the cliff which he could find.

The day was coming fast. Thorn had reached the gory head of the monster, shifted his hold from the rope to the thing's body. The two zorsals who could fly were following him up, screaming all the way. Simsa turned quickly now to Zass and made the spitting, excited creature let herself be stuffed into the baggy front of the girl's jacket.

Somehow, she did not want to watch Thorn climb the dangling body. She was fighting nausea, trying to keep out of her mind the knowledge that she must do this in turn.

Only . . . she had to see!

It seemed that in those few moments during which she had turned away, he had won a distance she could not have thought possible. One arm swung out, a hand had cupped over the edge of the cliff. She saw him hang so for a moment which was lifted out of normal time. Then he had pulled himself up—his head and shoulders disappeared, he must be wriggling so on his stomach—he was gone!

Simsa shut her eyes for a moment and then opened them again.

She found that she had grasped the belt about her, the rope of the carrier which she had tied there, with such force that her fingers ached. Swallowing hard, she made herself look up.

The off-worlder had returned to the edge of the cliff, but now he was facing outward, looking down to her. Though he must be still lying flat.

"This—about you—" He tossed another length of rope, which confused her, but that she must trust him she understood.

She leaped and caught the dangling end, felt that it gave so she could pull it down, tie it around her beside that attached to the carrier. The rope grew taut and she realized that he must be adding power to raise it.

Using the same actions as she had observed, she set her bundled feet wherever she might discover some hold, drew herself up, knew he was also taking much of the strain from her. The worst of her nightmare did not come, she could hold to the rope he had dropped, did not have to climb over the bloody head of the creature. Though once past that point, she put out a hand now and then against its scaled body and found the rough surface of that, while it abraded her hands, was secure enough to keep away the worst fear of the rope slipping through her clutch.

It seemed that she was trying to reach the top of a mountain and her struggle had no end. Already, the heat of the day struck against her back. Twice she had to fend herself away from the wall lest Zass be crushed. Then she heard a voice call:

"Your hand—reach to me with your hand!"

She groped upward blindly, felt his fingers close about hers. In a moment she cried out:

"Wait—there is Zass—"

However, the zorsal was already on the move on her own behalf. She pulled out of the pocket front, flapped, and now spun out to catch the rope for herself, crawling up and over Simsa's hands. Then the girl herself was brought up, scraping over stone, to roll out on a surface where the sand rose in puffs to make her cough. Before she could straighten up she felt hands about her middle tugging at the rope.

"Up with it—"

Hardly aware of what she did, only that she must do it, Simsa did not try to get up any further than her knees. She caught at the carrier rope which had swung back and forth across her and began to pull. The off-worlder was standing now, only more rigid with the strain of bringing that heavy burden.

The girl had no time to look around until that drew level with them, the starman's box keeping it under control. Together they worked to swing it in, scrambling back to give it room well beyond the cliff edge. Thorn went at once to the box, but Simsa sat back now to survey where all this effort had brought them.

Immediately before her and reaching well back into a tangle of rocks and thorn studded, dried vegetation, bleached to the color of bones—was the rest of the body of the monster. Here it was rounded to at least ten times its circumference at the point of the long neck. However, it displayed no sign of feet—tapering again so that the portion hidden by the covering from which it must have earlier crawled, was slimmed down like the tail of one of those small things the zorsals had fed upon during their night forage. She could not understand what had kept it so adherent to the rock that they had been able to use as a ladder without bringing the whole weight of it down upon them.

Apparently, this puzzle interested Thorn also for, once he was sure that their carrier was intact, its cargo undisturbed, he went to the side of the thing and strove to roll it over. However, it remained as tight to the rock as if it were indeed a part of the ground. Finally, he used a piece of stone to pry up a portion of the body so Simsa caught sight of a pallid half ring of flesh, before he was forced to let the weight fall again.

"Suckers, I think," he commented. "What is it called?"

She shook her head in bewilderment. "I do not know, nor have I ever heard of such before."

"Well," he half turned to face east, his hands on his hips, his head up, "there are the Hard Hills! Let us hope that such as this are not plentiful here." He prodded the carcass with the toe of his boot.

Simsa looked ahead. She had thought that the cliff up which

they had just fought their way was a barrier. Only, from what she could see now, it was just the beginning. Hills? No—these were sky scraping monsters of earth and stone. Still, they held one promise for any who had fought across the desert land—they gave foothold here and there to growth of some sort—sere and sun-browned now perhaps—but it had lived. Where that lived there must be water, perhaps game.

Heartened by that thought, Simsa got to her feet. They were still in the sun's full heat. Yet, surely in the broken country ahead, they could find shelter for the day—and perhaps even more. She said as much and the off-worlder nodded.

"We have to do some more climbing," he pointed out, "but you are right—where there is growth there must be water. And, in spite of the evil name of this place, I think we may find it more welcoming than the desert. But first we shall camp—and soon."

They were still in a depression between crumbling banks of sun-baked earth and long-dead brush. Thorn speculated as to whether they were not still following the path of a long-dry water course and that the cliff up which they had come had constituted a falls. There was a lot of sand through which they slipped and slid, sometimes ankle deep, hurrying now, while surveying the way ahead in hope of a place to shelter before the punishing heat of the day struck them down with exhaustion.

The dried up water course took a slow curve to the left and there was a rise of stone on one bank, half undermined, so that some had fallen over in a rough tumble which nearly barricaded the way. Thorn swung toward those and Simsa, at her old place of keeping the carrier steady, padded behind. Now, as they drew closer, she could see that those were no stones heaped by some whim of nature. These had been trimmed, set, and used, even though years, wind, and sand had eroded them into their present anonymous heaping.

Among those fallen blocks they found their shelter, a darkish hole which was still sheltered by half an archway. Inside it were steps leading down. Thorn switched on his light once again. Here was welcoming cool shadow. The zorsals honked and spiraled ahead eagerly. Simsa caught at the off-worlder's sleeve.

"Wait—let them search. If there is life denned below—" She could not help but think of the dead monster and that just such a hole as this could offer such a creature a home.

He halted, his head up, and she knew that, just as she did, he was listening. The zorsal calls sounded from below, oddly hollow, stronger as if some chance made those sounds monsters of *their* kind. Zass, from her seat on the carrier, thrust forward her head, her antennae advanced, her thin lips almost invisible, as she showed all her pointed teeth.

Simsa sniffed, trying to draw into her lungs enough of any odor which might lie below to judge what they could have to face. There was none of the smell of the Burrows, the mustiness of close and none too clean living. When the zorsals did not return to raise any alarm, she nodded to her companion.

"I think that nothing waits here—nothing living."

Though falls of dressed, if much wind-worn stone, half blocked that entrance so that scaling the carrier across it took patience and skill on both their parts, the stairs beyond that were reasonably clear. These were broad and the rises were shorter, so that to descend was easy enough. Save that they went on and on as if there were no end and that this long forsaken building had been raised on a foundation of long forgotten predecessors, as Kuxortal had been.

There was the relief that, the farther they descended, the cooler it became. Zass still hunched forward listening. From what seemed very far away Simsa could still hear the cries of the other zorsals. In the dark, they always hooted and cried continually since, she had discovered, something in their own screeching made it easier for them to elude any obstruction which even their dark-piercing eyes might not be able to see.

Thorn had once more switched on his belt light. When she turned her head a little and looked back over her own shoulder, the girl could see that the opening above had shrunken greatly. Yet the steps continued.

They stopped once, drank sparingly and ate, seated on one step shoulder to shoulder. Simsa inspected the supplies left. They could keep on going as long as they had water, but there would come an end if they could not add to their food and where, in this parched land, might they find any such? The scaled things the zorsals relished? She gagged at the sudden memory of the huge monster, now dangling dead across the cliff edge, which came far too clearly into mind. She had eaten much in the past which any dweller of the upper city would have disdained, but not that!

"Where do we go?" she asked, though she knew that he could have no better answer for her than some guess which she might make for herself.

"This might well be the remains of some outpost. That being so, there could also be a linkage by passageway to another and larger fortification beyond. In times of war, such would provide a secret way of supply."

"Why so deep?" Again she squeezed around on the wide step. That opening so far behind them now was made so small by distance that she could raise her hand and cover it with her thumb. Still the stairway went on down and down, for Thorn had gone to his knees and, having deliberately taken the light from his belt, swept the ray back and forth over what was only an endless stair without a break.

Her legs ached. They had traveled all through the night and she could not tell how far they were into the next day now. Surely they must have a time to rest, and soon.

The off-worlder might have picked up that thought from out of her head for now he said: "Let us go five tens farther. Then if there is no end as yet, we shall rest."

With a sigh, Simsa pulled herself up. The wrappings about her feet had worn very thin. Sooner or later, she would have to use her belt knife to cut strips from her coat to replace those. The only good thing was that they were no longer blasted by that heavy punishment from the sun. In fact . . .

Simsa's head came up. Once more she drew into her lungs as deep a breath as she could.

"Damp!" She had cried that so loud that, as had the early calls of the zorsals, the word was echoed hollowly back to her from down in the darkness, as if a line of Simsas stationed along the steps passed such a discovery from one to the next.

Thorn, his face only a blur in the reflection of the lamp, looked toward her.

"Yes," he agreed.

"Water?" Her fatigue pushed aside now, she got to her feet eagerly. Zass's antennae had curled slightly, while they rested and she had crunched with grunts of protest part of Simsa's food. Now she sidled towards the front of the carrier, both her sense organs extended to their farthest limit. From deep in her furred throat came chirps of impatience.

Still they descended. When they came to the fifty-step level Thorn had set for them, he flashed the beam along the walls. There were patches of damp, giving nourishment to queer growths of pallid white which formed as not quite regular balls, extending thread-like filaments outward to attach to each of the slimy looking sections of damp.

Simsa disliked the look of these and made certain that if she put out a hand to steady herself she would not touch one.

"Let us go on!" Though her whole body was one ache, she could not stay surrounded by this place which worked upon her inborne sense of danger to such an extent.

Thorn needed no urging. They had gone down perhaps five more of the wide and shallow steps when he uttered an exclamation.

The light hit upon, lanced along a level way. They had reached the end of the stairway at long last! Here the damp was heavy but the air itself was not noisome nor dead. Simsa whistled, and from not too far away came an answer. Then one of the zorsals winged into the path of the light, circled about her head.

"Look!" There was no mistaking the water sleeked fur on his forelimbs. The creature had very lately found a source of that great enough to soak as the zorsals were apt to do during the heat of the dry season—spending hours supine in the bowls of water that those who valued them always provided.

Tired as they were the sight of the zorsal, who uttered small cries of what Simsa well recognized as contentment, urged them on, and at this level they fell into a stumbling trot. Zass's demands set up an echoing of squawking which near covered the thud of their own footfalls.

Though moisture and the unpleasant growths still studded the walls, there was no wet underfoot. The girl noted that at the base of each wall was a shallow trench which perhaps was meant to carry off any runnels the plants had not sucked away.

Their beam of light suddenly was snapped off. Simsa let out a small cry of which she was ashamed a moment later. To allow the off-worlder to know that she feared the dark in any way was a humiliation. Then she could see his reason. Not far ahead, there was a haze of light, not as strong as that of his lamp, but sufficient to provide a guide.

As they approached, the girl noted that the source of the light seemed to lie to their left, being much stronger there. Then they came to an abrupt end to the passage, with a doorway on one side through which the haze came.

For haze it was, not the clean-cut beam of any torch or lamp. The effect was more as if they were advancing into a fog made of small particles of dim light which swam, gathered, and then split apart again. That zorsal who had circled overhead now gave an alert squawk and flew straight into the curtain which closed about him so that only muffled cries resounded.

"Slow—watch the footing—"

Simsa did not need such a warning from her companion. She had already cut her trot to a walk. The fog-stuff was wet, like sea spume, save that it did not carry the sting of salt in it. As it closed about her so closely that she was aware of Thorn as only a bulk moving through the mist, she felt thick moisture gather on her skin. This was like stepping down into one of those baths which she had experienced only twice in her life, when she had had a chance to gather enough extra silver bits to visit the one open to the most humble of Kuxortal.

The damp mist, though, had none of the strong perfumes which were a part of the city baths and which Simsa had never cared for. But she felt as if her skin, so dried and lacking in water's touch for many days, was growing softer, that her body, more than her mouth, was absorbing what she had lacked for so long.

As she had done in the heat of the day, she pulled at the belting of her jacket, opening that wide so that the touch of this fog, so soft, so healing (for it seemed thus to her) could reach all the areas of skin she was able to bare.

Where this mist arose from she could not tell, for there was no longer any sight of walls, only pavement underfoot, the outline of Thorn, and behind him the carrier which she no longer had to push this way and that to keep on the level and moving. Zass had flopped over, belly up, her head stretched to the full extent of her long neck, that she might so expose all of her body that she could. After the burning of the desert, this was like standing under the sky in the first of the wet-season rains while those drops still fell slowly and gently, and one was not yet battered by any wind.

Then the haze began to clear. Patches thickened, appeared to swirl this way and that out of their path, as if the fog itself held a sense of being, and would not impede their passage. Thus they came out of one last pocket into the full open.

Simsa gave a small sigh. Her feet folded under her and she dropped, her hands plunging into powdery sand or earth so soft that it deadened instantly all the jar of her fall. She slipped into it, her hands unable to find any firm floor to support her, and lay, her cheek pillowed on one crooked arm, surveying what small bit of this place she could see.

That it was totally unlike any site she had ever heard described by the most far roving trader, bore no mention in even legends, was very clear. They had come into a space large enough to be as wide as one of the market squares of the upper city. In shape, it was as circular as if they were caught up in the cup some giant, grown beyond human reckoning, had carelessly set down.

The outer walls were formed by the fog-mist which constantly moved, thickened, lightened, but never allowed one a clear view of what lay beyond. While sand in which she rested, feeling as if all energy had seeped out of her forever, was not white-grey like the fog, rather it held the glint of true silver—as if that most precious of metals (as far as the Burrowers were concerned) had been ground and reground until it was as fine as the flour from which the upper city baked its festival bread. Simsa sifted the powder through her fingers and was sure, that, though there was no sun to awaken any answering glitter, this was truly some precious stuff.

It spilled in an even rim about a regularly shaped pool. The water of that (if it were water) was a clouded pale silver-white—such a color as she had seen before. Her hand fell back into the sand, and she saw the ring again. Slowly, because her mind seemed so bemused by the waves of weariness which swept over her now, Simsa made the comparison. This pool was the very shade of the gem in the circlet she wore.

Simsa lay still. Zass hopped from the carrier. Using her one good wing as she was used to doing when there was need, she thrust the leather tip of that deep into the sand, leaned on it as she purposefully made for the water which lay so silent, nothing disturbing its gem-smooth surface.

Could she depend upon the zorsal's instinct, so much stronger than those of any of her own species, to judge that the opaque liquid was harmless? The girl tried to sit up, uttered a call which was only a soft murmur in her throat. Zass paid no heed, her dogged purpose was plain, as she scuffed through the silver sand and at last reached the water's edge.

With a small croak, she gave a last hop which launched her out into the pool. She did not sink, rather she floated as if that water might have substance enough to support her small body. The good wing was spread wide, the other as far as she could bend it. She had lifted her head to turn her long neck and rest her jaw on the edge of the good wing. Her large eyes closed, and it was apparent that she was at peace, experiencing now one of the highest pleasures of her own kind.

There was a stir at Simsa's other side. She was too drained to turn her head. Then into the line of her vision the off-worlder came. He had unsealed his garment, was stripping it down from his body with a purpose which Simsa could guess. Again a faint stirring of protest tried to raise her and failed.

Whiter than the mist walling them was his body. He looked somehow larger, more impressive than he had when clothed. Now he stepped across the narrow bridge of sand, turning aside to allow Zass full room to float in comfort. Rather than diving, he seemed to fall forward, as if his action had been the last surge of what energy he still possessed. Slowly, his body turned, sinking no further for his bulk than Zass had. He floated, face upward, his eyes slowly closing, his breast rising and falling as one who lay in the best slumber of the night.

Simsa watched and a longing grew in her. Whatever her two companions found there—that she must have also. She discovered herself crying weakly because she could not join them. From her tears and despair, she sank into a dark which closed deeply about her.

9

She was lying on such a bed as she had never dreamed might exist, one which accepted her slight body with a cool adjustment for every bone and muscle so that she was a part of the bed and its comfort wooed her to sleep. Still, somewhere deep within her, there was a nagging need for movement, for awareness of more than that lazy, insidious comfort, something which urged her back into the world.

Simsa opened her eyes. She was looking up at a rolling, ever-changing, slow-billowing of what might be cloud. Never in her life had she felt so content, so unaware of her body—as if that had been lulled into a peaceful slumber in which all pain and fatigue had been lost. She raised one arm slowly. For it seemed that, while caught in this delicious languor, she could not, nor did she need, to make any swift gesture. Her body moved also, even as her arm came into view. Whatever she lay on was not solid—

The slow languor vanished. Simsa slapped with both arms, rolled over, and her head and face went under. Startled, fear pulling her body taut, she strove to climb out, to fight back against what held her.

"Wait—lie still."

Simsa, thoroughly frightened now, splashed the harder.

Then her head was pulled back by an ungentle hold upon her hair. She rolled once more so that her face was uppermost and she could breathe. The hold on her did not loosen; instead, she was being towed through this stuff which was far thicker than any true water. She opened her mouth and screamed, all the sweet contentment of moments earlier gone.

Then her head was dropped to lie on a support which was firm, leaving her face well out of the water. She reached out, half expecting only water, but her hands discovered that she now lay only part way in the pool, her legs still trailing outward. By using her arms and hands, she was able to work her body up into a place where the powder-sand was near as soft a cushion as the pool's contents had been.

Simsa sat up. Against the silver of the sand, the opaque glory of the pool, her dark body was in vivid contrast. She was not wet. Her skin where she had won out into the air was damp, but it seemed either that moisture drained at once from her, or else was drawn as quickly off by the air. Even the mass of her hair, as she raised her hands to push it away from her brow and throw it back over her shoulders, was far less damp than it had been when she had come in from an early morning foraging in the dew which lay on the scrub growth of the river banks around Kuxortal.

If the water was not wet—it had performed something else which was to her comfort—that comfort which she had almost lost as her first bemused awakening. Her skin was firm and *clean* as she could never remember it being before. Now she wriggled her feet. Freed of the clumsy wrappings, the worn-out sandals, there were no bruises, no small pains of scrapes and abrasions. She had a body renewed, made whole, free and well.

She drew her hands slowly down that body, over her small, high breasts, over her narrow waist, her thin, scarcely rounded thighs. Her own fingers moving thus made her feel as if she were being stroked lovingly, given a pleasure so full that she answered with a crooning murmur deep in her throat, even as Zass answered when she was scratched along jaw line, and slowly, carefully, at the base of her antennae.

All the hunger and thirst which Simsa had brought here were dim memories. The desert journey was something that had happened to someone else. The girl surveyed her hand dreamily, and on her thumb the ring had moved about, the plain band facing the palm, the tower standing tall and proud. She was right—the rich, opaque shade of the unknown jewel was the same color as the liquid from which she had just come. She laughed aloud. Her feeling of well-being was as if she had drunk a full draft of rich wine. Once, one of the Burrowers, seeking to curry favor with Ferwar when the Old One was ill with pain that racked her limbs, had brought a bottle over which the woman had chuckled.

Ferwar had measured out its contents in hardly more than sips. Then, she had fallen asleep and Simsa, greatly daring, had taken the small portion which was left from the Old One's last pouring. The wine had been cool in her mouth, warm in her middle. She had felt for a while as if she so wished she might take wing to seek the upper air, as free as a zorsal in the night. This same freedom was in her now. She threw wide her arms, and trilled the notes which summoned her creatures.

They came, beating their way out of the mist, to whirl about her head. As she turned to watch them, she was aware that her hair lifted somewhat of its own accord. That vigorous life now within her seemed to give the damp locks freedom also. There was another call and floating across the pool came Zass.

Only there was something odd about the zorsal. She rested breast down on the surface, not sinking in—her good wing spread wide. Her good wing—? Simsa stared, startled out of her concentration on herself and what she felt. That wing which had always been bent, frozen into a crooked line, had straightened out. It was not wholly as it had been, not as wide-held as the other; still, neither was it crumpled as it had healed in spite of all Simsa's tending.

Zass swam to the edge of the pool, ran forward out of it. Both wings raised, to fan the air, the crippled one almost equaling the other. The zorsal cried aloud, prancing on all four feet at Simsa's side, both wings in motion. It was clear that she was demanding from the girl notice of this healing which had now come to her.

Then it was that Simsa fully remembered! She had not been alone. Nor did she recall ever entering that strange pool, of pulling off her travel worn, sweat-stiffened clothing. Where was he?

On her knees, she looked around quickly. The sense of being
inside a cup or basin was still very strong. There had been no
lightening of the mist. Indeed, to her, it looked even thicker. The
silver dust held no tracks—it could not. Move and it straightaway
fell into place so that not even the impression of her body was left.
A little distance away lay the muddle of her clothing.

Simsa stood, looking slowly around the circumference of the
pool. No one else was anywhere within the mist wall. What she could
remember last was watching the off-worlder shed his clothing. She
glanced quickly in that direction to see if there was that discarded suit.
Nothing there. What had happened to her?

He must have stripped her, put her into the pool. She reached
her bundle of clothing in a couple of strides, dropped down to
explore; there were those two bits of ancient jewelry, the bag of silver which had weighted her sleeve during all their journey.

Her nose wrinkled as she straightened out the breeches, the bits
of ragged under-linen, the heavy sleeved jerkin. The touch of them
now made her feel dirty and she felt as if she never wanted to see
them again. However, all she had carried was still there—a twist of
rag with the necklace, another holding the arm guard.

Here in this place of silver and milky-moon radiance, Simsa
freed the two pieces. The arm guard she slipped over her thin wrist.
It was not fashioned for such as she, the thing was too massive, too
wide. The necklace with its pale green stones—she brought out a bit
of the broken silver, twisted off a thin, stem-like bit to join the open
links, then dropped the mended treasure over her head. Cool to the
touch, it lay across her shoulders, the green stones fell between her
breasts, having been set in a longer bit which nearly touched her
waist. She liked the wearing of it. The metal felt right, good. As the
ring had done, to wear this gave her the sensation it was meant to be
hers.

She retied the bag of silver. He must have seen her treasures
when he took her clothing from her. If so, he had left them to her.
He . . .

But where *was* he?

The silver necklace slipped smoothly over her body as once

more she turned to look carefully about the cup of the pool. All three of the zorsals had once more gone back into the water, were floating there as Zass had been when the girl had first seen her.

Only there was no long, pale body also there, no pile of clothing on the silver of the dust. Nor—had they pulled the carrier into this place? Simsa had a dim memory of that. But it was gone. Her hand clutched, then tightened one about the other so that the tower of the ring caused a small sharp pain. She was alone, and she had not the least idea in what direction she must go to leave, from which direction they had come—where into the mist she dared venture.

That sense of content and well-being which had held her when she had awakened, floating in the water, was gone. She stooped and started to dress, though she hated the feel of the grimed and sweat stiff cloth against her body. The zorsals—if they could be persuaded to leave the pool, would they point her a way out? What had led the off-worlder to desert her here?

As she wound the belt about her middle, Simsa clucked enticingly. For a long moment or two, she thought that she could not draw them away from the pool. Then Zass, using her crippled wing better than Simsa had ever seen, turned and paddled with all four limbs, the two younger following her.

They came out on the silver dust and trooped to her feet, not taking into the air, rather squatting down to look up at her with those over-large eyes, the darker rings of fur about them seeming to give them a wide and knowing expression.

Simsa waved her hand in the gesture she had trained them to respond to—the one that when sent them out to scout, and uttered the alerting cry.

Obediently, the two younger arose, sending the silver dust fanning out by the motions of their wings. Their antennae uncurled with a snap as they began to fly around the edge of the pool, only they faced always outward, towards the swirling of the mist.

The girl stooped to catch up Zass, and settle her in her old place on the shoulder, taking a queer kind of comfort from the pinch of the large hind feet as they near pierced the coat to her flesh.

Simsa's head was up, she listened intently. So quiet was it here that she could hear the flap of the zorsals' wings in the air. Once, she half lifted her hand to her mouth as if to make a trumpet of that, shout through it. She did not quite bring herself to attempt that call.

Rather, she also began a circuit of the pond's edge. Some trick of vision made it look smaller than it was in truth, for, as she kept on, still she did not reach the other side of the cup. Then the youngest of the zorsals flashed overhead, straight into the mist uttering a signal, his brother hard on his heels.

Zass's antennae were rod-stiff, pointing in the same direction. Simsa drew a deep breath. Whether she was indeed on the trail of the vanished off-worlder she could not be sure, but the actions of her furred scouts made plain that something of interest lay in that direction.

She was strangely reluctant to leave the pool, the place where she had experienced such a quietude and joy of spirit. At the same time, she could not sit here forever. While the fact that the carrier had vanished made her believe that Thorn had meant to leave for good. Though why he had abandoned her . . .

The mist wall closed in. She lifted Zass gently from her shoulder, held the zorsal before her so that she could watch the signals of the antennae if they changed direction, which they did—now a few steps to the right, or one or two to the left. For all Simsa knew, they might be back circling the pool at another level, still she had no other guide.

Underfoot here was no sand, only rock. Her sandals and the cloth which had bound them to her feet were so badly worn that she could not use them again. So she must go bare of foot and be glad that her soles had been so toughened by years of such usage that, as long as the footing remained damp rock, she could walk it firmly.

Zass's antennae, her whole head, suddenly snapped sharply right. The girl obediently turned in that direction. She believed that the mist was thinner and, a moment later, was proven right as she came out in a dull grey funnel which fed into a narrower passage. Though she was sure that this was not the way they had come—this ran on a level, no stairs ahead.

The pavement remained smooth and she was sure not by

chance. However, walls were rougher, resembling more the stone of a cavern which had lain in a hill's heart since the beginning of time.

Her journey through the mist had not entirely stripped from her that feeling of well-being she had known after she had been drawn out of the pond. (Why had he done that and yet not waited for her?) She was not afraid—not yet. Rather, she was ridden by anger at her desertion—that the off-worlder had walked away and left her—perhaps to death for all he knew.

That anger was mixed with puzzlement. She could understand no reason for such action. Unless, her eyes narrowed a little . . . unless he knew far more about the value of what lay hidden in the Hard Hills and wanted no one to share any such find. Only then, why had he brought her along as far as he had? He could well have deserted her anywhere along the trail and so made *sure* of her death. Why that struggle up the monster-hung cliff? Why had he left her half within what she could only believe was a sort of healing water after her strength had broken at last? Simsa could not fit any of this into a pattern she could understand.

The light which the mist had provided diminished the farther she advanced into the passage. However, there was another gleam ahead, brighter—perhaps that of the day itself. She hurried her pace towards that, suddenly wanting more than anything to be back in an outer world she could understand, even if she faced desert once more, and that alone and without supplies.

What she emerged into was not desert—though the sky held the pitiless sun. Rather, she stood in a stone-walled pit—square in shape. In fact it might have been a chamber half hewn from the natural stone. Above her was a crazy patchwork of holes into which might once have been fitted beams to support other floors. The zorsals flew in a back and forth pattern and called to her impatiently.

However, she climbed with caution, testing each hand and foothold as she went. There was no stair here; perhaps when the floors existed the lower levels had been entered by trap doors and ladders. This close to the walls, first rock and then dressed stones fitted securely together, Simsa could see the marks of fire. Most had been weathered away, but here and there in protected places there were still black and direful tokens of disaster.

She reached the first large break in that wall, a niche into which she could pull her whole body and from where she could view all that lay immediately ahead. That this had been either a huge fortress, larger than any palace compound of a Guild Lord, or else a small city, there was no doubt.

Its walls had been remarkably well preserved in many places, but here also was greenery. So lush a growth, where she had been expecting to view more barren desert land, that Simsa blinked and blinked again, thinking at first this was some mirage such as she had heard might be sighted by those who traveled too far into the forbidden lands. The greenery did not vanish.

The complex of walls about her were so vine ridden that only here and there a protruding carved stone broke free. Those stones appeared to form a series and each was a head, easily twice the size of her own. Nor were any two of those she could scan from here alike. Some were animals—she was sure that the nearest was a representative of a zorsal, even though the antennae had been broken off quite close to the skull. Others were clearly of her own general species, yet each an individual, as if portraying someone who had lived here once.

Simsa could easily drop from where she perched to the top of another wall, one whose width near rivaled a lane in Kuxortal. Only, at her examination of that, the girl saw the first proof that the zorsals had guided her on the off-worlder's track. There was a pulpy mass of vine where something the length of the carrier might have rested for some time and beyond that a tree, lacking a branch, its leaves on those above and below scorched and drooping.

It would seem that for some reason this Thorn had seen the necessity to move this way, and perhaps swiftly, forcing a path through or against anything which would delay him. Simsa thought she did not need to fear coming on him without an alert—the zorsals would see to that. However, she was determined to follow, if for no other reason than she must know why he had gone.

The path along the top of the wall continued to display a

number of traces of hasty passage. As she went, Simsa's winged companions circled back and forth above her head. They were, of course, also by their very attendance, signaling to any who might be watching that she was here.

As she had passed the burnt tree, she had paused to examine it. It was well known that the starmen had fearsome weapons. They could blast into nothingness their enemies or their prey. However it was also one of their own laws, which they enforced rigorously, that these potent arms were never carried by any coming to a world such as hers. Only, neither were they supposed to bring any such marvel as the thing that had lightened the carrier. If Thorn had broken one law of his own kind, what would keep him from breaking another?

She did not like those signs of burning and edged past that place at a much slower pace. After all, who could judge the ways of an off-worlder? They had customs and codes of behavior far different, such that those of another planet might not even understand. Thorn was driven by a great need, or he would not have struck into the desert, would never have come this far.

Another wall arose before her. Here the stepping stone to bring her to its summit was a carved head was a face so horrific Simsa felt a chill. There were the demons and evil things used to frighten children, which one might dream about. As she stared at the thing which now confronted her squarely, she shivered at the pure evil in it.

She found herself making the finger gesture the Burrowers used to evoke fortune (a very fickle presence always in their lives). The worst of this image was not that it wore a grotesque mask of darkness and hate (rather it had a strange beauty which caught and held the eye), but that cruelty, lust, and evil knowledge shone through it in a terrifying way.

To reach the top of the next wall, she must mount upon that head. A smear of crushed vine across it proved that he whom she trailed had done just that. Yet, she had a feeling that if she drew herself up by its aid, she would not feel stone under her feet at all—rather flesh, cold and deathly flesh!

Simsa set her teeth. She must not allow such fancies to disturb her. She was of the Burrowers and had faced much which was of the dark of man's making, knowing it for what it was and refusing to be caught in any trap it devised.

Reaching out, she swung up on the head quickly. As soon as she had secure balance, again seeking hand holds of the edge of the wall above, scrambling, up and over that in a haste she could not suppress. The giant face was so real; not the fancy of some perverted artist, rather a true portrait. But if this one had been a ruler here once— then this was a city—or keep—which must have had a fearsome history.

From the roof on which she now crouched, for it was a roof and not another wall top, the girl could look down into a very large court—perhaps even a market square—where vegetation had grown unchecked for a long time. Vines interwove among trees, dead bushes were clasped tightly by their living descendants or by a stranger species which had choked them out. Immediately below her was a strip of bare pavement fully as wide as the wall top. On this stood the carrier, its cargo still lashed into place—not a single knot untied. Of the off-worlder there was no sign at all.

With a motion of her hand, Simsa sent the wheeling zorsals down towards that wilderness. They swooped above it, sometimes venturing to half alight on some top branch, leaning forward, their antennae weaving, always pointing groundward. Like most creatures who depend on flight as one of their defenses, she knew they were reluctant to venture any deeper into that maze of growth. However, the senses centered in their antennae must be well aware of any of the forms therein. If the off-worlder had tried to penetrate that choked pit of vegetation they would tell her. For the moment Simsa remained prudently where she was, watching the zorsals carefully, yet dividing her attention between them and what else she could see of this mass of crumbled building, or buildings.

Well beyond the farthest wall (she wished she had the distance glasses the off-worlder carried), she thought she could pick up another mountain looming above this lost place as the cliff had loomed above the desert plane. This might lay on a plateau or even be part of a valley with the real beginnings of the Hills beyond.

From the zorsals, she gained nothing. It became plain there was no value in her remaining where she was. Also, for the first time since she had awakened in the embrace of the pool, Simsa felt hungry. There was still food and water on the carrier, she could see the containers of both, and neither had been loosened. If the off-worlder had intended any long trek from here, surely he would have helped himself to supplies.

With caution she descended, using a swing of vine, already stripped of its leaves, the same way Thorn must have reached the ground. As she stood at last by the carrier, she could see something which had not been visible from above. The wall at either end of the bare walk on which their crude transport now rested was indented into a doorway, so deep set under an outcrop of a ledge as to be hidden except to one at ground level. While standing within each—

Simsa wheeled, her back against the carrier, her hand going to the hilt of a knife, far too puny a weapon to offer any defense against *that*—or *that!* This was the first time the zorsals had failed her. Why had they not recorded this peril?

She pushed Zass roughly down farther into the front of her jacket, striving to be free to climb to safety as she backed away from the carrier heading for that vine down which she had so foolishly slid.

There was no movement, no advance. The stiffness of those watchers never altered. Their eyes were on her, still there appeared to be no recognition that she was an intruder, the enemy. She halted, glanced to Zass. The zorsal was complaining, yet she never turned its antennae towards either of those *things* in the shadows of each deep doorway.

Her back to the wall, one hand on the vine, Simsa waited. Those two guardians might be chained in place, did they wait for her to come to them? Was that what Thorn had done—gone to meet death so?

None of her three furred people so much as looked at them. What defense did these watchers have to deaden the keen senses of the zorsals? The girl gathered Zass closer to her, turned the creature to face that figure at her left.

This was no beast. It stood on two legs, even as she, held a little forward two arms. Still . . .

Zass had at last uncurled her antennae, turned them in the direction of the waiting guardsman, then looked up into Simsa uttering a questioning and slightly guttural sound. No life? Naught but a carved figure?

The girl shifted the zorsal up to her shoulder and walked forward slowly, hesitating every few steps to survey the thing. Under that overhead was dark shadow. Only those eyes which had served her in night running, in Burrow delving, made out features of this silent watcher she could not catch when she had been more dazzled in the light. It was a figure, not of stone—no stone had such a sheen. But if it were metal then why was it so bright, so untouched by time?

Now it became plainer that withered leaves of other seasons, other debris from the growing place, had drifted about to hide the figure's feet, risen up to what might be its knees. Shaped roughly like her own species, yes, but never of flesh and blood.

Simsa walked steadily forward, no longer fearing any attack from its fellow at her back—for that must be twin to this. At length, she stood just before it looking up, for it was the taller— perhaps even more so than the off-worlder. The figure *was* of metal of some sort—a dark substance over which there was a patchwork of very faint color following no pattern at all. The head was a huge, round ball, the front of which was a of a different type of material— clear . . .

Having risen on tiptoe to peer through that, Simsa screamed, cowered away. Those dead dried things back on the beach had been noisome enough—but this shriveled, withered thing which stared back at her with eyes which were no longer eyes—it was an abomination she could not bear to look upon!

She turned and ran, back to the carrier, Zass screeching, both other zorsals now fluttering about her head, adding terrified cries to the din their mother made. Simsa tripped and near fell. She clutched the carrier with both hands and clung there, so sick and shaken that she could not even think. Always, she had believed that she could face anything—life in the Burrows was never for the squeamish—but this . . . this death of someone locked into metal, left so . . .

Who had stationed those terrible dead as guardians in a broken city? And why? They had been here a long time. Did the power which had put them there still exist? She yet held to the carrier, taking deep breaths, trying to get her emotions under control. The dead could not move, they held no harm in them. She need not—

Then once more she cried out. There *was* movement there; the thing, it was coming for her! She felt as if she were as securely rooted as the tangle of plants behind her, no longer even able to scream, for her throat seemed to close. One of those metal claws hanging by the guardian's side could have thus reached to cut off her breath.

10

The zorsals reacted to her fear, wheeling down, darting back and forth right over her head, their screams becoming screeches of rage. Zass fanned her wings frantically, the drooping one rising farther than she had ever been able to use it since her maiming, her head up, deep cries echoing from her. She had come running to Simsa down the carrier, to now face, with the girl, that figure moving out of the deep shadow that held the dead guardian, into the light.

Simsa would have fallen had not the carrier supported her: Thorn!

He edged around the stiffly standing dead thing to emerge into the sunlight. In his hands was a queer rod which Simsa had not seen him carry before. She watched him fearfully. His abandonment of her—were they not enemies because of something she did not yet understand?

Only there was no frown on his face, rather she read concern there. Or was that concern not for her, but rather because she had managed to follow him?

As he came forward, Simsa backed away, edging along the carrier, for at that moment she could not trust her own feet to support her unaided. She was still weak with the panic which had struck her moments earlier.

"It's all right."

She only half heard his words, still backing. Having reached the end of the carrier, she kept that between them. Supported as it was, riding higher than it had during the journey through the desert, it bobbed and shifted under her hold.

"It is all right!" he repeated. Now he paused as if she were a frightened zorsal that must be spoken to patiently and slowly until its inner alarm stilled so that one might approach and soothe it by touch as well as voice.

The zorsals themselves were quieting. She had half expected that, motivated by her own fear, they might have flown at him. Instead, they now settled beside their dam on the carrier, though they all faced him—their antennae outstretched and quivering.

Somehow Simsa summoned control. This was no nightmare dead thing. Strange as off-world powers might be, Thorn was a live creature who could be injured, fight, die; he was not invincible and she knew many tricks. Her retreat stopped, though she still kept her grasp on the carrier, one part of her mind thinking out a plan to push that forcibly into his path if he tried to rush her.

Though the actions of the zorsals continued to puzzle her. Zass, at least, had for many seasons been a weapon for her mistress, ready to attack upon command. Now it would seem that the older zorsal picked up no hint of trouble from the off-worlder.

Puzzled, thrown off of her usual alert reaction to any hint of danger, her self-confidence badly damaged by what she was now ashamed of—her display of fear—Simsa blurted out the last words she really wanted to speak.

"You left me." Those no sooner had been voiced than she would have given all she possessed to have not broken silence at all.

He still came no closer. That thing he was holding—it must be a weapon. Though it had no blade, no point, nothing about it which Simsa could recognize as a threat. She darted a quick look to her right—could she dodge into that tangle of greenery and so lose him?

"Yes."

His assent again threw her off balance. She had so expected some lie, some explanation, even some sign of shame or need to assure her that what she knew to be true was not. Now she simply stared at him.

She could be as blunt and she had to know. When he added nothing to that she demanded: "Why?"

The off-worlder had not put aside his weapon. Though the zorsals' attitudes would have her judge that he wished her no harm, that he was in no way hostile, yet she had the proof in his very word that he had willingly abandoned her.

"There has been death here." Now he held that weapon in his left hand only, with his right he touched one of those many things hanging from his belt—this a narrow strip of some dark material—which looked like metal such as she had . . . of course, it was like that substance which enclosed the dead guardians!

"There is still death here." She regained much of her self-confidence, now she was able to nod at the frozen figure behind him as if it were no more than a carving of stone.

"That is not what I meant," he returned.

"This," he unhooked the strip of metal from his belt and held it up. Her eyes were keen enough to catch a play of color across it. "This indicates radiation. My people are immune to a high degree. It is part of our history. There was once a war fought on my world, such a war as," Thorn looked around him as if he needed some inspiration, something he could draw upon to make things clear to her, "such a war as luckily this planet has never seen. Though it certainly has some surprises of its own to offer.

"There were weapons used which killed—"

She recalled the blasted tree, "By shooting fire? Such a thing maybe as that?" Releasing her grip on the carrier, she pointed to the rod he carried. "I saw—the burnt leaves, the withering."

"This is only a small, a very small example of such weapons." He did not explain, she noted, how he had come by what he held; she was very sure he could not have brought it with him through the desert. The thing was too large to have been concealed anywhere among their belongings.

"No," he was continuing, "there were other fire throwers, such as could consume all of Kuxortal within a flash of thought. Much of my world died so. There were left only small pockets which held life. And the few of my own species who survived—they changed—or their children did. Some died because the changes were such as they became monsters who could not live. A few, so very few, were still human in form. Only they were now born armored against the force of weapons such as those that had killed their world—unless the fire touched them directly.

"For it is also the curse of such a war that the very air was poisoned. Those who breathed it, ventured into certain places, died, not quickly as in the fire, but slowly and with great pain and suffering. Back there—that pool . . ."

"It kills?" she asked slowly. But she had felt no pain. Perhaps that was yet to come. She refused to allow herself to think that she might be akin to those withered, sun-baked things by the shore. Or, worse still, come to be what she had seen in the shell of metal.

"No, I think not." He looked honestly puzzled. "Tell me, how did you feel when you were out of the water—or whatever that liquid may be?"

"Good. And look at Zass." Simsa made up her mind she would not believe that she had been floating in something which would leave her dead. "She can unfold her bad wing; almost, she can fly again."

"Yes. It renews. Only there is something also near here which is the opposite; it kills!"

Now he did begin to move closer to her, but this time Simsa did not shrink away. He was holding out that strip of metal he had worn, in open invitation for her to look at it.

"When I came out of the pool—after I had drawn you in, since you were not conscious, nor able to help yourself—I found this thing you see. So, I pulled you part-way out and came to explore because of what can be read here."

Thorn placed his rod weapon on the pavement, pointed now with his free hand to the strip. There was a distinct line of red upward along it.

"This showed me danger—the very danger which my kind know well from their own past. It might have meant that before us was death—perhaps not for me, but for you and your creatures. I had to find the source, know whether or not there was a deadly radiation."

"You took the carrier," Simsa pointed out.

Again he nodded. "If there was the degree of radiation which this indicated, then the food, the water on it might already be poisoned for you. I had to make sure that you did not eat or drink before you left the pool chamber and I was not there to warn."

"And *is* what we brought poisoned?" She wondered if he knew that this tale was a weak one. She would have laughed had this been told to her by another, yet she could not judge the off-worlder by the measure of the men in Kuxortal. He was different—and perhaps she was a four-time fool to ever put any trust in him.

"No. The source of the trouble lies there—" He half turned, to point backwards at the Guardian, or perhaps to the passage beyond that motionless figure, from which he had come.

"And where did you get that?" It was Simsa's turn to point—this time to the weapon he had laid down.

"Where I came out into the open. It was just lying there . . ."

"But not of this city," she prodded when he hesitated. "How did a weapon from the stars—and those—" she indicated the guardian, "arrive here? Did they come then with your brother? Or were they on that ship which you said landed secretly? I thought that it was the rule that you did not bring such weapons to a world where they were not known. These who have waited so long, do they not wear the garments which are also of starships? I have heard of such—which allow one to walk on those worlds where one cannot breathe the air or live without protection. Who came thus?"

"These have nothing to do with T'seng. They have been here far longer and our people knew nothing of them. There is a small flyer, not one from the stars, but one such we use to explore new worlds. It rests beyond," he nodded again to the passage, "where it crashed. There was fighting here—a long time ago. Perhaps between outlaws and the Patrol." He stooped to pick up the weapon once again. "There is only a half-charge in this, less now since I tried it. Also, this weapon is of a type which is very old and not in use any longer."

He had an answer for everything, Simsa thought, which did not make her feel any easier. That wonderful sensation of well-being which had been hers when she had come forth from the pool, that was still a part of her body perhaps, but it no longer soothed and filled her mind. She was retreating fast into the mold of the Burrowers where trust was too high a price for anyone to pay.

"Was this really," she was guessing now but the thought which had come to her suddenly seemed to make sense, "what your brother sought here?"

"Of course not!" Impatience lent a snap into his answer. "But . . ." His oddly shaped eyes changed in a fashion to give him a speculative look, somewhat eager. She could almost see Zass in him now—a Zass who had sensed a ver-rat near to hand. "But perhaps this would explain better why my brother did not return!"

"He was slain by dead men?"

"This!" He seemed not to have heard her retort, instead he held that off-world weapon out at full arm's length, surveyed it as if he had indeed unearthed some treasure which would give him the wealth of a river captain after a full season's fortunate trading. "Tell me, Simsa, what would one of your Guild Lords offer for such weapons, weapons which can kill at a distance, putting their bearers in no danger, but blasting the enemy entirely?"

"You spoke of fire, of cities being eaten up by it," she pointed out. "What good would it do to destroy all that which could be traded for? No lord would send out his guards if he got no loot in return—not even one of the northern pirates would be so foolish. And they will risk more than any trader. The Lords live for trade, not the destruction of it."

"Only, such as this would not level a city. Its range is very limited. At its widest setting it could not destroy more than would be on this carrier."

Simsa looked from the slender rod to the carrier. She had seen the destruction on the upper wall, but what did any Burrower really know of the feuds of the Guild Lords or the thieves' leaders? Men died in formal duels, in feuds. There had always been raiding of the river convoys, pirates in the northern seas.

Weapons such as this would make a raid harmless for those who used them and they could take, say, the fleet from Saux, the richest prize ever to set anchor in Kuxortal. It would be as a flock of zorsals lighting upon a pack of ver-rats caught in the open with no holes ready gnawed for their escape.

"You begin to understand? Yes, given ambition, greed, the need for power over others—"

"You think of Lord Arfellen!" She made that a statement not a question. "Men have started talking of him behind their hands. The river trader—Yu-i-pul—last season he brought down such a cargo of weft-silk as most of the city marveled. He would not put it to auction after the custom, but held it, held it in Gathar's warehouse." (The significance of that—maybe it meant something). "Yes— Basher's story—Basher's story!"

It was like puzzling out one of the ancient pieces of carving and coming suddenly on a bit which, when fitted into its rightful place, gave meaning to the whole of the find.

"What was Basher's story?"

Simsa wrinkled her nose. "He is a great zut and would have men afraid of him—always he speaks much of what he knows—so that few listen to him and know that there is ever a grain of truth in his yammering. But he would have it that one of Yu-i-pul's guard got sick-drunk on that rot-wine in the Shorehawl and said that there was trouble, that Yu-i-pul knew an auction would not be profitable because of some meddling and, therefore, he would wait out the coming of the ship traders himself. Which he did, though all the city knew that Lord Arfellen was in a rage. It is said that he killed the one who brought him some news of the matter. But the cargo was in Gathar's warehouse in spite of the Guild Lords and Yu-i-pul took home more in trade than any river man has ever hauled upstream. There were five barges and his men were armed with good swords and spears which he had forged for them under his captains' own inspection.

"That was a season ago. Only—what Yu-i-pul has done, so can another river man try. If it goes so, and the auctions are used less and less, then the Guild Lords will feel the pinch."

Matters which had meant nothing to a Burrower, nothing to her save that it had been the initial coming of the very perishable cargo into Gathar's care which had led him to make the bargain with her for the zorsal use (there was a taste or smell to weft-silk which drew ver-rats as sweet gum could draw the Burrow insects).

"Have cargoes coming down the river ever been plundered?"

"It has been tried many times. Sometimes, such did change hands and those bringing the barges into Kuxortal have washed their blades of trader blood well up stream. But the traders of the river road are no weaklings. Such as Yu-i-pul have men sworn to him and his family, father to son. They have stakes in the selling and it is partly their own gain which they would fight for. Yu-i-pul has battled off several attacks in past seasons. They know enough of him and his men now to let his Red and Gold Serpent pennant pass through any of the narrows without challenge. That was why he could say no auction. The Guild wanted no fighting along the wharves, for threaten one river trader in the city and all will answer his warn-war horn, even if they would thrust him through the next day in some feud of their own kind."

"So," the off-worlder dropped down on the pavement, his weapon resting across his knees. He was no longer looking at her but rather at the greenery beyond her shoulder.

Though upper city feuds meant nothing, the more Simsa had talked, the more her own thoughts had leaped from one known fact to a new surmise. As he had done, she relaxed, seated herself, giving the carrier a light shove so that it bobbed a little away, no longer any barrier between them.

"You think that if Lord Arfellen knew that such as those," she pointed to the rod, "were to be found here, he would send men to seek them out, arm his guard, and venture up river to wait for Yu-i-pul? I think so, too. He is not a man to take lightly to insults and Yu-i-pul made him look small in the eyes of those who knew him best—if Baslter's story was the truth. Also, he would be afraid that your brother might discover what lay here. But would he not already have taken these weapons and had them hidden?"

"He could not hide what lies there. Any off-worlder chancing upon it would be required to report it to the Patrol. They would send in their own team, to clean up, to make sure that just that did not happen, that nothing of off-world weaponry would be available to such as Lord Arfellen. I do not know why the first ship landing in these hills did not pick up the radiation reports. Or if they did," he hesitated, "more may be behind this than I first believed."

There had come a change into his face which never seemed open to Simsa's eyes. Now there was a tightness about his lips, once more those lids drooped so she could not see what fire might lie in his eyes. There was something harder, stronger, closed and yet sharper about him, as if some emotion within had given him a new and keener purpose.

"You believe your brother is dead?" she asked quietly.

Still he did not look at her. "Of that I am going to make sure."

That was no oath sworn by blood drip or brother drink, still his words would hold him, of that she was certain. Watching him now, she knew that she would not want to be one to whom he threw a feud challenge.

"You think that they have been here—and Lord Arfellen might have sent them. But how would they know anything about it?" Simsa was suddenly struck by that. If a crashed starship, or even part of such a one, had been found, that story could never have been suppressed in Kuxortal. There was too much interest always in the spacers and all which pertained to them.

"They might not have known about this—at first. But there have long been stories of treasures hidden in the Hard Hills. So when my brother, an off-worlder, came to hunt for such, might they not have believed that he was in search of something more than the source of very old things?"

Simsa's Burrower shrewdness accepted that. Naturally, an off-worlder who came to search the Hard Hills would be assumed by Guild men to be hunting more than broken bits of stone, no matter what might be lettered on such. Though she herself had a lanquid interest in that direction because of Ferwar's addiction and the fact that there was a market among starmen for pieces, she would never have thought that anyone would cross space and then the desert land in quest of those alone, unless he was a victim of some madness.

There was the ring on her hand. She made a fist now by curling her fingers together so that the tower with the gem roof stood stolid and tall. There were those other pieces—the necklace which still rested its pale stones, like the tears shed by a weeping tree, between her breasts, the cuff—

She felt now within her sleeve pocket and brought that out. In the sun here it came to life, not brilliantly, but with a steady glow. At the same time, she jerked open the coat to show the gems resting against her dark skin.

"There may be treasure here also." Deliberately, she tossed the cuff through the air and saw him, in swift reflective action, catch it.

"These were the best of Ferwar's things. I do not believe that they came originally from Kuxortal. There is nothing about them which is of the city. Nor are the stones as are set here," she picked up the long, narrow strip which formed the pendant and held that into the sun in turn, "any such as I have seen brought overseas or down river.

"The Old One had dealings with faceless ones who made sure that they were not seen coming or going. I do not know from where these came. But it is true that seasons ago there was some small trade with the desert men. Then those came no more and instead there was a story of a plague which killed quickly—"

Though he turned the cuff about in his hands, his attention was no longer for that. Instead, he leaned forward, staring at her, his eyes wide open as they seldom were, eagerness visible in every line of his taut body.

"A plague which killed quickly!" he repeated. "Of what nature?"

Again, her thoughts took one of those sudden leaps. It was as if her whole mind could half sense what lay in his from time to time. She dropped the pendant back against her breast, waved her ringless hand towards that grim guardian which she could see the best.

"What you said of the air which could carry some poison in it where your weapons had been used—a plague!"

"Yes!" he was on his feet again in one fluid movement. Then turned to demand of her:

"This plague—how long ago?"

The Burrowers did not reckon time, they had no reason to. One season followed another. One said that this or that happened in the

year the river rose and Hamel and his woman were drowned, or in
the season that the Thieves took Roso to be a climbing man—that
was the way the Burrowers remembered. If the Guilds numbered
their years, Simsa had no way of telling by their time. But she tried
to think back to the last time that bone-lean man who had brought
Ferwar the most and best of her private gleanings had come to them.

He was a river trader of the smallest fringe of that order, one
who could never reckon more profit than might feed him and his
crew of two boys, as hungry and meager as himself, for more than a
voyage—-if they were that lucky. She began to count on her fingers.

"Twelve seasons ago—Thrag came. He had found a desert man
by the river, dying. He waited for his death and then took what he
had. But," she frowned, "the Old One said it was cursed. She paid
him, but said to bring no more and she wrapped it many times
over and had me bury it under stones. It was a jar of some kind. I
remember she asked Thrag what the desert man died of, and then
she was angry and told him that it was a devil and had doubtless
touched him also. He ran. Nor—it is true—did he ever come again."

One did not question the Old One, Simsa had learned that
as the first and foremost rule of her life, so early she could not
remember when she did not know it. Now thinking on what had
happened: Thrag, the dead man from the desert, the fact that men
had commented that the desert people in the following seasons had
disappeared, all came together in another of those quick forming
patterns.

"Twelve seasons ago, six of your years," Thorn was speaking his
thoughts aloud again. "These desert people could have stumbled on
a radioactive wreck, plundered it . . ."

"The plague being that kind which slaughtered your people in
the long ago? But there was no war here."

"No war for your people that is true. But two enemies, two ships,
one hunting the other, so driven by fear or need for revenge as to
loose the last weapon—a crash; it fits! By the Sages of the Ninth
Circle, it fits!"

"But you said that what you found was not a ship out of space,"
she reminded him.

"No. But it could have come from such a ship, used for escape by survivors who were still hunted men."

"And who now stand there—and there!" Deliberately, she pointed first to one of those guardians and then to the other. "But why do they stand so? I thought them guards. If they had died of plague or fought and killed each other, then why do they still stand so, one at either end of this way? That is the fashion in which guards of the Guild stand before a door which none but a high one can enter."

Thorn turned his head slowly, surveying first one and then the other of the motionless, suited bodies.

"You are right," he said thoughtfully. "There is something very purposeful in the way they were left, perhaps as guards—perhaps for some other reason."

"Were they—" Remembering what she had seen within the bubble-like helmet, she gave a small gulp, and then continued with what easiness she could summon, "Were these of your people? Or could you tell?"

"Not my kind," Thorn answered her decisively. "They were warriors. After the ruin which came to my world, our way of life was changed. We followed another path and that does not lead to war. If we kill—" she saw him shiver then and under her gaze it was as if his face grew gaunt and older in an instant—"if we take life knowingly and willingly, except to save ourselves or another, then there is that in us which takes command of our minds and we die. We are no longer men!"

She could not be sure of what he meant, but she knew that it was dire. Also, she believed that he should not be allowed to think on what her words had summoned to his mind.

"Not your people, then. But you know other worlds. Can you tell from which these came?"

"I shall find out!" He reached forward and dropped the rod on the carrier. She saw the roosting zorsals edge away from it, as if they sensed that it was a thing of dark power. "Indeed, I am going to find out!"

11

"So," Simsa also arose, "in which direction do we now search? The zorsals can find living things. Dead men wrapped in dead metal they will not hurt."

The two winged hunters were up once more from the carrier, coasting out over the thick stand of green stuff. Simsa could guess that they were hungry and went to prey upon what their acute sensors could pick up, even though day was upon them. Perhaps, because of that stand of thick green, the heat and glare were not so intense here. Or their interlude in the strange pool had heartened them, as she was sure it had done her, to the point that they could bear far more of the day's light.

"We?" then Thorn began and she already guessed that he was about to deny her any part in this. However, Simsa had no intention of either remaining here, overwatched by alien dead, or staying purposeless wherever the off-worlder would elect as a place of safety while he ranged outward.

"We!" Simsa repeated firmly. "You say you have found a broken ship. Even if it was not made for star travel, still it was not of this world. If it rode in the air, then how may it be traced to its home port any more than a seaship can be followed through trackless waves?"

When he did not answer her, she felt a small glow of triumph. Let this off-worlder not believe that he was the only one who could reason with good logic and to the point.

"It would seem that the way these were left," once more she indicated the encased dead, "has meaning. They are not as old as this place—that must surely be true. I think this was long forgotten before they came from the sky. It is—" For the first time she pushed the dead aliens to the back of her mind, thought of those faces she had seen so boldly carved along the walls, especially that special one which had so impressed her, leaving her feeling both frightened and, in a manner, unclean.

"This is," she continued after a moment's hesitation, "a place of *this* world. And the pool . . ." Hardly aware of what she was doing, she fingered the ring on her hand, rubbing across the stone which had held so much color of that "water" in it. "My people—we of the Burrows—swear by no gods or forces save Fortune. For it is true, I think, that there are none such who concern themselves with us and our fate. Still, in that pool there is life." She spoke as if something else fed the words into her mind. Yet, even as she mouthed them, Simsa was aware also that there was truth in what she said. "I do not know who they were, these people of the Hard Hills. However, it is plain they had secrets of their own, as powerful for us as the flame death is for those of your blood. How felt you when you came from that place?"

"There is some form of radiation there," again he was using a term out of his own knowledge. "Only it is such as I cannot measure. As to how I felt, I was . . . renewed, I think." He had been holding the cuff in one hand, as if it were of little or no importance. Now, she saw him suddenly slip it up over his fingers and palm, squeezing those together to allow it to pass. Even as he did that, he stood staring down at the band of metal which rucked up a little of the sleeve of his off-world garment.

"Why did I do that?" He seemed as bewildered as if he had been in the power of another, sent a task he did not understand in the least. "It somehow it feels right, but—" He stretched out the same hand for the stock of the rod weapon, jerked back with a cry of mingled pain and shock.

"I—it forbids me to take up that! But this is insane! The sun—I must have had a touch of sun to . . ."

Simsa smiled. So the wonders one could summon here were not so one-sided after all. She herself could supply something which would astound and dismay even one who talked of the destruction of worlds, and of wars flung wide enough to engulf whole legions of stars.

"Perhaps there are also weapons which *your* people do not understand." She pulled at the necklace on her breast, twirled the ring out into the full of the sun. "You hunt one mystery here, starman; there may be others."

He still stared down at the cuff, though he had ceased to try to rid himself of it. Nor did he attempt again to take up that weapon of his own kind. Simsa reached out her arm so that Zass could climb this bridge to the zorsal's usual riding place on her shoulder. A wind had been rising, sending branches and leaves rustling. Even though these grew so closely together here, one could not see how even the fingers of a light breeze could reach within the shadows to trouble them. The girl glanced at the sky. To the north clouds massed, a sight she had never expected to see over desert lands, or even this early in the season. Though this growing dark was no surprise to any who knew the way of the wet-time.

She turned to face the guardian in the other section of that way. "There is rain there." She pointed to the clouds. "Though a storm at this season is unusual, still I guess it best for us to seek cover. You speak of danger lingering in your broken sky-traveling thing, so perhaps it is best we take this other way."

A sudden heavy gust of air swooped down upon them, bringing with it the zorsals screaming with rage, and, she was sure, a beginning of fear. The creatures caught at the lashing on the carrier and held fast, their teeth fully displayed as they made apparent what they thought of such a freak storm.

The girl stooped and caught at the pull rope of the carrier. For the first time, she exerted her strength against the pull of that and felt the thing answer. Perhaps because she still held to that supply of new strength she had brought from the pool, she took pleasure in the fact that she was taking the lead in their journey.

Only Thorn reached her in two strides, caught the rope out of her hand. He had awakened out of whatever dazzlement or deep thought had entrapped him by the cuff. Now he moved with his old authority and confidence.

A second gust of air bore up sand grit to sting their faces and eyes, actually carrying with it bits of twig and torn leaf. It was as if something about this open space in the long dead keep or city attracted the gathering strength of the storm. Simsa, remembering traders' tales of certain rocks, peaks, even outcroppings of sea reefs, which did pull the fury of tempests, was eager to get under cover.

Their way was still blocked by the suited dead. The space on either side of that standing figure was too narrow for the carrier. Thorn did not wait to study the problem. Thrusting the lead rope of the carrier back into the girl's hands, he strode forward to grasp the shoulders of the figure. Though, Simsa was pleased to note, he did not stare at what lay behind the open part of that bubble helmet, rather kept his gaze turned to one side as he exerted strength (and it clearly needed full strength on his part; his muscles stood out visibly under the smooth fitting of his suit) to shove it to one side.

Some inequality of the pavement, or incautious movement on his part had a sudden answer. The dead thing tottered. Simsa cried out, her voice rising above the howling of the zorsals, as it rocked forward. Thorn stepped aside just as it crashed, to lie on the pavement, still as stiff and stark in its new position as it had been when it had denied them entrance to the way beyond.

Simsa sidled well away from it as she came on, giving a vigorous jerk to the carrier. Thorn stood above the fallen figure with clenched hands, looking down at its back almost as if he expected to see those stiffly suited arms go out, the legs move, and the dead arise to give battle.

The bottom of the carrier rasped across the bubble head of the fallen to nudge against the off-worlder. He gave a start, then stepped wide across it almost as if he feared the dead could reach out, catch at one of his scuffed boots. Then they were both beyond, passing out of the fast fading light of the day where the storm clouds swung slow, into a corridor.

Though this passage grew increasingly dusky, Thorn made no

move toward lighting the lamp at his belt and Simsa did not want to break the silence of this place by asking for that aid. For, even as they went by the guardian, the zorsals had abruptly ceased to cry.

Under her feet was the velvety gathering of long years of dust, as soft as the silvery sands which had encircled the pool. She glanced down at it now and again but they were already too far advanced into the twilight of the windowless and lightless passage for her to see if that was track-imprinted by any who might have passed this way before.

Outside, the storm hit at last with a roar, which followed them along the corridor like the outraged cry of a hunting beast through whose paws they had luckily escaped. There were flashes, too—lightning had been unleashed.

Still Thorn walked, beside her now, his hand on the tow rope not far from hers, allowing the girl to share his responsibility. Zass hissed into Simsa's ear after each lightning flash, flattening her body as close to the girl's shoulder as she could.

The passage was not altogether dark for the further they withdrew from the entrance of the guardian, the more visible came another gleam of light ahead. Twice, warned, or alarmed, by lightning which had given her a momentary glimpse of something leaning outwards from the wall, first on one side and then the other, Simsa had pulled aside only to realize that what she avoided were images nearly life-size which began to mark the walls at regular intervals. Her first thought was that these were more of the dead.

Perhaps Thorn had been startled out of his preoccupation by the same thought. For at last, he snapped on his lamp for a fraction of time, only to reveal the figures were of stone not metal. That flash of clear sight had given Simsa only a swift impression of something man-like, but she wanted to see no more of such.

Instead, she centered her gaze steadily ahead to that wan promise of more light. Doubtless, the off-worlder had some good reason for his now-cautious use of the lamp. Perhaps its power only lasted so long—even as he had warned her that of the box which lifted the carrier must be renewed.

They emerged at length into grey light again, though they were not fully in the open. Even as they stepped free of the passage, Thorn cried out, threw his arm about Simsa to hold her against him, pushing back into the archway behind. Down into the center part of the open space before them smashed a great block of stone, striking with force enough to crunch and send splinters flying in all directions.

Simsa stared up. They were under a roof in which there was a great jaggered crack, through which showed the night dark of the storm. She could see through this gloom other pieces of the dome which had fallen in the past. Thorn pulled her to the left, leading her under what seemed a much more secure overhang. Here she was as ready to hug the wall as he was to press her closer to it.

This space was no rough underground cavern. They were separated from the central cathedral and dangerous part by a series of pillars placed in regular order at the edge of the overhang. Each of these was carved in the form of either a standing figure, or a thick stemmed growth, half vine, half tree. All loomed well above even the off-worlder's head. Simsa felt a beginning of curiosity, a desire to inspect them more closely, but her companion did not linger, and urged her on by the grip he still held on her arm.

There were no more openings nor doors in the wall which formed the left side of this covered way. On that space were deep carvings, but no faces leered at her, rather these ran in lines as might some gigantic record left to puzzle those with whom the builders shared no blood tie nor memory.

She could not guess how far they had gone in their half trot along that wall when suddenly there was a flare of light directly ahead—darting upward, then spreading out to catch them both in its beam. There had been no more crashes of stone from above, yet the sound of the storm echoed hollowly here. Thus Simsa caught only a faint sound from her companion.

He dropped his hold on both her and the carrier, whirled to catch up that weapon rod awkwardly in his cuffless left hand. A leap carried him before her with one end of the rod clapped tightly to his side by his bent arm, his fingers hooked about a projection a third of the way down its length.

That flare ahead did not fade or fail, remaining near as bright as the sun. Simsa had involuntarily shaded her eyes at first, now as her sight adjusted, she first peered between her fingers, and then dropped her hand entirely.

This was not a fire, rather it burned steadily, as might a lamp. A camp? Of whom? No guild force or traders she knew of had such day-clear illumination to serve them.

Then—could the dead have left this on guard for some lost reason?

The girl, recalling only too well Thorn's tales of a slaying fire, reached out to sweep the other two zorsals to her. They had hunched their heads between their shoulders, half raised their wings as shields against the glare. She caught their honks of fear and misery. With Zass still in her usual place on one shoulder, the other two now crowded onto her arm (so heavy a weight together that she had to steady them against her body). Simsa backed against the wall, wondering if she dared to turn and run, believing she was too well revealed to try. She had no doubt that any weapons off-worlders might carry would have a range of least as far as a bow and she was well within arrow length of the light's source.

Thorn stood, his feet slightly apart, facing that beacon directly. Now he called out, waited, and called again—three times in all. His voice sounded differently. Simsa half guessed that he was speaking other tongues.

There came no answer save the continued flare of the light. From here she could not even see the source from which that sprung. Thorn raised his other hand so she caught the shine of the cuff, waved her to stay where she was. Then he began to walk steadily, with obvious purpose, toward the glare.

Simsa's breath came raggedly as if she had run some race. She waited for fire, for some other strange and horrible fate, to cut him down. There was no belief in her that there could be any friends here.

But no war arrows, cut to whistle alarmingly as they took the air, no spouting of off-world fire, followed. Thorn was merely walking as if back in the desert and that light was the cruel heat of the sun.

She could see him so clearly, though only his back now. Still he waited for death to claim him. Then he turned a little from the column of the light, passed to one side to hide—consumed?

The zorsals still cried and clung to her, showing no desire to take flight. Was it the light which kept them so? Or did they sense some greater danger? Their antennae were all closely rolled to their small skulls, and their big eyes squeezed shut.

Then, a dark blot which could only be Thorn—she was sure it was—showed once more between her and that light. While the light itself was reduced in both length of beam and harshness of glare, so she could see he stood there waving her forward. Because she must trust him, if she trusted anyone beyond herself in this place, the girl picked up the rope of the carrier, set herself to the forward pull of its weight and obeyed his signal.

By the time she had reached the source of the light, it had been softened to hardly more than that which a fire might give on a chill night of the wet-season's ending. Now she could see a space in which there had been set up what seemed to be a kind of fortified camp—if all those lumps of stone had been dragged there for walls of protection.

Piled against these blocks were containers and boxes—some of the type which she had seen unloaded many times from traders' rafts on the river. The others were of metal—surely off-world.

While the light itself came from a cylinder placed on a plate of metal in the middle of the camp, Simsa looked hurriedly around. Where were those who had set the light? She half expected to see, marching towards her, suited bodies—living bodies—of off-worlders. Dead men, she told herself firmly, do not make camps—they do not!

Only there was no one there save Thorn. He, however, had no longer any attention for her. Instead he was on his knees by one of the off-world containers, this one thin in width and slightly curved. Simsa thought it might just have been shaped to fit upon a man's back, for straps dangled down the inner side. Thorn had flung up the lid of that and was delving inside. Two small boxes, neither much larger than his own hand, had been set out. Then there was a larger one which flapped open as he pulled it free. Inside were blocks which fell out—one bouncing across to Simsa.

She had set the zorsals on one of the barricade rocks. Now she stooped to pick up that wandering square—and froze before her fingers quite touched it. She jerked her hand back, old half-forgotten stories shifted into her mind.

Caught—a man's, a woman's innermost spirit caught—fastened, made so a possession of another that such a thing could be used to summon, to torment, to—kill! Ferwar had laughed at such tales. But Ferwar—not even the Old One had seen such as this. For what she looked upon must indeed be the root of such stories. She was looking down—at herself. Imprisoned in the transparent cube was a figure so much alive that Simsa could not look aside.

That was how she must have appeared when she had drawn herself up on the silver sand of the pool, before she had pulled on again that dirty and confining clothing. The black skin of the prisoner was rounded, or spare—just as she was so shaped. If she could put finger within that transparent cover, surely she would touch flesh. That silver hair curled, as if just tossed in a loosening rain-wind. The ends lay soft across the shoulders, one strand half concealing a small, proud jutting breast. There was no coarse clothing, rather around the trim hips rested a chain as silver bright as the hair. From this, hung a kilt fringe of gems strung in patterns made by the use of silver balls between stones—just such gems as those of the necklace.

The small head was proud-high. There was that about this other Simsa—in the block—so great a pride. The living girl drew a deep breath. Through the hair on that high-held head was threaded another chain of gems, so that on the forehead rested a circle of them, pale and green, centered by another stone, opaque, the twin to the ring's jewel.

One of the image's hands held a small rod, appearing to have been wrought from some huge single white-grey gem. It was topped by a symbol Simsa had seen—one repeated several times over in some fragments the Old One had pored over, two curved horns turned upward, supporting between them a ball.

This was she. Yet never had she worn such gems, stood so tall, so unafraid, triumphantly proud. Was this that other her which some said dwelt within the body and went forth—no one could guess where—when life was spilled out forever? How could that be? She was alive here—Simsa as she had always been, had known herself, and yet—there was this other who was also her!

Though she did not realize it, she had knelt, was leaning forward now, one hand planted palm flat on either side of that amazing thing, staring at it, still in shock.

The girl was not even aware the off-worlder had come until his shadow fell across the other Simsa, half veiling her. She had raised her hand to brush that away. Then she looked up, met his eyes. For a moment, they rested on her—then on the other one.

He stared so long at the prisoner in the block that she began to feel cold. He knew—without her asking. Without answering, she also understood that he knew the truth of this thing, of what it might mean—and what it might do. She wanted so much to catch up that block, hide it away from his eyes, hiding this other self from his knowing—But it was too late for that.

Now he knelt, too, but he made no effort to take it from her. Could it be that there was a chance that he would let her keep it—make sure that she alone held safe this other self?

"It is—me—me!" She could no longer hold back the words. "Why is it me?"

She raised her eyes, hardly daring to look away from her find, lest he did take it. He had the strength to make it his, past all her defenses, even if she called upon the zorsals. Also, he knew what it was and how. . .

Simsa could not read his expression. She had seen him surprised, she had seen him angry, she had seen him push himself to the edge of endurance. This was another Thorn—one she must now fear?

"This—" he spoke very slowly and softly, almost as if he did not want to frighten her. "This is a visa-picture. It was made by my brother."

"Picture." she repeated. His brother—where? She looked around wildly.

"Like the bits on the walls, the heads," he continued just as slowly and carefully. "Somewhere my brother saw this—and copied it so."

"Me!" she insisted.

Thorn shook his head. "Not you, no. But plainly someone of your race, your own people, someone whose blood line might still have had a part in your own making. See—I would say she is a little older . . . and look there, do you have such on your body?" He did not touch the block which held the other Simsa, simply pointed with fingertip to the smooth skin just a little above that fringe of gems which fell between the slim, long legs.

Simsa stared. Yes, there was something there—a scar, hardly showing, except that it must stand out in a ridge above the rest of the skin. It was the same symbol as crowned the rod this strange Simsa carried—two horns guarding a ball.

"That—" he told her now, "is X-Arth indeed. Though this woman who wears it—wore it—is of no Arth race I have seen accounts of. Perhaps she was Forerunner—one of those who vanished from all worlds and space before our own kind came into being. That is a very old sign even on Arth, for it combines two forces, the sun and the moon."

"You say she is gone!" Simsa caught him up quickly. "But I am here. If she is not me, then she is kin, as you have admitted. Your brother—he can tell me—we can find—!"

The words poured out, she had not realized that she had reached forward and caught him by both shoulders, was even trying to shake him as if so she could better batter into him her need.

Now the expression on his face was changed indeed. It was not one of that strange softness which he had shown before, rather his features again set, his eyes narrowed and shut against her.

"My brother is—" for a long moment his lips did not move. Then he twisted free from her hold and stood up. "I can only believe that he is dead."

She stared up at him gape-mouthed. Then the full force of what he meant made her snatch at what he called a visa-picture, which she knew she must have. Almost in the same instant, she scrambled back against one of the rocks which made up that pocket of the camp. With that stone at her back firm, so comforting, she looked around again.

"How do you know?"

He nodded to the container he had been unpacking. "He would not have left that here, as he did the pilot—" Now he gestured to the lamp which still gave a day's light to them. "Those are intended as guides. They are—it is difficult to explain to one who does not understand our ways—but they are used in times of trouble to bring help. In them is an element which is set to answer to another whom those who may help always carry." Once more, he fingered one of those things on his belt of so many wonders. "When I came within the right distance—that blazed—to draw me. Just as it would have drawn any one of our service who came here. Had it not been for the fury of the storm, we might even have heard a call, for they are set also to broadcast sound as well as light.

"My brother would have had no reason to set this pilot light unless he believed he was in grave danger. Nor would he have left what he did in that," he pointed to the container, "unless he hoped that it would be found by someone searching for him."

"A message—" she had assimilated what he meant, "did he tell you somehow then what that danger was?"

"He may have." Now he went back and picked up one of the smaller boxes which he had taken from the container. "If he did, the message is taped here."

"But this—" she still had the block, holding it with great care. "Would he tell you where this came from? You talk of Arth, X-Arth—of Forerunners—of wild things no one has heard of—you know so much, you of the stars—tell me what you can of this one who looks like me! Tell me!" Her voice arose, she cried out with all the longing of those years in which she had been so much a stranger that she must hide her strangeness from her world. In a mixture of races, she had been the most notable that she knew. She remembered only too well again how Ferwar had cautioned her from her earliest childhood to conceal what she could of her strangeness. How many times had the Old One warned of the

Guild Lords who might have taken her just for her difference? She accepted the danger and had always done as the Old One said. She had been so long childish of body, she was near twice as many seasons as the rest of the Burrower girls when they were sought to pleasure some man. Partly, she had been safe because she so long remained a scrawny child. It was only when she had come out of that pool really that she had known pride in her body as well as in her wits.

"If I can find where that—where he saw it—" Thorn said, slowly, "then I shall take you there. If we come forth from this venture still alive."

She looked down at the Simsa in the block. He was right—she might want passionately to find this, but perhaps death stood in their way. Still, this much she had and it gave her a fierce joy of possession as she looked upon it.

12

Though the storm still rolled overhead, and there had been at least one more crashing fall of stone in the outer part of this great chamber, Simsa sat at ease. In one hand, she held a small container which Thorn had given her after showing her how to twist the upper part a little and then wait for a short time so that when it was fully opened, what it held was hot as if just poured from some inn kettle. She savored the rich contents, picking out bits which she handed down to the eagerly reaching paws of the zorsals, the three gathered before her and watching each bite she transferred to her mouth. Off-world food, with a savor she had never dreamed that any food could have.

Thorn had another such can by this knee where he, too, sat cross-legged. Only his attention was not for the food, but rather for the sounds made by the small box he had told her might contain any message his brother might have left. The sounds were not speech as Simsa recognized as such, rather a series of clicks as one might rap out with a bit of metal against stone. At her comment, before he had waved her impatiently to be still, Thorn said that this was a secret way of message sending and only one trained could make sense of those clicks.

The girl yawned as she scooped out the last large piece of food, then put the can down so that the zorsals squabbled over the chance to lick out its interior with their long tongues. She would have liked to have explored, poked into the remaining boxes and containers.

On the other hand, she also felt drowsy and, for the first time since she had left the pool, at ease and content. That the camp had not been looted, Thorn had said, meant that his brother had not been either killed or taken captive here. Thus, he appeared to believe that they were safe also—at least for now.

Simsa stretched out, turned her head a little so she could watch those lines of patterns across the wall. Among them she searched for that symbol connected with the other Simsa. Only it appeared nowhere here, at least not within the range of her sight. Then the clicking came to a sudden stop and she looked toward the off-worlder.

He had picked up the box with the message, was sitting with that closed-face look which she knew meant he was thinking.

"What did it tell you?" This silence had stretched too long—she wanted to know. Perhaps within those clicks was even the secret of what meant the most to her.

"He discovered that he had been followed. He had made a find—Arth—Forerunner—Then he saw the ship. There was enough about it—though he did not give details—to make him afraid that it might be the wreck of a war spacer. It was hot—radioactive—but he thought not too high for one of our blood to explore. He scouted and found indications that there had been others before him. Some of them, at least, were desert people; he discovered at least two bodies of those."

"Only," the off-worlder sat back on his heels, interlacing his fingers and turning them in and out, his eyes upon their movement as if so he worked some kind of fortune producing ritual, "he also came across signs that there had been another landing by several smaller ships—and not long ago. There had been a camp near there. A meeting place for those of this world . . . and others. Jacks!" The last word came as an explosion.

"Who or what are Jacks?" she pulled herself up. To learn all that from a series of clicks! But this was another starman's thing and so it could be true.

"Outlaws," he returned. "Just as you have pirates on your seas, so do we have their like along the star lanes. Such could provide the means for looting that war spacer. They would do so if the price was high enough. They have been and gone, but they had also left a beacon, something such as that—" he gestured to the lamp, "but of a different kind, in that it can be heard off-world by the ship for which it is set. When they left the beacon it meant they planned to return. It could be that they did not have equipment enough to start scavenging, or it might be that they needed more help, or—" He waved his hand as if there could be ten-ten reasons for such a visit and a promised return.

"They might want what they found for themselves; then the Guilds have nothing to do with this."

Thorn shook his head. "That camp my brother found remains of was laid out first by men of this world—the others were visitors. Also, it was set up several seasons ago and, therefore, whoever dealt with the Jacks knew well enough what lay here. Only that they themselves could not yet make use of it."

"If they knew, say, Lord Arfellen . . ." Simsa began once more to fit piece to piece in her mind. "Then why did they let your brother come here? He was off-world, he would know at once that this wreck of a ship was a bad thing. They could have easily killed him before he reached the Hills at all—"

"Unless they dared not report a death near their own territory—even by accident—of an off-worlder. My brother was no common man and the League and the Patrol keep their watch on all of us, especially when we come to hunt out Forerunner remains—or things X-Arth. Can you understand, Simsa? It is not the actual worth of bits of broken stone, or this," he tapped the cuff he still wore, "which matter. We seek out all we can learn because we must!

"My people spread out from Arth itself so many seasons ago that you would have difficulty in counting time. We found worlds with others living there—some were strange of body, stranger yet of mind. Some were enough like ourselves that we could interbreed. Other worlds were empty of life, yet held broken cities, strange machines, mysteries left by intelligent beings.

"All we can learn we must, for there were many, many powers which rose among the stars—and then fell. Some fell by war—we have discovered worlds which have been burnt black, holding only ashes—the result of the use of such weapons as we have come to fear and have outlawed. But also there were other worlds where all that remained appeared as if those who dwelt there had simply walked away and left great wonders to be toppled by the fingers of time.

"Why did they rise to power and fall? If we can learn only a little of their past, then we can foresee the way of our own future, at least in part. Perhaps some of the acts which brought them down we can then avoid."

"There is one world in our League where all such finds are gathered to be studied. The race who live there—who are so long-lived a species that to them our oldest known are but infants—study these finds, try to learn. Sometimes they themselves are the searchers, more often it is we of other species and races who collect the knowledge for them. Such a searcher was my brother—and he had much experience in these matters. When the first starships landing here brought back fragments of a much older time, and our traders brought ever more, he was chosen to come and see—to make records—report whether the remains here were such as would warrant sending in a whole ship of trained people to deal with them."

"My Simsa"—she still thought of the picture as that—"was she of your Forerunners? These people who rose and then fell, who knew once the stars and then lost them?"

"Perhaps—those symbols make it seem likely. Or she could be one born of this world who learned of such from other star rovers— those who were star rovers before my people lifted from their own world at all. I know now where T'seng found her."

"Where? Let us go there!"

"If you wish—" he sounded almost indifferent. He was more intent, she must accept, on his own search, the plans he must make. "In the morning," he added.

Simsa knew she must be content with that. Though she longed to set out at once, he had risen, gone to the lamp. Now he passed across it a disc he had taken from his belt. The light winked out. As its going, the zorsals stirred and the girl gave the signal which would post them as sentries.

She was sure that she could not sleep—that the need to see that other Simsa was so aching, tearing a feeling that she could not rest. But sleep lay in wait for her after all.

She awoke to the sound of water. Grey light from beyond the rock walls of the campsite shined through the broken dome so far overhead with the brightness of at least an hour past dawn. Across the camp's space Thorn lay, the arm with the cuff covering his eyes as if he had gone to sleep trying to shut out some sight he must rid himself of—at least for a while.

Simsa heard a soft chitter. The three zorsals were roosting on the top of one of the rocks, their softer, sleepy voices signifying they were settling for sleep. She got to her knees and looked out into the center of this space which was larger than any building in all of Kuxortal.

Now, in the better light, she could see that it was oval in form and that ranked above this covered, arched way which appeared to rim completely around the oval, were tiers of ledges, as if those had once furnished seats or resting places. People must have gathered here for some purpose. Probably to view action in the center where those lumps of broken masonry had crashed to crumble. She had never seen such a place and she wondered what could possibly bring so many people together—if all those ledges had once been filled.

The water she had heard running—that was funneled off from the ledges and the broken dome, gathering in a channel not too far from the camp. Simsa crawled over the rock barrier and went to it. It seemed clear and drinkable. She palmed up some, went back to offer it to Zass, who obligingly lapped her tongue twice across the girl's palm, thus declaring it all right. All that talk of plague from Thorn's "radiation" warning made Simsa doubly cautious, but now she drank and found it good.

"Fair morning to you, Lady Simsa—"

She had been trying to comb her tangled hair with her fingers, now she looked over her shoulder and smiled. Her waking here had seemed so lacking in care, as if they were safe in spite of all Thorn's tales. She found herself light of heart again, as she had been when she had left the pool.

There was something else she noted with a small inner surprise.

When he had called her "Lady" before, she had believed he had jeered at her, making it plain she was of the Burrowers, but—now— that title seemed right.

"It is a fair morning, Lord Thorn—" she agreed. "If you will toss me that water container, I can fill it before last night's bounty runs dry."

Already the run-off water stream was diminishing in size.

He did just as she had suggested, she using her lightning skill to snatch it out of the air, catching at its cording so it swung around her arm. This easily carried piece of equipment also had been among their finds the night before, and Simsa had guessed that its being left there was one more reason her companion believed in his brother's death.

She filled, rinsed, and filled it again. If they were to go on (she had already marshaled facts and plans), they could not burden themselves with the unwieldy and hard to handle carrier. Instead, they must draw upon the camp equipment. It would appear that was just what Thorn was prepared to do. Those things which had been in the one pack he had opened and explored so fully, he laid into a hamper, filling the first with ration tins and other things he sought from here and there among all which had been stored in the camp.

That light-weight, very tough, and yet silken-smooth square which had served as a folded pillow for Simsa was trussed to form a second pack which Thorn fussed over until he was sure that it would ride easily on her back. As he worked, he explained the use of some of the things they must carry. There were direction finders which would pick up those trail markings T'seng had set up leading Thorn along his brother's explored paths. In addition were some small, round balls Thorn explained were to be pressed at one end and then tossed. Almost instantly thereafter they loosed clouds of mist that would overpower any animal or unprotected humanoid creature. There were only four of these, but Thorn divided them, insisting that Simsa carry her pair in sleeve pockets she could easily reach.

She had already turned out of her right one the bag of silver bits—useless here, weighing her down when she could well need an extra lightness of arm.

When the packs were both put together, Thorn picked up the case into which he had fitted with great care all his brother had left behind in the way of information. As she stood waiting, Simsa thought she knew what he would ask for next. She put her hand protectively over that "picture" which she had wrapped in a sheet of thin protective stuff which had been rolled and cased to protect the mist balls. That was hers—she would not give it up. Thorn glanced at her, perhaps he read her determination, for he did not ask her to return it. Rather, he picked up the now lightless lamp, setting its broad base on the package he had fastened, carefully fitting it into place.

At first, Simsa did not quite realize the significance of his act. Then she took a long stride forward to stand beside him.

"You leave this so—because you believe we shall not return?"

"I believe nothing!" he retorted impatiently. "I only do what is customary."

"One man," she said, "went from this camp and you think died."

He did not answer. She needed no answer. Still her confidence was not shaken. There was always death. If one feared that constantly one had no time for life. One had this day—that was enough to concern one's thoughts.

They left the camp, Zass perched sleepily on Simsa's pack, each of the other two zorsals on a shoulder. When Thorn had offered to take their weight, she explained that they would not go to him, nor to anyone else.

The way was smooth enough walking and her well calloused feet had been rested, renewed and strengthened by the pool. He need not fear that she could not keep up with him, and she told him so.

Their door out of the huge chamber of the dome came soon enough, another passage opening to their left. Thorn entered without question, Simsa a step or so behind. This was so short a way that the light ahead, which was now sun bright, showed her once more those statues leaning outward from the wall which had given her such a fright the night before. She looked at each eagerly, hoping to discover some resemblance to her picture—but these were like the faces on the upper walls. A number were beasts of one kind or another, none she recognized, only that they seemed to be uniform in that they all showed fangs, claws, or gave the impression of being about to leap upon and slash down some weaker prey.

Three were humanoid, the faces bland, expressionless, with eyes which were mere ovals of smoothed stone. Yet she did not like them. The hostility portrayed by the beasts was open and honest. These others were masks which, she suspicioned, had they been living things, hid emotions and desires more subtle and far worse.

Beyond the passage was another wide space—a road or street. No slippery cobbles set here. The rain had washed across blocks longer than Simsa's height were she to lie full length upon them, still so closely knit together that though there was a crack here and there through which some thread of greenery had fought its way still the pavement was better kept that any of her home city. This highway was bordered on both sides again by tangles of lush greenery from which there arose buildings, three, four, even five stories high, slatted windows like tears along their sides.

Any walks which must have once led to these doors were long since lost in the luxuriant growth, and vines hugged the walls, forming thick cloaks for a good portion of their heights. Simsa thought that it would surely take the flames of the off-world weapon to clear a path to any of them. Thorn had brought that with them, still steadying it on his hip, one handed.

"Why not take that off since it will not allow you to use the flame thing?" she asked at last, nodding to the cuff.

"Because I cannot—short of cutting it," he returned quietly. "I have tried."

With a sudden stab of uneasiness, she turned the ring on her thumb, found it moved easily enough, that she could withdraw it and return it. Then she plucked at the necklace and it also hung free. Why the off-worlder could not shed his portion of her spoil she did not understand.

His "I cannot" had been short and sharp, making plain that he did not want to speak further of the matter. Still she might have persisted, when, suddenly, he made a quick stop, a half turn, to face the eternal mass of growth which stood between them and the buildings. At the same time, she heard, above the noise of insects to which her ears had now become accustomed, another sound, a clicking.

"That way—" Thorn started straight ahead for a wall of tangled brush and vine where Simsa could not distinguish a single opening. Then, as they closed in until the nodding ends of vines, seeking new supports, fluttered near them, she caught glimpses of withered growth, a blackened and scorched tree trunk. Someone had used fire to cut a path through here. Now Thorn fingered the rod he had carried so carefully.

From the end of that shot a brilliant, searing ray. The vegetation became ash, floating through the air. They had a narrow opening before them. What had grown there was but a screen of brush, for open to them now stood the arch of a door which had been completely hidden by vegetation, which now would begin to hide their own passing.

"You say," Simsa said, as she pressed along on his very heels, having a very unpleasant feeling that the vines and shrubs might begin to close in with an effort to take them prisoner. "You carry a weapon that is not allowed; how did your brother clear this path if he had no such weapon?"

"Well asked," Thorn commented. "But if he came the same way we did, he may have found that flitter and perhaps, the same as I, a flamer lost by the dead."

"By the guardians?" It would be long before she forgot those suited figures.

Thorn's answer was a grunt which meant nothing. He had stepped into a room with painted walls, though there was little light to see those because of the masking of the windows by the growth. Now he switched on his belt light to sweep the beam slowly across the nearest wall.

The paintings were faded but still the colors were visible. They showed odd, asymmetrical arrangements of flowers, and some flying things with brightly spotted wings. The zorsals, now out of the full light, seemed to waken from the stupor which had held them since they had come to Simsa earlier. The two on her shoulders suddenly took wing, up towards the high ceiling. One of them uttered a hunting hoot and swooped into a far corner. What he carried when he arose again made the girl flinch.

"No!" Simsa cried out as the ray of light caught and pinned the zorsal. The thing which he carried, clinging to the prey with his hind paws as he twisted off the head expertly with the front, was only too well known to the girl. What if? She caught at Thorn's arm.

"That thing feeds upon the dead," she said in a low voice, which yet sounded far too loud in this chamber. He gave her a slight shove which moved her away.

"Stay!" He mouthed that order even as he strode away. Simsa this time was willing to obey.

She saw Thorn's ray of light strike into the corner, hold steady for a long moment. Then the off-worlder was returning.

"Whoever it was wore Guildman's clothing."

The answer was so different from what she expected, perhaps from what he had also expected to discover, that they stood staring at one another.

"One of those who might have followed your brother?"

"Who will ever know now? Come!" The pace he set as he crossed the chamber was close to a lope. Simsa called the zorsals, but she knew that they would not return to her until their hunting hunger was satisfied. Under another arch man and girl went, and then they were confronted with a long flight of stairs leading upward.

Simsa was not used to climbing such, but the treads were nearly as low and broad as those they had descended into the place of the pool. They reached a level finally to which the vegetation had not yet grown and light came through the windows. There were no designs on the walls here but they had once been painted a plain golden color in which small specks of glitter sparkled tantalizingly as if marking corners of gem stones near buried from sight.

Another arch brought them out, above a sea of green, to walk a narrow bridge which had been built high in the air. Simsa clutched at a railing. To be so out in the air made her feel dizzy, as if she would begin soon to sway from side to side, as the boat had swayed in the hold of the sea; to topple over the edge, and then fall and fall until the ocean of green below would swallow her forever.

Thorn appeared to think this way of traveling entirely natural and was thudding on, never even looking back to where she clung to her anchorage. She set her teeth together and went forward, lest he vanish and be lost in that other building she could see ahead. *He* might be following that off-world guide which would take him along his brother's marked path, but she had none such to keep her from some wrong turning. For here, even the zorsals (within these tombs of buildings) might become lost.

She had to let go of the rail. Fastening her eyes on Thorn's disappearing back, she set out after him at a pace which fear increased even as she went.

They did gain the next building without missteps. Thorn stood within the entrance there, that disc once more in his hand, his eyes intent upon it. Simsa had expected to be led to another stair, to descend perhaps as far as they had climbed. Rather, the off-worlder wheeled, passed into a second room, going straight to a window there which was wider than the slits which lay farther down these walls.

He pushed himself up on the ledge to look out and down. Simsa could not see past the width of his shoulders and he said nothing, did not move. At last she could stand the suspense no longer.

"What is it?" She reached out to catch at the arm which wore the cuff, pull at the sleeve so tightly molded against the flesh.

"The end of a world, perhaps." His words meant very little, but he moved aside so that she could look down in turn.

Almost she cried out, but not quite. Then his hand slid across her lips as an additional seal upon secrecy.

Here there was no forest of green—instead a strip so wide its outer edges were almost lost to sight. In places it was blackened, scarred. While on it—

At first she thought they looked down upon a starship landing field with a fleet in port—a fleet of more ships than had ever come to Kuxortal in a season—in two seasons. Then she saw that most of these ships did not stand erect as if they had landed, as was customary, fins down, noses sky pointed. Two had fallen on their sides, plainly great damaged. Beyond them was a third which was of an entirely different shape altogether than that of the small traders she knew, a round globe from under which protruded a congealed mass of metal: a second ship upon which it had crashed. None of them were—

But, yes, there was one still standing, stark, sky saluting, some distance away. Its sides were smooth and clean where there were the marks of fire, wounds cutting across the others. It looked as if it would be ready to take off at any moment.

But if this was a graveyard for starships which could no longer fly, it was not deserted. Simsa saw what could only be men, men who wore suits like the dead guardians, but who moved, if clumsily. Several sat on carts which went apparently on their own power from one of the wrecked ships to another. Others walked, so slowly in those heavy body coverings, to pile things they had brought out of the wrecks, sorting them.

Thorn's arm shot out. He was holding the strip which he had told her meant the level of death which lay in such places. She could see that red line, which had been near the middle of the strip when he had first shown it to her, was now a finger-width farther up.

"A deadly place."

His voice was low, as if he were awed or shocked by the scene they watched.

"But they—"

"Are suited," he pointed out. "Still, so much danger; what could be worth such exposure?"

"Your weapons of fire?"

"Not just to trade to any little lordlings here," he returned. "Nor could your Lord Arfellen (though I have some idea he knows something of this) dare to come near what is being gathered. This is what is left of a war command."

"Your war—did some of your people flee after all their cities were destroyed?"

He was shaking his head. "These are not ships I know, and they are so old—maybe even Forerunner!"

His eyes were wide. "Forerunner arms! Yes! There would be fools on half a hundred worlds who would pay high for such knowledge, even if they could not touch the weapons themselves. You see these can be taken apart, studied, their ways of making taped. *Then* those who made this find—a find that would be blasted into nothingness if it were public knowledge—would have something to sell such as has never been sold before! *This* is a treasure of evil past any reckoning. We have found burned-off planets, but never before a fleet—or even one ship—which fought such wars! Arms to be studied and copied, the ships themselves. These looters can find buyers in plenty and it will mean ruin and death around the galaxy!"

"What will you do?" The force of his words made each come like a small blow. She could understand what he meant. Those working below would take apart these ancient ships and their arms of horror, learn, sell that knowledge. Who on Kuxortal could stop them, when to even go near that ghostly fleet meant death without protection such as only the enemy had?

13

Thorn turned away from the window, once more showing Simsa a closed face. His hands curled into fists, though the fingers of one were still tight about the off-world weapon.

"What will I do?" he repeated softly. He strode two steps across this chamber, turned abruptly and came back to her, to look down at Zass.

"I asked you once before," he said slowly, as if he were thinking his way from one half tangled and unclear part-idea to the next, "what will these do at your ordering." Now he nodded at Zass.

"How would you use them?" she countered quickly. To turn her creatures loose on those men below, who were not only completely enclosed in armor suits but were also working, if what Thorn said was true, in an atmosphere deadly to those without protection, was not to be considered.

Thorn was back again at the window, gazing at that scene of activity. "There is a signal, a way to call for help into space, in that wrecked flyer back there," he said. "If it is not damaged and it could be taken out there and set in the midst of that field . . ."

"Who would hear it?" she demanded. "Do you have a fleet out among the stars waiting for such a call?"

Now he did turn his head to look at her. "When I came here, there were those of my service who were suspicious. We reported our mission to the Patrol. This world is a call-stop mainly for Free Traders, smaller ships who deal on their own, captain and crew sharing in the profits. However, it is known that through the years, Jack ships—pirates—have set down here and sold their takes, gathered supplies and wares which were legal. There has been a watch on Kuxortal for some seasons now for that reason. Thus, there will be a Patrol scout on orbit soon." He hesitated and frowned. "It may already be there. But it will not touch planet until there is a signal broadcast to bring it down. If we could set up a warn-call—"

Simsa smoothed Zass's fine fur. Suppose that the zorsals could be led to do as he wished—and they died of this plague? What did she care for the concerns of his League if such action meant death for these who trusted her?

"It might be done at night," he was continuing. "But also success depends on many factors—whether the signal in the flitter is still usable, whether it can be planted out there, whether I could code in the right call—"

"And whether," Simsa broke in fiercely, "I am willing to send my zorsals to their deaths! You say that men will die down there if they do not wear those suits; what of these?" She held Zass closer against her, heard anxious twitters and chirps from the two males now drawn to them and fluttering about her head.

"If they go swiftly in and out . . ." but his gaze no longer met hers squarely. Then he added explosively: "I can see no other way, and this MUST be done! Would you see your world die in fire? For I tell you that such as would loot this place of the devices here would make very sure that no one else might come to pick through what they may have missed. They will not have long to make such choices—even in their suits they dare not be exposed to radiation so long as it would take to pick clean each and every one of those ships. What they take will be the richest loot. The rest they shall destroy— and to destroy with the weapons they will loose will leave a sore from which poison shall spread to kill and kill!"

"Your plan all depends upon chance and fortune," Simsa answered him. "Even if this other wreck of a flying thing has what you need, will it not be too old to work?" She did not know how much of what he said she could believe. Perhaps he thought he told her the truth, but perhaps also he was mistaken, or trying to frighten her into blindly following any action he planned.

"That much we can make sure of." Again, he flung away from the window as if he were impelled, an arrow released from a tight bowstring. He was already heading back and did not even pause to see if she followed. She did reluctantly, uneasy. Were his warnings true? Would those men working below either destroy the ancient ships when they had looted them or would they perhaps give flaming arms to those of the Guild who might have discovered what they did? It would be safer for them to slay out of hand any Lord Arfellen sent; they need not fear any trouble from the Guild, so far away and thus unable to learn what had happened until too late.

Once more she crossed that bridge, striving only to keep her eyes ahead, not to look down. Back they went, until they came again to the camp. Thorn lingered for some little time there, turning out boxes and making a selection of things.

It was when they came into the open space, passing once more the tumbled, dead guard, that the off-worlder spoke to her. He had been silently intent on what he was doing and until then did not even seem to note that she was still with him.

He shrugged off his backpack, but he did not put down that sack he had filled at the camp.

"Wait here," he ordered. "There is radiation around that flitter— but, as I have said, not enough to cause *me* trouble."

He was off again, squeezing by the standing dead, heading into that part of the ruins from which he had come at their earlier meeting here. Simsa sat down, shrugging off her pack in turn. She rummaged in it for another can of the off-world food. As she opened that, Zass and her two sons crowded up against the girl's knees, their forepaws stretched out, making small beseeching sounds. Already they were in thrall to these new tastes and flavors.

The contents of this can were more solid so Simsa broke off bits, sharing them with her companions who chattered loudly and grabbed, to stuff pawsful into their mouths until the cheeks bulged out alarmingly.

She did not like her thoughts. There were far too many ifs in the plan which the off-worlder had so quickly decided upon—*he* had decided. Not her. She still had a choice. The zorsals would never obey any order from him, for which fact she was very glad. That gave her a small chance to keep them safe.

That she could persuade the two males to carry a thing, if it were small and light enough for them to lift, down into that field of dead ships—yes, she believed that could be done. At night they might well be able to do so—unless the suited men kept glare lights on which would half-blind and confuse her creatures. Only what if there was no patrol ship to answer? And what could one ship do? And . . . and . . . ? Simsa shook her head, striving to settle her own thoughts into reasonable order.

Put it out of mind, think about something else, for a while. That was what Ferwar used to counsel when one was frustrated by some problem. Ferwar had always been so eager to collect her bits of the past, poring over them: the carvings, the bits of writing, the two treasures Simsa had brought with her. She felt within her jacket now, closed fingers about the jeweled pendant. But those fingers also brushed against the block and she pulled out that "picture."

In the light of day some of the details were plainer. The girl studied the other Simsa after tipping out the rest of the contents of the food can for the zorsals to squabble over and snatch in enjoyment.

That scar on the skin. Simsa pulled loose her inner belt and turned down the front of her pants to inspect her own smooth lower belly. Save that she lacked that, this was she! Thorn had said that his brother had left knowledge of where he had found that from which this had been copied by more of the off-world magic. If she had only made Thorn tell her how to get there! The place of dead ships—yes, that was of strangeness and perhaps of account as he kept saying. But *this* was of account to her!

The more she stared at the block, into the eyes of the Simsa imprisoned there, the surer the girl became that she must see, must know. Thorn had the belt guide his brother had left. She was certain that he would not yield that up for anything.

There was a city here, many, many tall buildings—she could

search and for maybe five seasons and never come upon the place she desire. But she must KNOW!

Was this Simsa a great lady—one who had ruled here among these very broken walls? Or was she, as Thorn had mentioned in his stories, one who had also come from the stars at a time so far in the past that even the stones of Kuxortal could not remember? If so— why had Simsa been born to wear her skin, her hair, her body, so many ages later? Blood-tie Thorn had said, but what kind of blood-tie could persist through uncounted marches of time?

The girl wished that the Old One was alive, that she could show her this. She wished she had been more demanding of Ferwar's knowledge, pulling answers from the Old One as to why she had been born among the Burrows, who was her mother, her father. Why, oh, why had she not learned more when she could?

Simsa held the long pendant of the necklet into the full light, comparing the gems in it, the way it was set, with that jeweled fringe about the "pictured" hips. This was no pendant! It had been part of a like kilt such as the woman in the cube wore. That was why it was in the form of a long strip . . .

The cuff? No, the Simsa in the block did not wear one of those, nor did she have a ring like that on the girl's thumb. Still, Simsa was sure that both other pieces had a place in the same time and world as that of the "pictured" figure.

She was excited, restless. Then she remembered that box which Thorn had stowed so carefully under the beacon at the camp. There might be something there—something which would give her the answer. There was no reason why she should not go to look!

Catching up Zass, the other two zorsals taking to wing over her head, Simsa skirted the fallen dead man, made her way back to the camp.

With care, she lifted the lamp from the box, half fearing that she might in some way set it to burning. Then she pressed the lid of the container as she had seen Thorn seal it. There were what he had called "tapes"—of no use to her. Under them some more of the blocks such as that she had taken for her own.

Each held a small, three-dimensional object. The first was a wreck—Simsa eyed that carefully, and decided that it was much smaller and of an entirely different shape than those she had seen scattered about the field. Perhaps this was of that "flitter" which Thorn had now gone to examine.

In the next was a doorway—not a plain opening such as they had passed through to get into the building from which the bridge in the sky had led. No, there was vegetation here which had been torn away, but the door itself was arched, with a broad band of color—or rather colors, one blending with the other in subtle combinations and shades—running completely about that arch from the pavement on one side to that on the other.

What was more important to the girl was that this archway was not open. It had a door across it and in the middle of that barrier, showing very plain in the representation was the symbol of what Thorn called "Sun-and-Moon" horns about the ball, even as the Simsa "picture" carried and wore.

Did this place stand somewhere within the ruins about her? Simsa pawed through the other blocks—there were three more. One of them was of the pool curtained by mist; this she discarded at once. Another seemed to portray a long section of wall on which ran lines of carving—some ancient record—of no use to her, and that also she dropped. However, the third, like that of the doorway, was meaningful.

It might have been fashioned by someone looking down a great chamber or room. The same colors which had played about the doorward were laid on here in wavering bands along the walls but only part way down the length of what Simsa believed was a long hall.

The colors ended abruptly in an expanse of silvery gray—a color which held both the sheen of the pool sand and the opaque beauty of the cupped liquid. This surrounded a dais on which stood—Simsa gave a small cry of eagerness; smaller indeed than the other picture she had treasured, but the same!—Here stood that other one, her other self!

Out there, somewhere among the ruins there was a doorway and beyond that—this! She need only seek and she would find!

Stowing those three blocks in her sleeve pocket, she hurriedly repacked the box to put it under the lamp, trying to replace all even as she had found it. Let the off-worlder worry about his wrecks and those who looted them, she had this which belonged to her alone, the secret which had become the most important thing in her life. Enough prudence remained for her to catch up and don her pack.

Then, with Zass perched on the pack, her head bobbing forward so that her mouth was not far from Simsa's ear, the other two zorsals overhead, the girl padded out once more to that road which ran through the vine and shrub shrouded ruins in search of the doorway—and of what lay beyond it.

The two male zorsals winged over her head. She wished that she could convey to them what she sought, but to show them the picture, ask them to find that arch—that was too complicated. She must depend upon fortune and her own two feet and persistence.

Simsa realized that the sprawl of ruins was far larger than she had first believed, as there seemed no end to the road, to the buildings which arose on either side. Her impatience grew but her determination did not falter. Somewhere here lay what she sought— the belief in that waxed stronger instead of less, despite the fact that she had found not a single sign of anyone passing the way before her.

The zorsals whirled in and out among the buildings. There were large insects which took to the air on lacy, near invisible wings, or on those which were dotted and splotched with vivid color which shone even brighter against the green of the plants from which they came. Still there was silence here.

Simsa went slowly, for as she passed each of the buildings, she looked for signs that the vegetation had been burnt back, that some-one had gone this way before her. There were trees growing tall, shading many of the lower stories of the buildings, so choked with vines tying one to the other that it was difficult to imagine that even a flame weapon could burn a path here.

The road curved to the right, in the direction of that distant landing field. Simsa, eager as she still was, drew closer now to the growth near to hand. Had some of those looters already come this way, or were they so intent on what they had found among the wrecked ships that this city meant nothing to them? She could not be sure.

A greater twist of curve, almost the road appeared to be turning back, curling on itself. Still she could see that it had an end. Narrowed, it led straight to—

Simsa's breath caught. She stood, small, dwarfed and made insignificant by that before her. Here was her door of colors! But it was an arch so tall and—

Her hand flew to her mouth, she found that she was pressing that thumb ring painfully tight against her lips as her head went farther back and she looked up and up—and up.

This was a building, not for men, but for some intelligence, some race, who were more than men—more at least than men of the kind she knew. Also it was totally different from the city in which it stood.

The city was old, Simsa had no doubt of this, but here within it was something far older yet. This held no kinship to the other buildings. There were no vines, no shrubs, no trees to veil it, and it was kin to the towered ring—truly it was!

From the ring to those grey-white walls, which also held a blue sheen, Simsa looked and looked again. There seemed to spread outward from it, from that gateway framed in the band of entwined color, a chill, a breath of such age as Simsa half expected to see it crumble and be gone to dust even as she walked slowly toward it. She could no more have turned aside now than she could take to the air as the zorsals had.

Three wide steps led to that door. Simsa climbed those, the towered keep rearing above her as might a crouching beast. That carving she had sold to Thorn—animal body, half human head. Now she stood before the door on which that symbol of X-Arth (or perhaps more than X-Arth; fragments of what Thorn had said flitted through her mind) shone with a pale silver radiance.

Her ringed hand went out. She must open that door, though somewhere, deep in her mind, some small uneasiness fought vainly to keep her from it. No—this was what she was *meant* to do. Old, old—forgotten—not wholly. She was breathing faster, her heart raced. Fear, awe, and something else fastened on her, made her one to be used, without any will of her own.

Her fingers touched the door well below that symbol, for the door was so tall she would have had to stand on tiptoe to touch even the lower edge of that. She planted her palm against the surface, expecting it to be cold as the stone in which it was set. But it was as if she touched a thing through which flowed energy. The gem on her ring sparked with a sudden explosion of colors, near matching those about the arch so high now over her head.

The door moved, swinging wide, though she had exerted no pressure, only touched it. Simsa passed within. Here—here was the huge hall-chamber of that other picture. She was only partly aware that the colors along these walls seemed to actually move, flow ceaselessly one into another, lighter to darker, darker to lighter. It was what stood in the center of that place facing her, though a long space lay between them, which centered her whole attention.

Simsa took a step, flinched—

Though she could see nothing, it was as if some cold, repelling mist hung before her, chilling her. There was such a darkness, not before her eyes, but within her. Yet she was also drawn. Without her willing it her be-ringed hand began to move, sweeping forth, and then from side to side, as if she lifted unseen curtains, clearing a passage through the intangible.

Step by step she went. Fear blackened the world about her, her heart beat so fast now that she felt it shake in her body, she could hardly breathe. Dimly she knew that she was fighting a barrier, a barrier which in its time had killed and would kill again. Still she could not retreat. That which waited drew her on.

It was a journey which might have lasted for hours, even days— here was no time as man measured it, only a war between two parts of her—one which was stricken with fear, one which yearned and drove her on. She did not know that she was crying, that small sobs from pain which was not of her body marked her torment. She was being wrung in two. And she knew that if she lost either part, if there was separation, then she would have failed—and that which was truly Simsa would cease to be.

At last she came to stand at the foot of the dais, looking up at the other who was she—or who was the essence of a race from which she had been drawn. Her arm fell limply to her side. That other was gazing down, the eyes were open, were fixed upon hers. Simsa gave a last, small, piteous cry and fell limply at that other's feet, her struggle ended.

Her body twitched, convulsed, a drop of froth trickled from one side of her mouth. She had entered her last defense, a withdrawal deep into her innermost part, abandoning all else to that pressure which assaulted her. Assaulted her? No, there was no desire to torment, to invade, to—

The girl lay quiet now. She sighed once, turning her head a fraction so that still her eyes met those of the other. Inside her mind, barriers weakened, gave away. She was as one who had been in prison all her life and was now suddenly lifted into wide fields under an open sky.

This very freedom was first pain in itself because it brought with it more overwhelming fear.

Her lips shaped pleas to powers—powers—what powers? There was one Simsa, now. Her body lay in birth pangs as her mind and soul formed another. She could not understand, she tried to flee from that act of birth, but there was no going back.

At length she lay, her last defenses breached, the sacrifice, the victim. A last, part of the old Simsa cried aloud that this was death— the end—and once more fear fell upon her as a dark cloud.

Through that terror pierced something else, clean, clear, free. She got to her knees, her hands going up and out to catch at the edge of the dais. She was so weak, so young and new, and this was—

Exerting what strength she could summon, Simsa drew herself to her feet, still holding on, for she felt as if the world were atilt and she was about to spin out among the stars . . . the great suns . . . the planets.

There was a whirling in her head, too, as if memory piled upon memory, though none was clear, and she felt that she was battered until her spirit was as sore as if she were a slave flogged for another's pleasure. Not *her* memories. When had she ever walked among the stars, when had she ever held power in her two hands and ruled a world and then lost that rule through the treachery of time?

She was young, at the beginning, not at the end.

As she clung to that thought, the memories grew smaller, dimmer, were gone, except that now and then a single blurred picture might rise for an instant, to disappear once again. As one who was just born she gazed still up at that other, begging silently for the warm comfort of aid.

Her hands moved over her body, stripping away the outer crust—the wrapping about the new born. Then she stood free of the past—the short and dark past, free, too, of much of the longer past— the bright awesome one. She reached up higher. The tips of her fingers could just touch the end of the rod that other held, that scepter of power and triumph.

Under that light touch it moved, tilted, slipped, so came into her hold. As she grasped it, so did the change come, nearly in the blink of an eye. She who had been the other, and was now only a husk, vanished as a husk would so when the power which held it together was drawn out of it. What had seemed a living woman became—a statue—leaving behind only that which had been of this world—

With the sureness of one who had done this many times over, Simsa reached out to take up in turn what was hers by right—the girdle of gems, the crown chain. As she locked those upon her body, she held her head high. By the True Mother, she was Simsa perhaps, but she was also the Daughter who had come into her heritage!

She turned to look back that way which she had come. There would be no barrier there for her now. A honking cry at her feet drew her attention to Zass. Simsa knelt on one knee, pushing aside with a frown of distaste the draggled clothing she had shed. She held out her hand and the zorsal came to her, wing dragging. With the scepter of power Simsa touched that ill-set wing, drawing the rod along its surface. The wing had become partly healed in the pool; now it wholly straightened, and Zass fanned it wide, hooting hoarsely. The power had lasted!

For a moment, she was caught again in that whirl of conflicting memories. Simsa brushed her hand across her forehead. No, she

must not push against what held her now. All would come right—
she need only wait. Wait and act when she knew that the action was
ready. This was a time to bide quiet and wait; there would come
what was needed to fill her, to nourish her.

She smiled and held the wand against her between her breasts.
No, she was not that one who *had* been waiting here through time,
but she bore the same blood, was a daughter tossed up from the age
flow of this world—perhaps by chance—perhaps through some plan
long past. This was where she had been called to be, now she would
travel on, returning that which she held in her to be once more
woven into the affairs of men and worlds.

Zass took to the air, screaming delight and triumph. The two
other zorsals flew to join her as Simsa sat back on her heels and
watched their dance of joy. Such small ones, so strong in their
own ways—a world could be fair—it was only with the coming of
another species that anger, hate, fear were made to last the length
of a day, draw blackness into dreams by night.

The zorsals winged back toward the doorway. Simsa, without a
glance at the skin of she who had not yet been born—the grimy
clothing, the pack—followed them. That heady joy in life which had
filled her when she had lain in the Pool of Renewing (that which had
been wrought by a younger and less people who had understood
only a little of true knowledge) was raised, flooded through her.

She threw her arms wide, half expecting to see the light of power
flame from each of her wide-spread fingers. Though it did not show,
yet it was there. And she was only newly born—there was much to
learn, to understand, to be.

Simsa passed under the gate into the open. The sun was low in
the sky, hanging over the ruins of the city. If she wished she could
call to mind who had dwelt there once for so long, the dusty burden
of their history. But that no longer mattered—it was gone past and
there was no reason to draw such back. For it was the same history
as all men faced, as all intelligent species faded. It had a slow
beginning, it arose to pride and triumph, it fell to defeat and decay.
It—

Simsa whirled about, the gems of her kilt fringe flashing. She stood, her nostrils expanding as if she could pick up danger by scent. Not scent, no, that alarm had come to her through the very air which pressed now against her body. There was danger . . . there—

Again she half pivoted, as if her body were part of an intricate device—her scepter turned and pointed now into the ruins to her left.

14

A figure moved, came into the open where the declining rays of the sun were already overshadowed, cut by the buildings around. Simsa shook her head, trying to so throw off that mixture of memories. Death had walked so, once.

There was another behind the first, a grotesque creature as if one of the carvings of stone had come to life to clump along on clumsy feet. Simsa's nostrils expanded again. The three zorsals above her head gave tongue, started to fly towards those two who were coming. Then with a burst of their highest speed, they cut away, even as that clumsy, stumping, second invader sprayed the air with a blast of flame.

Anger was born, cold and clear, in Simsa. Her glow of happiness and freedom was wiped away in an instant. She pointed with the scepter. From the twin horn tips which were a part of that ancient sign of the Great Mother-One shot in return glittering spears of light, no thicker than her finger but potent, drawing briefly from her anger and strength.

Together, those struck full on the weapon, that black, flame caster held by the suited one. There was a burst of white, a flare near blinding in its intensity. He who had fired upon the zorsals stood still. His captive had thrown himself flat even as she had raised the scepter, now he rolled—a maneuver which carried him behind a fallen column broken in its length across the open way.

Simsa, feet braced apart, stood wary and waiting. Now she could see clearly that one who was suited even as had been the dead "guardians," the men who had been at work in the landing field among the wrecked ships.

She caught her lower lip between her teeth. That flare of energy had been drawn from her own reserves of energy of body and mind. She was not yet ready to fight so—she could not summon strength for another such attack. There was so much which she must learn, must practice. She was still too caught by the Simsa she had lately been, fettered in spirit, clouded in mind—not what life had intended her species to be.

Still, that suited one did not advance. While his weapon—the girl saw what he held, a lump melded into his metal-protected hands—a stump, which still radiated heat, a heat she could feel even from this distance. The power of the Horns had turned back upon him the force of his own vicious weapon. So in a manner he had brought his own fate upon himself. She did not know he was dead, only that he was no longer a threat.

The prisoner he had taken appeared to understand this, also. He arose from where he had taken cover during that exchange of energies. For a long moment, he half turned, to view the motionless suited figure, then he looked to Simsa, his eyes once more opened to their widest extent, an expression of complete amazement giving away slowly to a just as astounded recognition.

Simsa walked forward, drawing into her by will alone, after a manner which she could not yet understand but which was as natural as breathing, energy from the air about. Perhaps even the dregs of that which had been expended in combat here came to feed her at her need. For with each step, her strength increased. There was no sound, even the zorsals held silence, no sound but the faint musical ring of the gemmed strings she wore.

"Simsa—?" Thorn had fully turned from his captor. His calling of her name was not quite recognition, rather his tone held a note of question, as if he knew that he saw her, still was not sure of the truth of what came towards him.

"Simsa." She made answer of her name. That was not a name out of that far dim past. However, that did not matter. In this time and place, she was Simsa and was willing that that should be so.

He came slowly towards her, still studying her with that intent stare. She pointed over his shoulder, to the suited one. "This is one of the looters? They know what you would do?"

He gave a start, as if she had shaken him abruptly from one line of thought to another. "They had a persona detect working—it picked up radiation from the signal when I brought that within their range. Also it proclaimed I was a stranger, not coded into their company. Having that they can hunt us down—"

"That one—" she tilted the scepter a fraction towards the motionless, suited invader, "is he dead?"

"With such a back lash he may be. What did you use on him?" Thorn demanded eagerly. She guessed that he would have liked to have taken the scepter into his own hands, to have sought to discover the secret. But that was not for him. He was a man—also he was of another race—a one whose blood flow, whose mind and body, could never feed the right form of energy.

"I used the Power," she said serenely. "Will there be more like this one to come ahunting?"

That question brought his attention back to the here and now. He looked over his shoulder. This much closer she could see that, not only was the weapon that invader had carried reduced to a fused mass of metal, but the whole forefront of his protective suit was blackened. Various other blobs which must have hung from just such a belt as Thorn wore were also sealed as useless knobs to the suit itself.

"Yes."

Simsa considered what might lay before them. She had used the Power this time without truly realizing what it might cost. Now she instinctively knew that she could not bring it into battle again until she had regained more of the life force upon which it drew. This thing out of time was not meant for sustained battle—for the defeat of men. Rather for healing—for . . . she did not yet know just all it might do. That, too, was part of what she must learn by very careful experimentation, drawing upon a part within herself which had just been born into life, a kind of life she might have never conceived existed before this had happened to her.

"I cannot defeat such again." She must make that fact plain to him. "There is a limit placed upon this. What would you do?"

He was versed in weapons and battle; this problem was to be solved by his kind of knowledge, not hers.

Thorn moved closer, still eyeing her as if he sought to learn some secret from the way her hair moved slightly at the tug of the evening breeze, from the way she met him eye to eye. She could sense the need in him for the asking of questions, but also there was the greater need for action.

"I have—I had—the signal," he spoke rapidly, breaking that bond of gaze between them, as if he must free himself in so little, in order to return to the pressure put upon him by what he considered his duty. "But I do not think that they know of the upper way we found to see the landing fields. Perhaps that one," he nodded at the suited figure, "is a scout who picked up the signal, so came to investigate. He took me before I reached the building—"

"And the signal?"

"Back there in the bushes. It must be planted. If they take off before it is—"

"Yes," it was her turn to understand. "Death will follow—not only on this world, but spreading outward, as do rings when a stone is dropped into a pool. Save that this stone is potent poison and an ending for all. There have been such endings before, doubtless there will be more to come. For their species is cursed with this greed, for domination, for the dealing of death."

Simsa spoke out of another stir of broken memory—then sealed it quickly from her mind. She must rather think clearly of what faced them.

"Will there be time to do as you have planned?" she asked then.

Thorn shrugged. "Who knows? But one must try."

"Always one tries," she echoed as memory also echoed, far and faint.

She whistled to the zorsals, softly. Zass wheeled, came to her, the two males flanking their dam on either side. When all three were just overhead, circling above Simsa and Thorn, she spoke again:

"Let us go there to where you left the signal."

She did not look at the suited one again. If the Power had added a third dead guardian to this city of the long dead, she did not want to know or remember her part in that act.

"Where did you get that?" Thorn pointed to the scepter. His strides were no longer difficult for her to match, as they sped down the wide avenue between the vine shrouded buildings.

"I found Simsa," she returned briefly. "I am now—whole." That was the surprising truth. She had been empty before, part of her missing, her mind stunted, narrow, unable to perceive what was of importance, though there had been an unrecognized ache in her ever for what was missing. How such as she had come into this world—what chance of birth had brought her body to match that of the Forgotten, that she might never know. However, she did understand that at last, her mind, her inner self, was now united with that body, fitting one part to another as it should always have been.

She knew he still eyed her, waiting for her to say more. Only there was no desire in her to share what had happened to her. Still, it was because of him—or his brother—that this wonder, this fulfillment had come to her. Perhaps so she owed him no small debt.

"I found other 'pictures' which your brother left. They led me to Simsa."

"The image! But T'seng reported on his tape there was an energy barrier of some sort—that he could not get close. Even that picture you claimed first had to be taken with a distant vision charger—"

He spoke of off-world things which did not matter. So perhaps that Simsa *had* been guarded until the proper time came. The girl remembered dimly how she had had to force her way through an invisible web to reach the place she had been meant to stand. But then she had been unknowing, another person. So the web guarded until the time was ripe, until the true blood returned to claim—

Once more the confusion of too-full memory struck at her. She resolutely broke that train of thought quickly.

"There was something. Yes. I could not see, though it tried to hold me back. But still I went on—to her."

"T'seng believed that place to be Forerunner, older than the city. The statue—you are now wearing—" He glanced at her meager adornment, then quickly away as if she might resent his eyes so upon her. Why should she? Her body was a part of her, even as was her speech, her thoughts. There was no reason to hide behind such grimed shells as she had worn before. Simsa thought with fleeting distaste of having such once more covering her own skin.

"There was no statue," she replied remotely. "There was Simsa and I am Simsa. She waited until I came. Now we are free."

He smiled ruefully. "Not for long if these Jacks have more trackers out. Though this is a good place to hide," he glanced about at the ruins. "Still we have no time for such games." Now his voice and face were both grim.

They had set a good pace and had rounded the curve of the avenue which led away from the castle-keep which was like her ring. The girl could see ahead the wall of that place where there were so many seats, and this side of that was the building where Thorn's brother had left his trail markers.

"Wait!" Thorn flung up his arm, but she had already caught that movement in the green beyond. No evening wind had stirred as vigorously as that! There was an ambush—

Simsa raised her hand, drew the zorsals to a tight formation just above her with a gesture. Together with Thorn she darted swiftly to the left, where they crouched together now in cover, seeking a hunt of what waited beyond.

"How many?" the girl wondered aloud.

"Can your zorsals discover that?" Thorn asked. "I no longer have the beamer. We cannot stand up to any weapon of theirs. This stuff—" He moved his hand slowly so as not to cause any betraying quiver of the vegetation around them, "is too thick for us to force a path through."

Simsa held out one hand, the other still clutched the scepter which was the most precious thing on this world she realized without being told. Zass slipped between two vines, coasted down, to alight on the girl's shoulder.

She turned her head a fraction so she might stare straight into the huge eyes of the zorsal. Almost she cried out. It was as if she had suddenly opened a book such as the Guild Lords were known to treasure. She was looking in. Before her lay an alien mind. Thought paths would clear for an instant or two, and then haze over, so that Simsa lost touch. Still in its way this other mind was complete, keen, knowing—

She had no time for exploration, all she could do was to look into those eyes and *think.* Zass uttered a very low, guttural agreement to that thought, before slipping away on four feet, wings furled, held tight to her body.

"What she can learn," Simsa reported to the off-worlder, "she will. Only I shall not let my small people be caught in that death-fire!"

He was watching her again with that wide-eyed astonishment. "What happened? You—you are—"

"I am Simsa," she told him firmly for the second time. "Your brother was right in this. Those of my blood once knew the stars—this world but one among many. Time is not to be counted by those who voyage so. A sleep, an awakening, a coming, a going, a lapping out, a drawing in. Once such voyaging was for us—now it is for you." She slipped the scepter from hand to hand. "Memory is a burden to which I cannot now submit. I am Simsa and I live. I do not care to know the why of that. Ah."

It was not Zass who returned in the same devious way that his dam had left, but one of the males. He squatted down before Simsa, staring up into her face. She reached out with the wand and touched him, where the wings joined his shoulders, with the two horn tips. He gave a small croon.

His mind was not so open. She could only read small, distorted fragments, but enough.

"There are four who wait. They have found that which you brought, but they have left it as bait. They are very sure of capturing you—us."

"Four," he repeated wryly. Her mind took another path, disregarding the strength of the opposition.

"This signal of yours, how large is it?"

He stretched forth his hands to measure a space as long as the zorsal before her was tall.

"How heavy?" she demanded next.

"About—well, I can lift it with one hand. They were made compact, you see. Sometimes they had to be set by men who were injured or who otherwise could not manage to shift heavy weights."

Simsa caught her lower lip between her teeth, thinking, easily and quickly, as if she saw exactly what must be done laid out before her as one of those "pictures" which had led her to Simsa.

"The box that you say nullified the pull of the earth." Fleetingly, she realized that she now understood exactly *what* he had meant, though her new flash of understanding was of no matter. "That lies still on the carrier?"

"No," he opened a distended pouch at his belt to show her the box. "I thought it was not wise to leave it."

"This thing can be in some way attached to your signal?" She was groping as well as hoping; the plan which seemed so clear to her would fail for just such a lack.

"Yes." He turned the box around to show her a small indentation in its surface. "Put this against what must be raised, press this, and the force is activated."

She dared to rise a little in their hideout to glance beyond leaves and branches to the sky. The low sun was already shut off by the buildings. Shadows now not only lengthened but also darkened across the ground.

"Give me this!" Before he could deny her, Simsa caught the box from out of his hand, taking care not to bring it near the scepter. She looked down at the zorsal, trying to make this thought command as simple as she could. Three times she went through what must be done, until she could read the reflection of her orders within the creature's own mind.

The zorsal snatched the box out of her hands and, with one fore paw holding it tight against his chest, scrambled back into the greenery. Simsa turned to Thorn.

"You asked before if the little ones could carry your signal down into that place, but you said exposure to the poison there might mean death. Therefore, they shall take it in their own way. With your nullifier to aid against its weight they shall fly it to the top of one of those dead ships, wedge it there. None of those who loot will, I believe, see them. Nor would those off-worlders search for a signal in the air above them—would they?"

He stared at her. "Your zorsals can do this?" he asked after a moment.

"I believe that they can. At any reckoning, it may be the only chance you have, unarmed and with those who watch and wait for you there. Can *you* hope to do as well?"

Thorn shook his head. Then he stiffened, but she had also heard a rustling, a snapping of branches, a rattling of vines. Perhaps those in ambush had begun to believe that their plans had gone awry and had sent out one of their number to see why.

The off-worlder's hand flew to his belt. She saw him touch that length of metal which he had said could measure the death breath of the ancient weapons of his kind. On the small strip the light line swung upward. She felt a tingle in her skin but was unafraid. There was no warning alert here but born out of the Simsa-of-the-past's memories.

"Hot—he's hot! Get back!" Thorn swept his arm back as if to sweep her away from him.

At the same time, a ray of light cut through the green above their heads, started to slice down towards them. Simsa threw herself to the right with that agility by which the other Simsa had learned to defend herself. At the same time she called out from the depths of her new half understanding.

"The cuff! Use the cuff."

He might have thought her urging foolish, but at that moment, he did not disdain it. Throwing up his arm across his face toward which that menacing beam swung, he brought the cuff between his head and that death-by-light.

The ray struck and spread across the surface of the cuff, then was radiated, swollen to twice its size, as the energy sent in to blast and kill was fed back along the same path by that defense. It happened in only a few breaths of time, but the reflected force set greenery to smoldering, swept back upon itself with doubled power—a power intended to exterminate helpless prey.

Thorn crouched, still holding his arm up. The cuff seemed untouched to the eye by the force feeding back from it, from him to the killer. Simsa fingered the scepter, longing to use it, yet sure that the off-worlder had a defense which would drain nothing from him in strength and still would save him.

There came a flare, a great clap of noise, with heat to follow. Simsa fell into the midst of a half withered bush, heard a crash from the other side. She clawed her way out of a mass of crushed leaves and spiny twigs, some of which punished her with raking scratches. Thorn lay still, his head and shoulders half hidden, his long legs tailing towards her.

On her hands and knees she reached him. His eyes were open, seemingly unfocused for a moment. Then they centered on her and she saw recognition in them. He raised his arm slowly upward, so that he could look upon the cuff without moving his head.

The ancient artifact was burnished, bright, even in the shadows here. It even glowed as if the fire which had struck it had supplied or awakened an energy which was truly its own. Still there was no mark upon it of any of the force which it had bent to crisp and kill.

Now Thorn did turn his head, look at her. "How, how did you know?" His voice, for the first time she had known him, was really shaken; he seemed vulnerable, no longer the superior starman whose people had key to secrets forbidden to the worlds they visited.

"It is one—" she tried now to find words which would explain something which she had not yet sorted out for herself. "That was one of the other Simsa's memories, one of the old defenses."

He put out his other hand as if to run finger tips over the surface of the cuff, but snatched them back before his flesh had touched the unknown metal.

"*You* are Simsa—"

"I am Simsa," she agreed. "Blood of her blood. Though I do not know that came to be, for she was . . . what your brother thought her to be. Long before the coming of those who built this city (and they also have been gone for tens-tens-tens past counting of seasons) she was here. Also she was the last of her people. But in some way, she must have planned that there would be one to follow her through time. I do not know how, but I am her child new born. Yet still I am Simsa. But why do we waste time now in talk? One found us. Others will come now to search."

Thorn sat up, holding the cuffed arm away from his body as if he still feared to let it touch any part of him. "You are right." He began to edge backwards, using the growth as cover. As Simsa started to follow, there was a shaking in the fire-touched brush. A small sapling crashed forward, falling outward towards the avenue, baring a new wide section to their sight as it came down, tearing half burnt vines with it.

Another of the suited invaders lay there, half covered by the mass that the falling tree had brought down with it, only his legs covered by the thick plating of the suit to be seen. Simsa had no doubt that he was dead. Also she was glad she was unable to see what havoc the return of his own fire had caused.

Thorn had suddenly paused, his tense attitude in the gathering shadows one of a listener. There were other rustlings—Thorn beckoned to her vigorously, his gesture made more emphatic by the gleam of the cuff which continued to hold a light of its own. She glanced at the scepter. Yes, there was also a very wan outline of thin light about the symbols at its crown. She held it in front of her, close to her body, feeling a gentle, pulsating warmth from that same set of horns which had unleashed death earlier.

With what skill they could, they had somehow found a way to a gaping doorway of one of the buildings. To try for the open avenue was to make them easy targets. The inside of the structure was a dark cavern, even though complete twilight had not closed in, but it was a promise of shelter.

Simsa could see that they had entered a single great room which appeared to fill the entire structure, there was no ceiling above, only a continued rise, though narrowing as it went, for the side walls were a series of steps in the form of balconies, off which were dark openings at regular intervals. The lowest of these was supported by carven pillars much like those they had seen elsewhere, stands of vegetation or monstrous life forms.

Thorn had gone to the nearest of these and was running his hands across the deep ridges of the carving. He looked over his shoulder as she joined him.

"These can be climbed. If those Jacks are all suited, they can't follow us. The suits are far too clumsy to climb in."

"And if they sit below, waiting for us?"

"At least we shall have a breathing space to plan something."

He was already climbing and she saw that he was right; the deep gouges left by those who had wrought this representation of a vine wreathed tree gave ample space to fit fingers and toes. She took the warmth of the scepter into her mouth and swung up easily behind him.

They lay side by side on the floor of the first balcony watching the door. Waiting came hard. Simsa again ran the smooth tube of the scepter back and forth between her hands. However, she was firm in keeping a barrier now against wandering memories. In the here-and-now she needed all her awareness for what might happen next, not for what had happened in the long-ago and had no meaning to her at present.

They heard the crunch of heavy footsteps. It was very dark now in the building—there appeared to be no windows at all. Simsa's night sight had adjusted only to the point where she could detect movement at the door gap . . . very cautious movement. Those others must have found the blasted body of their man, be fearing some attack out of the dark.

Whoever had hesitated there for an instant was again gone. Simsa could not tell whether out or in. Thorn's shoulder pressed against hers. He had turned his head so that his whisper came so low and close that she could feel the slight pressure of his breath against her cheek.

"They have a body heat detect—a persona. If it is with this party, they will know just where we are. They will try to keep us prisoned here until they can bring some stronger weapon out of the loot to finish us off."

If he were trying to prove to her how serious their position might be, she was already well aware of that.

"How long?" she whispered in return. Might they keep on climbing up from one balcony to the next?

No! The answer came to that as a wide beam of light which began a slow sweep around the interior of the huge hall, first at floor level, so each of those pillars, such as the one they had just climbed, stood out in sharp relief. Then at the far end of that sweep, on the opposite side from which they lay, the light arose to the second level. Thorn's hand fell heavy between her shoulders, forcing her against the floor.

"Stay flat!"

There was a solid balustrade for the balcony, reaching perhaps the height of her knees were she standing. Simsa wondered if that would be enough of a barrier to hide them both. Or if the seekers below would realize that they might be so concealed and begin an indiscriminate spraying with their flamers—a wild rush of fire they could not hope to guard against.

The light traveled. She had pillowed her head, cheek against her arm, and watched it sweep. Now the beam had nearly reached them, was turning along their side. Simsa realized she had been holding her breath. She had for these tense moments returned to the old Simsa. Her confidence, her feeling of superiority over these clumsy looters had ebbed. The scepter lay under her hand, but at that moment she could not have released its power even if she would. The sharp danger had swung her to the other side of the balance and she was only a badly frightened girl. That other Simsa—she *must* find her, *be* her again, or she might soon be nothing at all.

◼ 15 ◼

Yes, close one's eyes—remember only that Simsa! The Simsa who had stood proud, tall, knowing, unafraid. Do not think of the light moving closer, of alien death by fire, just Simsa.

She willed her heart to slow its beat, she willed fear to be her servant not her master. Even as anger can be willed to become a tool when the time comes, emotions can give greater strengths to one. She *willed*.

There was a sharp pain which ran from her cheek into her head—causing for a moment such agony that she thought hazily the flamers of the hunters had found her. Then the pain vanished as swiftly as it had struck, leaving behind it—

This was a strong return of that same feeling she had known in the hall of that other Simsa—that she was new, that she was now another. Dimly, the girl was aware that the hand, clasping the scepter with a force which made her fingers ache, also lay against her head. The ring—the ring had become a bridge!

How—or why—or what—? All questions which must be pushed aside for now. There was an urgency, a need, to act!

What she was doing was a matter of obeying commands, silent commands, delivered from a source she could not define, did not know, who had once been able to do this, and had used such action as a shield and a weapon.

Simsa opened her eyes but did not move her head. She saw the gem which formed the roof of the tower on her ring—saw that only.

It grew, spread, became like the pool in which she had lain, became more than the pool—rather a sea. Into that sea she made herself plunge—not the Simsa who was a body, rather the Simsa who dwelt within that body.

She sharpened her thoughts, her purpose, fumbling a little at first, then growing more sure, more adept. There was only the grey-blue-white sea which drew her thoughts, to form them anew, send them out as weapons.

Far away, she heard a whisper of sound, a rise and fall of cadence, of the reciting of a ritual in a tongue which had not been spoken for a thousand-thousand lifetimes. There was strength arising from that stream of words, flowing on into her as it grew louder, gathering energy for another in-pouring as it faded again.

Into the waiting sea spilled that force. Its surface was troubled so waves arose—not waves of any liquid, rather surges of power towering higher and higher. So—and so—and so—! Yes, this was what must be done, even as it had been evoked long ago. The power in her was still not great enough to move the very earth itself— though once such power had been so used—such cadences of rising and falling words had fitted stones into place, had lifted even great burdens skyward. She did not have that, but her efforts were answering in a different way—answering!

The rising turbulence of that sea closed around the essence of her own identity, caught and held her. She could have screamed aloud as that essence was rent by a tearing, a forcing of dismemberment. Now she was two . . . three . . .

Two and three—and still one. Simsa marshaled those others, those parts of her—they were her guardsmen, her warriors. Now it was time to send them into battle.

She looked into a great hall. There was no darkness there for her eyes, though she knew that in truth shadows hung heavy and long. Through the dark below things moved.

There was a haze about them. The haze of energy—two kinds of energy—one came from outward sources, one from inner. It was the inner which was of the greater importance—that source of energy which was born of life force, not from any weapon or rank discovery and foul use by those who meddled in what they could not hope to completely conquer.

Go—so!

Silently she commanded the two which had been born from her own essence, even as she had been reborn out of Simsa of old.

They blazed. They were light itself. And still they were her, night dark of skin, moon silver of hair, with the sign of the Great Mother blazing from head and hand. Two of them stood in the middle of that hall's darkness facing those who came.

The ones clothed in haze halted. She could see the ripple of their inner essence's diffusion which answered to every change of emotion. They were first astounded, then triumphant. One thought death—was moved to sight with his weapon to destroy. Two others quickly defeated his desires. She could hear no orders, but the thought behind their communication rang plain. The two she had dispatched must be taken prisoner.

There they stood. To lay hands upon them, to use an entangling device was a matter of no difficulty. Coils of thin white stuff spun through the air. The coils wreathed around the Simsas. It was meant to pull tight, to wrap them past all struggle for freedom. The coils slipped, fell to the floor where they writhed ineffectively as might living things which had been blinded, or broken.

Now he who had sought to kill from the beginning set his weapon on full strength and, over the protests of his companions, fired. Fire streamed, encircled, blazed with force. Those other Simsas stood unharmed.

There was dismay now. The in-hazed ones were touched by alarm, by uneasy awareness that they fronted something not within the range of their knowledge.

Slowly they gave back one step and then another. Simsa who watched gathered together all her strength, sent it flowing into those two others. Glorified by the light which was theirs, which they wore like robes of victory, they moved as one, following the retreat of the enemy.

They held no wands, but their arms arose from their sides, with hands outstretched. Fingers moved back and forth, leaving in the air trails of light which shone in the dark with the same radiance as that which cloaked them. Back and forth went those trails, where they touched they held.

There was a flicker of light. The Simsas were no longer facing the enemy, they were behind them. Before the suited men could clumsily wheel about, once more their hands were busy, weaving more streamers of energy which netted. Again they moved so, and again.

Those who had invaded the hall were now within a net wall of shining filaments, criss-crossing, floating up higher than their helmeted heads, enclosing them into a narrow space. They had all fired—first at this portion of the net wall—then at that. The raw energy they unleashed was caught in the spaces between the lines of that net, held there to render their prison stronger, more dangerous— a place for them to die should it grow solid with what they so unleashed in their fear.

They no longer used their weapons. But the fire which the net now restrained was not quenched, it still hung there, holding them. The two Simsas watched for a long moment, as if so they must make sure of their work. Then—

There was no sea now to draw back what had been sent forth. Simsa's own body arched with the sharpness of stabbing pain. She had given birth; now that life must return to her, and its entrance was more agonizing than had been the separation. She gasped, perhaps she voiced a scream. If so she only heard a faint echo of it dying away.

She lay on her back—then there were arms about her, lifting her, holding her as if to assure her safety and peace by firm grasp. She could not lift her hand, her eyelids weighed down to veil her sight. She fought that, looked up to see the blur of Thorn's face, his fear for her now easy to read. There was no alien strangeness about him now. She believed that she might reach into his mind if she wished, draw out thoughts he did not even know lay there—though that she would never do.

"It is well." she made her lips shape those words though they seemed stiff and hard to move, as if she had forgotten or not used speech for a long time. "All is well, I think."

He drew her higher in his hold. Her words did not seem to reassure him. Now she turned her head a little. Had that really happened, had those other parts of her appeared to weave the net of fire? Or had she only dreamed it?

"They—they are caught?" She asked it of him, for in his arms she still was not raised high enough to see the hall below, to know whether she had had some fantastic dream. Once more the balance was swinging—perhaps not so far this time. She could believe it had happened—with another's power.

"Look!" He steadied her with gentle care, drew her still higher, her body yet a limp weight, because she had drawn too heavily upon its resources.

Thus supported, she was able to gaze at what was below. Not darkness—there was a splotch of light within the space not far from the outer door. Irregular in shape it was like a great hearth fire burning. From it streams of light rolled slowly upward. She could see no lines of the net, but through the thin wall of the fire itself she sighted the three who had drawn together, facing the wall they could not broach, prisoners of the united powers they had unloosed here.

"I will not ask you how," Thorn said slowly, "or what you did. They are caught. Do you know how long it will hold?"

"No." Again that burst of inner knowledge which had led her to this defense was ebbing. It was as if she held a tattered cloak about her, some portions able to give her warmth and covering—rents elsewhere to leave her unprotected. She had been pushed too quickly, too far. There would come a day, of that Simsa was confident, when she could and would command all that had been poured into her through her heritage. But not yet.

"We must go then, while we can. But are you able?" He still held her, though he had gotten to this feet, drawn her up beside him. She discovered that she was able to stand, that the return of those others complete had renewed her strength in part. There was a place where that renewing might become complete.

"The pool . . ." she said. "If I can reach the pool—"

His understanding leaped at once to her meaning. Only the walls, the pit, all which lay between them and that haven . . . She would need his help to go there. Though she had immobilized these hunters below, there were others to come—that she knew. To reach the pool might well be beyond her capability, even with him to aid.

Need could give one strength, Simsa discovered. Somehow, she made the descent from the balcony, with her companion beside her on the round of the column, setting her hands to the holds, giving her support again and again.

She was able to stumble along, her stride growing more sure as they left the hall, making a wide circle about those still prisoned. Simsa could see the bubbles of their helmets but not the faces within. Could they be dead? She believed not; their life essence had not withered as the last of their own fire bound them in.

On, Thorn's arm around her now and then when she wavered, holding her upright as she paused to gasp, to hold the scepter close to her body. For it seemed to Simsa that out of the rod, came more energy. They were fleeing through the deep twilight now. Night had already brought stars into the heavens.

They came to the place of the camp. Others had been before them. Boxes were opened, their contents strewn about. The lamp had been melted down. But Thorn still had that light he wore on his belt. He paused long enough to snatch up a bag of provisions—then half carried, half led her on, past the dead—

The journey across the walls taxed Simsa's strength near to the end. When they reached that place where they must go down into the deep rock walled chamber, she wilted to the pavement, knowing that she could not descend on her own power.

Thorn dropped the bag beside her, vanished. She was too dazed now to even ask where he would go and why. Then he came back, a coil of thin, tough vine carried like rope across his shoulder. He pulled and twisted with sharp jerks, for testing its strength. Finally, he knotted the end about her waist.

"Listen." He had knelt, was looking into her eyes, his hands on her shoulders to hold her steady so that she could not droop away from him, "I shall lower you. Wait there for me—"

Simsa thought she smiled, perhaps her lips did twitch in a weak effort at such. There was nothing else she might do but wait. Did he believe she could go running off now into the dark?

However, she did make some shift to help herself by hand and foot holds among the sides of the descent, although she knew that Thorn was taking the most of her weight on the taut vine.

Then they were together again, along the passage. When she saw the mists of the pool, a last small surge of strength filled her. She pulled away from him, plunged on into that welcome softness which caressed her as if welcoming arms had been opened wide to gather her in, comfort her body, soothe her mind.

Here was the silver sand. Simsa fumbled with the catch of the chain about her hips, let her jeweled kilt fall. Still she took the scepter with her as she staggered on, dropping at last into the water, as one might fall in exhaustion upon a waiting bed. Around her, supporting her, was that liquid. She lay upon it, her eyes closed.

Sounds, clear, piercing sounds. Those struck sharply into the warm quiet which cradled her. She tried to shut them out, to bar them from this place so that she might not have to answer to them. That they summoned her she dimly knew.

At last she could not deny them. Opening her eyes, Simsa looked up for the second time into the rolling of the mist above the pool. She awakened slowly by degrees, shrinking away somewhat from the shadow of memory—intent on drawing about her only the peace and renewal of this place.

The sounds—

She turned her head, unhappy, uneasy anew.

Near her, their wings outspread upon the water, lying at ease on their backs were the three zorsals. She could no longer wall away memory; had they done what they had been sent to do?

Chirping, she called to them. Zass paddled with all four feet, after flopping over, came to Simsa, resting her head against the girl's shoulder, uttering new cries deep in her long throat.

Shrinkingly, as one might strive to use a limb which had been wounded and might not yet be fully healed, Simsa tried contact by mind with the creature. Again came that twist of alien thought, so difficult to follow. Yet she learned. It was as if she saw through other eyes, or through a distance glass such as Thorn had, but one which distorted in a manner which made her slightly giddy. There below her (at a different angle and in a fashion which accented things she felt her own eyes might not have seen at all) was that field of wrecked spacers. Things moved there even thought it was half in the shadow. Then there arose a rounded dome of what must have been of the ships. That grew closer and closer, a hole in it larger as she so approached. Within the hole—a broad beam of some kind immediately below. Out again, fast, fast, into the night—free, free to fly, to be in the air. Joy which was like a shout of triumph. Free to fly, free, free!

Zass's joy at her healing, her being once more able to live in her own element. But that ship, the beam within—surely they had meant that the zorsals had planted the signal—the signal which might or might not be answered.

Simsa lifted her head. Her dreamy content fled, awareness that they had in no way resolved this venture, crowded in.

No, he had not left her this time. He had been also in the pool. His body, so white against the silver of the sand, was bare of clothing. His head rested on his arm, was turned away. She thought that he must be asleep.

Reluctantly, she drew herself back up on the sand. There, coiled in a small shining heap was the girdle of Simsa. The girl reached for it, the links tinkling musically against one another with a small sound of bell notes. She had laid the scepter across one knee as she locked the chain once more in place, moving slowly because her body's awakening did not seem to keep pace with that of her mind. She felt physically languorous, unwilling to set her hand to anything.

Zass had followed her out of the pool, now squatted down at her side one small forepaw cool against the skin of the girl's thigh as the zorsal looked into her face. Simsa sensed a need for praise, for reassurance that all had been done well. She caught Zass up, held her closely, crooning, rubbed the small head behind the half unrolled antennae. The big eyes were near shut as Zass gurgled in vast contentment.

"They are back."

Simsa was startled, looked around. Thorn had rolled over. His head was now chin supported on arms he had folded before him.

"Yes, they are back, and I think that they have done this—" Simsa reported which she had learned from Zass's erratically contacted mind.

Then she had a question of her own: "If the signal has been planted and its message goes forth, when will your ship come? In time?"

"Let us hope so." The serenity which had been on his face when she had looked at him first was replaced by a frown. "But it is as fortune sends."

As fortune sends. The old, old words of the Burrowers by which she had always lived. One could give fortune a nudge now and then as they had tried to do. It remained to be seen how well. While— what did they themselves now face?

He was gazing at her as if she now were as alien to him as the zorsals' minds had been to her.

"What did you do, back there?"

What was the truth? That she did not know. She had wrought with tools she did not understand, to produce something which she could not explain. Still she must make him some answer. There would be many such demands upon her now, she knew—and what answers?

Slowly, fingering the scepter, looking more often at it than at him. (Why? Because she was suddenly so lonely, knowing that nowhere, even among the far stars now, would she find one who could understand what she saw?) Simsa told him of that strange birth of her other selves, of how they did, not what she had ordered, but what they themselves found necessary for her continued safe existence.

When she had finished, there was silence and that silence lengthened. At first, she had not wanted to look at him and see, perhaps, a shadow of disbelief on his face. Then, because of this continued quiet, she did not want to view what was worse—the agreement that she was alien, past contact with those of this age and time.

At last, refusing to surrender to the fact that she might be that indeed, that she was to be likened to one of the stone people of this city come to life, she made herself raise her eyes.

There was wonder in his expression. No—she wanted none of that from anyone, especially him. He had his mysteries brought from the stars, things which would make any of Kuxortal look upon him as greater than life. Was what she did any different in its way? There had been a people once who had mastered other forms of existence, who did not have boxes, and rod weapons, and ships, but held within themselves their own kind of knowledge to build in another way. It was how one used one's inner strengths and how one lived which must be the test of one's knowledge.

Once more, she began to speak, not slowly now, because she did not have to seek for words to describe things which were strange and dangerous, and very new to her also. No, this was in a way a plea. She who had never allowed herself to ask, even of Ferwar, what she wanted most—to find another who would be close enough to care where one walked, how one fared in the world.

"You have your nullifiers," she found her tone sharp, challenging, but she did not abate that note—let him believe indeed that she was questioning his way of life against this of her own—"all those death dealers out there!" She pointed to the mist still swirling hypnotically about them.

"You have also spoken of 'talents,' of minds which can meet minds, of other wonders. There are many worlds, many peoples, are there not? Both young and old. All have their triumphs and their failures. I do not know why I was born able to take that from what was stored here this knowledge. I do well believe that this may come to be a very heavy burden, one I would willingly pass on to others, if I could. But can you give your hands, your brain, that which is the very essence of you to anyone else?

"There are mysteries past solving. Is that not so? Did you not speak of how bits and pieces of those mysteries are carefully garnered and stored, studied? Did you not tell me of a race which is very old by your toll of seasons, which is also the guardian, the interpreter, of what can so be learned?

"Your brother came here seeking answers. He found puzzles. Some of them were only planted in greed and hate and were of your own time and the devising of your kind. But also he found Simsa.

"And because of that—I am. In Kuxortal, I was one who was like an unripened seed which would never have borne fruit. But chance, and you, brought me here. I found my soil, I was planted. I am now what that fortune which men seek, and sometimes fear very much, has made.

"I do not know yet what I can do. Great fear back in that hall forced me into action which was not planned by my mind. It may be that intentions and will and knowledge can live for ages upon ages— be given freely to one who is open to them. I only know that I am not she who you found in Kuxortal. Nor am I wholly she who resigned herself to waiting here. I am more than one, less than the other, but I am a person who is real and truly of herself. Though I am not sure as yet what I may be.

"You are of the stars. You have seen many worlds. I know that the race of Simsa was once also of the stars. Though of those I have been left few memories. She remained here. Again I do not know why. Perhaps her starship could fly no more, perhaps she grew tired of much traveling and wanted only peace. I," she lifted her hands, smoothed back her damp hair, "have only scattered memories and it distresses me—no, it is really painful to draw them back. I want no other life, only that which is now before me."

Then she smiled, a little sadly and added:

"If indeed we have any long life ahead of us. For if your ship does not come and these who burrow here, even as those other scavengers in the holes of Kuxortal, have their way, I do not see much ahead of us now."

He sat up straightly, tossed back that black hair which had grown since he had come planetside. There was no longer that awe—if it had been awe which she had shrunk from recognizing— in his face. She could see his chest arch as he drew a deep breath.

"I do not know either, my lady, who or what you may be. But that you are a wonder for which many men have sought for a long time and never hoped to find. That is plain. We have hunted the

Forerunners ever since our first ship landed to view ruins which were strange and empty. They are legends—so old, that even before my race ventured into space there were tales on Arth of earlier visits from aliens who traveled from far stars. That symbol—" he pointed to the horns and ball, "is known to us. We had priestesses in our own dim, long past history who wore such in honor of a goddess who was many things—dear companion to men, tender of the growing food, cherisher of children—and ready in her wrath to strike down those who threatened all such. Perhaps there was a Simsa there once. She was remembered for lone and long.

"But here you have accepted from the past what we have longed to know."

Simsa shook her head. "No, I shall not be another treasure for your people to hold. I am alive, a person, not an ancient carving, a handful of jewels set into some alien pattern."

She pointed to the cuff still about his forearm. Though he had shed all else of his clothing to bathe in the pool, still that was snugly fitted to him.

"Why did you not take that off?" she asked. "Do you expect still another attack?"

He glanced down as if a little surprised that he still wore it. Then his fingers fumbled, he turned it about and about, but the band would not slide from his forearm. It was not tight enough to pinch the flesh, neither would the cuff give enough for him to rid himself of it, in spite of his efforts, which she watched quietly until she said:

"It would seem that you, too, will carry a portion of the past with you. What will you do when you reach your home place? Cut off your hand that your kind may have what you wear to puzzle over? A lost hand, a lost freedom, neither will serve us. I shall perhaps talk to your seekers of learning, in my own time and place—if we ever leave this world. But I am to be no prisoner of theirs because they think me some 'treasure'!"

"They will not." He said that quietly, but in his eyes there was a stronger promise. How well he might keep that promise she could not tell. That, like all else, must be answered by time itself.

Suddenly, she laughed. "We speak as two who have the good

will of fortune, we who are not even sure we shall be alive with tomorrow's sun."

He did not look dismayed. Instead, he stretched wide his arms, as one who awakens from a refreshing sleep to face the brightest of good days on a morning at the first of the dry-season.

"I shall swear by fortune, Lady Simsa, who is herself and no other, that is what I believe. We shall live—and we shall seek the stars in freedom."

Now Simsa again smiled in return. She also nursed a promising lightness of spirit. Perhaps it was the influence of the pool's renewing, perhaps it was something else—his promise? Or maybe—she shied away from following that thought any farther now. She must learn herself before she strove to teach others, especially this man from the stars to which Simsa would return. *Yes!* That she too believed now, even as she believed in the realness of the sand about her, the shining of the pool, the heaviness of the ring about her thumb—that a new day would come tomorrow!

THE END

FORERUNNER:
THE SECOND VENTURE

This was scraped land, laid bare to heat-roasted rock, lacking a single lift of withered leaf or stem to break the unending stretch of gray-blue stone seamed with darker cracks. Still a cloak-covered body crouched above a winding fissure, one that ran from horizon to horizon across the desert world. Only in that fissure itself was there movement, a thick, ever-forward lapping—not of liquid, but rather heaving sand, swirling slowly along.

There was no sun to beat and blast this wasteland, nothing but open sky overhead. Open until the eyes reached above far enough to mark that screen of haze lidding this simmering pot of a planet.

The cloak shifted a fraction. Within the cave made of its folds there was small movement. The soft touch of tight curled antennae, the sharp prick of a claw against pillar of arm.

"Think you I have been a fool, my Zass?" The voice was not a whisper or a murmur, rather came as a croak from dried lips, the words hard shaped by a mouth as moistureless as the land. "Ah, Zass—there is folly, and there is choice—against that which is worse."

The mound of cloak heaved as the wearer it completely covered straightened, lifted her head to peer through the opening between two folds at that sliding of what was not water yet still passed walls of naked stone.

"Folly . . ." There was a bitter tinge to that single word. Even as she admitted to so much, another emotion arose, stark as the land, clear as the rock of any trace of life. Fear had moved her, brought her into this furnace of death, a greater fear than she had known before.

Again the cloak rippled. Simsa closed fingers tightly about that possession which, living, she would never discard. It was not a staff, not long enough for that—rather more a rod of office such as head-men of river towns in the world she had known might carry on occasions of state. Even under the folds of the cloak it shone—the disc at its head, the two curved horns on guard at the sides. Sun and two moons, she had once been told.

"Thorn!" Her tone made a spat oath of that name. The sound seemed to please her, for she said it once again with more force, a further unleashing of fury. "Thorn!" She did not call. Could any voice reach from world to world, lift upward through sky to the emptiness of space—wing from world to ship, ship to world, and bring it to the right ears?

It was Thorn who had introduced her to *them*—those cool-voiced, veiled-eyed men to whom he had shown respect, whom she had suspicioned from first meeting. She who was—

Again her shoulders shifted. Paws patted lightly against her firmly planted forearm, a small, sharp-snouted face turned up to hers. Those other thoughts, so alien and yet meant to please, to reassure, nibbled at the edge of her mind.

"I am Simsa . . ." She said that slowly with a space of a breath before each word. Simsa—and who else?

Once she had been a light-fingered errand runner for an old and crafty woman who knew much and told little enough. With Ferwar she had sheltered, as far back as her body memory reached, in the Burrows below the city pile of Kuxortal. She had soaked up, as might a sagser root given water, all that could be learned. Still she, even in Ferwar's days of whining command over her, had been free—

Free as she could, would, never be now! There were degrees of freedom; at least she had come to learn that!

Freedom she had won from the Burrows, only because she had had her fortune twined for a space with that off-worlder who had sought his lost brother—and the secret that brother had hunted in turn. Though she had inwardly rebelled, the stubborn-held life spark within that Simsa had sent her with him into a trap of ancient death and new-come disaster.

Then . . . She lifted her rod of sun-and-moon, with a hand she had not consciously set to that task, so that the tips of the curved moons touched her small, high, near-childish breasts. Her head snapped up; the flow of energy that she thought had forsaken that ancient artifact was not exhausted! Into her now flowed, not the power of destruction she had once called upon, rather a sensation of drinking deeply, feasting well. Through her coursed that reviving surge.

The girl closed her eyes to the opening between cloak folds, seeing once again the waiting one—the other Simsa, a mirror copy of herself. Or, rather, perhaps she was a reflection of that one. At a single touch she had become two, who for a space were wary, jealous of their mutual possession—the Simsa whose black skin now contained them both.

Only for a space had that been so. Then she was one again, but a new one. Scraps of knowledge, of which a Burrows child could never even dream, found space and rooted. She had been triumphant, proud, a great one in those moments. Even Thorn had seen it. Yes, but in seeing it he had also been aroused to make of her—

Zass growled deep in her long thin throat, her wings, covered in ribbed skin, lifted a fraction. Zass had always been able to catch Simsa's anger—or her fear. It had been Zass who had warned her into this last venture bringing them here.

"Forerunner," Thorn had called her—talking much of very ancient star-roving peoples unknown to his later kind, who had left their touch on many worlds, still puzzles to all who strove to unlock forgotten mysteries. Forerunner—booty. As much a treasure for him and his fellows as anything grubbed from the earth, shaken clear of age-settled dust. Simsa was to go back to those who searched for such booty. None had asked her consent, nor even told her clearly what was to come.

Thorn had disappeared when she had been escorted to that gaunt, space-blackened man with the eyes that looked yet did not seem to actually see. He might be gazing beyond one to search for some value. In her then the Burrows Simsa stirred awake, and even the ancient Simsa had withdrawn to consider and study and plan . . .

Save that they had not had too much time together, that first Simsa and she from the past. The Burrows-born girl had extended claws and waited to defend herself. Though she had known she dared not call upon the destructive powers centered in that very rod she fondled now, as she relived what had happened. An animal threatened will flee or attack. Simsa—neither Simsa had ever fled. To attack—that was also wrong, the wrongness ground into her sharply. Violence was not the answer to these space people. There were wilier ways. Wait, learn, the Elder One cautioned. Learn what they have to offer—whether it will be of benefit or ill. Weigh the ill—if it be the greater, then plan secretly.

So she had gone aboard the ship without protest. Three zorsals she had had, the two young males she had loosed to their freedom in the skies of their own world—her world. But Zass clung to her and would not be sent away. And, in a way, she clung to Zass as fiercely, a reassuring fragment of the life she had always known.

Simsa had never been aboard a sky ship before. Much was strange there, made even stranger by the fleeting scraps of memory that had awakened in Elder One when led to compare with the far past. She surrendered to that second Simsa all save a scrap of her long-held will, evading questions of these strangers, asking others of her own. Thorn might well have been within the metal skin of the ship which lifted with them, but she had not seen or heard from him.

In the small cabin they had given her for her own place, she had discovered, to her great anger, held rigidly in check, certain small hidden things by which she could be overlooked whenever these space rovers wished. The Burrows Simsa would have torn them loose, smashed them. The Elder One cautioned otherwise. Before each of those hidden spies she had used her rod. Then it was clear that anyone seeking to overlook her would see what was most in their minds concerning her. Meanwhile, she was about her own business—that of escape.

The finding of the spy things had not only aroused hot Burrows anger, but implacable purpose. These off-worlders wanted her for what they could learn. Just as they desired the place from which her twinned self found a storehouse of knowledge, though it was a tangle of ancient wrecked ships being mined by outlaws for unique weapons to be sold to the highest bidders on many different worlds.

From her these strangers sought to draw knowledge not theirs to have or hold, which she was in no mind to surrender. Simsa lay on the sleep place in that prison of hidden eyes and ears, Zass curled by her. And, closing her eyes, she began questing as she would never have believed could be done, but which the Elder One, pressing with her stronger will, found natural.

There was a wild whirl of thoughts pulsing throughout the ship. To plunge into that was like jumping into high sea surf where currents broke about reefs. Simsa of the Burrows struggled feebly, lost. She was drawn along as that other sought her own way of keeping track of these voyagers.

There were two who had centered their innermost attention upon her own self. Sealing away all clamor of others, Simsa followed those thought trails to what lay behind. One was a healer of sorts— a woman whose pitifully small fund of knowledge was considered large and imposing by these others. She was concerned with flesh and bone, and only a little with that which the body obeyed. Also . . . Simsa's eyes remained closed, but her lips lifted in the snarl of a Burrower's child—this one wanted fiercely to slash, to study, to even mutilate if she must, in search of something truly indefinable which was the force of life itself and which she did not even know existed.

The other, who would learn . . . Ahh . . . The snarl relaxed. Instead, her tongue tip smoothed across the lower as one preparing to savor an exotic but promising bit of food. He did have a glimmering idea of that which had been taken from Kuxortal's planet. Even now, he was considering one approach and then another. One could play sly games with such as he, if there were time.

Time! The very thought of that stung her. Thorn had told her openly that what she knew would be of great interest to a race allied with him, a people whose life-span was so long that they had turned long ago to the study of the rise and fall of species, keeping vast records. Yet the time before . . . ah, the time before was Simsa's alone and she was the guardian!

Only this ship's officer, who would make her prisoner even though as yet he had not shown his intent, had no idea of taking her to those of whom Thorn had spoken in awe. He would keep her, somehow train her, for himself alone. Now she laughed silently. Oh, little man, what would best shatter that plan of yours? She could do thus—or thus—Again she laughed without a sound, though Zass stirred against her and growled.

Let him play with his plans, that one. She had other business before her now. Just as she had sent forth seeking thought, so now she sought knowledge, not of what was living within this space-traveling shell but of the shell itself. Some things her older memory touched upon and recognized, yet the structure was different. As might well be, for long ages lay between the time of a ship that had once obeyed her and this one carrying a younger race.

She cared nothing about the source of its power. In the end, all such were not too different, and never had mechanics held any interest for her. There were other places—places that stored knowledge, places that might offer an escape.

The right knowledge she found while skipping randomly from mind to mind of the crew. Yes, there was an exit and those who were trained to use it. But as yet, she was not ready to bend another will to hers and through such a temporary captive learn—Success was again a matter of time.

Why that instinctive need for haste beat at her so, forcing her to wider and wider exploration, Simsa could not have said. However, the fear of her Burrower heritage melded with other uneasiness of the Elder One and thus she did no probing, made no attempt to bend any other mind within this shell to do her will. Not yet.

She was vaguely conscious of an increasing warmth. Even though her eyes were closed, Simsa sensed that the sun-and-moons of her rod were alight. In a way both fed her strength for this weird voyaging of thought—as well as building in her the imperative need for action. Was it chance, or some virtue of the rod, that led her into a thought leap to the mind of a crewman coming off duty and making his way along one of the narrow corridors to meet one of his fellows?

Duty—a regular duty for this one—checking. Simsa became sharply intent.

Beyond the wall where his hand now rested, she picked up the hazy idea of a cavity, within it another ship—a much smaller one. Yes, the Elder One identified, and the Burrows Simsa understood—an escape of a kind. Let this larger ship be injured, its powers fail—then some of those it bore across the star fields would have a way of seeking safety.

Duty—let him do his duty of inspecting the readiness of that Life Boat. The girl allowed herself to issue a thought order, uncertain as to how she could control this newly discovered power of which her Burrower half was still more than half-afraid.

He placed his hands against the wall. Facing the blankness in which her blurred half-vision could see no break, he applied weight. There was a parting of the corridor's skin and he went in, scraping his body in the narrow space between small ship and the wall of the lock that held it.

There was this to be checked—and that. Each Simsa listed, knowing that such information would never be lost to her now. Room for perhaps three bodies such as hers to lie in cushioned space. She followed his thoughts as he fingered a lever, a button. About them would rise the other simple controls—a foam of protective sealing to preserve the passengers against the shock of ship launching and of its landing.

That button set the strange brain of the ship itself at work, seeking out the nearest world that would give its passengers a chance for life. This lever would assert the right pattern for an orbital descent—and a landing. There were supplies that could be used for a space of time. Those, too, the crewman checked. Simsa released her tap upon his thoughts, drew back into her own inert body.

So, this ship was not wholly a space-borne prison as she had feared. Escape in that smaller vessel could be possible.

She centered a goodly part of her mind on that, leaving only a sentry of the Burrows Simsa on duty against discovery. There was, she realized, and knew she must busy herself with that, a good reason why the Elder One who had awaited so long the coming of her twin had not become sole ruler in her. The Burrows Simsa had cunning and training which that great one had never had to develop down the years.

Once more, she quested for that officer who desired her, who was tempted, who wanted power. He was not with the others but alone—and he was building thought-by-thought to action, examining one proposal against another. A net! Yes, a net such as a fisherman would draw. A net wherein to catch her—hold her. How? This ship he might indeed command. But she was certain that he proposed not to share with another any part of what he was planning. The Life Boat!

For a second, Simsa was astounded. Then she picked up the most vivid picture as if the eyes of her body saw this thing. Herself, drugged, sleeping and this would-be possessor of power casting off in the Life Boat, bound into space. Now his thoughts hazed, became a whirling circle of small bits of desire which might have been lifted from dreams. He strode through all of these like a conqueror in a world his own will might have laid waste.

Simsa opened her eyes, cut the questing tie. There was the slight sound of metal against metal as that hand-sized hatch through which had come food and water opened.

She reached out for the cup of liquid. It appeared pure water, but she distrusted now everything within this prison of a ship. Simsa offered it to the zorsal. Zass dipped a beak to stir the surface of what was within the cup. She did not suck, instead her head swirled a fraction on her long neck as she looked to Simsa, uttering the smallest of croaks, raising her wings a fraction.

Simsa sat up, setting the cup back on its tray. For all their greedy feeding when food and drink were before them, the zorsals possessed keen senses of both taste and smell, far keener than any humanoid Simsa had ever met.

She took up the rod and held it above the cup. Slowly, a greenish tinge, so faint that it could only be seen by one who, as herself, was searching, polluted the water. No poison. No, they were too intent upon squeezing her dry of all they could learn. Was this of the man's devising or a trick of that so-called healer who would be called then to minister to the ill and so get time for some of the examinations she wished?

It did not matter. Simsa slipped off the sleeping shelf and visited each of those spy buttons. Though the effort was weakening, she changed the projected images she had set up there—strove to seal new ones in place before she stood in the center of her small prison, Zass on her shoulder, her hands both closed tightly about the stem of the rod, thinking.

Had that drug been given by the man, then it was close to time when he must act. Of the two, she thought him the greater threat. How soon would he be on his way here to see how his plan had worked? If he was the one who spied upon her, and she thought he was, he would see her drink the water, fall back upon her bed, Zass also asleep across her breast. Would that image hold long enough? When she would not be here to reinforce it?

Already she had taken two steps forward to the door. It was undoubtedly locked, though she had not tried it. Now she traced the outline of its length and breadth with the moon crescent tips. The compartment door opened. Zass took off from her shoulder, hovered in the air beating her wings, her beaked head turning from side to side to view either end of the corridor before the curve of the passage made further sight impossible.

Simsa needed no contact with the zorsal. As all her kind, Zass had not only superior sight but also hearing. With the zorsal now on guard, the girl found the lock holding the Life Boat without any worry she would not be warned. Though, as she made her way there, she was surprised to find the passages so empty. It was almost as if they had been cleared to draw her into some type of trap. So strong was this impression that as she paused along the way, her attention ever upon Zass, she also released, in a little, her own questing sense.

Now at her goal, she opened the hatch of the small podlike escape ship—an easy exercise, perhaps made so by the very fact that those who might depend upon it for escape could come here injured or even shocked near to madness by whatever catastrophe made escape necessary.

For a long moment, she merely looked within, studying those same buttons and levers that she had seen the crewman test, drawing out of memory his knowledge of what was necessary for those taking shelter in the pod.

Now . . . the larger ship. Though Simsa of the Burrows had but the most limited knowledge of a space ship, and the Elder One whose awakened self had melded with hers knew ships far more intricate than this, she had some idea of the fact that there were indeed two spaces—one that made each star (to those looking up from planets) but a pinpoint of light far removed, and that other which was far different—a kind of timeless, distantless place or nonplace into which the ship entered for a lengthy voyage and which would be unmeasured by man, only by the highly developed, thinking machines. So might a ship travel between spaces Simsa of Kuxortal could not even measure.

Now—if an escape pod was loosed while the ship was in this no-time, no-space sea, would it indeed transfer those in it into real time, onto a real planet, or would it and its passengers be lost forever, to float in that place without future?

Still, it had been fashioned for escape. And all the accidents that could happen to the parent ship and make its use necessary—were they only to occur in normal space, in the orbiting of a planet, perhaps? If that were so . . . Simsa held the rod between her palms and it gave gentle heat to where the coldness of fear had begun to stiffen her body and send dark fingers of foreboding into her mind.

There was a sharp hiss from behind her—Zass had entered the lock and her message of warning was plain. Unconscious of what she did or why, Simsa slid into the Life Boat, the zorsal once more settling upon her, wide-held wings over her breasts.

Her entrance—what had she done!

Fear arose in a wave of harsh terror, which, once again, overflowed the ancient Simsa, leaving only the girl of the Burrows cowering against the padded resting place. Whether or not the Life Boat was

meant to be used now, it was reacting to her entrance as it had not
to that of the spaceman—

It was as if she had been felled by a blow struck by one of the
slinking lawless males of the Burrows. Into dark Simsa whirled, both
her selves cut off from light, thought, perhaps even life.

She awoke almost with the same speed as she had been struck
down. How long had she lain there? Time had no meaning. But her
thoughts stirred along with her body. There was no mistaking the
vibration of this small craft which held her as tightly as a shell
enclosed the shapeless form of ant-crab. The Life Boat was clearly
set on its own voyage—into the place where space was not—or
bound for the nearest planet, to a point where her recklessness had
launched it.

There was nothing she could do but wait—and neither Simsa of
the Burrows nor the ancient one she was twin to could lie easy under
that curtain of the unknown. Zass hissed but she did not move,
except to raise her head a fraction so that her large beads of eyes met
directly those of the girl. There was no fear in them, and Simsa knew
a spark of pain and guilt. To the zorsal she was the protector, the
all-powerful, and the creature was content to await the girl's action.

There was nourishment in containers within reach of Simsa's
hands as she lay. These held no threat of drugs so she shared with
the zorsal a bulb to be squeezed so that a slightly sourish-tasting
water refreshed them and she divided, amid falling crumbs, a cake
of compressed dry rations.

Time did pass under a fashion. She slept and perhaps Zass did,
too. There was no break in the vibration of the humming walls.
Purposely, Simsa tried to wipe from her mind all but a single fact.
The craft that bore her had been fashioned to preserve life. All the
efforts of those who had formed it had been bent only to that one
cause. Therefore, let her believe that she would emerge unharmed.

Three times the feeding procedure came and went and then
there was a difference in the feel of the craft. Simsa was tempted to
send out thought, but that needed another mind to link—and here
there was none save herself and Zass.

The vibration's thrum grew louder until the girl curled into a ball, her fingers thrust into her ears to deaden a sound that was as painful as any cut of a Guild Man's lash back in the stews from which the Burrowers came.

Pain from that rousing whine—then a crash. Simsa's body was driven back against the far wall of the craft by the force of that. Her head cracked against uncushioned metal above the bed place. But, through the agony of that blow, she saw that same door which had closed to entrap her raising in a series of jerks. Finally, it stuck and, on her knees Simsa now brought up both hands to push, for a moment forgetting the rod. Zass squeezed through the opened slit and a moment later, Simsa heard the zorsal give tongue in sheer fury and pain.

That brought her to her senses and she swung the rod upward, centering all her will on winning free. The door shuddered, began to glow. Heat from it fanned back against her own nearly bare body. Still she held until, with a last clang of protest, whatever had jammed it gave away and she was able to pull herself up and out—upon the refuge world.

That had been three days past. Simsa stirred within the cloak she had made from two stored coverings in the Life Boat. No moon, no sun—the haze would darken and so suggest night for a time, then flame again into this baking fury. The boat had landed close to this flowing stream of sand. Having no other guide, she had started to walk along that, well-aware that the downed craft would be broadcasting an alarm steadily. She had no mind to meet any would-be rescuers until she knew who—or what—such would be.

They had come a long way, she carrying Zass under the shelter of her enveloping cloak, for the zorsal could not stand the heat reflected from the rock. She had traveled by night and in the day, there was nothing in the way of shelter—only this ever-stretching rock and the moving river of sand.

Though she had dug a little into the river, she had found not a hint of moisture and she had no idea what moved it with a visible current. The bag of supplies from the boat were all that now stood between them and a death that would leave dried remains of girl and zorsal on the never-changing rock.

2

Though she had slept, or rather lost consciousness in an unquiet doze, Simsa was well-aware that she had near reached the end of her strength. There had been no change in the land, no sign that these plains of rock had ever supported life as she knew it. Still a feeling was also always with her, growing the stronger when she stopped to rest at the coming of greater heat, that she and Zass were not alone, that her shuffling advance was observed and weighed. She had searched the air uselessly for sight of a sharp-eyed flyer, glared back at rock until her eyes ached and teared. Nothing.

Nothing but the silent slip of the sand river. Not for the first time, Simsa put Zass gently to one side and, pulling the cloak well under her to shield her bare flesh from the heated stone, lay belly flat to stare at that strange ever-flowing current. There was something about the queer eddies that now and then troubled the yellow-gray surface that kept her from investigating by touch. Also, where could she find a branch or such to prod beneath that same scum-thick surface? Her rod she would not so defile.

She had no way of telling the passing of true time here, but she was sure that the haze was darkening and that soon it would be time to move on again. If she could force herself to rise, to set her feet on the still warm rock . . . But to go where? There was nothing ahead, certainly—at least she could see nothing. She did not even turn her head to look again.

Had she been an utter fool? There was still the craft down on a shelf of this same rock, and it would afford shelter of a sort, as well as the beacon calling for help. Simsa caught her lower lip between her teeth and bit down hard. To be forced to return, to be proven a failure—neither part of her welcomed that, as sensible as such a solution would be.

Below her, the sand eddied in a wider sweep. There puffed up into her face such a vile stench as set her coughing, gasping for air to clean her nostrils and lungs. Simsa raised herself on her hands but still did not withdraw from the stream side.

There was ancient rot in that puff of air. However, with it also a hint of moisture, befouled beyond belief, perhaps, but still moisture. Now she sat upright, allowed her cloak to slip away while her hands went to the single garment she wore. Since that Simsa of the deserted city had reached out to her, the Burrows Simsa, while standing alone in her gemmed crown, necklet, and bejeweled metal-strip kilt, she had taken the garb of that image from which the spark of life had come to mingle with her own. After, she had worn proudly the dress of that Elder who had ruled a people long since forgotten. Now she loosed one of the strips of the kilt, began to bend and twist it where it was made fast to the girdle until it snapped, giving her a silver metal strip studded with gems that could be cloudy or awake under certain lights to brightness. It was longer than her arm by a little. She held it firmly by the portion twisted free of the intricate linkage to plunge into the disturbance of sand which spread farther both up the river and down.

For a very long moment, she hesitated. Certainly that whiff of foulness was no invitation to investigate further. But the sliding sand was all that might stand between her and an impotent trip back to the Life Boat.

Her Burrows memory was wary, yet that also could give way to impatience. And now it did. As she might have used a short stabbing spear on some of the beshelled crawlers of Kuxortal's faraway coast, so did she bring the gemmed strip down with all the force of her arm.

It entered the sand easily enough, but—

Simsa flinched. Somewhere below that curling of gray brown,

she had struck opposition. Something she had attacked was moving, first threshing wildly about so that its frenzied struggle caused an upheaval not unlike a minor eruption. A bubble of the thick stuff broke in the parched air, releasing concentrated odor so foul that Simsa felt instant nausea.

There was nothing else moving, not even when she tried to draw forth her improvised probe. The metal held as stiff and straight and opposed to her strength as if it had pierced whatever it had first encountered, pinning it to the rock bed.

Simsa shrugged off the last part of the covering across her shoulders and arose to her knees, hands tightly clutching the strip. No strength she could put forth moved it. She began to weave the probe back and forth. At first, the obstruction was so great she could not stir her metal length no matter how hard she tried. Then it began to give. There was a sudden falling away on one side. Simsa answered that with as sharp a twist as she could deliver. Almost she lost her balance as the final release came. The strip popped up into view, scattering great sand droplets in all directions, bringing a miasma of the stomach-turning stench which it intensified to the hundredth part.

It did not come cleanly, though the sand of the stream did not cling to it. Rather, there was impaled on the tip, a thing as large as her two fists together. It was of that thick yellowish color shown by pus draining from a wound. And it moved constantly in a wild writhing, as if it strove to tear itself from the metal centered in its body.

In shape, it was an ovoid with no marked features nor any head or tail parts. From its underside spread, to lash in the air, eight tentacles all of the same size.

Simsa knew the dark spinners of the Burrows. But those were well-favored compared to this noxious blob. She held it well away from her and the rock shore, studying it as best she could. This was the first life she had seen since she had crawled out of the craft.

It was contracting those legs or limbs, wrapping them about its body as if, having found it could not escape through its original efforts, it was protecting itself as best it could.

Simsa blinked.

This nasty yellow blob was her captive. Had the constant heat, the lack of food or more than a sip or two of water so taken over her senses that she was seeing dream projections, like those the crax chewers were said to have haunt them in the latter stage of their addiction?

It was not true! Loosing the grip of her right hand, though still balancing the improvised spear with the other, she rubbed her fingers across the heat-tormented eyes in her seared face. There was now clinging to her rod a man! Fully humanoid, clothed, and no more than two fingers high. And when the man turned his face to look to her, she knew his face—too well.

To the credit of the toughness of the Burrows Simsa, and the command of the Elder One, she neither cried out nor dropped the rod. Instead, her wrist wavering a little in spite of all her efforts at strict control, she pulled the strip back from above the sand river and tossed it to the bare rock at a point as far from her as she could send it.

Zass's hissing, which had begun when Simsa first probed into the opaque flood, arose to a scream. In spite of the heat, the zorsal took to the air, flying over the girl's strange catch in the narrow circle of her species when attracted to some prey. Yet she made no move to launch herself into a swoop.

Simsa had to move the strip and shake it vigorously to detach her impossible catch. The little man lay on the rock, his chest heaving, his tiny hands pressed tight to his middle, the blood of a wound spurting a red flood over his body. His head turned so that he looked at her with such an accusing face that she dropped the strip, clasped her hands together so that her claws blood-scored her own skin. This was not the truth! Both Simsas clamored in her mind. She had not brought out of that sandy river this living miniature of Thorn!

Still the thing looked upon her as Thorn might have appealed for her help and she remembered all their wanderings and those days in the city of ruined ships, days in which, in a way she still did not understand, he had come to mean more to her than any one she had ever known—closer in a new way than even Ferwar, who had protected her since childhood.

"You are *not!*" She was not aware that she spoke aloud until she heard her own voice. Zass had fallen silent though she still circled in the air about the wounded thing which was not, Simsa insisted, real.

The Elder One within her now struggled for command. This once, Simsa of the Burrows did not instinctively brace herself in defense. Perhaps things as strange as this were common off-world, perhaps it was—

"It hides!" Again she spoke out loud, only now in the singsong that was the Elder One's own tongue. "It bends the sight, taking from the mind some favorite image to hide behind. But it is a foolish thing, else it would know the difference—"

So far had the reasonable explanation of the Elder One proceeded when the shock of new happening hit the Burrower girl. Even she could not believe in a manikin as big as her flattened hand. But— that was gone! Here was a full-sized man no different from the Thorn she had known, save that he writhed on the rock where his blood pooled. And there was the glaze of coming death in his dark eyes.

"Small to large!" chattered Simsa, her body ashake. "I know," she told herself, told the Elder One, "that this is not true!"

She grabbed at the strip of metal and used it fiercely to prod the dying man-thing—rolling it backward toward the river. It did roll— which, she told her dazed mind, no true man of proper size would do! So rolling, it was edged by a last push out over the sand flow, to strike the solid-appearing surface and be sucked under. While Simsa, breathing in deep gasps of the burning air, stared downward.

Illusion; both her memories, united, held to that stubbornly. Nothing but illusion. But what kind of thing could reach into *her* mind without her being aware and pick out such a memory, use it to protect itself? Was it in truth even that blob of yellow which she had first drawn forth? Or was its true body pattern something else again? Had it worked upon her with intelligence or by instinct? She thought of how she had kept so close to the sand river in all her travel across this barren world and felt more than a little sick. Her imagination was only too ready to paint for her what might happen to someone who lay asleep, who had no barriers. Suppose the projected Thorn had come across her in the early morning when she had made her rough camp here? Supposing he could have spun some tale of following her—yes, she would have been wary of him, of any spaceman now—but was wariness such as that enough?

Zass alighted on the rock not far from the puddle of blood left behind by the river-thing. It had been swift-flowing crimson when it had worn the seeming of Thorn. Now it was a dirty yellow, looking like rancid grease that had gone uncleaned from a pot far too long.

The zorsal extended her neck. Her feathered antennae pointed to the slight depression in the rock where that fluid had been cupped. Her pointed snout quivered. Then she gave a half-leap into the air, instantly stabilized by wing spread—and her hissing was sharp, so that she even seemed to spit in the direction of the congealing stain.

Simsa pulled up to her feet, drawing the cloak in folds over her shoulders. The place where the captured thing had rolled, to be once more hidden in the river, had not smoothed. There, the surface of the sand flow was troubled as a larger excrescence rose above the general level.

Bigger—larger—sand sloughed away from it. A thatch of closely cut dark hair first and then a face with those curiously tilted eyes that had been the first strangeness she had marked in her initial sighting of Thorn. The head arose until the sand formed a frill about the throat. The mouth opened, something that might even be akin to a voice topped the swish of the flowing sand:

"Simsssa." A hiss near in pitch to Zass's one of anger, a slurred attempt at her name.

The girl dropped her hold on the cloak so it fell to the rock, and the heat generated by the haze above lapped the black skin on her back and shoulders. She forced herself a single step closer to that thing in the turgid flood. Between her hands, both tightly grasping it, the rod of Elder One's near unknown, untested power pointed directly at the forehead of that illusion.

"Not!" She still had control of her voice. "You are not Thorn—you are not!"

As she began to concentrate her will upon action, she half-expected that the fire which the rod, the tips of the moon, the mirror of the sun, projected would come to her call and blast the sand creature into nothingness. Only there was no warming of the metal cradled so between her palms—no flash of energy. Once more, the mouth of the head worked.

"Simssssa . . ."

Her name—it could somehow have picked that out of her own mind. She held no wonder too unreal after what she had seen since she and the Elder One had fused, or not quite fused, into one. But she had not thought of Thorn, not that she could remember, since she had begun this journey across the endless furnace of the plain. If it drew upon her memories, old or new, why not Ferwar, or half a ten-ten of others she had known all her life, and known better than the spaceman with whom she had traveled so short a number of days?

The head—it blurred, as if her questions had somehow weakened the control of that which had set it—perhaps for bait. Still a man's head, but the black hair had blanched to pure silver to match the long strains now sticky with sweat that lay on her own shoulders, sprang wiry and alive from her scalp. White brows, which lashed about dark eyes—the skin as dark as a starless sky.

"Zzzzaaaaa . . ." that dark thing called.

"No!" Not the Burrows girl who answered this time, but the Elder One. Simsa held a fan of fleeting memories which reached from her to that bodiless head, strove to weave swiftly as a chain between them. The girl whom Thorn had known drew aside, the Elder One was there, and in her a new emotion stirred until she ruthlessly locked it tightly away.

"No!" She made no lengthy speech as the Elder One filled her. Instead, her hands moved independently of her conscious will, weaving back and forth so that the moon tips of her power rod might be scrawling some unseen pattern on the air between them. From her throat arose a low hum broken in rhythm now and then, as if she did voice words she made no attempt to speak aloud.

That black and silver head wove back and forth also, straining upward until there appeared the outline of a shoulder breaking from the shifting sands—black shoulder bare of any covering. Though the head kept its eyes fixed upon her, the mouth no longer moved. Yet its writhing against the hold of the sand, the arising and slipping back of shoulders, gave credence to a struggle, as mighty a struggle as Simsa had ever witnessed.

"Aaaah—Zaaazzza!" Thrown back, the head opened wide jaws to give utterance to a scream like that of a hunting zorsal. Its eyes were now pointed heavenward. It might have been demanding aid from some presence unseen to those from off-world. If it did so, it was not favored by the answer which it sought. For it was sinking back. The shoulders had already disappeared, now sand lapped up over the chin, sought the open cavity of the mouth.

The head was gone. A head was gone. Simsa would have flung up her arm to hide that hideous change from sight had it not been that she could not unhinge her fingers from their tight grip upon the shaft of the rod.

No head now, but a stretch of obscene, greasy yellow skin that was wrinkled about a single great eye. While the whole surface of the river tossed gobbets of sand into the air, spattering over the rock. A thing or a multitude of things was rising to the surface. Simsa of the Burrows would have fled. The Simsa of the Elder Ones only stepped back so that the spattering sand could not reach her. She watched the thing narrowly while the younger, lesser Simsa shared memories again—strange and horrible—of monsters and creatures so far from normal life that even to hold them fleetingly in mind made her shrink from a wash of foulness.

Still the rod wove and the Elder Simsa hummed or changed. Yet she was also on the move. Transferring her hold from two hands to one, yet keeping the horn points of the rod ever turned toward the wallowing half-seen monster that dragged itself out of hiding so slowly, the girl took up her cloak and the provision bag and the flask of water now near consumed.

Zass gave two screams, flying to the erupting sand and turning back again swiftly to circle above the girl's head.

Thus together they edged back and away from the stream that had been their guide across this stone waste. That which sought them had won free of the sand, which cascaded back into the bed as might water running from thick hide. The creature was ovoid in form, like that thing which Simsa had snared first on the strip from her kilt. Still it did not appear quite sure of its form. For there was a haziness about its outlines and within that veiling, there were changes, some lightning quick and only temporary, some more lasting. Of the weaving tentacles it sprouted, four firmed, stiffened to give it legs.

Face there was none, though a portion of it upraised to suggest a very ill-shaped head, that broken by a single unblinking eye. As it crouched on the same portion of riverbank where Simsa had made her camp, it shot forward ropy limbs or arms on which there were dark stains as might be given off by something rotting while still it lived. And from it, though there was no wind to send out any odor, there emerged a gagging stench.

As Simsa continued to retreat at an angle, one that would take her from the stream and yet not too far into the rock that she could lose her single guide—the sand dweller tottered up, to stand as erect as was possible on those stiffened feet. It ceased to wave its tentacles in the air, perhaps to concentrate all its strength on what it wished the most to do—take up the chase on land.

Zass screamed full-throated on a louder note than she had yet used, swung away from circling above Simsa's head toward the girl's right—the wider plain of the stone. Its surface was broken here and there by smaller fissures which did not offer any passage Simsa was aware of to a sand river. However, because they had no surface connection with one another did not mean they were not ponds or lakelets.

As might a fountain suddenly released flash the first burden of water in its pipes into the air, so above the lip of a near fissure flared an eruption of sand. Breaking through Simsa's hum came a dull thud of noise, one beat sliding into another as if the underside of the plain over which she was retreating was the surface of a drum answering to the blows of a threatening fist.

Back, she increased the speed of her withdrawal, taking the same way that had brought her here. The heavy light and heat of the haze was diminishing—though even when it reached its lowest point it still provided enough light to guide one's way.

Though she continued to keep the rod between her and that noxious yellow monstrosity, it clumped along, wavering from side to side its swollen, filthy body, leaving behind a trail of slick slime. Simsa glanced hurriedly now and then at that other fissure which still fountained, sand sweeping up over its edge to drift outward. The same partial haze that had half-hidden her first possible enemy was gathering on the lip of that broken way and she thought it well to guess that it heralded the coming of a creature similar to that which already stalked her.

The zorsal did not swoop any lower, hanging with fast-beating wings for a long moment over the fissure, screaming with rage and, the Simsa of the Burrows realized, fear. There was very little a zorsal feared—being one of the most fierce and practical hunters on its own world. It could even be flown at a man—or a woman—and swoop to tear at eyes and cheeks. Had she not seen Zass's two sons deal death to a serpent-thing a hundred times their size when she and Thorn had been trapped in another unknown wilderness? The zorsals had torn out the throat of a monster no man would have faced, even with the sharpest and keenest weapons known.

Yet Zass here made none of those punishing dives. Though she was ready enough to point out the danger to come, she showed no inclination to fight.

As another thought thrust in with a stroke of pure fear, the girl dared to glance over her shoulder. Were there any more of those fissures close to the path of withdrawal? One—she would need to swing near to the river to avoid that. Her eyes snapped once again to the stalker and then to the second fissure that had shown signs of life. Yes! A long yellowish tentacle waved into the air there, blindly, as if it sought for some hold aloft rather than swinging down to the rock edge.

The Burrows Simsa might have run until her lungs choked on the heated air—the Elder One held steady in spite of the rising struggle within the one slender black body. If the Elder One could handle this sand-slime, then let her do it—now! Burrow-bred Simsa could see that all that chanting and use of the rod made no difference to this thing. Perhaps a power designed to work on one world was useless on another. Could she tear loose another of the metal strips that made up her kilt—use that as a House Guard used a sword or spear? No, the length of the free limbs that had not adopted the guise of legs could outreach any such attempt she would make.

Out of the deepening shade of the sky haze there came a new factor into her forced retreat. The sharp crack of sound was unlike anything she had heard before—and the vibration appeared to linger on, actually echoing twice. Did the rock under her feet answer to it? She could not be sure. Perhaps the sudden movement was a shudder of her own body.

However, the effect on the yellow stream creature and that other one climbing out to join it was much stronger. Though that which walked had no mouth, yet from somewhere out of its body it uttered an answering sound—a thin wail—so high pitched the girl hardly caught it. Its globe body began to twitch, swaying back and forth on its pillar legs. One of those legs thinned, flipped outward, becoming once again a tentacle, so that the thing was thrown off-balance and, still fighting hard to keep erect, crashed to the rock.

There was a dull plop. The ovoid body burst like a container of foulness that had held its burden far too long. Before her eyes, the sand dweller began to dissolve. Twice, it reared up, strove to draw about it those rags of mist that brought it the power to change, to solidify and be a living force. And each time it did, the rod in Simsa's hands quivered also—faint, very muted, it produced the same note as there had been in that shock from overhead. Perhaps it had been at last attuned to service and was no longer so impotent.

That which had striven to climb from the other fissure showed no more tentacles and the sand thrown forth by its floundering was fast draining back into the cavity. Just so the substance of the one before her was lapping out as liquid now, a wave to flow along the slime trail its stumped feet had left. Back that noisome stuff flowed to the edge of the river. The horn points of the rod continued to sound forth their faint keening so that Simsa now marched forward, as she had before retreated, her rod pointing to the mess on the rock, driving it back into its own sphere with the fervent hope within her that it would not, could not, summon any power again.

3

Simsa swayed in turn as the zorsal flew straight for her, coming to perch upon her shoulder, its sudden weight threatening her balance. Zass's beak-muzzle slipped along the girl's cheek in one of the creature's seldom offered caresses. Did Zass judge the trouble over? Simsa gave the sky haze a single quick glance. She needed full attention for the fissures, to pick a way that did not encroach either upon one of those or go too near the riverbank.

Now that the enemy apparently had withdrawn for a space, she could think more clearly. That sound from the air . . . It seemed faintly familiar, as if she must recognize it. Some flying thing of prey? No, never had she chanced on any life as strange as the blob creatures. If they had some equivalent in the air overhead, then she would indeed have to watch with fear.

The cries of a zorsal—there were a whole range of those, from the sighting of prey to that squawk of triumph when the victim was safe in its paw talons. On Kuxortal, there existed fumga, which sought its food along the seas' edge, an eater of carrion—and the quef, said to dwell in the high mountains—of which she had been told, but which she had never seen. Now she turned her head a fraction and dared to withdraw a portion of her concentration from her route, reaching for the small entrance into Zass's mind which the Elder One had shown could be used to cement yet closer the winged hunter and the girl.

"What . . . ?" She did not truly think a word, rather she fashioned as best she could a need to know.

There was the usual misty image she could expect from the zorsal, barely recognizable, since Zass's power of sight was so different. But even as she caught that lopsided vision, Simsa also guessed at what she had heard. That sound had heralded the approach of a spaceship closing orbit upon this world. That distress signal which she had not been able to quiet had already pulled in a rescuer.

Simsa hugged her arms about herself, the warmth of the rod against her breasts. Someone from the ship she had been on? That might well be—if they had discovered her gone and had checked upon the Life Boat. If so, should off-worlders low flying sweep to seek her out, how long could she hide?

Certainly to descend into any of those fissures would be the height of folly. She wondered if she dared lie flat upon the heated rock, the cloak pulled over her to conceal. But she could not remain so for long.

Simsa frowned, remembering Thorn's talk of persona units, meant to center upon the body heat of another, devices as quick on the trail and far more tireless than any zorsal.

Certainly if they sought her, they must come equipped with every such device they knew.

She was also sure that there was one aboard that ship who would never let her go free if he could help—that ship's master who had seen her as a tool or weapon to move him into an area of power he had never hoped to reach. Yes, let him be in command of the search party and there would be very little chance of deceiving them by any ordinary means.

If the orbiting ship had not come from the freighter on which she had voyaged, then it would still be very sure that a search was made. They would discover the Life Boat empty, the supplies gone— therefore they would come looking.

If this had been a world such as she knew, with ground cover and even heights, she could have played a good game. She could have arranged a scene of accident that would have deceived—no one. Simsa of the Burrows spat. She knew so much, and still there were holes in that knowledge. What might have been possible untold planet-years ago could not be tried here. The discoveries of one race or species had to be refined upon by another, improvements made that could even be unknown from one ship to the next. She had listened, she had thought, she had studied all she could. No, she must believe that sooner or later those who descended from the hazed sky of this unknown planet would be able to find her.

Accepting that as not only possible, but extremely probable, Simsa had to work out her answer. That depended largely upon who those would-be rescuers were. If from the ship she knew, she would face stricter captivity. But if from another—sworn as they were to the space law of assisting any survival beacon—perhaps she could work out a story. Simsa of the Burrows took command. She had lived most of her life by cunning scheming; now let her loose her imagination.

The haze had been fast darkening. It was no more than that which might have hung above Kuxortal on an evening fast sliding into night. Her eyes slitting a little, she discovered that she was more at ease than in the glare of daylight. She gathered up her cloak and pulled it about her. Though she had gloried in the kilt and diadem, the dress of the Elder One was foreign to space travelers and she must conceal it as best she could.

She was faced with two choices—travel on into this unending rock desert with its threat of what might rise from any of the fissures, or return upstream to the boat. She could play a distraught and frightened survivor in the latter case.

In this now silent world, Simsa stared down at the rod. Zass had refused to quit her shoulder after she had recloaked. She did not try to read the zorsal's mind pattern again. It was plain enough that Zass sought protection where she had always sought safety before—close to the girl.

Simsa turned to go forward once more, heading into the unknown, careful only to keep far from any break in the rock. Her pace quickened to a trot as she still busied herself with thoughts of what she must or could do when the final test came and she had to face those intent upon her "rescue."

It was certainly plain that she could not remain on this barren world indefinitely, although the Life Boat, having once found a landing, would not rise on its own, being programmed only to carry passengers to worlds with breathable atmosphere where there would be a chance of life. In no way, Simsa thought, was it fitted to judge a strange planet for any other quality.

She was still considering what part she must act when, listening for any airborne sound to betray a flitter questing after her, she first noted that the haze, which not only cloaked the sky but also hid any sharp line of horizon on all sides, was decidedly darker in one spot ahead. This was the first change from the monotony of the plain she had yet sighted.

The stream she used at a careful distance as her guide angled slightly east. That dark spot lay to the west and was constantly thickening. Simsa began to trot. Heights curtained by mist? Then she might find a safe haven among those.

Shorter fissures pocked the plain closer to each other westward. Twice she made a sidewise leap and ran a few steps when an exhalation (or so it sounded) of foul air tainted the night. Still she heard no threatening lap of sand.

Simsa could soon see more clearly that which rose from the plain—a series of blocks, huge, but so squared in shape that she could not believe that they were natural formations. About the foot of three such plateaus of different sizes facing her directly the plain was darker—the dark of a fissure or another river of sand—too deep to be gauged from where she now trotted along. If that barrier followed the roots of those cliffs, she might have no way of reaching the heights at all.

The worst was true. She came out on the rim of a gully. Below swirled more of the moving sand, passing in its slow push, north to south, even as did the river she had quitted. Simsa swung south, eyeing those towering banks beyond. Though the rock rises had looked so even-surfaced from a distance, Simsa could now see that there were fissures of differing depth and length in their faces.

Only—those fissures were far too even! Nature might have begun the work of pocking those rocks, but some purpose not so slow nor unsystematic had then taken a hand. She might have been looking at sets of windows—perhaps even entrances, if there were ladders within to be shoved into place, or if the inhabitants possessed wings.

A hiss sounded below her chin, then the prick of claws followed as Zass changed her hold, suggesting one way of discovering whether they had chanced upon a rookery of another threatening form of wildlife. Though the zorsal strove to cling to the underside of the improvised cloak, Simsa dragged her forth enough so that the snouted head with its large eyes did face those patterned cliffs. The feathery antennae, which had been so tightly curled to the small skull, snapped open and out—stiff and straight, pointing to those stone rises.

Zass made no sound at all, and Simsa waited. Usually, there was a whine, a hiss, or even a short growl from the zorsal. Instead, the girl felt the furred body against hers quiver. The head turned slowly, keeping the antennae always pointing to the cliffs. Simsa tried mind touch.

The only emotion she could pick up was a blurred picture—a suggestion rather—of bafflement that was fast becoming curiosity. Zass raised a front paw to push aside the edge of the cloak, emerging completely out of cover, though clinging still to the coarse covering with all four paws.

Those antennae began to wave, combing the air, a sign Simsa knew of old. Zass was arousing to hunt, showing no fear at all now, rather more and more interest. Before Simsa could catch and control her, the zorsal took off into the dusk, climbing steadily through the air, then swung out across that other sand river, heading for a square of deeper shadow on the nearest of the cube cliffs.

Simsa whistled that sound which had always brought the zorsal from hiding. Zass did not reappear. She had gone into the door, window—whatever that opening might really be—not to show herself again. Nor could the girl even discover that in-and-out wave of thought pattern which marked her companion. There was only silence—the dusk, and that gaping opening, a mouth that had swallowed but had not closed.

That she could leave the zorsal never crossed Simsa's mind—the

Burrows Simsa who had considered the night hunter her only close touch with real emotion was now in command. She set her jaw stubbornly, advanced to the very edge of the gulf, her wary attention divided between the surface of the flowing sand and that window-door-hole into which Zass had vanished. There was no picking up the zorsal by mind touch, even when she struggled to the extent of the talent the Elder One had opened in her. Nothing! Still, Simsa was somehow sure that if Zass had gone to her death in that reckless flight, she herself would have known it.

Since the zorsal could not or would not answer, then the girl must find her own path. Slowly, from right to left and back again, she surveyed the sand stream. There was just one place where the rock walls confining it appeared to approach each other, and that was still farther south.

She counted aloud the openings on the one level, to set deeply into her mind the one Zass had entered. Then she strode determinedly for that narrowing of the stream.

Simsa was agile, her body fine-trained to many feats of strength that would have astounded anyone not used to the dangers of the Burrows and the skills one developed there merely to stay alive, but there seemed no hope of crossing this stream. On the far side of the narrowing there did rise the wall of one of the cube mounds, but there was a space between its roots and the edge of the river broad enough for a path.

In fact—Simsa's dark tongue tip emerged and swept over her lower lip as she considered narrowly the whole positioning of the rock ledges here. That shelf over the stream was cut in so far so that even a portion of the wall overhung it. Yes. She could mind-picture a temporary bridge here, one that could be easily drawn should any danger come from the rock plain.

If a bridge had been there, it was long gone. She dropped to sit cross-legged, trying now in her need to do what she had been wary of doing much since she had met and melded with that other Simsa. Her own only answer was a running jump to span the flood, and that she did not dare, even used as she was to falls and climbs in the lower depths of Kuxortal. So . . . what did the Elder One have to suggest?

Simsa strove to render her mind blank as far as her Burrows past was concerned. She and Thorn had both made climbs aplenty in the ruined city where the Elder One had waited in her great hall for so long. But there had also been vines and ropes and all else that intelligence could call into use as aides. Here, there was only rock, with not even a stunted bush or tree above, and sand which could hide—

Simsa shook her head vigorously. She was not going to remember that—not in any detail. What *had* the Elder One to offer? She squeezed her familiar self well back, called openly for the other to think or to plan, if there was any plan possible. And—

The answer was not quite an illusion, for it would be of this world, solid, supportive as long as it was held so by concentration. Concentration—her silver-white brows twisted into a frown and her shoulders straightened. She got to her feet, still holding the moon-sun rod in one hand, its symbol rising without her willing until the moon tips touched her own forehead above her eyes.

Warmth—

Without breaking that touch or changing the line of her set stare, Simsa reached to hook fingers in the cloak which had slipped down her body. With it in her left hand, trailing across the rock, she took steps that brought her to the very edge of the river's gully.

Her left arm whirled and the cloak arose with the gesture, stiff and heavy, dragging at her fingers. She willed with all her might—and threw—

The stiff, dark fabric went out, flapping edges like a creature of real life. It settled. One of its edges touched her feet, the other, bridging the sand flow, lay well into the niche on the other side.

"Believe!" She might not have shouted that order aloud, but it was so much a part of her that it filled her whole head. There was no longer any cloak—there was a bridge, firm and steady for her feet. This was the truth! The truth!

Holding the rod steady though its points were still warming—near searing hot now—against her skin, not looking down, for even to do that was to deny the needed belief a fraction, Simsa took one step and then again. She was treading on the cloak—no, not a cloak, a *bridge*, one summoned and held by will—her *will!*

There was a bridge prepared and she walked it. From the roots of her silver-white hair fell drops of moisture which ran down her face like tears, to drip from her chin to her breast and shoulders. The hair itself rose from her scalp in streamers that fluttered as might a lord's tower standard on a brisk and windy day.

The pain of the rod's touch was sharp. Simsa held fast. Within her, there was an outgoing, a draining—still she went forward on the bridge that was not a cloak. She stumbled, falling forward, her free hand clawing outward ahead to catch on rock. She made a last great effort and half-threw, half-twisted her body to follow that hold—to lie suddenly cold and very weak on rock while the warmth of the rod vanished as from a lamp that had been snuffed.

Panting with shallow breaths that seemed never to fill her lungs as she needed, Simsa shifted her body away from the edge of the drop. The ledge, which might have been cut to support a long vanished bridge, was narrow, so already she was back from its lip, bunching the now limp cloak under her as she wriggled along on her back. At that moment, she could not have again lifted a hand, neither to pick up the rod now lying sullenly cold across her breast nor to reach out for some sustaining hold.

This weakness she had felt before when she had opened wide to that one who could indeed use the rod, but never to the extent that she felt it now. She could not even raise her head, though she managed to turn it with great effort.

It was true. That was where she had been—over there! And here she was. The cloak was just a roll of cloth—yet—

Her eyelids seemed too heavy to keep up and slow, soft waves of drowsiness swept over her. No—she must not sleep, not just yet. It was as if that other part of her delivered more than safe passage and a warning. She did not know enough—she had no training in this power which drained so. She was again Simsa of the Burrows and as that, she dared not call on the Elder One, that other.

Thirst cut through her weakness first. Her mouth felt as if it were filled with sand from below. There were her rations from the

Life Boat—but water she had scanted on at every meal in this bone-bare waste. It was too bad that she could not command another illusion, one that would take on life once it was summoned—a stream of clear, pure—

Simsa's head jerked and the rock on which it rested bruised her painfully. She saw—she heard—she—smelt! Not water, that was the least of her worries at the moment. No, it was what appeared out of nowhere, leaning perilously forward from a window hold above her, its head downturned so that large faceted eyes met hers.

Feathered antennae curved forward. But this was not Zass. The great creature of the rock shared no other feature with the zorsal. Most of the face or forepart of the head was those two eyes, golden in color and broken up into many, many small circles, lidless as far as she could see and opaque when she strove to reach behind them.

Where a mouth and chin should be were small black mandibles or several pairs of jaws clicking together with the sharp sound that had first drawn her attention to the in-dweller. There were jointed forearms clutching with double claws the sides of its hole. What she could see of the body appeared to be covered with a thick plush of short green fur. The arms—or upper limbs—were black, the skin hard and shiny, a row of spikes running from the claws up to what would be a humanoid's shoulder.

Simsa at that moment could not have pulled herself up to any defense, and she glanced from the claws of the fore-limbs, those busy clicking, to the moving mouth with an uneasiness that began to be real fear.

Anyone who had ever visited a spaceport or heard the tales of the space rovers, knew that intelligence and "Human" classification came in many sizes, shapes, and colors. Her own striking appearance was unlike any of the other Burrow dwellers and, Thorn had once told her, totally unlike any that he had seen while he was a forescout and explorer for the Zacathan record keepers, despite the fact that they had untold species and subspecies indexed in their massive historical records.

That this thing so intently observing her now was not an "animal" or a "creature" on the same level as that she had fished from the sand river was something that seeped slowly into her mind. She gathered some of her depleted force to attempt such mind contact as she had with Zass, deciding that any intelligence possessed by this inhabitant of the rock pile might be very different, if no less keen than her own.

Her attempt was a failure. She could not even raise those in-and-out hazy "picture impressions" that were her communication in depth with Zass. For the moment, apparently, the thing was just willing to stand watching her (if standing was its posture), perhaps as baffled by her as she was by it.

Then, astounded enough to let out a gasp, she was sent rolling to the wall abutting on the ledge. The wrinkled rolls of her cloak had been jerked abruptly from her, though she could see no hand or mouth to grasp it. Since one end dangled well over the drop, she could only think at first that one of the yellow bulbous creatures had hooked it from below and was preparing to climb up to where she lay.

Only the dangling end flopped up, striking half across her body as it fell as the result of another unseen pull. There was something in this action that chilled her enough to leave her cowering against the wall, watching the square of cloth instead of the creature above her. Before she could grasp at it, or make herself put forth a hand to do so, the cloak rose, straightened out flat in the air as if it were one of those flyers Thorn had shown her in action—a manmade thing ready for flight.

Then it flipped over, to display its other side, before whatever power moved it so was withdrawn and the whole of it fell back. She had just time and wit enough left to grab it before its folds vanished down toward the swallowing sand. Once more, she was free to look up at the stranger above.

Sitting on one plush-covered shoulder was Zass!

The zorsal looked as thoroughly at home as if Simsa herself offered it a perch. But its antennae were completely uncoiled and the one nearest to the massive-eyed head touched a similar appendage on the alien, its tip curled a fraction about the much larger and more feathered sense organ of the stranger.

Swiftly, Simsa attempted contact with the zorsal and was again astounded. Only once before had she ever met such a wave of joy and sheer ecstasy. Once when, with her rod, she had managed to heal a broken wing that had so long kept Zass from the air and the flight the creature considered its proper sphere. Yet Zass had not been healed of any hurt this time. There was no reason for such waves of joyful emotion.

It was Zass herself who arose at last from the perch on the alien's shoulder. The inhabitant of the rock made no sign or move to prevent the flight, remaining motionless, its wide and lidless eyes fixed on Simsa. That it had some agency to lift the cloak she was sure, though for what purpose she had no notion—unless to impress her with the fact that it had powers she might find difficult to face.

Zass landed on her shoulder, pushing a furred body close to her head, nuzzling her cheek with sharp muzzle, Zass's bid for full attention and cherishing.

Absently, Simsa answered as she always had, putting up her left hand to scratch between the roots of the zorsal's antennae.

"Power—much power—"

No, that comment had not come from Zass, though in a way it had filtered through the zorsal's limited mind. Simsa was sure of the origin of the words which had seemed to boom directly into her ears, though all she still really heard was the clicking of a set of mandibles.

"Who are you?" she asked aloud, because that still came the easiest, but at the same time she thought—tried to think—to Zass as if the zorsal were one of those communication devices she had seen in use by Thorn and the other space people.

"Come!" The big head leaned farther out of the rocky opening, loosing both appendages from their claw grip on the stone, stretching down toward her.

Simsa wavered to her feet. Her body still felt as if she had suffered a perilous illness. This ledge led no place and it would seem she really had no choice now. That she could once more make the inanimate obey her command, fashion a bridge, she doubted completely. The Elder One had withdrawn to her own place for now, only Simsa of the Burrows was here.

She looked at those claws which moved slightly, thinking of them curved about her wrists, choosing to tighten—to cut—Yet that instinct of awareness of danger which had been her shield so often in the depths under Kuxortal did not come to life now:

Simsa somehow knotted the cloak to hold about her waist, then planted herself facing the wall, outward from the overhang. Drawing a deep breath, she thrust the cloak's edge between her lips and bit down fiercely on it. That she dared not lose. Then she extended her arms and hands as far as she could upward.

Zass had left her shoulder and was up there again with the alien. Simsa both saw and felt those claws close about her wrists, even as she had half-feared that they would.

4

She was wafted aloft as easily as if she wore one of those gravity-nullifying cubes Thorn had used during their exploration of the forgotten city in which she had found her other self. But this wafting was by no machine—rather, through the strength of the rock dweller who slipped back into the shadowed window hole even as Simsa was drawn upward so that when the grip was released, she stood on her own two feet inside a dusky hollow. There was a faint light which issued not from any crack in the rock walls now closing about her, but from the body of the creature who had brought her here.

It stood taller than she—perhaps able to match height with the untrustworthy officer on the spacer. There appeared to be no neck. The round ball of the head, with the still clicking mandibles and the huge eyes, sat directly on its rounded upper torso. That was a well-stuffed oval of the plush fur connected to the lower portion of the thing's body by an overly narrow waist. The lower portion of the body was nearly twice the length of the upper and banded across the fur by stripes of a darker shade. The hind legs were the most strange of all. They were very long and powerful and, when the alien squatted back on the middle joints of the appendages, they reached above that thin waist. Like the upper "arms," these bore no masking fur, only two rows of spikes erect and as menacing-looking as the claws which scratched the floor when it moved a fraction. The bottom of the lower portion of the body also touched the floor, apparently giving the stranger balance.

Zass had been flying in circles; now the zorsal settled down once again on Simsa's shoulder, claws digging painfully into the girl's skin. Bending her head closer, Zass rubbed cheek with Simsa.

"What do you?"

An abrupt question delivered with a sense of impatience. The girl looked around at the zorsal and then at the waiting monstrosity. It was plain that they could communicate after a fashion, but only through the aid of Zass. For when she tried with all her might to center thought toward the waiting stranger, Simsa received nothing in return but a sickening, whirling sensation which made her close her eyes for a moment and hold on tightly to that which was real—that she stood here with Zass and that—that—thing and was not tossing elsewhere in a place that had no safe anchor.

"I run," she returned, simply because she felt that only the absolute truth was possible with this one. Zass could pick her thought out from her words, or her head, but enough of the old Simsa remained that she must speak aloud in order to hold on to reality at all.

"What runs behind?" At least the answering message relayed through the zorsal was logical.

What did run, in truth? Perhaps the officer from the ship she had fled, perhaps another of his humanoid species. But mainly, Simsa knew at that moment, she ran not from any person or living thing, but because of her own fear—her own determination that she would remain free within as well as without herself.

She could never free herself now from the Elder One. That she had faced and admitted. At first, she had been welcoming, aflame that she had found something, a part of her that had been lacking all her life and that she must have. Then she had realized that, to this new inner dweller, there must follow a surrender of that other Simsa whom she knew the better. Free? Inner freedom she could not control, but freedom without she could.

"I do not know." Again it was the truth which that other drew from her.

There was no expression readable to human eyes on the big-eyed round of the greenish furred face. She would not try again to reach the other by straight thought. However, she did aim a question of her own, determined somehow to keep a kind of parity with the alien, not to be as a small child answering questions of an Elder.

"Who are you?" She tried to make that emphatic, hardly knowing how it might reach the other through the filter of the zorsal's skittery thoughts.

"Fear."

For a long startled moment, Simsa thought that that other had also answered simply and with a threat. Then the rest of it, fading in mind touch but still understandable, came through:

"You fear—" It would seem that the other was simply going to ignore Simsa's demand. "There is a right to fear—"

Again, Simsa was startled, this time into jerking back a space and throwing out the hand that held the rod as a barrier against a wriggling blot struggling freely in space before her.

One of the sand swimmers in all its slimy ugliness, so real that she was almost certain she could touch and feel the soft pulpy body. Then, as instantly as it had made its appearance, it winked out. Hallucinations! Even as the sand swimmer itself had used that talent against her.

"You fear—" Again the words squeezed past her amazement to deliver their message.

No yellow blob this time. There was—the figure was not as clear cut or as well-materialized—perhaps it was too strange and alien to this other that it could not be fashioned sharply. But nonetheless she looked at a ship's officer.

"It is strange." That was conveyed to her although the thoughts coming through the zorsal had no expression of bewilderment. "This one—your kind?"

Simsa shook her head vigorously. "No kin." How that definition would fare in Zass's receptive thought she could not tell. The zorsals were mainly loners after they reached their second year, their mating being a hurried affair, immediately after which they separated, one sex from the other.

The tenuous form of the space officer did not blink out so quickly. It might be that the alien was either trying to refine it into better detail or was comparing it closely with Simsa to refute her own quick denial that it was like herself.

"What do you?" The first question of all was repeated.

Simsa took a deep breath. She would be guessing, but she believed that this creature wanted from her a deeper reason for her flight—for her fear—not just what had set her wandering across the stone-clad landscape.

"I have—power." She cupped both hands about the rod of her power staff and held it a little out from her body. "He—wants that power."

The light that came from the alien body flared as much as if it held one of the lights Thorn had carried months ago, much plainer and sharper than a torch.

And, in answer, for she had certainly not called upon any of the skill of the Elder One, the moon horns, the sun set between them, flashed into life also, giving off a radiance that warmed Simsa's body where it reflected that gleam from her black skin. Once more, she felt her hair stir and guessed the ends of it were rising. But this time, there was no feeling of being drained. No, she was pulling strength from without, not from depths within her.

The glow of the alien's body faded into a faint sheen, almost flickered. Now the life in the rod was withdrawing also, still not outward but inward so that she no longer felt any lack in her body. Simsa might have eaten well, drunk deep, slept soft. She was completely restored in her inner strength.

"You—have—the not-haze—" Zorsal folded her wings, shifting from one foot to the other on Simsa's shoulder. The girl was not sure what was meant by that. Then one of the long spined "arms" moved at the center point, flailing forward, the claw at the end indicating without any mistake the rod.

Simsa clutched her treasure a little tighter. Was the alien striving to take her one weapon? But the claws did not quite touch the horned disc at the end, only held so for a few breaths, as if the creature were in some odd way measuring it. The joint creaked again and once more the long arm folded back as might that of an insect of her own home world.

The creature hitched around somewhat awkwardly, using that pointed end of its abdomen as a pivot. It did not turn its head to look at her again, but the order came clear enough from Zass:

"Come!"

The front appendages dropped to floor level and the back ones moved apart, giving the alien a strange likeness to an animal keeping its head down to sniff out a trail. The upstanding antennae smoothed backward, their tips well down on the wearer's back. The alien no longer moved jerkily, even though its posture made it appear so, and it moved rather swiftly. Simsa, lingering only to gird up the folds of the cloak knotted about her middle, had to trot in order to keep up.

There was no light except that subdued lumination that came from the large furred body before her. They had entered a tunnel through the rock, smooth of wall and floor, slanting downward after a few more swift strides, so that Simsa had to move with caution for fear of a stumble, the clawed feet of her guide apparently finding this surface less slick than it looked to the girl.

At spaced intervals, there were other openings, but, though she peered into each as they passed, Simsa could see nothing. Therein the darkness was complete.

The gradual curve of the descending way became steeper and Simsa tried to find, first on one wall and then the other, some manner of handhold to which she might cling if she slipped. She was about to appeal to her guide when she was aware of a splotch of brighter radiance on the floor. Before she could step aside, her foot pressed a thick stuff which clung, even when she stepped, almost leaped, ahead.

When she planted the light-smeared foot again, she found that her skin clung to the stone and steadied her, yet it yielded easily enough when she would move forward. Then she noted that a second large drop oozed from the thick body before her. For a moment, she was revolted and would have tried to wipe the first coating from her foot with an edge of the cloak, but then, as if Zass had told her, she knew that this was not waste from the body ahead, but a gift meant to aid her.

Sure enough, as the creature deposited a third and final discharge, it turned and thrust its foreclaws deep into the mass, drawing them forth brightly shining. Then it flung these out to both walls, where they caught and held. The alien doubled its body in upon itself as if it were deliberately striving to break its own narrow waist, to bring chest and abdomen together, then hurled itself forward, the clawed forearms outheld to catch at something ahead.

A few steps farther on, the floor vanished in a great hole as dark as any of the doorways they had passed. Simsa gasped. The rock dweller had swung across with the ease of one long accustomed to such feats, but she could not follow.

Or—could she?

Light blazed up beyond and she saw the alien waiting at the far edge of that trap. That increase of light displayed to Simsa against the left wall a ledge, so narrow that only if one turned one's head against the rock and squeezed along its surface could one pass that way.

The girl made sure that her cloak was knotted as securely as possible with the power rod in its fold still pressing warmly against her flesh. She studied the toehold path, liking nothing she could see of it, before taking a first cautious step forward. Perhaps it would have been easier to face the wall and not the abyss as she made her hesitant way onward. Except that a stubborn core of the Burrows Simsa was determined to look at danger in all its blackness, not to turn her back upon it.

She had no way of telling how deep that hole was. It appeared utterly black. The alien and Zass, who had already winged to the other side, were quiet; thus the dark was also silent except for her own breathing, which was in time with the fast beating of her heart.

That black hole so near her feet seemed to have a power of drawing her, so that she scrambled with outstretched arms on either side trying to find some hold, no matter how tiny, to sustain her. Thus she inched along. She was near enough to the far side where her two companions waited to feel the beginning of relief when the silence was broken by a sound. As if in the depths of that blackness something stirred—perhaps a creature winged as Zass but greater in size, beating those wings, about to take to the air.

Zass responded with a squawk that Simsa readily identified. It was not surprise—rather fear. Yet the zorsal did not fly away, but, on the floor of the farther side of the hole, jigged from one foot to the other, its mouth a little open, still uttering no sound. The alien creature which had been her guide this far raised one of those long jointed arms in a quick beckoning gesture, urging the girl to hurry. Simsa, her head snapping around so that she faced that well of darkness and what might move in its depths, slipped along one foot and then the other. The anchoring substance that the creature had exuded was wearing thin. She was losing her sense of being firmly rooted each time she put her weight fully on one leg so that she might either extend the other or draw it to her. Below, that sound grew louder. She could imagine wings stepping up action—some grotesque horror about to climb the air—for there was a distinct upper-reaching current from the hole.

Two more steps—

Zass gave tongue at last, a screech that meant defiant warning. The black in the hole appeared to possess more density, but the girl could not be sure whether she saw with her eyes or in a picture raised by fear to unnerve her just as she was so close to steady footing. Certainly there was movement from below, and she could see a kind of circling in the dark which was not unlike the whirling of the sand stream when those horrors that dwelt within it were minded to seek the world beyond.

She clamped her teeth hard, refusing to be panicked into a misstep now to carry her down into—that!

One step. She brought up her eyes, refusing now to watch. The movement of dark within dark reached her as a sick giddiness. Instead, she forced her head around again and eyed the goal toward which she edged.

Out of the hole arose what looked like the spray of a fountain. Was it liquid or a reddish light formed of so many brilliant sparks that it could well seem a liquid? Against all her determined will,

Simsa's attention was drawn to it. Like the whirling of the dark that appeared to give it birth, it caught and held the eyes—drew—

Pain, so sharp, so intense that Simsa could not suppress a choking cry following upon its first throb. On her bare right arm was a wink of light, a drop, a spark, of that which was playing higher and higher, spreading out farther and farther to encompass the whole of the dark well.

She caught her breath in a second sob and, with one of the greatest efforts she had ever made, tore her gaze from the enchantment of that fountain and took the final step which brought her to the safety of the tunnel floor. But she slipped and began to topple back into the column of silver-red flame.

Once more, those claws locked on her flesh, this time on one shoulder, sliding her along the floor, her flesh scraped raw by the harsh stone. On her arm that spark still lived and ate into her flesh viciously.

Beside her on one side squatted Zass, her wings fanning, uttering small mewling cries of distress. On her left settled the ponderous green body. The claw passed from her shoulder to the wrist of her painful arm. That was drawn upward even as the alien crouched yet lower. Then the girl felt the scraping of those mandibles across her skin and she shuddered in spite of the pain that already bit into her. That touch repelled her as much as if one of the tentacles of a river dweller had grasped her. A liquid flooded the place where the spark clung and drops of a strong-smelling gel ran sluggishly down her forearm from the point of claw contact.

The angry fire in the spark was quenched, though Simsa felt still an ache such as a bad bruise might well leave. The claw grasp loosened and Simsa swiftly withdrew her arm. Although this touch had been for her benefit, and she had no doubt of that, still the contact had brought distaste, even nausea.

She had no trouble seeing that the alien had left a gob of gel over the wound and that it was hardening, for she could feel the pull of it on her skin. Again the long, furless, doubled-jointed arm swung out, but not this time to grasp any part of her; rather, it struck her almost with the force of a blow, pushing her farther from the spouting fountain, on down this new portion of the corridor.

For a moment, she sprawled from the vigor of that shove and then she raised from all fours to her feet and came halfway around. Zass, with a second croaking call, took to the air while the inhabitant of these ways, again on all fours, butted the side of its head against Simsa, sending the girl on. She received a fleeting message, far less clear than the others, yet warning enough.

What wrought now within the well could not yet be through with them, not if they lingered near that fiery fountain. Simsa began to run. Her large companion, for all the awkwardness of its person, moved with a swift glide that took it to the fore until, with an appearance of exasperation it snapped out, its mandibles catching the untidy ends of Simsa's cloak. There they held with the fierce might of a metal trap so that the girl was drawn along at a speed to set her gasping.

They rounded a twisting turn in the tunnel and Simsa near lost her footing at that sharp pull which started her in another direction. Having left the light that the well fountain had given them when it streamed, Simsa could see only dark walls a little away as they passed, and those because of the emanation of the huge body beside her. There were more openings which they passed at racing speed, a second turn, and then ahead was light bright enough so that, even at this distance, it made Simsa blink. For the first time since she had begun her journey past the well, she became aware of the warmth of the rod against her body.

That this thing of power had faded completely out of her mind during her escape from the fountain-thing broke in her thoughts as an unanswerable puzzle. Simsa of the Burrows had begun to believe the rod had no limits. Even the Elder One had not roused in her when the pain in her body had come as a warning. The intrusion of the Elder One into her mind, which she generally half-resented, now completely surprised and frightened her by its absence. Simsa of the Burrows, the girl knew then, had been uppermost during that encounter. She had, from the first moment of finding her likeness and opening herself to that inanimate material which had held for so long, come to depend more and more upon the Elder One—to believe that she was invincible, to resent the knowledge held by her. Now this. Where was the Elder One and why?

The alien bore her steadily along toward the distant light and they emerged from the tunnel into a place so utterly different from the barren rock of this world that Simsa was astounded and could only stare and wonder.

This was not a desert land. If the great basin or hollow was indeed floored with rock, there was no sign of it. Growths certainly large enough to be termed trees were set in ordered rows, an opening—a path—between their ranks directly before the three from the tunnel. The boles were not too large; Simsa could probably have clasped arms about the nearest and interlocked fingers on the far side. In color they were a smooth bluish green, lacking the roughness of bark. But at a height to clear the round head of the alien, who now rose to sit as it had when it first confronted the girl, they branched thickly with fine stems which bore long ribbon leaves of blue, rippling continually, though Simsa could feel no hint of any breeze.

Behind these guardians of the path were masses of shorter foliage changing in color from a deep true blue, through green, to yellow. And those, too, rustled and trembled as if they provided hiding places for all manner of would-be ambushers. Zass gave a cry of triumph, soaring up and out to fly above the trees in the manner of her kind, and when Simsa's eyes followed her, she saw an oddity about the sky. That haze that had prevailed over the rock land looked much thicker here, though more luminous, and the stifling heat of the outer world was tempered by many degrees.

The tree-guarded path ran straight and even on it, there was no hint of rock or sand, but rather a thick growth of what appeared to be very short-stemmed, thickly packed vegetation in patches of color, some yellow, some green, some blue, and here and there a showing of silver white. The farther the path ran, the taller grew the guardian trees. But those were not high enough to hide what was at the end of the way.

Like unto the rocky upcrops that walled in this oasis of vegetation, there stood a structure: a square cube of blue which shaded to green at its crest. And its green crest was patterned with evenly spaced windows or entrances open to the air with no suggestion of any barriers in the form of doors. Appearing at some of these were creatures that so well-matched the one accompanying the girl that they could have been cloned. These took off from the openings in easy leaps, propelled by their heavy back legs. They might have been diving down into the mass of growth below them like swimmers entering a sea. Once they were swallowed up by the reach of tree and bush, they vanished completely from sight. None of them had appeared to notice the three who had come out of the dark rock ways.

Zass wheeled and turned, coming back to settle on Simsa's shoulder, rubbing her furred head against the girl's cheek.

"It is the place." The alien accented the explanation beamed through the zorsal by a jerky movement of a clawed forelimb.

"The place? What place?" Since that compelling hold had been lifted from her, Simsa had made no attempt to go farther into the open, to step upon the plant carpet of the road.

"The place of the nest." Zass's thought had, the girl decided, an impatient twinge, some emotion of the alien carried through. Perhaps to their guide this was like Kuxortal, so well-known a landmark that the whole world should recognize it.

Having so answered her, the big green creature dropped once more to four feet and scuttled on. Nor did it look back when Simsa made no attempt to follow. She was curious, yes, but her caution had been triggered by the inhabitant of the sand stream, by the well, and certainly by the alien itself. That wariness which had served her so well as a nameless, kinless one in the Burrows came to the fore. Thus she deliberately squatted down on her heels, narrowly surveying all that lay before her. The one who had brought her here appeared to have forgotten her entirely, and suddenly pushed with force between two of the tree trunks into the deep curtain of the foliage and was gone.

Simsa absently rubbed the fountain wound, where soreness still made itself felt. Under the touch of her fingers the jellied stuff stripped away and she looked down to see there was not even the thin line of any hurt. On impulse, she took up the rod in her two hands clasped together and let its head sway forward so that the horn of the moon pointed toward that building. There was no more coming or going at the high windows. It might have been deserted long since.

Without any willing or conscious movement on her part, the rod began to move. She stiffened her grasp, fighting to keep it still, and discovered that all her strength was not enough to bring it into the same position. The horns were above, they were below—they were this side and that—but Simsa, for all her trying, could not hold them in a line with the green-crested block.

She let the rod drop to her knees to think this out. The rod could draw upon power—it could transmit also the power within her. It was a weapon as well as a warning shield. Therefore—she attempted to reason carefully and coolly (as she would have done having found some mysterious thing buried back in the Burrows, something that would be worth much if she could only solve its purpose)—therefore, perhaps there was a defense here. But why? Was it—Simsa sat up straighter and her lips parted a little, her heart beat faster—was it that such as the Elder One had been known here in long-ago times and that, thus, there had been good reason for the indwellers to learn how to withstand the power that Simsa could call upon?

Elder One—her thought was as sharp as a call—Elder One! Though she strove to throw down every defense, there came no answer this time. She was still the lesser—the Simsa of the Burrows, for all her rod and her jeweled trappings. She was—alone!

 **5**

It was the needs of that third part of her, her body, that broke through Simsa's absorption. Hunger and thirst at last overcame such reviving effects as the rod had provided. She surveyed the vegetation now with more than just an interest in the fact that it existed at all. Searching the pocket within her cloak, she found a half-packet of survival wafers—thin and tasteless stuff, meant to contain in the smallest possible portions enough nourishment to keep a humanoid alive and moving. There was no more of the precious water, only a soaked area about the flask in the cloak to betray its loss.

Though Simsa in this lifetime had never before been off her home world, she well knew from warnings aboard the ship and from the stories of the space crew that, fair as a new planet might be, any of its liquids or natural food might also act as swift poison for the off-worlder.

She held a half-wafer in her hand and it crumbled yet more in this aridity. To attempt to eat that was to choke on dry crumbs. All this growth below argued that it must draw upon real water—and surely not some stream of moving sand.

She was aware that Zass had dropped out of sight, gone questing lower in the brush behind the trees. Hunger and thirst—answers to those were more important now for her continued existence, than thought-searching for a second self. Surely, the Elder One had never been bound to one world in her own time—Simsa had too often caught hints of a wide-roving life before that one had chosen to wait in her own way for deliverance by a far descended female of her blood.

Simsa's lips quirked in a half-smile. Let the Elder One sulk or haughtily withdraw. But somehow, she was sure that were she to make some wrong choice, to endanger her body, there would be a speedy warning. This was a part of their unwilling partnership that she had never put to the test before.

Under her feet, the splotches of mosslike vegetation that carpeted the roadway gave forth a sharp scent, but not an unpleasing one. The odor certainly had none of the rankness of the Burrows' ways, nor any warning stench such as the sand river had given. She walked forward with an outward air of confidence which she held to as she would have held the cloak had it been cooler here. As she turned her head from side to side, striving to pierce the wall of thick growth that twined and matted behind the tree columns, she could see no possible opening, no hint of any fruit or berry ripening there, certainly no sound or scent of water.

Into her mind thrust the raw triumph of Zass. Somewhere in that maze, the zorsal must have made a kill, for only freshly slain prey could bring that particular involuntary instant of communication. Zass had killed, but what and where there was no answer. And, if the zorsal feasted on some form of life subject to the aliens—perhaps so much the worse for both of them.

Firmly, she pushed the new stab of fear to one side. She had come close enough to the cube building to see that the only openings at all, on this side at least, were those at the edge of the roof. Between the ground and those was only a smooth wall. Perhaps the aliens, with their own sticky body fluids, could make such a climb with ease, but there was no such opportunity for her.

Simsa stood for a long moment, her head held high, her nostrils expanded to their full extent, as she turned very slowly about, testing each possible way. There were odors in plenty—none of them obnoxious, some close to the perfume of flowers. Then—water!

She had heard that certain off-worlders could not scent water, though all of the lesser life-forms could. Evil-smelling as the

Burrows were, one must, for very life's sake, cultivate an inward listing of odors in defense. There was water, not of the sea as it might have been back on Kuxortal, but rather stream clear—in that direction!

There was also no opening in the brush and she could not soar above its curtain in Zass's way. Simsa worked with her blanket cloak—there were thorns on brush stems, she had seen that from the first. What protection she could give herself she would. She had already frayed and pulled a hole in the middle, now she let her head slip through and the other folds she draped about her, flipping the ends up to cover her arms.

Then, rod in hand as a tool to hold back the entangling sprays of leaf-covered vine or branch, she advanced into that wilderness. As she took her first steps, trying to hold aside what was too thorny to break and throw from her path, Simsa was at once aware of the rustling which was brought about by no wind. Only the branches and leaves were aflutter, the disturbance directly before her. It was as if these rooted plants and trees were communicating one with the other, resenting her coming, urging each other to a stiffer defense.

With her cloak covering held by a thicket of thorn branches, Simsa was brought to a halt. One such swinging stem, as thick as her forefinger, looped down before she could dodge and caught in her hair, its movement not concluded until the silver strands were well-entangled. Now she could not even move her head without an answer of sharp pain from her scalp. She had seen insects so captured by sticky cords produced and woven by creatures much smaller than their prey. Only here it was the vegetation to which she was prisoner.

Sharp pain in one cheek followed the flailing of another thorned tip and her cloak, which she had planned as protection, became her downfall. Something seized its folds so tightly that even were her hair unentangled, she could not have slipped free. The girl pursed her lips and whistled. Zass had found prey, she must have escaped this trap, therefore—

Only, before she heard any flapping of wings, there came again that sound which had saved her in the rock desert. The mist over this basin valley—she could only see a fragmented portion of it, her head held as it was now—was thicker than the haze above the desert. Not even a shadow showed through its padding of what should be open sky. Yet above that, sounding very near now, came the throb of a flitter's passage. Nor was it only bound across the valley . . . Simsa thought that from the continued sound it was circling.

Persona signals—from the first, she had thought that perhaps without her knowledge, she might be carrying a direction clue for hunters. To her, many of the machines of the space people approached magic. And always it was machines that served them so. During her imprisonment on the ship, she might well have been subjected to a scanning, some strange and terrifying treatment that imprinted her scent, her person, the cast of her thinking mind, upon one of those machines.

One thing for this moment was more important than a possible captor out of sight above. The branches that had so efficiently captured her became motionless at the first sound of that off-world ship. A moment later, they went into quick and painful action. She was literally dragged forward; the clutches in her snarled hair used to pull her were enough to bring tears of pain to her eyes. Though she tried hard to free herself, flailing about with the rod, that action won her nothing but bleeding scratches, some of them so deep as to be close to wounds.

She could not see how those clutches on her hair and her body were transferred from one bush to the next, but somehow that happened. She was sure that bits of her hair, together with her scalp, were left behind. Blood dripped down her face. She could taste it as it touched her lips. Still the bush tore as one growth sent her stumbling to the next. Their rustling was a buzzing in her ears which seemed even to go deeper—into her very head, stirring her thoughts into wild panic.

Attack from creatures one could understand, but to have plants rise up against one was a kind of madness. Inside she cowered and tried hard to fight her fear. Then she was whirled, gasping, bloodied by scratches, half-deafened by the rustling, into an open space. Open as to the ground, but here were trees in a circle. Their branches met and interlaced over her head so that she could no longer view the haze. Though still, now that she was free of the side growth, she heard the flitter—the beat of its return growing louder as it seemed to head for the space just above the trees now roofing her in.

Simsa tripped and fell, the last of the brush having handled her so fiercely, and hit hard against stone. However, this was not the rock of the outer desert lands, rather a coarse gravel which skinned and pocked her knees and the palms of her hands. It was of a bright orange color and it helped to make a setting for what was undoubtedly a pool.

There was also the play of a fountain—though not one of fiery particles such as had arisen in the well of the tunnel. Rather, this leapt and then cascaded back into a wide, shallow basin, the heart of which was carved stone in the form of three loops, the center one footed between the sides of the other and wider two. Around the basin came a pattering of smaller feet on the loose gravel and Simsa faced her errant zorsal, who, by the dampness of her fur, had been sporting in the water.

Simsa crawled to the pool side to plunge both of her scratched and smarting arms into the liquid. It had not the clarity she associated with the water she knew, being faintly green, but the scent!

She cupped her hands and scooped up what she could, to drink and drink again. This water, if water it was, tasted like the potent wine old Ferwar had kept jealously for her own comfort on the wet and cold days of the leafless season. It was strength itself as she swallowed and felt it within her throat, somehow both comfortingly warm and refreshingly cool. Before she drank for the third time, she bathed her face. Those scratches burned with renewed fire for only an instant or two, and then the pain was gone and she could see in her reflection that even the most wicked of those tears in her skin appeared to have closed. Such comfort she had been able in the past to summon—or the Elder One had done—from the rod. Here, where nature was cruel, there seemed to be other kindness.

She was still bathing her throat and shoulders when the same brush that had used her so badly swung all to one side, without any forcing pull that Simsa could detect. Through the opening so made there came the alien, or an alien. At least it resembled to the last hair of its antennae, as far as she could detect, the one who had brought her here.

The creature halted beyond the edge of the basin, facing her across the play of the water. Zass, who had been paddling with both front paws in the fountain spray, gave a leap and flutter of wings to reach Simsa's shoulder.

"These . . . are your hunters?" The alien did not glance upward at the sound's source, which at that moment seemed directly overhead. "Or have you called them?"

The words dropped clear and cold from Zass's thought to hers. Simsa believed there was an aura of menace about them. Words could deceive if the one who uttered them was clever enough, but thoughts . . . If they could only speak directly without the shifting through the zorsal!

Moved by some inner push that Simsa had no time to explore, she sat cross-legged on the gravel and thrust the smooth end of her rod into the loose stuff. When it was rooted firmly, she slid her fingers up, tilting the tips of the horns in the direction of the other, and, not now beaming directly to the zorsal as she had before, she began to present what she wanted to communicate as shortly and clearly as possible—pausing now and then to try and order her thoughts.

Her reason for escape from the spaceship, with no choice of a landing save such as the equipment of the Life Boat offered, her travel across the waste of rock, the battle with the sand-stream horrors—

As she marshaled all these into proper sequence, she strove to picture in her mind those actions and beliefs that were concrete, together with the nebulous things that were her own guesses, colored by her emotions. After all, she had no suspicion of that space officer, of the medic, that she could prove true. Though she herself was convinced that the fear that drove her from the galactic voyaging ship had very real roots.

If she were reaching the alien in this way, and not through Zass, she had no evidence of success. But she was startled out of her concentration when she saw issuing from the brush and coming into the clearing of the fountain more of the green-furred creatures—at first glance complete duplicates of the one who had brought her into the valley. Their great faceted eyes centered on her and they squatted down, their large knees near up to the level of their heads—a silent and, to her, a disturbing circle, so that now her thought stream faltered and she held to sending by all the force her will could summon.

It was completely silent. Even Zass huddled down voiceless—quiet except for the buzz of the searcher in the air, whose passing sound grew stronger, then faded in a regular pattern. The flitterer must be circling, that circle growing the tighter with each passage.

Remembering what she had seen of the valley from the mouth of the tunnel, Simsa believed there was no cleared space wide enough to let the other-world carrier ground. Why did it remain above? Perhaps it was broadcasting directions for search to a party on foot.

"What have you that these want?" That demand was sharp and clear, and it had not come through Zass. She—or rather this other—had made contact at last directly with her.

"It is what I am." Simsa stirred. The rod was warming in her hand. The Elder One who had withdrawn, leaving her alone as she had always been to fight this battle; surely she awoke again. Even more slowly and with greater effort, Simsa launched into the time before she had been escorted aboard the spaceship ("honored guest" they had been too quick to tell her, but her senses, honed to a fine edge in the always perilous Burrows, had answered "captive").

Was this big-eyed nonhumanoid really able to catch and understand her tale? How much contact had this barren world ever had with spacecraft and those who flew from world to world? Might the whole concept be wild fancy in their minds?

There flashed into her thoughts now not the pictures she had been fumbling with, trying to build, but something else—a holding to her conceptions she did not understand at all. No! Simsa of the Burrows screamed noiselessly. She was being fast pushed into an impotent captivity once more. Each time the Elder One returned was with stronger hold, more in control. Simsa shook her head from side to side as if she were threatened by a winged creature flying for her eyes, her mouth, to attack. Only the attack was in her head—not without—and she could not so loosen the will of that other.

The flicker of truly alien thought was like a flashing light shone brutally into her eyes. She thought she saw fragments of strange pictures. Buildings stood and were gone in an instant; shapes that moved and might be either intelligent beings or threatening animals rose and vanished in the space of a breath. It was like listening to a speech one should be able to understand but was spoken so swiftly that thought could not translate word.

Now the rod was bending in her hands, making her battle for mastery over a length of metal. Only for a fraction out of time could she put up a show of defiance. Then her hands no longer obeyed her. The rod was inverted so that the points of the horns touched, bit into the gravel. Her fingers were under the control of that other one and with their support the horns dipped, pushed away, came back—swung to this side and that.

There were loose markings in the gravel now, half-seen patterns. Then five of the aliens were leaning forward, their eyes no longer holding Simsa's gaze but fast upon that which the horn left as it moved. Also she could read that message, almost—though it caused sharp pain between her eyes when she attempted to hold those lines in sight and think of them.

Then—there was no trouble at all. What the rod of power had so drawn was a symbol of power, one from the far, far past. It was a mark of identity, a request for aid, a warning. Each small, stark line could have more than one meaning, and some such she could only inscribe because time beyond time had always made them so.

One of the aliens, not the one who Simsa believed had been her guide, moved around the edge of the fountain to squat opposite the girl, studying the lines. A hand claw swung out to alter two rays of the pattern in a modifying way. Then mouth mandibles sent up a loud clicking and two of the others thrust back into the brush and were gone.

The one who had recognized the pattern now began to gesture with its claws, opening them to their greatest extent, bringing them together with a rattling snap. Dimly Simsa recognized a rhythm in that crackle of horn-covered flesh. Not speech, something else, more powerful than words. Perhaps even a weapon.

She who was now in command of the girl's body brought the rod back so that the horns touched her breasts. Through her body began a humming vibration which rose steadily until Simsa of the Burrows knew fear. Something had awakened in her to answer the claw-clicking. Humming linked with click. No, that vibration, she knew now, was not aimed at her body. It was fortifying whatever powers had been loosened and—waited.

Part of her answered the click and hum, but another bit of her, Simsa of the Burrows loosed for this duty alone, listened for another sound—the buzz of the off-world flyer. Surely it was louder again!

The clicking claws moved faster and faster, advanced out over the pattern. In her own grasp the horned rod dropped forward, once more pointing at that stretch of earth on which that design had been set.

And—the earth began to move. Even as the sand had fountained up to emit the many legged horror of the stream, so did an ever-lengthening rope of the gravel arise, thicken, take on solid form. It spiraled up and up, although Simsa could not raise her head to watch it. That other held her solidly prisoner, eyes upon the rooting of that column in the pattern.

All the lines of the pattern had now disappeared, disturbed, pulled into the being that was growing. Toward the pillar flashed water from the basin, combining with the earth and gravel, licking quickly up and around, binding the other into a truly solid shape—not unlike the tentacle of a sand beast, yet already far beyond such in length of reach.

The alien had shoved back from the column, which drew more and more of the earth's substance into it. Simsa followed, rising to her feet. That spinning length was thicker than any of the trees about them and still it grew, faster to reach above, but always adding to its girth as it went.

The color was changing now. Having pulled the gray-brown gravel into it, it was adding to its substance earth from below that covering, and to that dull brown were streaming torn leaves from the brush, longer ones from the trees. Still it spun as now there came from its core a growl which deepened as the reaching spout became thicker and taller.

Zass was on Simsa's shoulder, her talons clamped tight as if she feared that she also would go flying to make a part of that force-born column. The roar reached into Simsa even as the hum, the clatter of the claws had done earlier. She could no longer see the alien or the others who had been there. The solid stem of the growth cut them off.

There was a last high note of protest, perhaps the earth of the valley crying against the loss of its covering. Then the column whirled loose from its rooting, spiraled up as straight as a well-cast spear into the air.

Simsa discovered now that she could watch it going, her head well back. The tip of it had already vanished into the haze, the rest and thicker part of it fast following. And the sound it still made was the roar of a storm-born tempest. Out and out—

The Elder One was too exhausted by whatever had been wrought here to hold her other self longer in check. Though the girl had no idea what had been done, yet she found herself listening with some eagerness for the sound of the flitter, if such could ever break through the whoop of the storm wind.

What had they wrought? A thickening of the natural roofing over the valley rendering it even more opaque? Or something else?

She could see no difference in the haze. Instead, there grew in her a certainty that what had been born here was no defense, but a weapon aimed at those who searched. Sturdy as a flitter was, there could be danger from wind, sand, a whirlpool in the air.

Simsa's teeth closed upon her lower lip. Had she not wanted escape? Could she, with her so small influence over what—or who— dwelt in her, dictate what kind of escape? Yet she shuddered now, and not from the demands of the power. She could see, impressed against the veiling of haze, a picture that might be all too true: a small craft caught in the fury of earth and air, crushed, downed, buried even as it fell, and with it humanoids, perhaps not kin, yet—

Thorn—his face flashed over the scene of the struggling, doomed ship. They had stood shoulder to shoulder once. If he had not delivered her into the hands of those others with their ever-demanding quest for knowledge, if he had foreseen . . . She was not certain, she had never been, in truth, that he had betrayed her knowingly—only without thought, because to him she was a treasure. Thorn—

The smooth-faced off-worlder about whom she had built up so much resentment, had dismissed as useless in her own struggle for freedom from the system he had been so eager to serve—she could see him now.

She could see him now!

There was only that face on the underside of the haze through which the swirling pillar had completely disappeared. But she could see Thorn. His eyes, set obliquely in a face where the flesh was so much lighter than her own, were closed. The mouth which had been always so firmly held was gaping a little, and from the gape ran a dark trickle. There was no life in that face.

Thorn dead? To the Elder One, his vanishing had meant little, but this Simsa had always clung to the hope that if she could reach Thorn, in some manner he could point a way to her freedom—even though he might have thoughtlessly betrayed her in the beginning.

She stared as one confronted by such a horror as moved in the sand rivers. Then she broke—through the tight control of the Elder One, through whatever bonds that other and the alien had woven to do what they had done. If it had been Thorn in that flitter, and that other part of her had killed him . . .

She did not care if the whole of an off-world ship had been blasted into nothingness—but Thorn was a different matter.

"Zass!" The zorsal might not understand her words, though she had always answered to her name. "Thorn! Seek!" And to the words she added the imperative mental command that could arouse the creature to action.

With a spring into the air, Zass took off, her skin-covered wings beating as she followed the whirling weapon of gravel up toward the haze—though she did not take the same path but rather headed out toward the north in a way that would lead her across the valley to the guarding cliffs. If Thorn was out there—Zass was a hunter with talents no humanoid could equal.

As the zorsal flew, Simsa thrust the rod back into her girdle. It was no longer warm against her flesh—the power was gone, perhaps exhausted by the work it had done. Just as the Elder One was once more lapsing into the quiet that covered her when Simsa of now was free. She spoke to the green aliens directly and with the vigor that anger gave her. Someday she would learn the key—how to use the Elder One's knowledge without losing also that other person. Now she must make the most of the time in which she was free to be herself.

"What—happens—to—the—flyer?" She spaced her words, speaking them slowly and emphatically as if so she might project their meaning without Zass's translation.

There was no movement, no change in the two who were still with her. She could have ceased to exist for them. Both of them stood erect, their bodies at an awkward angle so that their heads were turned up toward the haze. There was still the whining of the whirlwind, but it was dying. And no buzz of flitter broke through it.

Simsa caught up her cloak and stalked around the pool where the spray that had fed the pillar was once more but a small play of water. In spite of her distaste, she put out her hand and caught at the arm of the nearest of those watching. She gave a hard jerk and the tower of green fur near toppled on her, the faceted eyes dropped to meet hers.

"What has happened?" demanded the girl, determined that the other would neither shake her off nor longer ignore her.

6

Above opened one of those squared apertures of the blue bulk of the building. Once back at home—"nest"—her companion shook off Simsa's clutch as easily as though the horn-smooth covering of the slender upper appendage had been greased, twitching even the spikes easily through the girl's fingers. Paying no attention at all now to Simsa, the other began to climb the wall—up to that gaping mouth or entrance. Though from the outer rim of the valley, she had seen much going and coming from these apertures, now they appeared blank, deserted.

Simsa sought holds for her own hands, but, to her groping fingers, the surface was smooth. The claws of the valley's inhabitants were more useful here than fingers could be. Zass? She could recall the zorsal—but to what purpose?

She started to walk around the base of the huge cube. The vegetation wreathed it for a space until bushes and trees made up a walling. But no entrance on this level appeared.

Taking a deep breath of resolve, the girl called—not aloud with the whistle that was Zass's own summons, but more awkwardly with her mind, sending out a need for help. As she did so, she watched keenly the openings above. In none of those dark hollows did anything stir.

All right! So be it! She was left with only one chance—to return by the same underground way that had brought her here. Nor did she stop to wonder why this need drove her. There was safety here, of a sort, so why venture forth into the waterless rock world? Why?

Her hand smoothed the rod. This was what she had sought—freedom. The aliens had offered her no threat. They had indeed called upon the Elder One's skill to serve their own purpose. So well had they succeeded in that, that they might well look upon her as she looked upon Zass, a lesser life-form but a useful one.

If what they had summoned up had dealt with the flitter, as she guessed it must have, what should that matter to her? It only assured what she wanted—freedom from the off-worlders' avid curiosity, their desire to make of her a tool, one that she had no mind to be. Let well-enough alone—that had always been Ferwar's own saying, drilled into her fosterling from childhood.

There remained Thorn. They had fought as battle comrades, yes, but any debts between them had been canceled in full long ago. And it was Thorn, was it not, who had drawn the attention of those beyond space to her own existence? She owed him nothing at all.

At the same time, Simsa assured herself vigorously that this was so, she swung around to face the clear road leading under the arch of the trees back to the tunnel mouth. Nor could she battle into surrender that in her which led her from one hesitating stride to a fuller one in that direction.

She had filled her water carrier at the fountain after she had bathed her scratched face. Now she noted that there dropped from the walling trees fruit, deep blue in color. Saliva filled her mouth at the thought of food as she picked up one that had fallen close enough to brush against her shoulder. To eat of this might mean death. However, the water had not poisoned her, but rather revived her, and she must have food.

Simsa broke the ovoid apart as she would a survival wafer. A golden pulp burst forth to sticky her fingers. She licked, first cautiously and then greedily, before she spit out a reddish pit. Now she avidly harvested a goodly store of windfalls, tying them into a corner of her cloak, as she headed toward the tunnel.

Even as the rich flesh of the fruit slid down her throat, she was thinking of that back trail. There would be no luminous guide this time—she must take the road completely in the dark. What of the pit where the fire-thing leaped? Without any light she could well tumble into that unwarned. To edge along the narrow path to safety a second time . . . Simsa swallowed and swallowed again, the soft fruit all of a sudden too much to easily get down.

This was folly—the worst of folly! For a Burrows-bred fosterling to risk all for a stranger! Twice her steps slowed, the second time at the very edge of the tunnel. She paused there to look back over her shoulder, for she had half-hoped. But there was no stir at any of those openings. She was on her own. Was it because she wished to succor one of their enemies? Or could it be that they were very willing to have her no longer their concern—to see her dead in the barren land, perhaps, offering no threat to them at all?

Rubbing the fruit juice from her hands down the front of her cloak, Simsa took hold on the rod, facing into the dark of the tunnel way. She was using that thing of power as one blinded might use a cane tapping the way ahead.

She rounded the turn in the passage, half-expecting to see before her the glow of that flame which had awakened at their coming here. It remained thickly dark. The Burrows had often been without any lights, nor did those who laired within them depend upon torches or lamps too freely—most of their errands had been solitary hunts which they had no intention of sharing with others.

Now Simsa drew upon memory—not that of the Elder One (she wanted no loosing of barrier there), but on what she had learned in this time if not on this nameless world. Unconsciously, because the habit had long been engrained in her by training, she was counting off steps. So many to that trap, then so many along the toehold at its side.

One hand for the tapping of the rod against the tunnel floor, one to the side so her fingertips slid along the wall. She gasped when those suddenly met with nothing, then remembered those many dark niches or doors that had been spaced along the corridor. Her head up, she also used what gift of scent she had. There was a musty odor which she associated with the passage itself, interwoven with the faintest trace of a metallic effusion such as she had always connected with the various machines of the off-worlders.

She slowed, stopped to wrap the cloak the tighter about her, and then went to her hands and knees, creeping at hand-by-hand's length until her fingers met nothingness and she knew she had reached the pit.

Refusing to look down into the blackness lest she see that whirling which heralded the flame fountain, Simsa felt along the lip of the gap until she discovered that narrow ledge she had struggled across before. There was a stickiness which she stirred with thumb and forefinger, certainly the remains of that liquid emitted by the alien.

Simsa sat back on her heels. If she got across without arousing the danger below, if she found her way out onto the barren rocks, if . . . Her lips twisted and she spat several words well-known to Burrowers, blistering in their meaning. Why? Who told her that this must be done? It was not the Elder One, she was too well-aware of how that one could flash into command upon occasion. What set her to risk this? A vision on the haze of a man who was doubtless already dead? She was more than a fool—she was mind-twisted—and for the sake of her own kind, she should have been eliminated long ago, as was done to any lacking in sense and reasoning power.

Still, even as she lashed herself so, she was certain that she could not retreat. From Thorn, before those others had arrived at his call to take control, she had learned a great deal, not learning as the Elder One would measure it—though oddly enough in some things there were likenesses in acceptance of aid. Upon a strange world, when there was danger, off-worlders drew together—unless they were utterly mind-warped as had been those who had come to plunder on Kuxortal. She was no space-goer. And she had more to fear perhaps from off-worlders now than she had from the alien life. But it had been she, or a part of her, who had raised the thing she was sure had engulfed the flitter. And if Thorn had been aboard . . .

Simsa thumped her forehead with the palm of her hand. Thoughts, why must she deal with thoughts? If she could not justify what she did, not to herself—so be it. She only knew that it was as if she once more hung from the compelling claws of the alien. She had no choice against these invisible claws that had come into being when she had seen Thorn's face, perhaps his *dead* face, backed by the haze in the valley.

Hating what led her, but no longer fighting it for there was no use in such a struggle, the girl got to her feet to begin edging along that narrow strip of walkway, the pit at her back, teeth set hard against lip as she strove to move without a sound to betray her.

What if the thing could not hear, rather sensed? She did not look over her shoulder, but scraped along the rock so that its surface abraded the cheek she kept to it as she moved. Without even viewing it, Simsa was aware that once again, there was movement in the dark. Sweat ran down her face, smarted in the raw places on her skin. One step, another, this part of her memory was stubbornly blank. She had been too fearful before to reckon; now that same fear was rising in her like a smothering of her lungs, a choking in her throat.

On and on. In her own ears the beating of her heart was a drum for votive dancers, deep and calling, while breath came in shallow puffs. She would not linger. To stop moving was perhaps to anchor her immovably to await the torture of the spark fire to whip her down.

So far no light—she clung to the darkness, which now meant safety. Step, hold, bring the other foot along. Again. Again! Then she became aware of heat against her body. Even as the alien had a glow to light the way arising from her own frame, so did there arise radiance from the rod. Simsa could not spare the hand to tuck it farther out of sight. It was responding to power—to energy she could neither understand nor control.

She was certain, if she were able to look down, that that which lay in wait would respond. Step. Hold. Step. Sound now—a spitting such as might come from fat meat placed too close to a flame. Yes— there was brightness growing, not only between her body and the wall, but behind and below.

Light, enough to see!

Simsa hurled herself sidewise as well as forward, landing with bruising force on the tunnel floor. Behind her the infernal sparkling fire fountained upward a first questing tongue.

She turned her back on that growing brilliance and ran, half-expecting it to launch an attack upon her, as had the thing from the sand river. Only speed was in the fore of her mind as she scuttled ahead.

It was light, far too light in the tunnel. Simsa gave a gasping cry as a spark swooped into her line of sight, seemed to strike straight at her, as might a well-aimed weapon loosed in fury. More sparks in the air, they touched and bit, leaving smarting if tiny hurts behind them.

Simsa fled on. There was other light ahead, faint but there. Still refusing to look behind, she panted into the room within the shell of the outer cliff into which the alien had first drawn her. Only then did she face about to see that, though they had not followed her into this rough-hewn chamber, there danced in the air of the tunnel she had just quitted a cloud of flame sparks, multiplying constantly. She had the frightening feeling that they were merely building up to collapse into a more solid flame—a creature that not even the Elder One could handle.

She threw herself at the window opening that had been her doorway. Scrambling up on the ledge, she swung over and dropped to the shelf where she had taken refuge before, then leaned against the rock, her breath coming in racking sobs. This was sheer panic such as had not gripped her since childhood. As she got her breath, Simsa could see that there were no sparks flying now from above. Since the heavier haze which was night on this world was tight drawn, those would have been instantly revealed.

She would not, could not, linger too near. Whether that which fed the sparks dared venture out of the dark well into the corridor, she had no way of knowing. Only she must put between its source and herself as much space as possible.

Thus, even as she had climbed there in her hunt for Zass, so did she now scramble down, fighting to remember so that she would miss no finger- or toehold. It was not until she had reached the foot of the cliff and looked up at the dark opening above that she was angered at her own fear. There were indeed those raw and smarting places on her skin to make plain the threat offered, but now she had a feeling that she had given way far too easily to what was more threat than attack.

Before her was that slowly flowing river of sand. She had crossed that with the bespelled cloak. Now she hunkered down on that carven place where a true bridge must once have been end-rooted. Sliding out of the cloak, she laid it flat on the stone, her flesh cooled by puffs of a wind that did not ripple the sand below but was becoming swiftly forceful.

Trying to beat her from her perch into the sand river? No! There was a danger in such a belief. Had it not been belief that had forged the bridge for her on this very place? She must not speculate, must keep closed those corners of her mind into which could intrude and be nourished the thought of dangers.

She ran one hand across the rumpled cloak, her fingers catching in the edge of the hole where she had torn a place for her head. Then upon it she laid the rod from her girdle. There was no warmth in it. There had not been since she had dropped from that window above. There could be tens of tens reasons why. The Elder One—

Simsa shook her head and grimaced. This she must do herself, for to loose that other one, to call upon her . . . That one might well have no sympathy for what Burrows Simsa was doing now. The Elder One would have no reason to succor any life she had helped to warn of. She might perhaps even try to extinguish it with her own power. Simsa of the Burrows must go forward now, and how she could do that?

She got wearily to her feet, tugged on the cloak again, swung the rod back and forth as if it were only a fishing spear. North or south? She had come in from the northeast when she had discovered this place. Surely, the swirling sand flood could not cut it off entirely from the outer world—she had never heard of a stream that ran in a circle with no inlet or outlet.

South, then, for she had already made the journey along the northern way before she had found the bridge place. It would not be easy—but what had been on this world?

There was no "beach" along the edge above the sand river, nor would she have gone too close to what might climb out of the water.

Rather she continually climbed and descended a series of tumbled rocks or edged fearfully along slides of gravel where a wrong step might send her spinning down into that noxious flood.

Zass had not returned, and she had flown north when leaving the valley. Therefore, she herself might have a long march back even if she could locate a crossing of the flood. And she was tired. Night and day flowed so easily one into the other on this world she had long ago lost all sense of time as an exact measurement. But now her flesh and bones measured for her. There was just so far she could force her feet to carry her, and realizing that she was near the end of endurance, Simsa dropped down behind a large boulder that formed a small wall of its own, shutting her in so that she need not watch the stream. She took a scant mouthful of liquid from the flask she had filled at the fountain, ate two of the sticky fruit. Then with the rod upon her breast as she had slept ever since it had come into her hands, Simsa forced her mind quiet, for she needed a clear mind and a rested body. She walled fiercely away all thought of what might have happened to the flitter and those within, and sought sleep.

Here where there was no rising sun one could truly see, no cry of bird or buzz of insect to disturb slumber, she did not know how long a time had passed before she wriggled in her pocket of rock and wall and moved stiffly to sit up.

Those small burns the fire had left her all sprang to life. She saw the spots of seared skin on her arms and hands, felt them on her cheeks and throat. There was no healing from the alien source this time; she shrugged and looked over the edge of the rock that had sheltered her.

And there—she had been so close! A few steps more and she might have—Simsa again shook her head at her thoughts. To have taken that path when she was so weary would have been folly. There were at least two places to pass that would require all her courage and strength.

At some time in the past, there had been on the other side of the stream another outcropping of the blocklike rocks, not quite as tall as those to her right. There was very little regularity to that formation,

so she could believe that it had not been shaped by intelligent
endeavor to form an outpost for the valley defense—save that one
corner to the east was acute- and regular-angled. The rest of it had
been shattered. Some mighty blow had crushed the stone, crumbled
it to a riven mass.

However, a portion of that mass had landed in the sand river,
supplying an impediment where the thick stuff parted to flow, a narrower ribbon right below her perch, a wider one to the east. She
could drop to that mass. The first of the streams was small enough
to leap. The second one—let her reach it, and she could see better
what was to be done!

She ate and drank sparingly, made sure that her supplies were as
safe as she could make them. Then she descended to a rock where a
center ridge afforded a precarious perch.

Did it offer enough of takeoff for a leap? And what of that gap
farther on? She studied her possible landing and decided that the
gap was better than her present perch. Working her way to the end
of the ridge piece, she saw to the safety of her cloak, now twisted as
tightly about her above her waist as she could manage. Also, she
brought forth the rod and thrust it in twice to make sure that she
would not lose it.

The rippling of the sand at the foot of her rock was steady, but
Simsa would not allow herself to look. Instead, drawing upon the
skills of her lean body, she jumped, landing only barely on the other
rock, fighting desperately for hand- and footholds. Here she lay for
a space, breathing fast and staring up into the haze. It was midday
or later, and now she was conscious of the heat both of the air and
of the rock beneath her.

Rolling over, she crawled on hands and knees to the other end
of the rockfall and there surveyed the rest of the passage. This break
was wider than the other portion of the stream and it had no good
landing strip beyond. Simsa refused to accept that. There must be a
way.

Looking higher, she picked out, partly shadowed by a tumble of
rock, a darker spot, which, as she studied it, took on something of a
likeness to the window holes in the fortress? home? city? behind her.

Had she had about her all that she carried in the Burrows when about her nearly illegal business—a stout rope, with a small knife that opened into a grapple—the crossing would have been, perhaps not easy, but possible. But she was not equipped as in the old days.

Still, that thought held in her mind—a rope and a grapple. If the grapple held true, she could swing across above the surface of the sand, reach the narrow top of one of the tumbled rocks just below the suspected opening.

Simsa shed the cloak. The rod? It was too precious to risk. That left the metal strips of her kilt—which she had been so proud to assume and which she had since worn even when it would have been better not to in order to avoid attention. One strip still lay back beside that other river where she had been tempted to fish with such ill results. But with two—four more . . .

She speedily loosened a pair. They were limber in her hold, not stiff, but they were also hard to bend, and she had to pound them against the rock with the help of a small stone until she had them entwined together, with two prongs pointed outward in opposite directions.

Rope? There could be only one source for that. Simsa now fell upon the cloak and tore a wide strip, or rather worried it loose with the edge of her grapple. Into this she fitted her small store of supplies—it would make a pack she could bind to her back. The rest of the tough material she tore, pulled, cut, and knotted into an unwieldy length of line perhaps half the width of her palm in thickness.

Knotting this to the improvised grapple, she again tested each and every knot. She was not depending upon illusion, or will, or power now, but on knowledge she had learned for herself, and that thought strengthened her determination to succeed. If she fell, she thought wryly, then that Elder One, with all her learning and skills, would end just as quickly as the beggar-thief out of the Burrows. Save that she was set on victory this time on her own.

It took three casts, even in the full light, to bring the grapple within that broken window place. Then Simsa threw all her weight backward, not just once but three times. Without realizing that she did so, she was mumbling one of the charms Ferwar had always sworn by and made her learn to summon fortune.

She was very careful in tying on her improvised pack, allowing herself two swallows of water. Her skin was slippery with sweat now and she deliberately rubbed her palms across the rock surface to pick up any grit that might adhere.

"Ready as I shall ever be!" She said that aloud stoutly as both a challenge and encouragement. Then, the awkward "rope" in her grasp, she cast herself directly into the hands of fortune by jumping from the end of her perch.

The swing of her rope took her only an arm's distance above the sand, and the force of her jump brought her up against a far rock with such a blow as nearly drove all the air from her lungs. But she held and began to climb, her feet braced against the riven face of the rock, her hands and arms cruelly strained. She reached the end of the rope, swung up one hand to hook over the edge where the grapple was fixed, and at last tumbled head forward into a cramped hollow where she merely lay, her breasts heaving from the struggle and the fear which, at the last moment, broke through the guards she had set.

She was safe across and, for a time, that was all that counted. Her many bruises and scratches joined those earlier hurts, and she felt as if she wanted nothing but to lie where she was indefinitely. To be back on her pallet of rags in Ferwar's smelly burrow with a pot of fish stew and edible fungi boiling over the fire under the tending of her foster mother—that was sheer luxury. Why had fortune not granted that she remain so for her lifetime? She had meddled with things that were better left to slumber aeons longer. Now, it was as if she were one of Lame Ham's people, made of sticks and rags, which he so skillfully used to summon up a crowd on market days while his partner Wulon plucked purses from the unwary.

This could be welcome sleep and a good dream. Yes, she was in no rock hollow, but underground, sheltered as always, where she had learned to be quick and clever and had few equals. There was Ferwar true enough; she need only put out her hand and she could clasp the edge of the old woman's outer cloak fashioned of patches upon patches.

"Ferwar?"

At her call, the other swung around. Her face was very wrinkled and there was a difference in her eyes. She answered, with a zorsal's loudest scream.

❖ 7 ❖

"Zass!" Her own cry of recognition roused Simsa out of the deep exhaustion that had held her.

The zorsal perched on a point of broken wall well above the girl's head, nodding so that the stiffly held antennae were a misty pattern against the haze-shrouded sky. Zass was licking her paws with smug satisfaction, cleaning sticky patches from her claws and then her coat. The smell of overripe fruit reached Simsa, and she knew that her companion had been raiding those supplies she had brought out of the valley. Or had she? A quick glance at the bundle showed no change of wrapping. But Zass had the gift of wings—what did that lengthy journey through dark back to the valley mean to her?

Simsa whistled weakly. The zorsal paused in her leisurely toilet to look down. Her muzzle wrinkled, and her tongue shaped one of the low cries that the girl knew of old. Zass was very satisfied with herself. Now the small furred body rose as the leathern wings unfurled and she flapped down to squat once again, this time beside the girl's body as Simsa fought bruises and stiff muscles to sit up.

Zass's self-satisfaction was familiar to Simsa. Just so did a zorsal signify a successful finish to any hunt. Then it was true—that last small doubt was gone. Thorn was here, somewhere in this wilderness of barren rock, and Zass had found him.

The girl ate a little of the fruit, too, soft now, not far from spoilage under the glaring heat of this outer country, allowed herself sips of water. She offered some to Zass, but the zorsal refused it.

285

It was hard to reckon time, but the sky haze was darker close to the eastern horizon and brightest behind the tumbled rocks, the upstanding cubes. She had best be on her way. Simsa grimaced sourly as she got to her feet. Those burns from the tunnel's sparks, all the scrapes and bruises of her journey made themselves into small torments when she strove to stretch, to rub muscles in the calves of her legs which knotted painfully. As she shouldered the bag of supplies she spoke once more to Zass, trying at the same time to empty the fore of her mind of all but that face she had seen on the haze of the valley.

"Thorn!"

Zass clapped her wings, producing a smacking sound which echoed among these rocks or ruins, whichever they might be, then took lazily to the air. She flapped about in a circle as Simsa worked her way out of that foreguardian of the valley world and trod once again the rock plain between cracked fissures. Having seen the girl so prepared to follow, Zass's flight straightened into a line pointing east yet, to Simsa's surprise, south. The girl had expected a northern pathway.

Nor did Zass keep to the air, but returned now and then to perch on the girl's shoulder and chitter what Simsa understood as complaints. Always the zorsal disliked any long march since, winged, she could outfly those moving on the ground, and this was difficult ground to cover because of the constant breakage of the fissures. Sometimes it was necessary to detour for a space to get around one, and Simsa remained alert to any movement within, expecting at any moment to witness an upward surge of sand heralding the emergence of a monster. She swung the rod back and forth at waist level, always careful to point the horn tips toward any fissure she had to pass.

She was suddenly aware that the wind was coming in faster puffs than usual. Then her head came up with a jerk, and she faced directly into the lightest of breezes, still near furnace hot from the day.

Burning. Something burnt, and a stench of other odors that she had not breathed since she had left the foul agelessness of the

Burrows. She moved the rod up and out. It was warmer in her hand. Another of the beasts about to attack?

Zass took off, her claw tips scouring Simsa's shoulder where there was no longer any protecting cloak. The zorsal angled even more to the right, heading over two large fissures and giving a loud squawking cry. Simsa began to run, though her way was a zigzag and not a straight path, to where the zorsal was again circling in a wheeling pattern of flight, continuing to give voice.

The other river! Simsa made herself slow lest she suddenly skid over some lip of rock into that flood. What had Thorn to do with rivers—such rivers as befouled this world?

She came upon disaster so warned, but still astounded. Zass had settled down—not on the rocky shore of the stream, but on a mass of broken metal which protruded out of the ripples of sand that must be tugging at it, though so far not able to swallow up the wreckage.

A flitter right enough, but one that looked as if a giant had caught the machine out of the sky and twisted it between his hands even as one might twist reeds to fashion a basket—only this had then been idly thrown aside. Marks on the rock showed where the flyer had skidded after a forceful landing, heading straight for the river which now held a good third of it in its thick grasp.

There were no signs of life about the cabin of the downed flitter. The rough, transparent, glasslike substance the off-worlders used to give vision but also withstand any attack of enemy or nature was so crackled that she could not see inside. The worst was that the skid that had taken it into the river had landed it against, and well up on, the far bank. Between Simsa and the wreck was a broad band of flowing sand.

The girl dropped her bundle and grimaced at being faced again by the problem of sand rivers and their hidden inhabitants. There was a chance that she could leap from the solid base of this shore to the top of the wreckage, but she did not know how well-based the latter might be. She might land on a mass which would then simply tip her off into that muck which she had no intention of entering.

The zorsal was walking across the clouded upper portion,

pausing now and then to lower her head and peer into a portion fairly clear of such veiling. Then she fanned her wings and sank her claws, extended as Simsa could see to their fullest reach, into one of the cracks, rising in a small jump with the aid of her wings while all four limbs were anchored in the shattered material.

A crackling answered her and Zass bounced higher into the air, bearing with her a three-cornered fragment. With a series of splitting sounds, the rest of the badly broken window dome fell out and slipped down the tail of the flitter to cascade into the sand, where it speedily disappeared.

Simsa had no difficulty now in seeing bodies trapped in the wreckage; two of them, wearing the shining, one-piece uniforms of spacers, were wedged within. One had fallen forward, his or her head resting on unmoving knees. But it was the other Simsa saw and knew.

Her haze-borne vision in the valley was true. Thorn, his head up and back, sat pinned there. His eyes were closed and there was that thin runnel of blood coming from the corner of his mouth. Dead?

On her hands and knees, lest she somehow lose balance and fall into the sand trap, the girl crept to the very edge of the cut in the rock that held the river, and tried to distinguish any signs of life. But he was too far away.

"Does—he—live?" She aimed her most urgent thought, adding to it all she had learned, at the zorsal, uncertain whether Zass could even pick up that question. Surely she knew the difference between life and death. Any hunter would. Simsa watched the zorsal alight again and move forward, with a strange caution. Zass might be approaching some trap which she must spring. With her hind claws caught in a pinch grip on the frame of the one-time viewplate, she folded her wings and swung head down, her front hand-feet widely spread apart.

A moment later, those closed one on either side of Thorn's lolling head, and shifted it around a fraction while the zorsal studied the bleeding mouth, the closed eyes, with the experience of predator.

The sensation that was her answer reached Simsa just as the

zorsal let go and moved over to test in the same way the other body.

Alive! But how badly hurt? And was that flitter equipped with the same help-summoner as the Life Boat carried? Would it summon assistance in time from wherever this party had planeted? It might well be that all her solicitude was not needed, that already help was on the way, help Simsa had no intention of meeting.

The second one was dead—again an assured report from the zorsal. Zass had tugged the other's head up, and Simsa saw that this was that woman whose mind she had touched only to be revolted and frightened. This was that one who would seek out secrets with a knife, or by machines that would maim and kill! Knowledge so sought was debased and vile. Before she thought, Simsa followed the customs of the Burrows and spat as she would have into the footprints of one upon whom she called ill fortune. But there was no need for that. The ill fortune of her own kind—the fortune they believed the worst—had already struck.

Her own kind? Simsa straightened and clutched the rod as if to turn it on herself. No! Not now—but there were no barriers that she could hold for long against that moving inside her. Out of hiding, or the resting place into which she had retreated after she had worked her power, the Elder One was again emerging.

There was already that slight shift in Simsa's sight. Some things sharpened, others faded as if there dwelt in her now another range of vision. Yet when she looked at Thorn, she knew that this was a task from which she would not be allowed to turn, even if she wanted to—that that broken body set just out of her reach had importance not only to Simsa of the Burrows, but also to her who co-dwelt within.

Zass loosened her hold on the woman, allowing the dead to crumple back. The zorsal did not have the strength or means to free the spaceman—that would lie with Simsa. And the Elder One—by all means the Elder One!

It seemed to Simsa, even as she yielded once more to the other, that each time she did so, the Elder One grew stronger, more ready to take command. Only, having once begun the withdrawal of herself, she had always known she could no longer withstand the other.

What could the Elder One do here that Simsa could not? Build a bridge? Of what? The cloak was shredded. And Simsa would not go down into that flood of sand and what it must conceal to reach the broken flyer.

The zorsal had returned to Thorn, settling on the edge of the frame that had enclosed the broken transparent bubble, and once more set her foreclaws again expertly to cradle the unconscious spaceman's head. This time she turned it cautiously so that his closed eyes were directly facing Simsa. Having adjusted the hold to her satisfaction, Zass raised her own head and gave a chirrup which was a bid for attention.

In Simsa's hand the rod moved, or rather the Elder One moved it. There came a beam of light, green-blue—rippling as if it spouted from a fountain, narrowing until the ray appeared solid in its intensity. It struck directly above and between those closed eyes.

So it was held steady, not by Simsa's will, but by that other's. The knowledge of what was happening was not shared. Simsa could only guess that this was meant to benefit. Then that beam flashed off as speedily as it had first shown.

Now it returned to alter target, striking upon the wreckage itself. No narrow beam now, rather a new kind of haze, puffing forth to envelop the whole of the broken flitter, encasing it, growing ever more dense. Simsa, who must stand by and watch while the Elder One was in command, uttered a cry.

The wreck, which was now but a black shadow within the haze the rod had engendered, slid away from the other bank, dropping its crumpled nose into the sand river. Yet the girl was certain that the Elder One had no mind to lose Thorn. Why then let him fall into the hidden territory of the slime blobs?

The haze thickened below, thinned above. The broken observation bubble was nearly clear, while the underpinning was hidden. Yet still it moved.

It moved and, within her, there came in answer such a draining of energy and life as she had never known, even when the Elder One had ruthlessly used her to some purpose such as the releasing of the valley whirlwind. There was no way to fight, to protect herself—she could only give and give.

Having woven its web of haze, the rod flipped back against her breasts and again Simsa cried out—this time in pain, for it might have been a glowing brand held forcibly to her skin. Nothing drifted or spun from the horns now. And there was nothing left within her to give. What the Elder One had wrought exhausted her. She fell upon her knees, the rod dropping from her grasp as she braced herself with both hands and straightened arms to keep from crashing headlong on the rock.

There was an impatience rising in her now—not borne from her own thoughts or desires, but out of the wishes of the Elder One. It would seem that she found this Simsa too frail, too feeble—

While the haze-enclosed wreck was down across the river now, it had not dipped into it as she had expected it to do, rather seemed supported by the haze upon the surface of the flowing sand. However, as she watched, the even flow of the sand was troubled by a dimpling of its surface; small hillocks broke out of the flow. And from these grew, like upside-down roots of hideous and poisonous plants, the weaving yellow tentacles of the blobs, small at first but spreading ever larger, longer.

It would seem, however, that the rod's haze bore within it some ingredient that held them back. For, though they strove to penetrate it with tentacle point, those strings of unwholesome flesh were powerless to fasten on the wreckage.

The flitter's movement toward where Simsa crouched was very slow. She could see that the whole of its bulk had cleared the opposite shore and was pointed toward the rock rim immediately below her. She had to brace her head upon her folded arm, lying near flat on the rock now, her strength seemingly continuing to drain without visible threading through the rod.

"Will!" That command was like a shout, cutting through the tangle of her thoughts and fears. "Will!"

Will the broken machine to her? Simsa of the Burrows could see little aid in that. But ruthlessly this other was taking over more and

more of her mind, centering all her thought upon the wreck. *Will*—
yes, let it come to her, come to her. It rang like a chant and, though
she did not know it, she was sitting up, her face frozen in a mask as
she intoned aloud, though not even her own ears—only her body—
knew the rhythm of that call:

"Come—come—come!"

She knew nothing of the forces that other commanded.
Seemingly, she was now the tool in place of the spent rod. Her
hands raised from her knees, weakly wavering, but still motioning,
emphasizing her chant.

"Come!"

There sounded the cry of a fighting zorsal. Simsa heard it only
from a distance and as something that had no meaning now. All
that did matter was that dark core of the haze moving toward this
bank.

Splashing, a sucking, coughing sound. Still Simsa was not free to
look, to break the compulsion holding her.

"Come!"

Something moved within the haze—something that hunched
along the length of the flyer, answering to her beckoning even as the
flitter appeared to do.

"Come!" One small, helpless part of her shivered, if a thought, a
memory, could shiver. Did she summon one of those blob-things
which had climbed to ride the wreck? In spite of that tremor within
her, she waved and called for the last time: "Come!"

The crushed nose of the wreck must be now against the rock
shore below her. Once more she was herself, the power flowing out
of her and leaving only a weakened husk of a person behind. The
haze was fading, but that which crawled along the dark shape
reached out for the rock—reached with a hand, not tentacles.

Simsa stumbled to the very lip of the rock, caught those groping
hands in hers, then was herself thrown backward, another larger
and hard-muscled body covering hers. She looked up into the face
of Thorn.

In that face, the eyes were still closed. Blood trickling from his
mouth spattered on her. She had strength enough to wriggle out

from under his inert body, leaving him facedown and unmoving now upon the rock.

There was a sound as if some great creature had sucked or inhaled. The haze was abruptly gone. She could see the yellow horrors from the river climbing in a solid mass upon the wreckage, bearing it down the faster with their weight. Luckily, they were more conscious of this invader of their own place than they were of those on the bank.

Zass cried again—a battle cry that brought Simsa's attention to where the zorsal cruised back and forth upstream. The whole surface of the sand there was pocked and heaped. There seemed no end to the creatures moving toward the wreck.

She crept forward and caught Thorn by one shoulder. To turn his body over was a task almost beyond her much-impaired vitality, but she managed it. Now she unsealed the uniform he wore, much as she had seen him do, in a search for injuries. Catching up the rod once again, she passed it slowly over him, hoping that through it, she might learn if his hurts were critical. She thought a rib was broken, there was a contusion on his head just above the nape of his neck, and the blood, she discovered when she was able to pry his mouth open, did not come from a punctured lung as she had feared, but rather from a tear in his lower lip.

Ferwar had been, in her time, one wise enough to care for hurts such as come easily to the Burrowers. Simsa now stripped off a section of the rope she had made for crossing the other stream and tightly bound the rib. She washed the graze on his head, separating the short strands of blood-matted hair. A second piece of her rope went into the dressing of it. Last of all, she dribbled a little of the water from the valley's fountain into his slack mouth, holding it shut until she felt him swallow.

When she loosed that last grip on him, he stirred and muttered in a language strange to her. His eyes opened and he looked up at her, but they did not focus or show any knowledge that she was with him.

Zass flew in from the river. Now she streaked back and forth, shrieking on a note so high that Simsa's ears could barely catch it, and the girl knew that the zorsal was aroused to the peak of rage and fear.

Just as the attack of the river-thing had earlier summoned its fellows from the inland fissure, so did the uncommon commotion about the wreck, which had nearly disappeared beneath the sand, draw the others once more.

Simsa and Thorn were on a small height of the rock and the nearest fissure lay some distance away. Still the girl could see weaving yellow ribbons of unclean life streaming, jerking up into the air, across the stretch between her and that pile of rocks which had once formed the outer point of defense of the valley. They were cut off. Even if she could get Thorn aware and on his feet, she could see no chance of their escaping in that direction. And the fissures lay north and south, as well as west, while the river was east. They were boxed in.

There was a thing with a handgrip fastened to the belt she had unbuckled and thrown to one side when she had searched for the spaceman's hurts. Undoubtedly, a weapon of sorts, but how one used it and whether it would be effective against the sand river monsters the girl had no idea.

Only they could not remain tamely where they were, to be pulled down, torn by those deadly weaving ribbons. And she could not carry Thorn. It would seem that the Elder One had given her this duty and then withdrawn—again, leaving her exhausted and without resources.

There must be a uniting between the two of them. Simsa at last accepted that, though all her normal instincts rebelled. Back when the Elder One had first entered her, she had been exultant, feeling whole and full of such energy and power as she had not known could exist. Her disenchantment had come little by little—to have one full memory and another that was only shatters of half-seen, never understood pictures, had been a true and growing torment. And then, when the off-worlders had thought to take her apart as it seemed, to shatter *her* for that broken memory, she had thought of the Simsa of the Burrows as her shield and escape—having from then on fought to contain those complete memories as well as she could.

Which had sent the Elder One into hiding and brought her, Simsa, into choices and action that was left unfinished—weak, drained, unable to fight—

Zass swooped down and settled on Thorn's body, her wings fanning, her head slanted so her feather antennae were turned straight at the girl.

"Go!" That was as potent an order as her own "Come!" had earlier been.

Go she might be able to do, yes. Though at the moment she did not feel she had the strength to take more than a step or two away from this one stretch of unfissured rock. But though Thorn's eyes were open and he rolled his head back and forth against her knee, crying out whenever the bandaged head wound touched the rock, he was certainly not conscious of where he was.

She leaned over him, trying to sight some knowledge of her in his open-eyed gaze. Then she thought out carefully the speech she had learned from the ship people. To speak to him in that tongue might have some effect.

"Thorn Yan!" Once he had told her that that was a "friend name," used only in comradeship with those he trusted and his kin. "Thorn Yan!"

The blankness of his face was troubled by a frown.

"We must go. There is trouble." She spoke slowly in the ship language, making each word as emphatic as she could. Reaching out, she drew that unknown weapon from the belt holder.

"Trouble—" She dangled the weapon before his eyes. A hand-grip together with a tube. What would issue from it and how one could make it work she did not know.

Thorn's lips moved. He turned his head to spit a mouthful of blood onto the rock. That small bit of action seemed to recall him to himself. Now he looked at her and his frown grew the stronger.

"Simsa—"

"Yes," she agreed. "Thorn!" Now she dared take him by the shoulder and give him a small upward pull, once more holding out the weapon.

"Look!" Purposely, she did not point to the riotous scene at the wreckage, but rather to those things issuing from the fissures inland—the ones that drew their slimy bodies purposefully toward their own perch.

She had steadied his head as he lifted it against her arm, and now look he did. Then his hand fell on hers and twisted the weapon out of her grip, striving to steady it as he viewed their attackers.

 **8**

"Greeta! Greeta!" Thorn shouted the name of the dead woman—but even that part of the flitter which contained her body was lost to view. The creatures of the sand crawled and heaped themselves most thickly on that section of the wreckage and had, by their weight, pushed it completely under so that although here and there, an end of broken metal might be seen and the tail of the fuselage was still tilted above the surface, the rest was only a writhing struggle of the yellow things.

"She is dead," Simsa said sharply. "You cannot bring her forth from that!" She waved a hand toward the struggling mass of ovoid bodies and tangled tentacles.

Thorn gave her a quick glance, and there was certainly no sign of friendliness or gratitude beneath those knotted brows or in that rage-thinned mouth. That deep anger filled him, making him forget the pain of his own hurts, Simsa sensed without being told.

He crooked his left arm at eye level, used it so to steady the barrel of his weapon. Down into that heaving mass of filthiness shot a ray of fire so brilliant Simsa closed her eyes for an instant that she might not be blinded.

Deep inside of her mind arose a scream—not from any fear or torture wreaked upon her own body, but surely coming from those sand-dwelling things now feeling the searing pain of the attack.

That faint stench which had first guided her in this direction was now a fetid cloud.

She reached up, averting her gaze from that beam, to catch his elbow with a fierce grip.

"No!" Both by word of mouth and in her mind she shouted that. "She was dead when I found you—you can do her no service, only bring those things upon us now. Would you sacrifice your life for the dead who are safely past the Star Gate and no longer aware of this world, or any other men know? She was dead! By this"—with her other hand she waved the rod before him—"will I swear it!"

For a long moment, he either did not hear or else had no belief in what she said. Then that beam of deadly light was cut off, and his weapon-holding hand fell to his side, though Simsa kept her grasp on his other arm. She dragged Thorn around, his back to the river, to face the long space that lay between them and that outcrop of rock which was the tricky entrance to the valley.

She had been very right to fear those fissures. Now, as she looked out over the broken surface of the plane, most of them were throwing out gouts of sand, or there were tentacles fastened on the rock that bound them at the surface, and here and there a gob of yellow was already well out of the depths and turning toward the two.

"What are they?" For the first time, Thorn spoke to her with a rational voice.

"Death," she returned briefly, and then added, "Here they rule. There"—she pointed to the pile of rocks which was throwing a longer and longer shadow across the plain, reaching for the very foot of the small rise on which they now stand—"there is hope—a little . . ." She was bitterly frank, for she was sure that his useless attack on the flitter's blobs had done much to arouse even the most sluggish of the crawlers. "If we can reach there. But how? Can you burn us a path, out-worlder?"

He raised his weapon again to closely examine the butt of it. Simsa was able to see a thin bright red line there, as a hidden line of fire might show.

"I have half a charge still." He might have been speaking aloud to himself, for he had not looked toward her at all or made any comment on what she had said. His free hand broke out of the loose hold she had kept on him and went to a row of tubes set endwise along his belt. "Two others—that is it."

For the first time, he at last regarded her.

"If we reach there"—he gestured to the distant hump of stone— "what then?"

What then indeed? She had purposely tried not to think beyond reaching the rocks. Back across the river—finding the tunnel—the valley? But the dwellers therein had already attacked Thorn once— would they raise a single, jointed, hook-haired leg to aid him? This might be only a perilous interlude between two deaths. Since the Elder One had helped to raise the storm that had brought down the flitter, the valley people might be a little more merciful to Simsa. However, could she count on that? You could not guess the many turnings of the path in any alien mind. By her act in saving Thorn— momentarily—she could well have condemned herself in their understanding.

Yet she had nothing else to offer but the ruined block tower— beyond the faintness of the hope that, if they could hold off the crawlers for a space, the valley people might just be moved to take a hand.

All this had passed swiftly through her mind, so she could not be sure that her words of answer did not follow directly on his question.

"I do not know—for the future"—she gave him the stark truth— "but it was once a place of protection, and I feel that these crawlers cannot venture too far from their holes." She said nothing of the valley dwellers.

She saw that he was continuing to watch her from under scowling brows.

"Was it of your raising?" he asked grimly.

Simsa did not understand. "What of what?" Had he acutely and correctly connected the storm that had downed the flitter with her fellow dweller in this body? She pressed the rod against herself and withdrew one step and then another, her attention divided between his scowling face and the weapon in his hand.

"Yes!" His scowl smoothed away, but now there was a sharp

purpose in his face as his weapon swung around and up to cover her. "It *was* you!"

She retreated no farther. Confrontations back in the Burrows had taught her something of such a game, though this was no time for the playing of games when the yellow ovoids on the plain and their kin in the stream closed in.

"I do not know of what you accuse me." Which indeed was no lie. She only guessed at his thoughts, would not attempt to use the skill of the Elder One to truly read them. "But if you wish to front me with blade and skill"—she fell back easily into the speech and custom of the Burrows—"it would be better to wait—we have a common enemy now."

Zass's screech nearly drowned out the last word of the girl's speech. The zorsal dove at a yellow tip flapping along the edge of the rock where they stood and tore at it viciously with both tooth and talon, sending out a spurt of black-green fluid which nearly touched Thorn. Startled, he swung swiftly to face the zorsal's opponent and aimed a beam of fire down into the owner of that questing tentacle.

Though that finger of light was far less in its brilliance and sweep than the power he had summoned earlier, Simsa once again heard the dying shriek in her mind. Zass was voicing cries of triumph, planing out from their stand toward the interior and the rock tower as if she, also, urged on them that way.

The nearest of the fissures had already proved a doorway for one of the monsters. Although it swelled into greater bulk upon coming into the air, even as they all were doing, it was not developing such a size as either Simsa or Thorn. Having apparently made up his mind, without any further argument, to their journey across the plain, the spaceman once more took careful aim at that crawler. With a sharp burst of energy, he turned it into a stinking mess of well-charred fibers.

Simsa leapt lightly to the rock level where the creature had died, keeping well away from the mass. Its thick, sour odor seemed to cling to the air and pass from that to her skin and hair so that she gagged until she was able to control herself.

Thorn had not kept up with her, and Simsa did not need Zass's warning croak to look back. The spaceman stumbled a little, one hand to his bandaged head, yet aimed his light weapon once again and took out, or at least badly wounded, another creature sliding from its fissure to cross her path. There was a humming, unlike Zass's shrieks of defiance or the sizzle-purr of the off-world weapon in use. For a breath or two of time, Simsa thought the sound was coming out of the air, some form of communication between blob and blob to rally the sand creepers emerging ahead of them into an array they could not hope to blast their way through.

Thorn's weapon failed. He stood, swaying a little, as he dug another cylinder from his belt loop and, shaking one such from the butt of the hand piece, forced the other in with a sharp smack. Not from him or Zass came that sound—rather it pulsated in the air weirdly as something within her stirred and answered to it.

Simsa waited for Thorn to catch up. As he raised the weapon again for another shot to aim at a well-grown sand-thing, she caught at his wrist a second time. That murmur of sound was akin to the power raising of the Elder One and the yellow valley dweller.

Zass stopped in midshriek, rose higher into the air, circling about the two on the ground, the path of her circle growing farther away with every revolution the zorsal made. But it was the monsters that now surprised the girl—that and what she held in her own hand.

From the horn tips came a soft diffusion of light as unlike the killer beams from Thorn's weapon as morning mist is unlike lightning. It curled out about the two of them, enveloping them even as the wreckage in the river had been earlier hidden from Simsa's eyes. She almost expected to be caught up, taken helplessly into the air. But that whirlwind magic had been partly of the valley inhabitants—this was wholly her own.

The Elder One again—still that iron will did not move to take her over as it had so many times before. Perhaps this was only protective, preserving her from harm because of her usefulness in some future ploy. At any rate, she and Thorn must take advantage of it.

She crowded close to the spaceman, aware of their closeness of body that she had resented before.

"Together," she breathed, "it will hold us together—free from them—your weapon—" There was a glistening line of blue encircling the weapon's handgrip and even as she spoke he uttered a cry of pain.

"Sheathe it!" she ordered. "It is not akin to what would serve us here."

Though he had never completely lost his look of aloofness, he did slip the weapon back into the loops on his belt while the haze thickened about them. Now their clear vision reached little more than an arm's length ahead of them. Simsa thought of the fissures and wondered if their present blindness might bring them to worse than an encounter with one of the monsters. But her wonder was fleeting as she heard Zass's call from overhead. They had played this game before on night foraging when the zorsal's eyes could outsee her own. She need only to listen and Zass would guide their route for them.

At another ranging cry from Zass, without asking or seeking at all, Simsa hooked her fingers in Thorn's belt and gave him a strong jerk south and forward. It would appear that he understood, for he made no resistance to her urging, though he kept his hand ready near the butt of his weapon.

They stumbled on, for Thorn's weaving progress became more and more unsteady. Yet, when Simsa wished to lend him her strength, he muttered and thrust her away, though she did not loose her hold on his belt. There was a stain on his head bandage. When she could catch words he said over and over in a low, monotonous stream, she could understand none of them. This was not the trade-lingo of Kuxortal or the sparseness of space speech. She thought it might be his native tongue and wondered fleetingly how far he had come from the world of his birth.

Once she must have misheard Zass's warning cry, for they nearly blundered straight into a mass of waving yellow tentacles before Simsa could brace both feet against the stone to drag Thorn back.

Then the haze descended once more about them like a wall and they pushed on. That curtained journey across the rock floor of this world seemed endless. Twice they stopped to rest as Zass came flitting down through the cloaking mist to perch on Simsa's shoulder and thrust her long muzzle in a moist caress against the girl's cheek.

On the second such halt, the girl offered her water bottle to Thorn. Although his belt had a number of pockets of small tools thrust in loops, there was no sign of any liquid carrier. Perhaps all such supplies had been in the flitter and had sunk with its dead passenger into the sand. He took several lusty swallows. Simsa had her hand raised half in protest, ready to wrestle their store away from him. But she was sure that he was only dimly conscious now, and she must keep him going on his own, for she could not handle the weight of a flaccid body should he fall. To stay here waiting for their strange cover to be penetrated by any seeking blobs was the depth of folly. Let him have the drink if it gave him the energy to keep onward.

Doggedly she kept her mind from any future—let them just reach the outpost of the valley. *Then* she could decide on the next leg of their trek.

It was getting darker and, twice, Thorn stumbled so badly that he fell to his knees. Luckily, some instinct within him kept him struggling onward, though the girl was sure he was no longer aware of her at all. Then, when it seemed that the darker haze, which was the night here, and the mist about them were so mingled together as to give them real darkness, Simsa saw a black blot of rock loom out of the curtain ahead. She loosed her hold on Thorn, but she could still hear the click of his metal-soled space boots on the stone behind her as she lurched forward to fall against the sentinel rock, her breath coming in ragged sobs.

This beacon she knew, mainly because in setting forth from the ruin she had marked its fanciful resemblance to a head, the head of some grotesque creature of the never-seen, such as had been carven on the walls of that long-forgotten city on Kuxortal where the Elder One had waited so long for escape. Simsa gripped the stone with one hand. Her other fingers were so locked about the rod that they seemed numb, grown together with the force with which she held on to that weapon.

Zass's squalling cry split the gloom of this double mist as the zorsal winged down to sit on the rock. Simsa leaned against it, spent by all her efforts. The clang-clang of the footplates did not fail. Thorn came to her and oddly enough much of his wavering unsteadiness was gone. His head was a little forward, as if he fought for clarity of sight, and for the first time in what must have been half the night he spoke to her:

"Simsa?"

"Yes, it is I."

He kept on until brought up against the same rock that supported her. Now he put out a hand to touch her arm a fraction above the wrist that was cramped against the rod.

"We—we thought you—probably dead . . ." he said slowly. "There is no shelter—and your Life Boat was deserted, the direction call half-failed. Why?"

"Why?" She rounded on him. Within her flared all the frustrations and trials that had beset her since she had made her blind landing here, bringing an anger from which she drew strength. It had always been so—that anger could burn away fear, or help her forget it a little.

"*Why?*" She echoed his question hoarsely. "Ask that of your friends, off-worlder. Ask it of Lieutenant Lingor, of Medic Greeta—no, she is dead. If she was a great good friend of yours . . ." That thought pricked at her. What if all of his pushing her toward those off-worlders, his stories of the Histro-Tecks—those long-lived Zacathans who would treat her as a living treasure—had been false? What if such thoughts as she had picked up from Lingor, the medic, also had dwelt in Thorn's mind—that she, Simsa, was no person but a thing, as much without life or intelligence as one of the small metal images that could be dug up in the Burrows, and sold to upper town dealers for the price of a drink or a couple of stupefying smorg leaves. What had been her price to Greeta, to Lingor—above all, to *Thorn?*

As she pushed away from her rock support to face him now, the anger in her indeed giving her strength, she was all Simsa of the Burrows. The Elder One slept or was gone. Fair enough, this was her quarrel—wholly hers!

"I do not understand." There was weariness in his voice as well as in his bloodstained face. There was also stubborn determination, such as she had seen during their journeying upon her own world when he had refused to surrender his will in spite of all the obstacles that had ringed them in.

"Play not the unmind with me," she spat. "No, I have not striven to read your thoughts," she informed him as a shade of distaste seemed to come into his eyes. "Why should you think that? Were you not at ease knowing well your job was done when you betrayed me to those friends of yours! Lingor—he thought to make some plan to use what I might summon as power to make himself master among his own kind—*No!*" She gestured quickly as she saw his swollen lips open and was sure he was to dispute her words. "You need not tell me that this was not so, for that I did read in *his* mind. He was so sure of me. And she—that dead one—Greeta, who was supposed to be a healer, not a destroyer, what did she want of me? This"—she slapped her hand across her breasts—"my body! That she might cut and trace and learn how one who was supposed to have died perhaps a million cycles of Kuxortal ages ago could walk the earth! That, too, I read past any denial. Only, I do bear her with me ever indeed—this Elder One—and by fortune her fair self, I did not ask for that burden. She summoned me, as well you know, and I could not stand before her.

"In that hour when she came into me, I felt—perhaps just what she wished me to feel to keep me to her task—that I was whole, that a part of me long severed had come back. But she is very strong and I think that she could make anyone believe as she wished. When I am threatened, she awakes and sometimes it is she and sometimes it is I, Simsa that always was, who stands to arms and awaits battle.

"She led me to read minds and then I could plan. Do you think I survived my years in the Burrows without knowing when to fight and when to run? Run it had to be from that Lingor—and your Greeta. Once that starship planeted again they could have taken me. I know so little in this life of your ways, star rover. I would have been as an unarmored as a lizard is to Zass—sweet and short picking. Perhaps together, those two even thought to crack my bones and get all the meat! No, the spaceport was their Burrows, they would know every turn and twist therein. Thus, I made sure that they would not take me there."

"This is a dead world," he said slowly. There was not so much disbelief in him now, she thought, but of that she could not be sure.

"You are saying that this is a place of no refuge," she caught him up. But, of course, he did not know of the valley. Perhaps it was best. No, she could do nothing about that; the valley belonged to the green folk and she would take no intruder into it.

"A place of no refuge," she repeated, hoping that he had not caught the pause created by that thought. "But it is one I chose—one where I and any off-worlder hunting me can be equal from the start. I knew that the signal of the Life Boat might summon a ship. So Lingor turned back, did he?"

"You do not understand." He placed his weapon on top of the tall rock by which they stood. "They could not have done as you thought. There was—"

"As *they* thought," she retorted. "You delivered me up. They had me on their ship well between worlds. Yes, they were very sure of me—you were all very sure of me. Let me say this, off-worlder, it will be better to die of hunger and thirst or by blundering into the reach of one of the sand-things here than to be prisoner of those you chose to give me to!"

"I did not *choose* anything!" From the sharp note in his voice she found she had indeed pricked him then. "I am a member of the Rangers attached to the Hist-Search under the orders of Hist-Techneer Zanantan. You could have stayed on Kuxortal. I asked you to come with me to meet those who have spent long lifetimes unriddling the secrets left behind—perhaps by such as your Elder One. It was for your own safety that you were given a single cabin, guarded—"

"Against your own officer, against such as Greeta?" she interrupted. "Do not speak such foolishness. The cabin—yes, it was safe enough! There were hidden places through which I could be watched, every movement of mine noted. But the Elder One could meet them trick for trick there!" She laughed.

"Not so!" His hand formed a fist which he slammed into the rock, not seeming to notice the pain that gesture must have caused him. "You would be an honored guest. As for leaving Kuxortal, how long would you have lasted had any one of the lordlings of the upper town known the power you could wield? Speak of having your secrets out of you—they are experts at such games and far rougher than any off-worlder can guess."

"So!" She cut him short. "The Elder One could have handled anyone coming with steel and fire. But suppose your officer, your Greeta, came to let into my 'safe place' some air to breathe which would have tied me into sleep. That was but *one* of the things they considered. Though they were not working together. No, off-worlder, I would rather take my chances on this rock than with them. The ploys of the lords I know—the crafts and slyness of your people are something else again!"

He shrugged and slipped down, his back against the rock, his hands dangling between his knees, nor had he again taken up his weapon. It was Simsa who gathered it up and tossed it to thud on the rock before him.

"We are but at the gateway of a place we may be able to defend. And the fog which protects is going." The cooling of the rod within her hand was a warning, and the drifting of the curtain was indeed showing thin.

He did not answer her, only pulled himself up once again, holding on to the rock. It seemed to Simsa that there was now a grayish shade to his face as though the color of the rock had somehow oozed into him even during the moments that he had been resting.

She did not wait to see if he would follow, but was already in search of that way down which she had found before. Along that she climbed, the rod made fast to her girdle, using hands and toes with all the dexterity she had learned in Kuxortal. When she reached the top of the second and much taller block, the haze that had surrounded them in their journey hither had indeed threaded itself away. The sky was darker than she had ever seen it.

Calling Zass to her, she settled the zorsal on a rock point from which she could view most of the surrounding territory, including a bit of that second sand river which might offer a new threat. Simsa rolled what she had left of the cloak-made rope into a mat and settled her head upon it. The Elder One might have in her time gone without sleep to a great degree—Simsa had come to suspect that when she discovered she needed less and less rest since her body had provided shelter for the ageless one—but a body was only flesh, blood, and bone after all and also had its demands.

She was straightway plunged into a deep dark where no dreams troubled her rest. If Thorn joined her on her perch, she neither knew nor cared. She no longer depended upon anyone or anything but herself and the zorsal, for Zass's single-minded loyalty had never changed, and as a camp guard the zorsal was the best.

There was the contrasting brightness of the midmorning haze when she opened her eyes again. An arm's length away lay the spaceman on his back, his eyes closed, the dried blood on his chin cracking and flaking off as he drew in long, slow breaths. Zass's cry came—faint, but growing stronger as Simsa sat up and shook loose the silver lengths of her hair, combing it clumsily with her fingers. The zorsal made her usual circling descent and landed just in front of the girl. Her forepaws were tight to her body and so sheltered and protected she carried there a branch heavily laden with fruit. There was only one place the zorsal could have found that—she had been within the hidden valley. But it was what was woven around the branch that caught Simsa's attention a moment later. A tubing of some kind, transparent enough to show that it was filled near to bursting with the blue water of the pool—and that was not Zass's gift! Someone of the furred ones had wished the girl well enough to send that.

Simsa gave a sigh. For the second time in her life, she felt at one with something larger than herself. The first had been when she had fronted that statue of the Elder One which had contained the essence of she who had waited and watched for so long—and now, when she could believe that those of the valley cared, even in so little!

9

Simsa scrupulously drank and ate only half of the bounty the zorsal had brought. Like it or not, the sleeping spaceman at her side was still her responsibility. Zass squatted down, clapping and folding her wings, to sit licking at her body fur where sticky smears suggested that she had fed well before she returned to the two now stranded on the rock ledge.

Having appeased a measure of her body's need, the girl went to the edge of the block on which they had taken refuge to survey the narrow ribbon of flowing sand that lay between them and the barriers of the valley. There were no ominous writhings on its surface, nothing to suggest that there lay danger beneath that smooth roll. But she did not in the least believe that if she ventured into that murky stuff (and she had no idea as to how deep it was), she would not be in such danger as her imagination was only too willing to suggest.

Her hook and rope trick could not work again. There was no convenient hole in the rock across the stream to catch her grapple and she had sacrificed so much of the rope length since she had knotted it together she was sure it would not span that space. Through squinted eyes, she viewed the escarpment on the other side. The haze appeared a fraction brighter, nearly as irritating to her sight as the fire in the dark tunnel had been. She dug into the memory of Simsa of the Burrows and tried to pluck forth an answer to her problem.

There was a chance—she looked to where the zorsal squatted. Zass had moved closer to the sleeping or unconscious spaceman, now and then stealthily putting forth a paw as if to touch him but quickly jerking back the limb before the gesture was complete. The zorsal apparently found the man the object of infinite curiosity— even though she had once traveled for days in his company on Kuxortal.

Simsa turned to face the plain over which they had come. Though none of those ominous lumpings of sand were being spit forth from the fissures, and no yellow tentacles had thrust up into sight, she knew that to set foot again on that surface was to offer a challenge to the sand dwellers.

The Elder One—she shook her head violently. No, she would open no doors, would have no part in lending her body to the other's superior wisdom! No appeal to the Elder One. *She* was the Simsa of the here and now, and as such she would solve—

Her thoughts were broken by a hacking cough. The eyes of the man were open, and he had lifted himself up to lean on one elbow and regard her.

After one measuring glance, his gaze shifted to the rocks about them, the heights beyond the sand stream. The tip of his tongue crossed cracked lips. Simsa moved, bringing to him half of Zass's bounty, which she had spared in spite of her own thirst and hunger. Thorn sat up, squeezing first a portion of the water into his mouth.

"Where does this come from?" He weighed the still not empty tube in his hand. Perhaps it was the needs of his body that made his voice so harsh.

Simsa could see nothing to be gained now in keeping the valley oasis a secret. Without his flitter, Thorn could not return to any of his own kind who might be encamped where she had brought down the Life Boat. Nor did she undervalue the dwellers within and their powers. They had already brought an end to one invader of their world and could hold them both at their pleasure.

"There." She pointed to the rock wall that raised such a formidable barrier against them. "There is water, fruit—a place of growing things."

"There is also more, is there not?" he returned, breaking one of the blue fruit apart, licking the pulp from his grimed and stone-bruised hands. "That whirlwind which struck a little too quickly and accurately. Your people—your home world?" He gestured with sticky fingers at what lay about.

"No!"

"But one you know well enough to be not only able to survive, but to protect yourself against any dangerous surprise."

She was not aware that she had once more pressed the crescent-crowned rod between her breasts until there was a feeling of small warmth in it. She glanced down and saw the points of light like two gleaming Caperian sapphires, glistening where there was no sun to draw such an answer.

She did not know this world. But—did the Elder One? At least that inward dweller had matched the power of the furred one quickly enough. They might have been old partners in such a defense, or weapon.

"I do not know this world." She held her voice steady; in at least half she was speaking the truth. "You are a star traveler—I am not. I cannot read the star maps. And Life Boats choose the nearest world which has breathable air for those seeking escape—so your own instructions to voyagers read. If this was the nearest world on which we could breathe . . . then that was it. I did not pilot the Life Boat. Who can?"

"Still, there is other life here besides those monsters of the sand."

He chewed the last of the fruit skin and swallowed it. Then he picked up the water-bearing tube and swung it slowly back and forth as if intending by this gesture to refute any easy lie that might occur to her. "Your zorsal did not fill this—that I will not believe—no matter how well the creature has been trained."

"You do not truly train a zorsal!" she snapped, playing for time before she made that other answer which she must truly give. "Yes, that was filled—by others—another. But I know no more of this world than that others *do* abide. And they are not humanoid, though they appeared to me well-intentioned."

To her, perhaps, but she did not forget the raising of the

whirlwind—nor, apparently, did he, for he gave a harsh sound that might have been laughter, except there was no lighting of that in his expression.

"They are well-intentioned?" Thorn made both a question and an accusation out of those four words.

"To me—to Zass—welcome was given."

"But not to any scouring their skies—is that it?" He had lifted himself as far as his knees. Now with effort, Simsa making no move to aid him, he got to his feet and crossed to her side where he might look down at that sinister, half-solid flood circling there.

"How did you cross before?" he wanted to know, having stood a long moment in silence.

Tell him of the light path of belief—No! But the grapple anyone knowing of the Burrows would well accept as natural. She explained what she had done and that it could not serve them now because of the lack of torn-fabric rope and the fact that there was no anchor on the other bank.

Thorn did not even answer her. Instead, he leaned well out, back once again on his knees, looking along that section of this heap of stone which fronted on the river.

"If I knew how deep . . ." He might have been voicing some thought aloud. Now he slipped from its loop on his belt the ray weapon he had used in their flight. Knocking the small charge from the butt into his hand, he examined it closely.

"To set foot on that—" Simsa did not know what he intended, but she was sure that anything venturing on the sand stream would sink beyond aid, even if he or she was not attacked instantly by the dwellers therein. But Thorn was not peering downward. Rather, he turned his head to the left to inspect the edge of the platform on which they now perched. The new vigor of his movements revealed he must have made up his mind about something as he got to his feet. He spoke with the old authority she remembered well from the days of their first meeting on Kuxortal.

"If that rock—the one with the three lumps along it—is under-cut, it will fall forward. Two more cuts there and there"—he used the barrel of his weapon as a pointer—"ought to bring down a rockslide. Let that reach this river and we may well have a dam over the top of which we can pass—if we are fast enough."

"You can do this with your weapon?"

He nodded, but was frowning. "I believe so, but it will also near exhaust this charge, and if we meet with trouble beyond . . ." He shrugged.

He was not fashioned to show much patience in the face of danger. Simsa had sensed that from the hour of their first meeting. Neither was she. But the path on the other side of that flood was a rough and narrow one, twice forcing her farther away from the proposed crossing to cling like a nix-beetle to the stone and edge along. If the inhabitants of the stream were aroused, a mere crossing of their dwelling place was not going to bring much safety. On the other hand, to remain spinelessly where they now perched would achieve nothing either.

Simsa turned the rod around in her hands, rolling it back and forth between her palms. Might this weapon-tool of the Elder One serve also? Best not try, she decided swiftly. She needed all her native wits about her; she had no idea of turning any part of their escape over to that indweller. It might well be that the Elder One had no wish to get Thorn free of the valley or even continue to allow him life.

Her own attitude toward the off-worlder had made such a number of subtle changes lately that she could not be sure she would be able to rise and combat the Elder One on that point. So she remained silent, offering no assistance.

He was very careful in the aiming of his weapon, several times lying belly down upon the rock and then getting up to move again when the proposed angle of the beam seemed not to his liking. But at length he fired.

The ray that shot from the barrel was wider than before and there was also a puff of acrid smoke which set her eyes to watering and made Zass squawk indignantly and take to flight. Nor did the zorsal return; rather, she winged out and up toward the rim of the hidden valley.

However, the fire sprayed across the lumped rock that was

Thorn's choice for undercutting, the stone disappearing as if it had never had existence. The block fell forward. To Simsa's astonishment, for she had not really believed in Thorn's promise, two other huge stones followed, crashing into the first and driving it on into the river.

There was a dam almost before she could draw a deep breath again. The first rock had disappeared, eaten up by the swirling grit, but the second, which had followed, kept its upper surface above the rising sand.

Thorn returned his weapon to its loop with one hand, the other one caught tight about her wrist.

"Jump! Jump!"

She could do no else than follow his command, for he had already moved to leap and would not release his hold. Thus, they threw themselves forward together, he loosing his hand only as they left their rock of refuge. Simsa fell as she had been trained, adding new bruises to her score.

Thorn was already up, once more reaching for her. The sand was banking higher, rivulets forced their way across the lower edge of the topmost block. There was no time to hesitate. She sprang first, reaching a higher landing on the other side, swinging around to narrowly watch the sand.

That pocking and lumping which had been the signal for the monsters' attack before was beginning again. Simsa brought out the rod. It might well be all that was between them and death now—if, as he feared, his weapon was exhausted.

Just beyond was a narrow strip of small stone-marked beach. Where they had landed were rocks and already Thorn had his back to those, was glancing from the weapon he had drawn again to those movements of the sand about the improvised dam.

Simsa looked up hopefully. There were no promising hollows here. The cliff wall was sheer above a level with her head. Zass, who had returned to circle over them on that wild venture across the fallen rocks, gave a series of guttural cries and rose higher in ever-widening circles, one of which finally reached beyond the edge of the cliff. She did not return. The girl felt the warmth of the rod and knew that if they must make a stand, this fight was again hers as well as his. Could the haze that had been before summoned once more give them cover?

Deep in her there was a stir. The Elder One was rousing and, seeing a tentacle stretch from the river toward her, Simsa knew that this time perhaps a surrender on her part to that other personality might be their only chance at safety.

"Can you cover me?" Her companion's demand was sharp, and Simsa, concerned with her own apprehension at the stirring of the Elder One, looked at him in confusion.

He was wrestling with his weapon, turning its butt around in his hand, tapping it against his palm.

"With that thing of yours"—he was even more impatient now— "can you hold them back for a space?" He nodded at the rod.

"What do you plan?" she asked, then swung the rod around so that the ray shot from the tip of the nearest moon crescent to transfix a yellow sucker-marked pointed ribbon, as thick as Thorn's wrist, which flailed at the spaceman's scuffed and battered boots.

"We need stairs. Hold them and I shall see what can be done!"

Almost mechanically, and without aim, she swept the glow of the rod across the now fiercely troubled sand surface. Thorn wheeled about to face that expanse of sheer rock. Did he think to bring down another rockslide? But what would that profit him if they were buried in it?

What shot from the barrel of his weapon was not the wide beam that had eaten out the rocks and reduced the monster company to odorous ash as they crossed the plain. Instead, a ray no thicker than her smallest finger was aimed steadily while a blackened hole appeared. Another and another, each some distance apart. Yes—a ladder which would not give under their strength but instead afford them a way out!

Reassured that Thorn knew what he was doing, Simsa kept to her own task, that of driving the sand creatures off. Perhaps they had learned the threat of the rod from her earlier attacks upon their kind, for they were in no hurry to crawl out of their holes. Tentacles waved and were reduced to oily smears. Then, though the sand heaved and whirled in an even more frenzied manner, there came no more signs of creatures emerging.

A muffled exclamation brought her head around for an instant or two. Simsa could see that the ray from his weapon, thin and light as it was, had begun to ripple along its length, and she guessed that the source of its energy was failing.

Thorn flitted it more quickly now from the carving of one space to the gouging out of the next, racing against both time and his dwindling resource. The last dark splotch before the ray utterly disappeared was hardly more than a very shallow groove. Tucking the now useless weapon-tool back in his belt, Thorn knelt to jerk at the latches on his space boots, freeing his feet and locking the footgear by their fastening to his belt.

He gave a last glance to the boiling surface of the stream and then jerked a thumb at the cliff fast.

"Climb!"

Simsa resolutely shook her head. "Go yourself. I will stay and buy us what time fortune will favor."

Thorn stared sharply at her and then centered his gaze on the rod, almost as if he would will that into his own hand as he had made the rocks earlier do his bidding. But it was plain, without any more words between them, that this game must be played by her rules and not his.

He turned and caught at the first of the holes he had cut in the barrier while Simsa, drawing upon all the depths of will within her, allowed the Elder One to venture forth.

Ah, this space-going intelligence was apt in a point of peril. Yes, one must well keep one's eyes upon such species, for they learned so quickly that they often neglected the proper controls in their search for raw power. However, this was no time to argue the points of any such case. Simsa, the Elder One, flourished the rod as she would a whip to send some shadow lurker squalling. The bluish ray became a cloud to thicken and slide across the sand.

Thorn made good time up the rock ladder and Simsa, tucking the rod to safety, followed. But as she climbed, she discovered that the failure of the weapon he had used was marked by the shallow indentation of the high holes. She did not look down or try to squint upward at the other climber. Instead, she slowed until a voice from above brought her to a stop.

"Not so fast—these are the hardest—" Thorn called hoarsely, as if the effort he had forced his body to was sapping once more his small measure of strength.

How long did he believe she could continue to hang there by her fingers and toes? This was proving a far harder journey, even with no darkness and no pit of flames, than the first she had taken into the lost valley.

She could hear a scrambling sound, the hard breathing of one putting his body to an ultimate task. So much did Simsa of the Burrows hear, but the interpretation came from the Elder One.

This new race of space-faring species had determination, even if their unopened minds hampered them so much. Tools were things outside themselves, dead things of wood and metal, until they were roused to limited life. It seemed clearer and clearer that they were unaware, totally unaware, of other potentialities. What could they not accomplish if they learned—

And how would lives across the star lanes be changed if they did? For good or ill? Those two on the ship who had thought to use her—*her*—for their own knowledge, were there an overnumber of such among these new people?

The Elder One speculated and her thoughts passed through Simsa's mind, hinting that perhaps, when there was time and space for privacy, she might be set a number of difficult questions by this other self of hers. For the moment, that strength which filled the Elder One kept her as tight and safe against the stark wall as if she stood on a well-balanced ledge. She did not fear that her grip with fingers and toes might be lost.

More scrambling sounds from above and then something dangled down the cliff face to nearly strike her in the face. The belt of the spaceman, its loops stripped of all the tools and weapons that he might carry, swung close to her left hand, and she dared to loosen her hold to seize upon it.

But she did not rest her full weight upon that tie; rather, she still climbed, with the belt wreathed tightly around her arm as a support. Then a hand reached down, laced fingers into the jeweled belt that held her kilt, and heaved her up and over the lip of stone, grazing her flesh in the process in a rough end to that journey. Once more they had found refuge on a flat level of rock—one so wide she had begun to think that they had lost the valley descent that lay to the north and that this was merely more of the plain raised to a greater height.

The sky haze was thick, seeming to curdle about the two of them as though it were a serpent winding its length back and forth across the sky, now nearly touching the rock at their feet, now capriciously raising to give them great range of sight.

Simsa saw Thorn sitting only a little away from the cliff edge, his belt in a coil about his feet, his bandaged head and arms limply forward as though he had spent the last of that burst of strength which had brought him this far.

She scrambled up to stand gazing north and west. Somewhere there cut the valley with all its promise of food, drink, and shelter—or perhaps its threat from the furred ones who had already brought down the invading flitter. They had welcomed her after a fashion, but how would they greet Thorn or treat her for bringing him hither? Simsa of the Burrows arose in her to demand that from the Elder One. But the latter was still in command of her slender dark body and was turning her a fraction to face what seemed a deepening of the haze.

The penetrating cry of Zass broke the silence of the cliff top as the zorsal planed down to Simsa's shoulder, nuzzling against her cheek with soft chirrups. Then, through that heavier gathering of the haze, came moving shapes. The girl braced herself. Perhaps none of the blob-things could climb this high, but it was plain that someone—or something—had come seeking them.

🔳 **10** 🔳

The first of the half-seen shapes emerged from the mist, one of the green furred people of the valley. Simsa half-expected to sight a weapon in those claws of the upper appendages. Or was this creature only war-armed with such mysteries as the Elder One had helped them to call up? There was no way of reading either anger or suspicion on a face that was mainly huge eyes and a mandible-equipped mouth.

Thorn fought to his feet, wavering there as he stood to confront the newcomers. On impulse, the girl moved closer to him, not to help but because she intended to knock from his hold any weapon he might produce for attack. But both hands dangled at his sides. He seemed to be expending the full amount of any energy left him just to hold up his head in order to face these newcomers squarely.

For more than one of the valley dwellers followed in the wake of the first, moving out to form a half-circle, all the two humans and Zass. Simsa had seen enough tapes, enough strangers from off-world in flesh, fur, or scales, not to be surprised at the strange forms into which nature had fitted intelligence on other worlds. Somehow she was sure that Thorn would realize that now they dealt with "people" and not with monsters intent only on the hunt.

But it was the Elder One who was still in charge and Simsa found herself mouthing strange syllables which she could not translate but which she knew were a mingled greeting and plea for understanding. Judging by the only standards she understood—those of the Burrows—she was content to let this other carry the argument.

Having uttered that strange hum-hiss of speech, she remained where she was, the rod now held up before her, as a runner on her home world, sent to clear the road, might carry the House-crest of a lordling as he sped ahead of that lord's entourage. She felt the combined sight of those others. How she could sense such impact she could not explain. It was almost as if the dead Greeta had, in a manner, achieved her desire, and all the parts that went to make up Simsa's black, silver-haired body had been laid open to be observed, weighed, disputed over—or accepted.

The leader of the valley force went to all fours to approach closer, the clack-clack of those long claws sounding louder. Simsa looked to Thorn. The man had somehow conquered the weakness he had before shown and stood with straight shoulders and upheld head. His hands moved in a very ancient gesture of peace, which was common enough to the species she did have knowledge of. Both his hands were held on a level with his shoulders, his bare palms exposed to the strangers' sight. He wanted no struggle.

"This—one—from—overhead?"

The question was awkwardly phrased, but Simsa understood.

"Yes."

"From—this—you—ran?"

"Not this one." Simsa was willing to give Thorn the benefit of the doubt. After all, he had never held such thoughts concerning her future as those other two revealed.

"Why—here?"

"For me"—she could not evade that—"but he is not an enemy." Was she right in declaring that? Even now she could not be sure.

"What does he, then?"

"He is a hunter of old knowledge. He believes I have such knowledge—he would take me to those who gather it."

"He is—not—of—the—home. He is of the short-lived kind."

If thoughts could hold contempt, that fairly dripped from the speech she caught with the Elder One's aid.

"He—not as those you know." A flash of knowledge came to her then, such as so often broke through the barriers set by Simsa of the Burrows' wary mind. These creatures were female—or at least of a sex approaching what her own kind thought female. They equated Thorn with a state of being to which they had long ago reduced their own male counterparts—a small but necessary evil. Certainly very short-lived, if they had their own way in the matter.

"He is a hunter of knowledge," she continued sharply. The shadow thought of what was expedient to do with mere males had come too fast upon the uttering of the judgment of his usefulness.

"Paugh!" An exclamation of disgust was not easily translated to words, but came from the spokeswoman of that other party. "What has such as he to store knowledge in?"

On impulse, Simsa spoke aloud to her companion. "They—I do not know how much you may have picked up from thought reading—but these hold males in contempt. Will you open your mind to them—and quickly."

She was not even sure that the spaceman could "think" a message plainly enough. Her own hold on such powers was shaky and she was only sure of success when the Elder One was in control.

There flashed speedily a series of pictures, aimed surely for the furred doubter or doubters but as easily picked up by the girl.

It was like watching one of the reading tapes run a little too fast to be enjoyed but showing so many changes and hints of knowledge as made her feel breathless. Then she saw the leader of the valley ones squat back on her lower abdomen, balanced by the two long folded legs. She swung up a clawed forelimb, the murderous claws held well apart, perhaps her own type of peace signal.

"A Memory one!" There was an exclamation of wonder in that mind speech. "A Memory one, be it male or not. Tshalft must suck this one for herself."

"No!" Simsa took a wide sidestep, which put her between the valley dwellers and Thorn. There was a connotation to that word "suck"—or so it had sounded to her—that carried a dark meaning.

"No harm to it," came the quick promise. "It has too much to give. We try—our Memory ones are few—and there come many hatchings before one is discovered in these days.

"To have new knowledge, that will be treasure for the home. We shall do it no harm, even as we have done none to you. But will it be hunted again? Has it laid some trail for its kind to follow?"

"Will you—" began the girl, when he spoke swiftly, proving that he had read that mind speech.

"The flitter is down. But there are others on the ship which landed here. When they cannot raise any call from us they may write us off—for now."

"But not forever?" Simsa prodded.

"Zasfern is not easily thrown off the trail of anything which is as great as the discovery of a true Forerunner," he answered her. "They may not be able to search now, but in time they will come, yes. My immediate superior, Hist-tech Zasfern, has power with the service."

"It speaks of others," came the thoughts of the valley leader. "Who are these others?"

Thorn raised his hand and pushed fretfully at the bandage about his head. "Answer for me," he said to the girl. "Ask them not to mind read me now—I—" He stumbled half-toward her. Unthinkingly, she took his weight, which bore her with him to the stone.

Over his body she looked up at the others. "He is hurt."

"That is so," conceded their seated leader. "Now his thoughts go all ways, as the guden fly when it is time for a harvest. What would he have you tell us?"

"I know little more than you. But he has said there is a very ancient race whose mission it is to collect all knowledge and store it. They are very old, but it is true that most they gather is from such a long time in the past that they do not understand much of it themselves. They only hunt and hunt for scraps to be fitted into a whole. They have said that is why I must be brought to them. For they think that I—she—can match some of these scraps for them."

"So they will be led to seek here. When?"

"Sometime hence, I think." Simsa shifted Thorn's head upon her knee. He gave a small moan and rolled his face toward her so that she felt the light flutter of his breath against her skin. "He must have help." She found herself adding that plea.

"It is well—for now. Yes, we have much to learn—Tshalft would wish us to do this."

A click of claws summoned one of the others. With no visible sign of any discomfort because of his weight, the speaker plucked Thorn out of Simsa's half-hold and placed him on the back of the follower squatting before her. One of those claws grasped both of the dangling arms of the spaceman, imprisoning his wrists in a single hold. Then the creature turned and started away three-legged, but seemingly not in the least slowed or disturbed by that. Simsa and the speaker followed.

This time there was no journey into the dark, but the top of the barrier was wide and they were soon near curtained from each other's sight by a thickening of the haze. Simsa found her own wrist caught in the claws of another, steering and drawing her onward when the haze at last thickened into a roof too dense for the eye to pierce beyond a foot or so.

They came to the top of a stairway and the grasp on Simsa fell away—only the one pointing claw directed her downward. The steps were stone, chiseled out of the rock. For her feet they were narrow and, since so much was hidden from her, she took them one at a time, her right hand braced against the side wall, her fingers ready to cling to any projection they might chance upon.

She had lost all sight of Thorn and his guardian and tried to force out of her mind a suggestion of danger—a fall for the awkwardly laden valley inhabitant and perhaps the end of the unconscious man as a result.

Down and down wove the stairs—there were no landings where one might pause to get one's breath, summon up courage for further effort, and the fog was as tight as a cloak about them. Then that began to thin and wisps of it moved away as clouds could be driven across the sky by the wind—only here there was no wind.

She could see the way ahead for a much farther space now. But there was nothing but more and more steps. Simsa might well have given out long ago, but that extra energy which the Elder One always brought with her sustained the girl even when the presence of the Elder One herself began to slowly retreat into that part of Simsa which she had established as her own abode for all time.

The last of the haze was tattered strips. Here and there she could sight a tall standing tree of high-growing vegetation, much like those that had formed the avenue at her first coming to this place. The zorsal uttered a small cry and took off, winging ahead, apparently diving into the massed vegetation which Simsa would have thought was far too thick to allow any wing spread. They reached at last the floor of the inner valley. She could smell the heady scent of dropping fruit and she licked her lips, the odor immediately bringing with it hunger.

There was a path here, not as well-marked as those she had found earlier, and it did not stretch straight forward but wound around among bushes that were taller than the girl's head. Palm-wide flowers clustered thick over these, weighting those toward earth where crawled a number of green winged things which in a minute way were not too unlike her guides. Among the bushes, some of the furred people were moving. These claws which could threaten so menacingly worked here with delicate care, loosing one after another of the busy feeding insects, holding them above jugs until, from the tip of rounded green abdomens, a drop of clear liquid gathered to drip into the waiting container. Its donor was then returned to the grazing ground of the flowers.

At the appearance of the party from the cliffs these harvesters drew together and stared silently, nor did Simsa pick up any thought save once or twice a feeling of dislike or alien aversion radiating from them, something she had not felt before. It would seem that her presence, or Thorn's, or both, was a matter for resentment.

Yet there were no claws raised even a fraction and their own party plowed ahead through the wandering trails of the flowered-bush land without any communication she could sense. In a few strides, they left the workers behind.

This was a wider way they had now turned into. Ahead, though still some distance away, the girl caught sight of that odd dwelling or fortress she had seen before. However, they were not headed for that. A side way opened in the brush and into it stalked the furred one carrying Thorn, then the leader of the company, raising a claw to beckon Simsa to follow. The others kept on in the open and were quickly lost to sight as this side way made a right-angled turn. It would appear, Simsa thought, that they were heading back toward the cliffs down which they had just come. But when they emerged from the growth that was so thick a screen here, there was again a wide space as there had been about the fountain.

No spray of water spun into the air here; rather, the open place, a triangle, cradled what Simsa first thought was a giant egg. At least it presented a solid-looking ovoid to the newcomers. Their party halted just at the verge of the open space and the leader advanced, not with that measure of authoritative stride-hop, which she had shown earlier, but slowly, using the claws of a right fore appendage to tap out a rhythm on the bare ground.

Though the tapping was so small a sound that Simsa could barely hear it, there was an answering in the ground itself which ran along the surface of the earth, even into her own body so she found herself moving with the same beat, her rod nodding in turn in her hold.

It appeared that whatever or whomever the leader so summoned was not minded to answer. Yet the tapping continued patiently. There came at last a sharp pop. Across the surface of that giant egg appeared a ragged crack. A portion of shell detached, to fall upon the earth. Then a second and a third, until the shell was in fragments. They were fronting now another of the furred ones. In size she was smaller; she had been cramped and fitted into the egg without much room to spare so that when a forelimb moved slowly into the open it did so feebly, as though any effort were nearly too much for the slowly arousing creature within.

There was a sleekness, as though it had been immersed in water that now dripped and runneled to the ground. Then the faceted eyes which Simsa had thought were blind centered upon them.

"Why—come—disturb?"

There was anger bordering on rage in that demand from the egg prisoner.

"A Memory one—from far—sky." The leader braced both

forelimbs on the ground and lowered her own antennae-feathered head so that those lacy sheaths nearly brushed the pounded earth.

The other had managed to pry her body free. With her last jerk what remained of the shell crumbled into powder on the ground. She made a slight gesture with one set of claws and the leader hastened, still on all fours, to approach near, pausing at a small distance which Simsa read as one of respect, to unhook a smaller edition of the harvester jugs from a belt and offer it to the newly hatched. Greedily, the other seized upon it and drank until at last she turned it upside down to prove its emptiness.

She moved alertly now and Simsa was able to note the differences between her and those other of the valley dwellers the girl had seen. The head was certainly out of proportion, larger, and the fur was lighter, banded with a very faint darker striping.

"It—was—not—time," the egg-born announced. "To disturb is forbidden—only a matter of great importance—"

The leader echoed that last expression. "Great importance!" She must be slightly servile to this other, but she was standing her ground about what she had done.

Simsa was aware of the huge eyes (they looked even larger than the others of this race she had yet seen) turned on her. Movement beside her came as the bearer of Thorn released her burden to sprawl on his side. But it was Simsa that the strange one first surveyed. And it was the Elder One who moved forward to receive that searching, inimical stare, eye to faceted eye, until the egg born said:

"This one—in the time of the lost moon—this one—"

"Not so," the Elder One answered at once. "My blood kin, perhaps—not me. I am new into the world as the Most Strong Memory herself."

"Too much—too long—then the egg again," the other thought. "If not you then—why you now?"

"New come from egg, I seek my people."

"Did they not guard—wait—know the signal rightly?" There was a note of indignation in that. "There must always be those who know—who can call."

Simsa the Elder One shook her head. "Too long—too long. Those who might have watched went I know not where."

"Yet you stand here? What loosed you, then?"

"The coming of one reborn, of my kin reborn—she I summoned—but I had no body. My egg did not hold me, so thus I am in her."

"Ill done. Seek you a body, eggless one?"

"This one serves me well—it is kin born and so mine. We walk the same path and all is well."

"What seek you here?" The fur of the other was rapidly drying and the darkened stripes were more sharply defined. It put out one forearm to its head as if to support that still too large cranium.

"Safety—for a space," Simsa returned promptly.

"This other—" The large eyes for the first time regarded Thorn. "Is he dying? Have you already quickened and used him and now await your own body eggs? If that be so, why bring him hither? Let his body return to the earth since he is of no further use."

"He is not my seeder of egg life." The Elder One seemed to know exactly the right answers. "He is a Memory Keeper."

If a furred, facet-eyed creature could look affronted and disgusted, Simsa believed that this one did.

"He is male—they are good for only one thing. There has never been a Memory one among them—never!" There was angry indignation in that.

"Probe and see, Great Memory Keeper, probe you, and see."

Simsa found herself moving slightly away from the prone spaceman as if to clear a wider path for the other's thoughts. On the ground, Thorn stirred and made a querulous sound.

The girl had an impression of a thought stream almost as visible as an outpouring of fluid, and the greedy sucking up of the same. Yet the Elder One did not share what was happening.

Simsa could set no length to the time that exchange continued. Again, Thorn raised a hand to his head as if to protect himself from some blow. He muttered unceasingly. Simsa picked up words of the trade-lingo, but she was sure that he also spoke in several different tongues during that weird communication—if communication might be the term to apply to this one-sided interrogation. Then he was at last still and the big eyes lifted from his face to rivet their full attention on the girl.

"It is true! Memory cannot be kept hidden from a rememberer—or, it is said, in any way altered more than the alteration which occurs from the event's action appearing thus to one, otherwise to another. These Zacathans—these who seek memories, not to keep them in trained minds but in other ways—he is of importance to them?"

"Judge that for yourself from what you have gained from this man. He served them as the tenders serve you, bringing bits and pieces he has learned for their combined memory."

"But they have no true memory—no true rememberer." Again that feeling of hostility.

"Each to their own, Memory One. If knowledge be kept, what matters the exact way of its keeping?"

The other raised both claws to her oversized head. "I have a this-way, that-way in my head, egg-born. Too much, too fast, and I not yet ready to break shell when it was loosed upon me! Let this one be kept—and tended—and you—be welcome among us. But we are the apart ones and if any more strangers come seeking, let them hunt out on the plain. For we shall set up the barriers. Much—much to think on—to sort out. Much!"

She seemed to crumple, to draw in upon herself, squatting down among the remnants of the egg. Now the one who had borne Thorn here picked him up with the leader's aid and turned abruptly, even as two of her kind came bursting into the clearing. They pushed aside Simsa and the leader to close upon the Great Memory, stroking her fur, holding forth another jug, a much larger one, for her to drink from, while those with Simsa and Thorn urged retreat.

They were not to be quartered in the tower that served as a residence for most of the valley, Simsa discovered; rather, they were taken along the cliff side to where there was a cave that gave a measure of shelter. Long plant leaves were brought in bundles by the furred ones and then were speedily teased into two beds. Food appeared in the form of fruits spread out on another large stiff leaf, and Zass found her way to them just as Thorn roused. The furred ones were gone so that they were alone.

He levered himself up on one elbow with a groan and looked around him, plainly puzzled. "Where is this?" he asked in trade-lingo. "And where is Zasfern—he was waiting for my report. I do not understand. I was in the foreroom of the ministry and Zasfern was asking questions. It seemed as if he asked hundreds of them—all about our past surveys. Why—"

The spaceman might have been talking to himself. Now he saw her. At that same moment, the Elder One also loosed her grip and it was the Simsa he had first known who faced him.

"Where is this place?" There was more force and spirit in his demand. "I take it I was not with Zasfern, so who turned my mind inside out?" He rubbed the palms of both hands across his forehead as if seeking to erase pain.

"It was the Great Memory," Simsa began her answer, not sure he would believe her, and related all that had happened from the moment they had met the furred ones on the cliff top to the present.

"A memory trained to hold all knowledge—" Thorn repeated when she had done. "I would have sworn that was impossible. But perhaps on this forsaken world, there have been so few happenings of importance that it could be done. If you saw the great banks of computers in Zath City . . ." He shook his head and winced. "That is now the memory for most of the known worlds, and it would take a thousand Zacathans a good thousand of their life years to begin to shift it all. No one could hold that. But this Great Memory does believe I came here to gather knowledge rather than harm her people?"

"You came here for me," Simsa responded tightly. "That I have not forgotten even if you suddenly choose to do so."

11

Here in the valley, the thickening of haze marking the nighttime was stronger. Simsa, sitting at the mouth of the cave, gazed out over the expanse of brush and trees where shadows appeared to gather and wrap around each living thing. From behind her came the low, even rhythmic breathing of Thorn's sleep. His ordeal of mind search at the hands—or thoughts—of the Great Memory had undermined his strength more than he would admit, and he had slept away most of the rest of the day since they had been left at this refuge.

There had been no guards set to see that they stayed where they were. Still, Simsa did not doubt that, if she descended that slope into the cover of vegetation, she would not move without eyes upon her. There might be a very thin line between captive and guest.

Zass, wings furled, was curled next to the girl, the greater heat of the zorsal's body warm against her flesh. For the moment, she was alone again—the Elder One was gone from the forepart of her mind. She was thinking fiercely, making one plan and discarding it as quickly while she sat there motionless.

Food and water, all her body might need for existence, were here. But she had begun to understand that it was entirely possible she was as firmly a prisoner here as she had been in the ship. Only— Simsa smiled crookedly—*then* she had had her own plans. The difficulty that now lay before her was that her plan had succeeded. She was free of the ship, from the designs the officer and Greeta had nursed in their minds. But if her future freedom was to be encased in this valley, of what benefit was it to her? No, she had been too quick to move when she had stolen the Life Boat and come here. She should have waited until she was closer to the well-traveled star lanes where planets able to support life would have been more abundant.

Between her idle hands the rod twirled. It was without light now, just an unusual artifact of a race long since disappeared. It would seem that in her way she, too, was such an artifact. Perhaps even a possession to be fought for. Where did she go now—what must she do?

That she would meekly go to ground here . . . no, that was not for her. Though Simsa sat statue still, restlessness fired within her. Surely there was a way out! She refused to believe that this early in her wanderings she had been brought to a firm stop.

"No moon—"

Those words out of the dusk of the cave at her back startled her. It was easy to forget Thorn's presence for long moments at a time.

"Why did you come?" she demanded abruptly, not mind to mind but in trader tongue.

"You were—are—here."

"And what is that to you, spaceman?" She was glad she could get such a hard note into her voice. "How well were you paid to bring me to those? Or had they not yet paid and you would not lose your prize?"

"I cannot believe—"

Simsa did not turn to look at him, rather dug the point of the rod into the grayish earth. "Do not, then. I know what that officer, that woman of your breed, would have of me. And who knows what else their superiors might plan. If I could tear out of me now that other one, I would give her to you—or sell her." Again Simsa grimaced. "I am of the Burrowers and one sells, one does not give. Yes, I would sell her to you readily enough. When she first came to me . . ." She returned in thought to that moment in the strange temple where she had found her double frozen in time, undoubtedly worshipped by the forgotten race who had succeeded her own. "Yes." She spoke more swiftly. "When she came to me, I felt—whole—greater—alive. Until

I knew that for her I was only a body, by some chance of strange fate, a body born later in time and yet of her people, by resemblance. Then . . ." She bowed her head a little, trying in her own mind to sort out what she had felt then, that the Simsa she knew was a nothing, a spark that could be easily extinguished by this great fire. Yet, stubbornly, she had risen to the challenge, to fight, to remain at least in part what she had always been.

"Was it not better"—his voice had the old calm she had known during their first journey together—"to become the greater—rather than the lesser?"

Simsa's mouth worked, she spat defiantly, even though he might not see the whole of that gesture of repudiation since her back was to him.

"Speak not of alms until you wear the beggar's sores," she repeated an old saying. "I know only that, at times, I am one thing and at some instances I am another." She turned her upper body a little to one side so she could see him where he lay stretched on one of the bed bundles, his arms folded under his head to raise it a little.

"She—I—brought down that flitter of yours! She—I—joined in with these of the valley and caused one death of your people and meant no less for you. Do you still speak for her?"

"Yet you came to find me, and else that had not passed, I would have died. Why save me?"

"Perhaps she had a reason."

"Not you, then, but this other?"

Somehow, he was forcing the truth out of her. "Have it your way, star rover. Yes, I came for you. There was too much in the past that I would see you dead without a chance of defense. We walked strange trails together once."

"Just so. And now we would walk others, it would seem. They will be searching for the flitter, you know. I do not know how good the sand river is at burying what it takes, but the flitter recorder will continue to send messages for a space—a beacon."

She pounded one knee with her fist. "Your lieutenant must be very sure of what he wants."

"What did you discover which made you do this thing?" He

hoisted himself slowly to a sitting position. "You said that that officer wanted you for what profit he might make, that Greeta wanted you to—"

"To cut flesh from bone and see why I am what I am, yes! I told you they set me apart in a cabin with hidden peepholes that they might watch me, perhaps test me in some way. She—the Elder One—found those with no trouble at all and made for them covers—hallucinations. Tell me the truth, spaceman—if you had gotten me to these Zacathans of yours, would they have done any better?"

"They do not work in that way."

"Ha!" She seized on that instantly. "But they would have studied me in some other way, would they not?"

"They would have asked you to share memories—"

"Memories for their storehouse. Now let us see . . ." Simsa dropped the rod across her knees and leaned back a little. "What can such memories consist of? My own of the Burrows would have no meaning for them. Thus, they would have summoned that other and strengthened her, fed and nourished her, until she was and I was not. Is that not so?"

"What do you want?" he queried in turn. "Do you want to be of the Burrowers once again, to shut from you all the wonder and freedom and—"

"No!" Again she rolled her hand into a fist, thumped it painfully into the ground beside her knee. "But you—you cannot guess how it is—"

How was it, then? For a long moment, she was caught up once again in that outflow-inflow of identity change which had been hers in the ruined temple. A warm richness spread through her. "Come . . ." It was a whisper. "Come—be—whole!"

So easy—a surrender that would be so easy. But beyond that lay what? All the fears of the Burrows were cold in her, rising to blank out that gentle warmth. She would no longer be what she had always been, and even more then would she also be a prize to be fought over.

"Zasfern understands." Thorn's voice reached her only dimly. "Talk with him, with any of his people. While you fight so, you are denying half the protection you say that you need. Was it you or the other who escaped the ship? No matter what you do now, they will believe only in her existence, not in yours."

She knew that he spoke the truth. One of her enemies had been killed—but what was one among a number? She knew only Kuxortal, unless she unleashed the Elder One, or awoke her. But men were alike across the stars. They hungered and they knew greed on other worlds just as the lords of the upper city in Kuxortal maneuvered and fought openly and in secret for advantage over their fellows. She did not know whether the Elder One had powers enough to keep her freed from such demands and she wanted—To learn the height of power, she would have to surrender herself, and to that she was not agreeing.

"So there will be other officers and other Greetas, and these among the Zacathans, too?"

"I think not. They are old, they live much longer than any other race or species we have found among the stars. To them, knowledge is great, for they are the guardians of history, the stories of many empires which have carried conquest from world to world, of races who knew the stars before my own developed. Yet the Forerunners—of them they have only bits and pieces, mainly guesses. To Zasfern, you would be a treasure to be guarded with his life—but only if you are willing."

"Think on this Zacathan lord of yours, picture him . . ."

For the sake of knowing a little of the future, she would dare so much. She saw Thorn's eyes close, felt for herself the inward turn of thought. He was concentrating with the skill that made him what he was—one in search of the always new.

Between them was a stirring of the air, a stirring she could see more than she felt. At the center of that stir there was something materializing—Thorn's thought? No, the power of the Elder One was at work again. Perhaps as much as Simsa, that other was curious, was near desperate to discover who had inspired Thorn and meant so much to this space rover that he risked death in service.

That fog-thing might well have been fed by the haze which was ever-present here, but it gathered substance enough for her to see.

Humanoid in that it had a manlike body, legs and arms clearly
defined one from the other. But there were webs between the
fingers, and on the scaly round head there was an upstanding crest
of ribbed skin which wavered a little in the air as if it acted as
antennae to reinforce sight or thought. The features were saurian in
outline, with teeth surely meant to rend and tear flesh. There were
no eyes in those dark pits—or else Thorn's thought did not supply
them.

Only for two breaths, no more, did she see that; then it was gone
and Thorn opened his eyes and let out a deep sigh of relief. There
were beads of moisture on his face, shining on his ivory-colored skin
as if he had been weeping.

"That was Zasfern."

How could he be so sure that she had seen anything?
Apparently, he believed she had.

"You have showed me his outer shell only." Simsa rose abruptly.
"I must think." In spite of the eyes she was sure watched them from
the underbrush, she strode away from the cave, along the roots of
the cliff, battling one thought against another as she went.

There was a breeze moving under the trees, not to form any
more specters out of Thorn's past but to cool her body. Then Zass
cried out from overhead and came to take position on her shoulder.
Thorn really believed in his mission and in this lizard-faced
humanoid he served. Of that she had no doubts at all.

She crossed the empty ground at the cliff's foot to set her back
against the bole of a tree and relax. But the thoughts that were
crowding in upon her were like sharp-pointed thorns from some
vine ringing her around. Surely, her escape from the ship had been
prudent? Who could be sure what outré weapon they might have
used to cow her into obedience or drive all consciousness from her.
Thorn believed in his own truth—but that was not hers.

Simsa found herself listening, her head turned slightly to the
north. The hum of a flitter! Thorn was so sure they would come
hunting him. But if they found nothing, or only indications that the
other machine had sunk, would they then linger? And if they went
from this world . . .

For the first time, something other than the nameless and unsorted fears of the girl from the Burrows ebbed, and she was confronted with something else. Spend the rest of her life here in this valley? She stared about her, wondering. Never in her life before had she accepted imprisonment—she had been wary enough to escape it when she had run the Burrows ways. No matter how strong the door barrier of one of those underground dwellings had been, there had also existed bolt holes, the secrets of which were jealously guarded. It had been through one such that she and Thorn had made their way to freedom on her last night in Kuxortal.

There could be bolt holes aplenty here, also. But what lay beyond? Only the seared, scored land which could support no life such as her own. That was so to the north and east—there remained south and west.

Intent on driving this new set of shadows back into oblivion, Simsa rose and began to walk, determined to make a complete circuit of the valley wall.

Once more, she found the flight of steps down which they had come. She shrugged off any idea of another climb to the cliff top as yet. There would just be more rock, though twice that had been broken by crevices which might lead to caves such as they had left her to shelter in, or perhaps even to the mouths of passages—she marked each carefully in memory and continued.

When she reached a fringe of vegetation beyond which she could hear the play of water, she was sure that the fountain she had discovered on her first visit was there. Simsa then became fully aware that the cliff side here showed a number of indentations—shallow yet forming a pattern that ran horizontally and not vertically as if meant for a ladder out. These were so rounded of edge, so worn by time, that she could not be sure of any of them or their meaning. That they were not just intended to be decorative she was sure.

A little ahead, the cliff burgeoned out in a wider curve, cutting into the valley itself. Here that pattern was not so faint, so worn. It consisted of a number of holes of equal proportion bored into the stone in clusters, but in few of those did the same number of holes appear, nor were they arranged in the same grouping.

Old Ferwar had been an avid collector of scraps of parchment, of any bits of stone bearing a strange design that could be writing. From her earliest essays into Burrow combing, Simsa had been alerted to find such, and many a sweet or copper piece had she earned from her old guardian when she'd brought one back.

There had been a number of scripts of different kinds on those fragments out of the past—wriggling lines running without a break across a crumpled bit of rotting parchment, or words set out in stone, often broken in the middle and the rest missing, in some tongue she was sure even Ferwar did not know. Now she was certain that what she saw was an inscription of such importance that it had been painfully and carefully drilled into the rock.

She rounded the outer bend of the invading rock point and once more faced the darkness of a break in the wall. The edges were uneven. It was apparent that the same hands that had carved a message into stone here had been busy again.

But at the midpoint of the stone arching above that entrance was something more than mere pitted stone. Nearly as badly worn by time as the rest, it hung there, blind-eyed and anonymous. It could be intended either as a warning or a welcome. The triangular head of one of the valley inhabitants was depicted, eyes not to be mistaken, many times life size, and with the effect of a never-sleeping sentinel.

With a hand gesture, the girl suggested to Zass that she invade that dark space. But the zorsal refused with a whimpering cry. Nor did Simsa herself want to go ahead. A temple, a palace, a prison—it could be one or all three. It was not in the least like the residence of that moundlike erection at the valley's core.

She sniffed. Temples usually, to her Kuxortal-trained nostrils, burned some forms of scent. There was no sound of any movement, no sign of any path recently used here. For there was a clear drift of leaves, dull brownish through death, right across the entrance.

All peoples, Simsa had learned enough from traders to know, were jealous of the dwelling places of their gods or objects of power. For a stranger to enter such without the proper ceremonies was sometimes merely another and very unpleasant way of committing self-killing.

In spite of every suggestion her mind made, there was another part of Simsa that would not let her move on past this place without learning more about it. Step by cautious step, she moved toward the entrance and, as her feet crushing the dried leaves gave forth the smallest of crunches, she halted between each step to listen, turning her head from right to left.

Also, she held the rod well up and gave full attention to the horns. There was no warning heat, no coming of the light. Judging by this, there was nothing of alien power housed inside.

Zass chittered in her ear and was ill at ease. Still Simsa could not break that compulsion which sent her on, over the threshold into the darker opening beyond.

As wide as the doorway was, it proved to be funnel-shaped, narrowing steadily on both sides so that to go forward, she had to enter a passage that must have been designed to admit only a single one of the valley folk at a time. Being lesser than they in bulk, Simsa walked easily.

There were no breaks in the walls that closed about her—no doors into dark, secret ways, as there had been in that other chill passage she had entered. Here, sheltered somewhat from the weather, both walls were studded with pits or the holes that could be warnings, exhortations, even hymns to be sung—or thought—to some greater form of life.

The small amount of light that entered here from the valley was shortly gone. Simsa faced the dark with no light from her rod to supply her. Zass's whimpering cries grew stronger. Yet the girl received no clear warning from the zorsal, only that there was something here the creature did not like. Simsa paused, waited for a long moment, curiosity and prudence at war. Then she opened her mind in the way she had learned to do since the Elder One had come to her.

Thought quested ahead far faster than she could have run. And encountered—nothing. Or was there too *much* nothing? Simsa considered that thought silence carefully. She had discovered a mind shield on board the ship and at the port before they had lifted. Most of them the Elder One had contemptuously considered childish attempts and had let Simsa know that if she wished, they might be penetrated easily, not that the girl had cared to try them.

But this was, in its way, very different. As Simsa considered why she believed so, the Elder One stirred. It would seem that she also could be moved by curiosity. Because there was more than just that emotion moving her, on sudden impulse, Simsa stood aside—not waiting to be overtaken by that other—to afford the Elder One a free passage through the channels of her mind.

There were wisps of pictures, none of which she could seize upon long enough to clarify—buildings, places out-of-doors—temples, fanes, sanctuaries which the Elder One knew. Some with powers still there—others lost and forgotten, the powers dead with the people who had worshipped them.

Then came a delicate kind of prickling—yes, Simsa of the Burrows had been right. This was not one of those forsaken shrines—something waited ahead. Or did it slumber long past an awakening? The dark silence was far too deep.

She was not surprised when the moons glowed with their tip lights again. Zass was suddenly silent, enough so that her head brushed against the girl's cheek with every small snorting breath the zorsal drew. Once again, but for the first time since that hall when she had rushed into what she'd thought was completion, Simsa was with the Elder One, not pushed to one side, a spectator in her own body.

Those inscriptions on the walls were thick here, the lines of pits crowding in upon one again. Then they came out of that passage into a cavern or hall which was so large, so cloaked in darkness, that the rod's light was no more than a feeble candle end, showing no more than a few steps before her.

To venture out into the middle of that, away from the small sense of security that the wall itself gave, was hard. But Simsa had courage to match the Elder One's now. So they came to a large pit in which no fire burned, nothing stirred. Instead of light, the depression was filled with fold upon fold of thick black, and when she lowered the rod and went down on one knee to see the better there was a heaving and a stirring of that dark as the sand had heaved and been troubled by what dwelt beneath.

"Sar Tanslit Grav!" The Elder One's words—or call—or greeting—echoed, with each echo growing the louder instead of diminishing, until Simsa wanted to cover her ears with her hands and could not.

"Sar!" As if that were a command which could not be disobeyed, the roiling of the dark grew. Faster spun the layers of it beneath.

Up from the heart of that troubled mass of nonlight came a long finger of the same thick blackness. And finger it was, as much as one upon her own hand, marked by the joints, a pointed nail on its tip— and yet that finger was near as tall as she.

It had risen straight upward and Simsa waited, shivering, for the hand to appear, but it remained a finger elongating itself as it rose. She caught another flashing picture from the Elder One of a finger that had once so risen from a grove of trees to beckon and she shivered throughout her body, waiting for that to beckon her, knowing clearly in the same way that if it did so, she must follow.

It was beginning to incline in their direction.

Simsa flung back her head. In her upraised hand the rod twisted and turned. That reaching finger quivered—flashed out. Hallucination? But what had triggered it?

As she had done when the furred one began her spelling to bring down the flitter, so the girl began to hum, and that thrum was in some manner picked up by the rod and intensified. There was light now, fountaining forth from the rod itself, drawing a circle of radiance first around Simsa and then reaching out to encompass the pit. In its core there was the flood of black quiescence now—but only for a moment. As the hum grew louder and the light stronger, the pool of dark began to rise again within the stone cup that held it. There was a compulsion in that sound Simsa did understand. As if sound itself could accomplish that which she would believe only hands and body strength could bring about.

Once more the Elder One cried aloud through her lips:

"Sar—sar . . . Grav!"

Something broke the surface of the pool. It was not a giant fingertip reaching out to seize what it might crush upon the rock. No, that which was relinquished slowly, reluctantly, was a vast mass giving forth a stench that was not of any organic thing rotten, but rather like the smells Simsa remembered from the spaceport, from the ill-running machines that her own people—or the people of Kuxortal—did not know how to tend properly.

The bulk of it was nearly at the edge of the pit now, the blackness bearing it up. Then it washed forward so that Simsa had to leap back and away to escape the wave that brought it and then receded, leaving what it had so borne to drip ooze on the rock flooring. The Elder One moved her forward as a game piece again to stoop and touch the light of the rod to the black slime the thing was shedding.

There was a flash. Fire, which was like honest flames burning, ran outward from that touch, ate greedily at the ooze and drip until all she could see was a huge mass of burning stuff, from which she staggered back coughing as the reek of it bit into her lungs and brought tears from smarting eyes.

12

The fire ran fiercely, then smoldered into dark patches with dull crimson gaps where the flames still ate as they died. This was no machine such as she had seen in company with the off-worlders, nor did it have anything of Kuxortal in it. It was a mixture of solid plates and branching ribs—a carcass and yet not one of any once living creature.

Made by the hands of others, not born by the way of nature. Simsa was ready to swear to that. What it might be she could not have said. There was a rain of sooty bits flying from the structure as if it shook itself to get rid of the last fragments of that covering.

"Yathafer . . ." It was not Simsa of the Burrows who had breathed that name, though her lips had shaped it. Just like all her touches with the Elder One, this was only part of a mystery. Looking upon that blackened thing, she saw it not, but rather a glider, soaring great wings against the sky, a sky that was not curtained in the haze that covered all here, a sky clear and faintly golden. And he who so winged about, using the upper drafts of air to raise and ride, he was—

The faintest of memories struggled in her. No, it was not *his* name she had spoken a moment earlier. It was that of what he did—wind riding, freeing himself from the clutches of earth to soar and swoop and be borne by the breeze's will. He was—

"Shreedan . . ." Yes! That was the name, but where was that flyer? And how on this world of bare rock and traveling sand had Yathafer's wings come to be hidden?

That congealed darkness which filled the basin had drained away. She looked into a black hole where nothing moved. Yet before her was that which was of her people. Why had it arisen to her now? Or was this merely another manifestation of the rod she carried— that it could in truth control all of the foretime?

Tarnished metal showed as the black ashes fell away. She saw the body swing and it was intact, as were the wings which had been closed, one overlapping the other, following custom when the Yathmen stored their craft.

Deliberately, Simsa edged by that craft to point the rod straight down into the basin from which the thing had so emerged. There was no trickery or hallucination leading her to see what was not. She had already reached forth a hand and flicked more ash from the wing edge, felt the solid metal. So—what else might lie hidden below? Simsa was certain that the rider of the Yathafer could not lie here. Or, if he did, his life had long since fled. But she wanted to make sure—she had to! The excitement was like a lash laid about her shoulders, driving her along to more discoveries.

Fixing her mind firmly on the problem, the girl summoned whatever else might lie before that was or had been made by hands. There was no roiling of the dark in answer, even though the light of the rod grew stronger as she poured into it all the energy she could summon, reaching a peak of power that she had held only during the ceremony with the valley seeress when they had summoned the whirlwind.

She saw the sides of the bore and then there was utter dark which swallowed up her light. Either this was strong enough to hold any other prey, once it had been alerted, or else there was nothing left.

At length, Simsa realized that she was expending power for nothing and she loosed control and concentration, turning instead to the machine so oddly revealed to her. Slipping her rod into the girdle about her waist, she caught with both hands at the edge of the folded wings and gave a slight pull. There was no resistance; rather, the wing moved easily. Nor did it fall apart as she half-expected it might. So she was able to push it before her, shedding more of the ash all the time, heading for the entrance.

Her people—Simsa of the Burrows stirred. No, the people of the Elder One—they must have been here, too, in the forgotten past to leave this artifact of their own design. But why had they come? She was sure that this was not the world that had first shaped them—what might the Great Memory be able to tell her concerning that past?

She had to learn so much. From the star rovers of this day she had plucked some things, but always warily, afraid ever to reveal herself entirely. On Kuxortal, she had been an exile; was here another exile of her race awaiting discovery? Know—she must know!

As the girl drew the long-hidden flyer into the open, she found herself no longer alone. Here squatted the strangely banded one who had been—who was—the Great Memory, renewed within the egg, ready once again to serve her people. On either side of her, two of the larger valley females reared high, their upper limbs free and claws clicking softly.

Behind them was another party. Thorn, on his feet, his arms stretched wide apart, each of his wrists in the claw hold of a valley guard, stood there. Though human or near-human eyes could read no expression on those large-eyed faces, still Simsa was sure that peril was with him. Yet she did not pause—or that one within her would not let her, as she came fully into the open, pulling the machine behind her. The light caught painting on the upper of the folded wings—a spiral of blue flecked with glistening stars which did not appear to need direct sun rays to give forth diamond splendor in flashing points.

"What—drew—you—from Pool of Forgetting—" The mind search of the Great Memory quavered in the girl's head.

"That which was of my own people," Simsa replied. "How came it here?" Even as she asked that, her mind was busy trying to storm a door stubbornly shut against her. Blue—and diamond-bright sparks—those had a meaning—what—how—who?

The Great Memory, still on all fours, advanced a single step. Her head turned up at an acute angle so she could center the gaze of her eyes on Simsa, hold the girl so. Simsa was aware of a steady and ever-strengthening thrust against her, as if the Great Memory would encompass her about and squeeze from her what the alien wanted most to know.

"You have troubled the Place of Forgetting." That was a forceful accusation. "Why?"

"Why do you seek to renew memories yourself, egg born?" countered the girl. "I was led here—" How true that might be she did not really want to know, but she suspected much. "To learn what pertains to me and mine. Now I lay upon you, Great Memory, by your own rules, tell me of this thing—or who flew it, and where, and when—and why."

There was a long moment of silence. Then: "Since the pool has given it back to you, your power is attuned to it. Back—back too far, egg sister, rides *that* memory. Perhaps there was another like you who came hither in an earlier day—perhaps once this whole world was like the valley until death struck and struck."

Simsa stiffened. A cold wind might have blown out of the cavern behind, lapped her around.

"What death?" she asked, and feared the answer. Had those who had nurtured her fought these? If so, how could there be any link between them except one of enmity?

"Out of the winds it came, and it shut away the eye of day. It slew all which lived upon the earth, save here where there were the ancient guards and they held, but it was many times the toll of egg years. Marsu was Great Memory and lived out ten egg turns thereafter, for there were none born after the death of the Eye and its closing for long and long who tested for memory. After her there was Kubat, but the memory was less and it was only because Marsu could not take the egg again that Kubat, the most promising, went to the first transferral—five egg times was *she* Great Memory. After her, there were many, many." Tshalft clicked one set of foreclaws as she counted out those names that perhaps even memory could not string like beads in a line forever.

"And there was never any end to the curse of those from the sky—only here. Thus it was."

"Those from the sky . . ." Simsa pushed herself to ask the question. "They were kin to me?"

"Not so." She was so ready to hear otherwise that the girl gave a small gasp of relief. "For there were those like unto you who strove to aid when the Death came. And death claimed them also. One alone won to this place of strength and hiding and in the fullness of time, he fell into the great sleep, nor could he tell us how to rebuild his egg so he could come forth again. Then we took that"— she indicated the flyer with a claw—"to the Pool of Forgetting, which holds all that is not to be brought to memory again. It was a thing we had not learned to use and memories without use had best be forgotten."

"And from where did he come, this one who could fly, and the others with him?"

The answer she expected came clearly: "From the sky also. But they wrought not in death. They treasured life whether it be in their form or another's, which was not true of those who brought the death. Long ago that was a very small memory and one which fades even when the egg renews."

"Of what manner of form were they—these dealers in death?"

The Great Memory swung a little about, her claw stabbing the air in the direction of Thorn, where he stood prisoner.

"I have searched the Great Memory and the lesser, the newer and the elder. And this one bears the look of those who brought the Death."

"He may look like those," Simsa countered, "but they vanished with all their kind over the years. This one comes from a new people, a people which are as nestlings late out of the sack. He is not your enemy."

"There is a memory like unto him," the other repeated stubbornly. Her thought sending was gathering strength and, with it, Simsa could sense an impeccable will which carried memories through years of hibernation and rebirth in the service of the rest.

"Memory is of two parts," returned the girl slowly. "There is that which shows itself a picture, there is another of the inner part no one can see—save through experience. He may wear the guise of that ancient enemy—but he is not kin, nor blood, nor bone of theirs."

It was difficult to judge what impression she was making when

she could not read any facial expression. Now she added what she
hoped would be further proof of Thorn's innocence.

"This one found me egg-bound, as I might be said to be, on
another world and helped to loose me. Would he have done so had
he been as those who strove to destroy your world?"

There came no answer from the Great Memory for a long time,
too long. As when they had stood in the valley before, she and that
one who had controlled strange forces, there came the sound of a
flitter faint in beat but not to be mistaken—seeking—from the
northeast.

Thorn might have heard it first. His head was up so his eyes
could search the haze.

"Again, they come in search." It was one of the guards who
broke mind silence first. She pointed with her mandible-set lower
face toward the cliff. "He calls and they come!"

"You set up a direction call?" For the first time, Simsa spoke
directly to Thorn. "One to lead them here?"

He shook his head. "There is one such on the flitter. It was
triggered when we crashed. That will be their direction."

She raised her hand and Zass, who had floated out of the haze to
take position on her shoulder, now stepped onto her wrist. Simsa
looked deeply into those feral eyes. "Watch—watch—unseen—" she
beamed an order.

The zorsal flapped wings and cried out hoarsely, then sprang
into the air, soaring deep into the protective curtain of the mist,
beyond the power of Simsa's eyes to follow her. Now the girl looked
to the Great Memory.

"If it is the flitter which they seek, perhaps they will find it—but
the rocks hold no track prints to bring them here."

"They will not come." There was something very final about the
Great Memory's reply. "If they seek, they may find." She turned her
head but a fraction, but Simsa knew as well as if it had been shouted
aloud that these would make use of Thorn as a final answer to any
such search—that a safely dead body could not betray them.

She moved swiftly, pushing past the Great Memory. The rod's
tip flicked from one to the other of those claws that held Thorn's

wrists and the creatures dropped their holds, their limbs falling as if stricken powerless against their furred bodies.

She need give him no orders. He was already alerted, leaping from between his late captors to Simsa's side, his hands instinctively on his weapon.

"No!" she uttered aloud with force. "These have good reason to fear your kind. Prove yourself peaceful and you have a chance with them."

Then her mind spoke to the Great Memory as one to bargain.

"I, too, have a quarrel with those you hear. But this one is not of their kind—"

"He came with them!" was the instant interruption.

"Yes, but in his way, he is also subject to them. Now he is free of them, he wants no more of their company." She was improvising. She turned her head a fraction to speak directly to Thorn.

"They will destroy those whom they believe seek them out here. In the past, some humanoid race blasted their world into what you have seen. My people, they tell me who were here for another purpose were also brought down. You must be dead—if you want to live." She smiled grimly.

He rubbed one wrist with the fingers of his other hand.

"If they do not find me . . ." he began slowly in trade lingo, and then continued, "Yes, it might be so. If they locate the flyer and I am not in it, they can believe that I was—" His mouth moved in a twist of disgust and she knew what he thought—of the tentacle things that had taken so eagerly what fortune had brought them. That they were killers and doubtless carnivorous she had no doubt.

"But . . ." He stared at her very directly. "If they believe me dead as Greeta, they will lift ship and—"

"You shall remain." Simsa beat him to that protest. "How soon will they lift ship?"

He shrugged. "There will be nothing to make them linger here. They will believe you dead, also—once they have seen what preys out of that sand trap."

She looked about her, needing no thought contact with any of the valley dwellers to realize that these would do nothing, except perhaps, in a grudging way, provide some shelter. To spend a lifetime on this scraped rock world which had a single cup in which life could continue . . . Her own desires protested that. How much harder must it be for this space rover trapped now with her, whose whole life had been given to the stars?

"Perhaps . . ." She was forced into this. It was her fault that he was here and she no longer believed that he had any desire to wish her ill. "Perhaps you might be found—"

"Dead!" That word snapped into her mind and she knew that the Great Memory at least could dip into her thoughts and see what lay behind any speech her lips shaped.

"Not so!"

There were small sparks dancing at the tips of the rod horns. Fight—no. She had no wish, no will to blast any from her path except those mindless things that swelled and crawled from out the sand. The valley inhabitants had every right on their side.

"Not so," she repeated firmly. "Cannot memory be altered, or is this not the skill of yours, Great One?"

There was a moment in which she could read startlement and near repugnance. To alter memory for this one would be breaking belief in all she had been taught to hold the most sacred.

"You do this?" There was vast distaste in the question she threw at Simsa.

"I can make one see what is not . . ." She held the rod between overlapping hands. "Look you!" she commanded, pointing to a rock, a battered crown showing between two tall growths. The girl concentrated, narrowing both vision and thought to a single thing. On the rock there sprawled one of the yellow horrors from the sand holes.

With a loud mewling sound, one of the guards launched herself at the apparition just as Simsa broke the picture. Claws scraped bare rock. There was nothing left of that obscene intruder.

"It is forbidden to play so," the Great Memory flung at her.

"I do not play—I merely showed what can be. If people can be so deceived as to sight, they can also be deceived as to what they *have* seen."

"Forbidden!"

"To you, not to me," Simsa responded. "Let me take this space-man to a place near his people. Then I shall set in his mind a crooked memory and this I can do."

"But you shall have still the real memory and what if that is read?"

The Elder One drew up Simsa's body proudly. "These are but children when it comes to forces of the mind—and memory—Great One. Do you believe that such as they stand any chance of winning of any thought I am not ready to supply fully?"

"And what do we know of you?" The Great Memory was far from being convinced.

"That I have helped. Ask your singer of storms what I did with her. Those who so labor cannot close evil thoughts and show only the good. So do I swear upon this—" She held the rod higher. Now from the tips of the horns there shot larger sparks of blue light which flew as might some insects into the air about them. "I swear that I mean you and your people all that is well—I swear that *my* memory shall be locked while I am with this one from the skies—and that when he is set among his people once again he shall forget all except what I shall allow him to recall. And—"

Once more the sound of flitter, this time nearer, beating steadily, not circling as the first one had done. Zass came out of the haze and sought a landing place on Simsa's shoulder.

"Flying thing—bad sand—goes—" She lifted the words from the zorsal's mind.

"They are centering in upon the place where the other flitter crashed," she told the Great Memory. "We may have but little time. Shall I do this thing or will you tie here one so different that he will leave an ill memory behind him—of death when it should have been life?"

The Great Memory hunched herself together and the claws on her forelimbs clicked. She had closed the passage of communication between them and Simsa stood ready with the rod. That she must defend Thorn now was a duty she wished had not been laid upon her. Though she did believe that he had not been party to the exploitation that the others of his kind had wished for her.

"Your flitter," she told him, "is centering in on where the other was sand-trapped. I trust that they are armed—"

"Yes. What are you going to do?"

"Return you to them," she said promptly.

"And you?"

"That choice remains mine. I have not found such a welcome among your kind that I care to repeat a trip with them."

"But you cannot stay here!" He looked around him. "There may not be another chance for you to go off planet."

She glanced at the winged machine which had come to her call. There had been no escape for the one who had once used that to soar above the barren rocks of this trap. Yes, it was a trap, but it was a trap she could master after a fashion. The trap that was offered by his kind she doubly feared.

"You know nothing of this world," she evaded him. "What have you seen of it? A small portion only." She held the rod between them; those awakened tips sent their spill of sparks in his direction, forming a wheel about his head, spinning faster and faster until they made a ring of fire. She felt his instant response of fear, of danger signaling his body into action. But he only had time to jerk his head a little.

Then, he stood statue still and Simsa began her task. There was again the flitter sliding into the morass of the bubbling sand. This time, no compulsion of hers brought him out of the wrecked ship; rather, it was his own effort that led him to leap to the ground from that unsteady and perilous perch.

He wandered, he fought the blobs, but Simsa was not a part of the action which was all his. He had that implanted with a skill that haste did not destroy. He did not come into the valley—he had seen nothing of those who dwelt there. Instead, he had sheltered on that rock perch reaching out from the ramparts of the cliffs and there he had been successful in fighting off two attacks of the sand creatures.

Skillfully, the Elder One wrought and Simsa herself knew a chill of fear at that skillful weaving. She was sure that this was not the first time the other in her body had worked such a transformation of what had been into what she wanted it to be. Would she someday turn on Simsa and blot out all memory of the Burrows—of the real girl she had been? That was what she had feared from the first, after her exultation at finding the Elder One. She might resemble that other to the last fine silver hair springing from her black scalp, but she was not the Elder One—not yet.

Thorn stood quietly, staring straight before him. What he was seeing, she knew, was not the valley but that plateau of rock, and he would keep that in mind only until they were back at that point.

"You have changed his memory." The Great Memory drew farther away from her.

"I have saved his life," the girl answered. "But there is one thing more."

She brought to mind another vivid picture—across the barren rock just below the height on which he perched was a broken body and though he tried fiercely to reach it, to beat off the two creatures who dragged it away under the sand, it was gone, all that black skin and silver hair swallowed up forever. To satisfy the valley dwellers, to end any more questing, Simsa gave him her death.

13

While Thorn was still bemusedly reliving the false memory, Simsa and two of the guards took him back up the valley stairs, sent him down cliff and across the rude dam of the fallen rocks by the uniting of their will. Simsa watched him stagger up and out upon the tongue of rock. Between him and her, now there swirled a thickening tongue of the haze. Those who found him would not seek farther, not after he had told his story. He was only a darker shadow in the haze this far away and yet she stood watching him.

By the beliefs of the valley folk she had done wrong. She refused to let herself think ahead to what the future might hold for her, another exile on the seared world as had been the one who had soared and flown in earlier, brighter days. Could those wings still bear one aloft—and, if they could, would she attempt such a flight once the skies were free of the flitter whose beat overhead sounded louder and louder? Zass descended to settle on the girl's shoulder, but she did not need any message from the zorsal to realize that off-world aid was at hand for Thorn.

The mist distorted but it could not entirely hide the figure of the man on that rocky rise beyond the cliffs. Out of the haze, a flitter settled in a straight line from the sky. There was another aboard who swiftly lifted the overhead cabin cover and leapt from the machine to front the waiting spaceman. They were too far away for voices to carry, to know what Thorn reported. Would her conditioning hold the false memory? Simsa's body was tense as she waited, half-expecting them to turn in her direction. But they did not. A moment or two later, Thorn, the pilot's hand on his arm to guide him, returned to the flitter. With a rumble it rose from the rock.

As it was swallowed up by the haze, still Simsa waited, listening, telling herself that what she had done was the best for all concerned. Whether she had lost the favor of the valley ones or not did not matter. They had shown no desire yet to exile her from their refuge and thus she still had access to life-sustaining supplies.

She stroked Zass, taking comfort in the rubbing of the soft antennae-crowned head against her cheek. In so much she had this one to cling to. And—for a moment she hesitated, wondering if such a thing could be so, could she also by will alter her own memories— wipe from the past all that would make her restless and discontented with this cup in which she might well spend the rest of her life?

There was something within her—and it was not the Elder One—that suggested she had chosen wrongly, that her place was out there, no matter how suspicious she was of the motives of Thorn's people, seeking new things ever. The Elder One? No, she could not now contact that one. Her fear of being bound in this prison was that of the real Simsa—and to it she could not yield.

Once more in the valley, she sought out that cave in which Thorn had been sheltered for a space. She curled on the mat bed place where he had rested, willing sleep. It came. The last thing of which she was truly aware was the nestling of Zass beside her, the small warm body against her own breast and the low, contented crooning of the zorsal lulling . . .

She must have dreamed, but none of that dream aroused her into the wakefulness. Her arms were about Zass so tightly that the zorsal protested and nipped at her hand. There was the dampness of sweat along her body and she was breathing in short gasps as if she had been running for her life before a hunt of vastly superior power.

Her mouth was parched—she might have been shouting for help for hours. Help against whom and why? Simsa did not believe that the valley dwellers had sent such a thing upon her. No, it was the old, old law which Ferwar had so often quoted to a heedless girl child. Use any power for the bemusement or ill of another and it recoils upon the sender a hundredfold. Only she had not meddled to Thorn's hurt, but for his own safety!

She licked dry lips. Outside the narrow niche of cave the haze was that of day. Here, it was easy to lose all sense of time with no real night or sunlight to measure it for one. She might have slept for hours; the painful stiffness that hit her as she tried to move suggested that indeed a lengthy time had passed.

Zass was gone, doubtless to hunt. She herself was well-aware of a hunger pang like a knife thrust through her middle. Crawling out of her rough shelter, she rose to look about.

A short distance away, purple globes hung from the boughs of a tree scarcely more than her own height. She headed toward that, uncaring at the moment whether the fruit would be safe eating for an off-world digestion or not. It was full ripe, giving forth a good smell as she twisted a globe from the branch and mouthed it.

Sweet, but with an undertaste of tartness, its juice trickled down her dry throat. Nor did she hesitate or wait after the first mouthful to test safety. Having eaten a half-dozen of the fruit, she sought the water basin.

There were three of the valley dwellers there, drawing water into jars. At her coming, they each glanced once at her and then pointedly away, making it very plain that they intended no contact. Simsa waited until they were gone and then fell on her knees to draw her sticky hands back and forth in the water before drinking. Once more that liquid invigorated her.

When she had done, she started in the direction of the structure that was the heart of the valley. Twice more, she met the furred ones along the paths, both times having to take a hurried step out of the way when it became apparent they had no intention of giving any room to her. It was as if she had really become one of those illusions she had spun in the ship's cabin to deceive those who would spy upon her.

So plain was this nonrecognition that Simsa found herself rubbing her left hand along her body in reassurance that she was indeed there and that this was not a very realistic dream. She never remembered eating or drinking in a dream before—but that was no promise that one did not indulge in such satisfactions for an ailing body. Perhaps, as Thorn, she was afevered and walked only in spirit. No, such a thought was foolishness—she was alive and awake. But that she was so overlooked meant trouble—trouble that could only come from what she had done to Thorn.

Memory meant much to those of the valley—so much that it would seem they bred or carefully trained their holders of recall. To force wrong memories on someone who could not withstand her power to do so . . . yes, to them that might be worse than the outright slaying of the prisoner. Yet she had done just that as much for them as for him. Surely, they did not want to have descend upon them those such as the officer and Greeta, greedy to learn the secrets of others. Now after Thorn's false report, the ship would take off, and there would be no future exploration—they were safe.

"Not so!"

Simsa wheeled to face a wall of the thorn-bearing bush that walled the pathways before she realized that the words had not come to her ears but into her mind. And the thought, from the force and vigor, that was the Great Memory, or else she who had raised the whirlwind with the Elder One's help.

Simsa hunted the first opening in the thorn bush and pushed through it into another of the clearings. No water basin here, no glittering shards of broken egg—only four of the people. There sat the Great Memory, the claws on her forelimbs turned into fists to better support her more upright stance, and beside her the priestess or chieftainess who had summoned the whirlwind. It was she who made an abrupt gesture with her right claw which brought Simsa to sit cross-legged facing them all.

"They are gone—back to their ship—back to the sky which gave them forth," the younger leader thought with vigor. "Yet you remain and, from the memory of the one you favored, you took much. Why is this so?"

"That he and those with him would do as you have said—leave this world and seek no more. He now believes me dead."

"As you showed to him—" the Great Memory came in. "Why?"

"Have I not said—some of those are my enemies." Simsa was

puzzled at that question. "Believing me dead, they seek no more, leave your world. Is this not what you have wanted, Great Memory?"

Leaning her weight heavily on her left arm and fist, the older one uncurled her claws and, on a patch of hardened clay before her, drew with claw tip a series of what looked like a mixture of coils, one slipping into another. Between these she then inserted deep holes, boring claw tip well into the ground. When she had done, she looked to Simsa almost triumphantly, the girl thought, if such faces could reveal any clear expression.

All four of them were still, waiting. Undoubtedly, she was expected now to answer and she did not even know the question. Was that muddle of lines and pits on the ground a message? If so, she had no chance of reading it and there was no value in suggesting that she did.

She pointed with the tip of her rod to the lines. "I do not know the meaning," she thought slowly and, she hoped, with emphasis enough so that they would believe her.

But even as she tried such communication, the rod shifted in her hands, turning, with forces she could not fight, to interact with a portion of the pattern. And there uncoiled in her head—"Hav bu, san gorl—" The words were not only fiery pictures in her mind, she was speaking them aloud. The Elder One knew. This *was* a challenge, a contest of wits and of memories, something that had happened long and long ago and had never been forgotten. The rod trembled in a game of sorts, one in which the stakes were very high—even life or death. And it was a game that was not native here to this forgotten valley. Who had he been—what had he been—that lost, air-soaring one who had sheltered here until his years ran out?

She had a flash of picture, of ebony skin and a mane of silver hair, of brilliant jewels aflash as bodies crowded about two who sat and played for stakes that would condemn one, exalt the other. This was deadly contest and she came to it with a riven mind.

Again, she was not one but two. One of those twins was impotent, a prisoner who could only watch a game not of chance but skill. There had been the flyer and another—another whose face she could not see clearly, blurred as if the years between them had worn it away, even as wind wears away in time the hardest of stone. Yes, the player and the flyer—it was his fears and longings that she touched upon for a moment of keen despair.

Exile. That was the price for the loser. And what the gain? Change—a change he could not allow. This was all a whirl of shadows Simsa could not pin down to understand. Mind power against mind power, desperation against rising triumph. Even as Thorn had been molded and sent forth to play *her* game, so was this one being mastered to act for another. Knowledge was power—and power was the ultimate goal for any living creature.

Wrong! Deadly wrong; something struggled within the prisoner Simsa. She had known the power of the half-barbaric nobles of Kuxortal and had taken her chances with it. There had been the infinitely greater power of the space people and here—here of the valley dwellers, the power she had dared to draw to her to turn Thorn's life from one path to another. Power—always power! Within Simsa a bitter struggle began, a lost one, for the Elder One was clearly awake and lying in wait. *Her* game had been successfully played out. She was not going to withdraw now.

There was a tearing within the girl, a supreme effort which the watching Simsa thought she could never have made. But she was no longer the one who triumphed, but rather the winged one. And the fire that filled her was the flame of his despair and need. Only a glimpse of that ancient battle was she allowed, and then—

Darkness—though she knew that she did not sleep or wander in any land of illusion. There was a spark of light. She somehow felt the pain of that which held her stretched upon rock, bruising her body. There was the ship—not the one that she had voyaged upon and fled from. The faint outlines she could see rising from that core of light were different. A ship lost in time—an ascension from this world even as Thorn and those who had rescued him would go—if they had not already gone. She was left alone as it climbed skyward, then she was alone again. What had she won? Doom for herself and perhaps no victory for those for whom she had fought her battle. She willed the dark to close utterly, that she might know that all changes were past, that she must live and die as that sky rider had chosen.

She must have passed out of the far time into the now in sleep. For when she again battled with the dark, it was to awaken in that same shallow cave where Thorn had sheltered. For a long moment, she did not move but lay there staring up at the ragged rock about her, wondering at what she had seen and its meaning. Time, she had all the time in the world now to think about what she had done, perhaps not once but twice, as the wheel of the great years made its slow turning. Had she indeed savored the last confrontation of the flyer and one of his people? One who successfully built false memories could never again trust his or her own.

She pulled herself up to look over that valley of life in the midst of so much desolation. Simsa had always prided herself on her self-sufficiency, that after she had been able to walk, talk, and feed herself, she had progressed steadily toward full independence. Yes, she had shared with Ferwar, but somehow the old woman's attitude toward her had been one of very casual interest after she had dinned, beaten, bullied the fiercely independent girl-child into abiding by the only rules that meant safety on Kuxortal. Simsa had come these last dozen years or so to think of herself as one free, in no way forced to another's ways.

Certainly, she was now freer yet, for there was not one left on this unnamed world who could lay any task upon her. The valley people were apart—she could expect nothing from them, save perhaps food, water, and this rock over her head. She had the zorsal, but as long-lived as Zass might be, she would not spend too many more weary years here.

Nor—Simsa sat the straighter and her mouth became a determined line—nor need she stay here, either, to dry away into nothingness because she was forced idle. What had she seen of this world after all? The fissured plain in which the sand rivers flowed and this valley! But that was not a world, only a very small part of it! There was nothing to prevent her going forth again, with supplies she could cull here, to advance her wanderings. What had brought that first ship, the one of the flyer, to this world? The impression lingered strongly with her, *not* at any nudging of the Elder One, that there had been a reason—no casual or unplanned voyage as her own coming had been. There was no suggestion either that that exile had fled and been followed as she had been. Therefore, let her see what had drawn those others, even though time might have nearly erased all signs or traces!

The need for action had always been a part of Simsa of the Burrows. Perhaps it had also tinted the musing of the Elder One, for the girl was aware now of a flow of strength, as if that other part of her agreed, was impatiently pushing her toward faring forth.

It was dawn. Her "sleep" must have lasted hours. And she felt the refreshment of her body. Simsa swung out of the cave, went down to the fringe of the green stuff.

How many memories did she ride now? She tried to control the shaking of her hands. How was it she knew that if she broke from the parent branch two of those paddle-shaped leaves and pressed their edges closely together, she could fashion a bag, one strong enough to carry water? Her hands were already busy at the task and, cautiously, she sought the Elder One. There was a blotting out there, so—*No,* she had had a hard enough time as two people. She would not welcome a third—the hovering identity of the flyer—too!

Yet, when she was fully equipped with two water bags filled and sealed and fruit she had examined critically that it be not too ripe, she felt free enough. East lay the river of sand, the plain over which she had come. Nowhere in that journeying had she seen more than dead rock and a blasted world. Not east, then—west? And that direction also had the advantage of being away from the landing place of the Life Boat and presumably where Thorn's ship had also set down.

She whistled as she headed toward that stairway up the cliff. Zass came winging, circling about Simsa's head, complaining with a hoarse croaking at what lay in her mind. Yet the zorsal made no move to remain behind, but went with the girl as she climbed steadily to the top of the cliff wall again. That flyer, he had not even had such as Zass to bear him company—she was not as bereft as he.

Now she set him firmly out of her mind as she tramped along the lip of the cliffs working her way to the opposite side of the valley.

The haze was always thicker in the morning, and as she looked down into the cut before leaving she could hardly see the highest crowns of the trees. They had their own protection from discovery. When she tried to stare ahead, she could see only a little. But it was enough to locate where a fall of rock gave her a place over which to scramble down.

That river of sand flowed here, too, but in the place below the land slip it was narrow. Rocks tumbled to leave only a space over which she dared to leap. When she crossed, she stood staring keenly about her. To find such an aid to return to the valley was almost as though her mind had moved the cliffs to achieve it. But she must be aware of the ease which the haze might spin her around into losing it. She reached among the debris of the slide that had fallen on the other side of the stream and picked out any pebbles she could find that held a glint of pure yellow. Several such had been fractured in the crush of the fall and gave off bright sparkles from their scraped surfaces. These she chose first.

Setting, as she hoped, straight out from the valley toward the unknown west, Simsa left a train of such pebbles, one dropped every twenty strides. The haze was thinning and seeming to rise into the usual ceiling across the plains, so she could see and easily avoid any of those threatening fissures. Though the air was warm and the rock actually hot under her feet, there was still no sign of the haze thinning enough to let in the sunlight.

Zass now and then raised in flight, which carried her out of sight into the dimness before she returned again to settle with complaining grunts on Simsa's already talon-scratched shoulder. There was no way of marking any hour, just as there appeared to be no end to the monotony of the other plain. She had chanced upon no more rivers of sand, and even the fissures were smaller and farther apart.

A seam of reddish yellow drew her to one side. Simsa hoped she had chanced upon a vein of more of the colored pebbles she could use for markers, as her supply fast diminished. But as she came closer, she saw that it was not a mineral that had raised that streak of color but seemingly a plant—the stems thrusting upward from rosettes formed by flat leaves against the stone, some tipped with bright red blossoms. At least, she thought, they might be termed that, though they were not open, but rather appeared as tightly rolled cylinders.

There was not only plant life, but insects that hovered over those blossoms, unrolling tongues almost as long as the rest of their small bodies to thrust those deep into the flowers. Zass croaked with interest and then appeared to decide that the feeders were too small game for her to exert herself to catch.

More and more patches of the vegetation spread in streaks along the rocks and those were rising in a ridge—a slow upward slant which did not require too much exertion to follow. The insects whirled away on almost invisibly thin wings and then resettled as she passed. Now there was a second type of growth, this anchored on the level surfaces of the stones over which she climbed. Like the things that lived in the sand streams, this was deadly to the smaller life-forms, for it threw out long limbs patterned with thorns. Simsa strove to avoid their seeking claws. Not all travelers were so lucky. Simsa caught sight of a white blob on the ground. One of her jumps to avoid a thorned lash rocked the blob and sent it spinning over so she could see the eye holes of a skull, though she had found no other land animal hereabouts. These remains of a victim made her look more carefully for any trace of such life.

At one or two places, the moving tentacles of the plants raised such a barrier that Simsa leaped the obstructions, fearing to feel the rake of entrapping thorns on foot or ankle as she crossed there. The larger they were, the more she could foresee trouble if she kept on a direct course. Then both plants ceased growth abruptly as a last jump landed her on an expanse of what appeared to be ebony-hued glass, so that she slipped in spite of desperate efforts to keep to her feet, sprawling forward, luckily out of reach of those flailing vegetable arms.

Zass had leaped to wing and now screamed with rage at what she considered hard usage, drawing Simsa's attention aloft. She sat very stiff, her eyes trying to take it all in, even as she had studied the ruins of faraway Kuxortal.

No vegetation masked this place, but there had been far worse things that had happened to what had manifestly been a building or collection of such which in size far rivaled Kuxortal itself. These buildings had—melted!

Before her, walls were half-buried in a hardened ooze of their own substance. Simsa could see that beyond the pools of glasslike puddles were other walls rising three, four, and even more stories high the farther her eyes peered through the haze.

Nor had those higher and less damaged walls been fashioned of stone. Even in the hiding of the haze they gave forth a metallic sheen, bearing no resemblance to the rocks on which they stood.

Unlike the mound buildings in the valley, these had openings at ground level where they were not entirely melted into formlessness, and they were closer to those she had always known. A palace, a fortification, a city so built that only narrow paths, rather than broad roads, linked or divided? She did not know what she had chanced upon or—

Within her was such a strong surge of memory that the Elder One won control before she was prepared for any battle.

"Yi—Yi Hal . . ." The strange words she uttered echoed from one building to the next, carrying on hollowly from where she faced the wreckage, deeper and deeper into the mass before her, until she almost thought she was being answered by something hidden in the haze.

"Yyyyiii—Hhhalll . . ."

But in truth, all she heard was Zass's scream as the zorsal planed down to sit on the nearest mound of circled rock.

Pushing against the cry of recognition came another memory. Not—not home—never Yi Hal again. Only this which looked enough like it to deceive at first glance.

Simsa clasped the rod of power closer to her so that the points of the twin moons pricked her flesh. Never again Yi Hal! Simsa of the Burrows had no site that had ever been truly a safe and happy refuge from the world—but now she wept the Elder One's tears as memories lived, flickered, died, and she sat alone in the ruin of what was not Yi Hal.

🔲 **14** 🔲

That abiding trait which all her life had drawn Simsa into adventures and had at last landed her on the present glassy puddle, stirred. She was curious. This was a dead place and still it drew her. Back on Kuxortal, she had grubbed for those finds out of the past that had been hidden in the walls, the roofs, the footpaths of the Burrows. This was like the Burrows, a dead place—waiting—to offer the intruder what? She rubbed the grief tears away from her cheeks with one hand. What did she know of that past? she asked herself fiercely. Nothing! Let the Elder One mourn if she would—Simsa was more intent upon what lay before her.

She crawled on her hands and knees across the puddle of glass until she could lay hands on stone. The footing was slick and she had no mind to fall.

Thrusting the rod into her belt, Simsa worked her way along the walls, part of whose substance had bubbled down into such a trap. There was the opening of a dark doorway and, calling on all her boldness, Simsa pulled herself within. Whatever, whoever, had built this massive pile had been not much taller than she. Half-consciously she had been watching for some carving, some runic inscription or sign. The dead city she and Thorn had found on Kuxortal had had such. And there were those ancient eroded markings on the cave wherein she had ventured in the valley. But here were only walls, and a kind of grimness which began to dampen her eagerness.

The room within was as bare of wall as was the outer husk. Yet, the surface was so smooth to the touch that she could believe that if the melting blast had not licked within, there would have been a metallic surface that resembled the rock without. Dull gray, then—

Simsa went into a half-crouch, her rod jerked forth and up in threat or warning. That shadow before her aped her own stance. A long moment of tense apprehension passed before the girl realized that what she did see was her own reflection as hazy of outline as if a tendril of the mist outside had been drawn with her.

She walked forward, ashamed at her reaction to such a thing. Putting out her hand, she touched the surface of a mirror far more accurate in reflection, as she slid her palm along against that other hand raised to meet it, than the polished metal discs so used on her own world.

She studied the figure she faced. Her hair floated free—a ragged mass of fringed stuff about her head and shoulders. Her black body faded from sight in the dim light of this place. All she could see clearly was that hair, her jeweled kilt, the rod in her hand. Her other palm against the surface slipped slowly to the right, then met nothing. A moment later, she discovered that the mirror was not part of the wall, but rather screened another door behind. The purpose of its setting puzzled her. Could it be that those who had once lived here announced their presence as visitors by such reflections cast on the mirrors?

She slipped behind that barrier to go on. Oddly enough, though she could not distinguish any source for it, there was light of a sort— enough to show here the blank walls of a passage. Zass croaked and gibbered impatiently from her shoulder perch. Her neck at full length, her antennae weaving back and forth, the zorsal projected a feeling of excitement, as if they were approaching another grove of trees from which she could take her fill of prey. It might be that in this dark gloom, Zass remembered the warehouses on Kuxortal where her kind kept under firm control the destroying vermin that scuttled among the bales.

Of course—the wuuls—the rod swung in Simsa's hand before she began to marvel at that snatch of other memory. Something that was gray-white and crept upon its belly, though its weak-looking legs could ensnare and hold with the force of a trap—the wuuls that feasted on both the dead and the living.

"Wuul?" She questioned aloud the picture that had snapped into her mind.

She answered herself with an exclamation that was both fear and irritation mingled. Wuuls came from no place or time she, the real Simsa, knew. Yet, the thought of them was so real she found herself straining to hear, slowing her own pace to watch and listen—for what? Something that must have lived elsewhere and long since become dust. This was a memory of the Elder One or that other which intruded now and then—the flyer.

If traveling through this place was going to release such scraps of alien memory, it would be better now to retrace her steps and leave the ancient pile to its death sleep.

Only when she had decided that this was the choice to be made, she discovered that she had no means of carrying it out. Simsa was not aware of the Elder One in control, of the haunting of that other exile. To all tests, she was in command—of her thought, perhaps, but not her body. That carried her on into this ruin which was fast becoming a maze.

The corridor she followed split and split again. Never did she hesitate at such a branching. As if someone far stronger than she held her by the shoulders, she was turned briskly right or left to march on.

There were openings along the sides which might indicate rooms, even as in the underground ways the valley dwellers had traveled. But none of those did this pressure allow her to explore.

Twice, she was out-of-doors for the space of a stride or two, always sent ahead into another door across that narrow way, until she began to believe that this compulsion was carrying her directly into the center of the city, fort, palace, or whatever this pile had once been.

There were no relics of its earlier inhabitants—just the smooth corridors down which she was marched, some straight, a few curved. Then the way began to slope upward, not by means of any stair, but rather at a gentle incline until, at last, Simsa emerged into one large room without a ceiling. There was no sign of metal above—perhaps this had always lain open to the haze of the sky.

In the center, was a pool—an oval with a raised rim about it. And even though there was no sun to bring out their glitter to the fullest, Simsa could see that it was encrusted with a pattern of brilliant stones, gems to which she could not give names.

Making a half-circle about the rim of the pool were seven chairs—or thrones, for they possessed such adornment of jewels as to be the seats for great nobles. And inlaid on the back of each was a symbol.

Simsa's rod swung up, the horns of the moons pointing.

"Rhotgard." She signed to the first in line. Then—

"Mazil, Gurret, Desak, Xytl, Tammyt, and Ummano—"

She threw herself down on the pavement before those thrones, the rod falling with a clatter across the stone, as she folded her arms over her breasts and weaved back and forth in the age-old way of one who mourns. Within her, fear swelled to panic—to such terror as left her weak.

She could not control that which was in her. Never again would she be what she was. These others—the Elder One, that other faint shadow who had done the naming of names—they were taking her over, tearing at the small part of her that had kept an imperiled freedom. Once she had welcomed knowledge, now she would flee it—rip the encroaching others from her own flesh if she could.

Instead, that which used her to ride into life was making her crawl in her debasement, reach out hands to the water of the pool—for there was water there, though dark and turgid so that one could not see what lay below it. This liquid which lay in that place—her skin was roughed by the breath of her terror—still she could not draw back.

Her fingers forced themselves into a cup, swooped to break the quiet surface of the pool. Somehow, she had expected the water to be night black as it lingered in the hollow of her palm. But it was green like that of the valley, cool but not cold.

Her mouth opened against her will as her hand rose to her lips and she drank. That liquid which seemed so cool in her hand—as she sucked it up from her palm it was bitter, warm. She might have been lapping from some muddy-bottomed footprint left on a trail or from one of the ill-smelling, stagnant seepages in the Burrows. Still, she swallowed, unable to reject what she mouthed, not only that but two palmfuls more.

Bitter and hot in her mouth, growing hotter in her throat, pain spreading into her middle, until she bent over, both hands pressed to the place between her breasts where that pain seemed to eat the worst—dully at first and then with quick thrusts. Poison! A safeguard that had been placed here and to which her own disturbed inner struggle had treacherously guided her. She would die. She fought to raise a hand, ran her finger into her mouth, her throat, that her own muscles could eject this torment. But her hands were no longer hers—they betrayed her, too, though they continued to nurse her middle.

The *High Cup!* Memory warred with memory. It was as if her own trick with Thorn had certainly been forced back against her again. Of old this was—not to show pain, to sit unbowed, serene as the poisonous fire ate, until her own talent—power—could render it harmless.

She uncoiled from her huddle of anguish on the floor. Even what was left of Simsa of the Burrows understood this. She had been struck, perhaps past any defense, but the girl who had made her way through all of Kuxortal's fetid trails unmarked, cunningly, able to face down any opponent—save Ferwar—that girl came out of hiding to give her the pride to stand straight and tall fronting the chairs of the missing. She seized upon another trail of memory. An initiation of sorts, though the reason for such had long ago disappeared and what she had to offer might be worthless now. If she had been tricked and trapped . . . well, she would play it through! Fight what gnawed within her, not by the rubbing of hands, the voicing of any pain cries—fight with the mind! Just as she had wrought with Thorn, overlaying true with what was false, so must she work here. There was pain, but it was fading. By concentration, she forced her trembling hands away from her body and held them before her as they shook, and the fingers writhed with the torment.

No—that was growing less. Think it off! Instead of the poisonous draft she had swallowed, she forced into her mind the memory of the drink from the pool in the valley, sweet, cool, refreshing. That was what she had drunk.

Hands, be still—fingers, together; no more trembling, no clawing at the air. Coolness within her. Sweat gathered on her forehead, dripped down like the first of a spring rain from her chin and cheeks to her breasts and shoulders. The effort wrenched at her almost as much as the pain had done. And, behind it all, those two others waiting—the Elder One, the flyer, waiting for her failure.

Which would *not* come!

Do not think pain—think something else. What was the greatest thing that had ever happened to her, which made all the rest of her life small and mean and of no account? That moment when she had stood before the statue that might have been her own likeness, when she had first known the Elder One and—welcomed her! When she had first believed that she could rise to greater heights, before the seed of doubt had been planted, before she had known what she might represent to others.

That was the hour, the endless moment in which she had been really whole, when she had been born anew into a different world. Here was a place that was also one of birth—

The thrones were empty. They had long been so. There were none in this hall to judge her endurance, her talent, only herself. Simsa held her body tensely erect as the gnawing within her twisted and tore afresh. Do not think of what might have been, what once had been. Think of now and the next moment and the next. Pit all her strength against the pain and that which was meant to finish her if she did not fight it.

Her hands—they no longer trembled. She willed them to spread fingers, contract them again. Her arms next—the scarlet thread of torment which ran like the blood in her veins. That was *not* greater than she could bear. This she had done before and came out the victor.

She? The other she. Who was she now—the thief from the Burrows or that much greater one? Both—they must be fitted together or she was left with death. No! Keep her mind free from such a thought. This was the place of trial. She did not shrink from what it would bring her.

Arms—the hot pain was less, surely it was less. Feet—the heat within them that seemed to char its way outward . . . There was no heat! She would walk where she willed and there was none who could say her nay! Not now, not ever!

The twisting pain within her, coil upon cramping coil . . .

She stood, she breathed, lived, and she would continue so. Simsa drew upon that pain, surveyed it as she would a new road opening before her. Simsa! Not the Elder One, not the thin shadow of the flyer—no, she herself. She was one!

"One—one—against you!" She shouted aloud her defiance to the empty thrones, to the shadows who had once been seated there. "I am Simsa!"

Even as she turned, all the power she possessed to hold on that thought, using it as both shield and sword, the dark roared in upon her. Nor was she aware anymore of her body, which held the pain, of anything save that she was Simsa and so she would be unto death itself.

There was no pool, the thrones were gone, she moved through a place of drifting shadows. They might have been those cast by others like herself, wanderers in a place that was meant for searching—and which she must best not by aimless hunting but by finding!

Some were like trails of silver smoke with no hint of form about them. Others were faceless men and women floating. The shadows of shadows that clothed them were strange and varied from one drifter to the next. Twice, she was sure that she had sighted figures in spacer clothes, a woman in a robe of the desert people, and others—so many others. But she refused to be a shadow, refused even to look down along her own form to see whether she matched these lost and wandering ones.

Rather, she put purpose to her own drifting, forged ahead as if to some goal. She had come here to hunt. Therefore, to be about that task as speedily as possible was what she must do.

Beyond, the shadow people arose—and then became tenuous wraiths of their own—buildings, tall towers, squat blocks, things of vivid beauty, darker structures which in their way threatened . . . The people, the kingdoms, the worlds—

Her hands moved and still she would not watch them, only fasten her mind on what they did. For in the air of this place of shadows, her fingers moved with a purpose. On the air itself she sketched it—the rod with the sun, the horned moons in protection on either side.

That was no shadow; rather, it was light, dazzling light that did not hang there. It was moving, her guide through this place to whatever lay beyond. Perhaps, this was the world of the dead. She had heard many beliefs and fragments of beliefs in the past. There were temples aplenty in Kuxortal and Simsa had shunned them all in her time—finding in none of them any stronger will than her own.

What lord ruled here—or what lady? She need not ask. The answer was ready in her thoughts: Soahanna.

Again at the thinking of that name, the orb before her sped the faster and she urged that which was left of her to course behind it. It appeared now that the dark in which all those mist figures moved was thicker, was attempting to slow her, hold her back.

All her will concentrated on the one thing, that there was a power, a will, a force here which she must front and upon that fronting meant all that would save her from becoming one with the other drifters.

The dark thickened. The other shadows were very few now and only the thinnest trails of mist were visible. Yet the orb pointed her on. And she would go—the stubborn will that had been born in her from the beginning held her to that.

The last of the searching shadows was gone, dark pressed tight on her in another form of pain. But that dark could not hide the orbed light nor stay in its forward flight. Perhaps that symbol in some manner cleared the way also for her. She continued to concentrate upon it fiercely.

There was no more dark. Here was the arid, scraped plain; the river of sand; the fissures that hid death. She was back; yet there was a kind of lifelessness—if rock and sand ever held life—and the orb swept ahead.

Was she going back? That fleeting thought nipped at her concentration. She expelled it firmly.

No more rocks and whirled sand—this was the ship cabin in which she had known, being spied upon, that she must take charge of her own life again. Only a flash of that—

The spaceport at Kuxortal where the whole of her story had started, where she had seen Thorn and marked him down as the perfect customer for her bits and pieces dug out of the past.

That, too, was gone in a rippling as if it had all been painted upon some curtain which was now yielding to a rising wind. Here was that other city, ancient beyond the counting of Kuxortal, the city in which she and Thorn had found the smugglers, and that field of spaceships which would never lift again—the city in which she would discover, on her own, the Elder One.

The hall now, the very place where she had made that discovery. Only she did not see it as one who entered but rather from the dais as one who had waited and waited for years out of time's flow. She was the Elder One!

And again, there was a shadow—one who came even as Simsa of the Burrows came to wonder and to break time's lock. The globe swooped toward that shadow. It disappeared and she was again able to move. But she knew her first meeting had been the right one. When she doubted then, she had unconsciously attempted to rend something that had been meant to be sealed. Yes, she was Simsa, but—

By the light of the orb she could see the two hands that reached forth. She seized upon the rod and brought it to her. This was what she had sought—this was the binding beyond any cutting of bonds.

Dark again, but now no whirling trails of mist people. Simsa opened her eyes. She lay on her side, her knee nudging the rim of the poison pool. Pain . . . she waited for the pain to begin again. Then she realized she had learned, she had gone beyond. The very ancient final test for travelers had been given her and she was the victor. Yet, when she tried to pull herself up, she was very tired, as worn as if she had hiked for days or labored past her bounds of energy.

She heard the scream of Zass and the zorsal spiraled from the sky haze overhead, to claw a hold on the back of the middle throne. Suddenly, in a rising tide of laughter, Simsa felt within her relief from all that had happened since she had found this chamber.

"Ha, Rhotgard, wherever you may be—see what wisdom has now come to seat itself in your place." She moved too fast and grimaced as limbs that had been cramped protested. Making a wry face in the direction of the pool of initiation, she pulled forward her own leaf bag and took a swallow of the water she had brought with her.

The pool was no longer calm, glasslike as a mirror, nor was it aripple. Still, through its depth so that she caught glimpses now and then, she saw movement, the movement of those shadow people who lived (if they lived) now apart.

Her fruit was overripe and smelled as though it were close to rotting. But she conscientiously ate it and, with the water, it was summoning back her strength. Zass walked the length of the throne seat and came so to peer into the pool herself.

She flung up her head so that her antennae tossed like plumes and spat—the ultimate in her gestures of disdain.

"Be not so bold," Simsa warned her. "It is a test, but it might be more for an impudent zorsal." She scrambled awkwardly to her feet and then began stretching and bending each limb, turning her body this way and that. How long had the shadowland kept her? She could not tell—time itself was forgotten here. But the pain that had racked her was gone and what she felt now was only the complaint of cramped muscles.

She stooped at last and picked up the rod. Perhaps it had not shared her venture, but its essence had brought her through. It would be long, she thought, before she would learn *all* it was capable of in her hands, even though the Elder One was no longer pushed aside but shared the high seat within her.

With half-recognition, the girl looked around. She might never have trod the rock of this world before, but this chamber was familiar to her, a place that was to be found in every sector center where the Kalassa went. Kalassa—she had a name and with it a flood of memories which she banished for the moment. Time enough to pull upon those when she had not her own work to undo. That which she had wrought in fear must be broken. Such fears were like the drifting shadows, things now without any real substance at all.

From this world, there was speeding a ship and on board it, one with whose memories she had meddled. As the valley dwellers, she realized fully now what her fear had led her to do. She had made of him also two people and who better than she could understand what that would mean to any living creature? He would dream and awake with bits of dream so real that it would shake him, his belief in himself. He would walk down some street on another world and see an object that would bring a flash of recognition; he would be talking to friends and suddenly wonder why he had used words . . . He would—

No!

If she had learned anything in this time of trial, it was that none should be two. Perhaps, the memory self she had set on Thorn would not be as known to him, as much of a burden as the one she had borne, but he was to be freed from even the shadow of a shadow.

She put aside her bags and set her improvised pack to one side. With the rod firmly in her right hand, she approached the throne nearest to her.

"By thy leave, sisterling." She had not said that aloud, but she was certain that it reached whatever shadow had once had form and had sat there judging. Seating herself forward on the throne, she passed the rod with a wide swing of her arm across the end of the pool nearest to her.

For the first time, the surface of the water was broken by a troubling which sent wavelets skidding outward from an upsurge in its center. That troubling of the water brought with it a puff of odor—not as foul as one would believe could rise from a poisoned pool, rather one that made her think of a field on Kuxortal where she had once lain down under the sun of spring and spent a quiet hour such as those of the Burrows seldom knew.

Staring down into the troubled pool, she began tentatively with some fear, which she quickly choked off lest it weaken her, to search. What she had done tied them. The Elder One knew and feared such ties. For if ill came of it, both the captured and the captor suffered. So it was with a sense of duty as strong as any order laid upon her that Simsa began her search.

First, she visualized her Life Boat, how she had left it among an upturn of rocks that had the appearance of a forest of stone trees stripped of all save their broken boles. He had been there—it was what had sent him questing out across the rock plain. So—

"Thorn?" No call echoed aloud, but such a seeking as this world, this galaxy, had not known for a thousand years' planet time—or more. "Thorn?"

In the pool, she used the troubled waters to build his reflection. So lay his dark hair—so were set the planes of his face, his slanting eyes—so had he looked with that intent study when they had sought the answer to the death that had lain in the ruined city for countless years, with the threat of returning to trouble life-forces again. There were his shoulders, wide under the tight-clinging fabric of his spacer's uniform, his narrow waist so supple when he moved—Bit by bit, calling her own memories of him to the fore, she built his likeness upon the water.

Now—she edged forward a fraction on the throne—*now* she must see him as he went from her the last time, wide-eyed but sightless for a time, his wound dressed with the rags of her blanket, his head still up as if he, too, heard the hum of the flitter come to take him back.

He was a man, no illusion that she might have constructed to save herself for a space. And because he was a man she owed him—Simsa fingered the rod, drew fiercely upon that other memory—a debt to be paid and only she to pay it.

🔳 **15** 🔳

Farther—out and out—she had tied a bond between them; surely, she could ride that road to find him. The rod blazed high in her hands and the water in the pool now churned from side to side. Still, below its surface, she could see an outline of a shadow—a ship—the ship that should have borne him away. But that was still standing on its fins, pointing skyward. Not off-world yet?

Simsa pinned that shadow with part of her will, held it steady, as within it she sought that which she must find. There were living things encased, yes. She brushed past minds, impatient to discover what she sought. None of them—then where—

Thorn! Of his name she made a cord of concentration, of demanding.

Thorn! At last she touched! As Zass might use her claws to capture prey, so did Simsa fasten on that other one. Thorn!

Yet his shadow grew no clearer as she strove to break through the wall she had so harshly and strongly built to control his future. He was like those spacemen clad in armor whom they had fought together on Kuxortal, impervious to the very will that had sent him forth.

Thorn! she demanded again.

He was gone!

The strength she had put into his summoning swung back upon her like a blow until she felt as if the last thread of breath was almost driven from her lungs. She dropped the rod and caught with both hands at the arms of the throne chair lest she be thrown into the fury of the pool before her, whose contents seethed as if all the fires in the world were bringing them to a boil.

Simsa swayed again, braced herself. She had so strongly believed that what one had wrought might be also dismissed upon willing. But Thorn—she could not even hold any longer to him at all! Hers the deed and one she would have to live with.

That backlash of the power she had used was exhausting itself. She felt sick and giddy as she huddled in her seat, watching the whirling of the waters.

"Elder One." She did not cry aloud, but the petition of that name echoed through her spare, taut body. "Elder One?"

Wildly, she threw open her mind, summoned—what, she did not know. Somewhere, there was an answer. She had been so confident that she could break the bonds laid upon Thorn. The valley people had been right in their judgment of her act. She had called forces she could not even put name to and now she would dare to try again— if she could—for her will was a limp thing, drained of all energy, a feeble tool she could not depend upon.

The tumult in the pool was subsiding and the haze overhead was thickening for night. Still, Simsa crouched within the curve of the throne and Zass, perched on the taller back of the one in the middle, let out a small cry—a querulous one demanding attention.

At last, Simsa gathered up the rod that lay at her feet and stumbled down and away from her perch. She caught one foot against her pack and would have fallen, looking at it dully. Then, she gathered up her water bags and what else she had carried, turned her back upon the pool and the thrones, and wavered toward the entrance that had brought her hither. Zass cried out again and flew a circle over the girl's head as Simsa took hesitant step by hesitant step, unaware of the tears wetting her thin cheeks.

She had been so very sure that she had at last come into her real heritage, that there would no longer be a cleavage within her. But when she had tried to project as she was sure that the Elder One had been able to do—perhaps she had bested the Elder One in spite of herself. Sometimes that which one wanted the most slipped through one's fingers. And she had been for all this time trying to push away from her that oneness which she had first delighted in.

As she went, Simsa made no choice of passage to follow. The long, dimly lit hallways fed into one another and she was so weary. Yet, she could not rest here in the place of her great failure. Let her win out of this shrine of the dead, be again under the open haze of nighttime. That she wanted more than anything now with a dumb, inner aching. Twice, the zorsal returned to ride for a short time on her shoulder as she stumbled along. But whenever Simsa stood for a moment or two, supporting herself with one hand against the wall, Zass uttered chirruping cries in her very ear as if she would spur the girl on to greater efforts, as though she knew ahead lay something better than the gloom of these stark corridors.

At last, a final door stood open and there was more light before her. She wavered out into the open, the stark-walled buildings behind her.

Here was a platform overhanging a dip in the contour of the land which descended in a series of wide ledges or steps into such a tangle of vegetation as she had seen in the valley. The buildings or building lay entirely behind her and she was free of its hold on her. Simsa crossed the first of those ledges and, on the second, as far from the door through which she came as she could go, she dropped to the stone, the zorsal taking off into the mists of the night with a cry that sounded like a shrilling of triumph.

There was food and water. Most of the fruit was too bruised and spoiled to eat and she hurled it from her into the growth beneath. She allowed herself only a few sips of the water, not knowing when she would find another spring, and curled up; the weakness and fatigue she had carried as a burden since she came from the initiation chamber finally crushed her. Though there was only the hard stone to lie upon, Simsa drowsed.

An aching loneliness closed in, flooding her mind as the fatigue tore upon her body. Was this how the flyer had felt when the past was cut from his life and he had been left here alone? She herself had cut off her past deliberately, and now—Was it worth what she had done? That was her last thought before sleep, deep and dreamless, closed upon her. Did she dream? If she did, there was no memory upon awakening. It was Zass's shrilling cry that pulled her out of that depth. The zorsal walked up and down the ledge within an arm's length, her antennae weaving furiously. Plainly, she was disturbed or highly excited. It was midday by the look of the haze overhead.

For the second time, Simsa had awakened so cramped and sore of body that it was a minor agony to move. Before prudence ruled again, she had taken up the leaf carrier that held water within—the other being already flattened and dry—and drank deeply to clear her throat of the dust of this place which still choked her.

Zass's talons clicked against the rock of the wide step as she came to squat before the girl, looking up into her face with an interest that demanded attention.

"Others—"

"Others?" queried Simsa. What others could there be, unless that wide stretch of vegetation to which the steps led was another inhabited valley. She tried to pick up from the in-and-out emissions of the zorsal's mind some hint.

But while she looked to Zass for aid, there came another sound out of the haze overhead, one that made her drag herself up, striving to find the last rags of energy to carry her. Where? Back into the place of the long dead—or forward down the stairs into that green-gold covering? A flitter! She could not mistake that!

But Thorn—surely he had been firmly under the altered memories when he had left her. When? Days earlier? In this haze, it was easy to lose all track of time. What else would he do but quietly and obediently return to the outer world, wait for his people? There had been no break in the shell she had built about him—that she could swear to. Or dared she swear to anything? Hallucinations might have betrayed her instead of him. Still, she was not ready to confront any off-worlder.

Simsa pushed a heavy lock of hair out of her eyes. She made her decision quickly as the sound of the flitter grew stronger. There was an odd glow on the haze some distance to the north—as if the machine itself was emitting light in order to break up the haze. Or perhaps these off-worlders with all their bits of knowledge regained from the shattered past could use some mechanical means to so penetrate that curtain which cocooned this part of the planet.

At any rate, these tall bushes and trees ahead promised better hiding. Were those aloft in the flitter to sight the buildings, she was certain they would land, perhaps upon the very ledge above her, for exploration. Her cramped body protesting every movement, she started running for the end of the second ledge where she had slept, then across the next one. Three such she descended without seeing more of the off-world machine than that spot in the haze, but the sound of the engine was steady—a heavy beat—and it was moving at a pace no faster than a walking one. They were spying below—they had to be.

She had seen on screens within the spaceship pictures taken from at least six different worlds. They had tried to interest her so, she had thought, that she would not be aware of their intentions concerning herself.

Her foot came down on a rotted fruit, perhaps one of those she had flung to the winds earlier, and she skidded, flailing arms to try and retain her balance. Her efforts brought her to the right-hand side of that wide flight of stairs so that when she fell it was not on the worked stone but on the earth beyond. She had only a second to ball herself as well as she could. Then she struck with a jolt that drove the air out of her lungs and rolled on down until she hit against the thick stem of a plant that was tree tall and tossed its leafed head from the shaking she gave it.

For a moment, she could only lie there. Somewhere Zass was airborne and calling to her. But she believed that the zorsal was wary enough to keep away from the flitter still, by the sound, cruising overhead. As soon as she got her breath back fully, paying no attention to bleeding scratches or abrasions, she crept on her hands and knees farther on until she was sure that she was under cover. Then she rolled over on her back and stared up at the leafed branches overhead trying to think, to subdue her rush of panic.

Why had she believed that the ceremony of the forgotten people had made her invincible? That independence which had

been hers from birth had made her believe that she was a worker
of wonders—

All right, let her now work one of those wonders on this
hovering sky spy. Dared she try to reach any aboard that flyer with
a talent that she admitted now she was untrained to use? Had it been
her seeking for Thorn at the hall of thrones that had brought the
space rovers out again to hunt? Her foolishness was enough to
shame her many times over. To attack an enemy when you did not
know the range of any weapon that might be brought against you—
to overestimate your own . . . Yes, she was a fool and they could be
only playing with her in order to cow her into their hands to do their
will with even less freedom than a zorsal on a flying leash.

Thorns tore at her shoulders. A vine, locked about her throat,
brought her close enough to the choking point to make her fight
vigorously. But all this was under the reaching roof of the trees, and
perhaps she passed unseen. Or did they have such spy weapons as
could pierce through that leafy covering, center on any life-form
that moved below? Simsa all her life had heard so many tales of the
invincible machines and installations of the spacemen that she
could believe anything might be true.

There were no paths here, or at least she had not chanced on
one.

One path—just one path—she had no idea why that meant so
much to her, unless it promised speed. What did she flee? Some
reaching bolt of energy from that flyer overhead? The sound of its
engine deepened, almost like the roar of a canzar from her home
world.

Then there was wafted through the moist air that hung under
the larger trees such a putrid stench that the odor alone halted her
mad flight. She eased back on her heels and sent a short mind call
for Zass.

Deep within her mind something stirred. This was no longer the
Elder One awakening—she *was* the Elder One—but that fragment
of other memory was not hers by right. She gained a fleeting mind
picture of what? Not a reptile, for it had no marked head, only a
round pulpiness of wriggling grayish body. Then it raised one end

of that body and she saw an opening, a dark red maw surrounded by two circles of crushing teeth.

"Wuul!" Not her own memory—that other's wuul! She snatched at what that other knew concerning the loathsome crawler.

Killer—with no mind to be touched, to command, although those who had built the ruins behind were long gone, this creature of their own world was free and coursed the mangled planet left to it.

Panting, Simsa set her back to the nearest of the tree-sized plants, readied the rod. The smell was choking in its nauseating heaviness. She retched in spite of her fight for control.

"Wuul!" Frantically, she tried to gain more from those two who had accompanied her to this outpost—the Elder One, that far-faded remnant of the exiled flyer. All she received in return was the wariness of one, the stubborn desire to fight of the other.

She purposely tried to put the hum of the flitter out of her hearing and settle upon the here and now. The bushes were rent as a tree fell to her right. Small things skittered and ran blindly, most of them making for other trees. There was a sullen crunching as the tree that had been downed thrashed from side to side. Its root end was being furiously and thoroughly shaken.

Simsa slipped back, putting the bole of the growth under which she sheltered between her and the thing. Then she turned and ran back the way she had come, branches lashing at her, blood welling from cuts across her arms and legs. There came the crash of another tree just as she reached the end of the vegetation that lapped about the bottom ledge. She threw herself out and forward on the stone and scrambled somehow onto the next higher.

That blot in the haze hung just about her now, pulsating. Another tree went down—she gasped and made it up a third ledge. Of Zass there was no sign and she hoped that the zorsal would have intelligence enough to keep off from both the flyer and her own position.

Once before she had seen Zass and her two sons fight and kill a monstrous thing out of the wilderness. But that was on another planet and the thing was not a wuul. The stench of the creature preceded it as another tree, this time on the very edge of the opening where lay the bottom ledge, crashed.

Wuuls could eat anything, even rock that bore such lichens as she had seen before the other entrance to the ruins. But all would infinitely prefer meat—and she was meat!

She thought of the ruins, of that maze of hallways. No, to be trapped in there by a wrong turn or choice—that she dared not chance. Not in haste now, but as one making a last stand against impossible odds, Simsa stood ready. She held the rod tightly—it was her last hope. Yet both the Elder One who had carried this and the lost flyer feared the wuul.

Into the open pushed a mass of gray, unwholesome flesh, heaving as the jaws ground along the tree it had brought down. It had no eyes—

No, meat it hunted by heat, the other part of her memory supplied. There was no way she could shut off that kind of body radiation which was drawing the thing. She was a large section of meat raising in it a stronger call. The pulp of vegetation leaking down it, the thing raised the blind end that faced her. The roll of the jaws never stopped, though now they spat forth green sludge which had filled its mouth, preparing for the far more attractive prey ahead.

As it reared part of its forelength from the ground, the end weaving back and forth, Simsa could guess that it was near the length of four or five of her own kind, monstrous as the things that bedded in the sand river.

The things that bedded in the sand river?

No! Hadn't her building of hallucinations failed drastically once with Thorn even after she had given her full stretch to their weaving? This thing had no eyes. It sensed by other means, although it seemed now to be in no hurry, as if it savored her disgust and strictly controlled fear as another part of the feast.

The things that bedded in the river—

Simsa ran a tongue across the dryness of her lips. That would not leave her mind! She could not be sure whether it was the last stupid thought of the Simsa who had been—or a part of the new Simsa who was.

The things that bedded in the river! But she must withdraw, put aside thought and fear of the wuul, if she would try this. And that might condemn her from the start.

Nevertheless—the people of the Elder One, her people if she believed that she was of a freak birth that brought into being one of the true Forerunners. If all Thorn had said was the truth—if that were so—and if she had passed the initiation by the pool, then—

Simsa deliberately closed her eyes to the weaving forepart of the wuul, to build in her mind the largest, the most active of those things that had threatened her from the fissures of the rocky plain or had crawled from the river. Its leprous yellow hide, so swollen of belly until it seemed all stomach and guts with only a vestige beyond, save for those sucker-pocked arms—many of them—reaching out.

"Come," she demanded, putting into the order all the strength she could summon. If the fissure thing was as well-protected as Thorn—if she failed—

Something stirred. She touched and clung with her thought, prodded and pricked. It was not too far away! Perhaps there were fissures here as well as on the plain, having each their inhabitants.

"Come!" This time she reinforced her mental order with a shouted word.

Along the side of the slope, away from the ledges, there was a crumbling of earth. Lumps fell outward, there was a trickle of running sand which edged out and down.

Why did the wuul hold off its attack? She wondered for an instant or two, then realized that she must concentrate instead on that which she called.

More and more of the earth was slipping downward. Then, as if an inner dam had given way, a whole cascade of the running sand washed aside two lumps of earth near as large as her own body. From that hole which had hidden there waved the end of a tentacle.

Shock struck Simsa. Somehow she had not believed entirely, she had expected failure in one small part of her. Now her will soared like the battle cry of fresh troops sent in to make or mar the victory.

"Come!"

She waved the rod in a wide gesture as if she would clear the way for the creature. The bubbling, flowing sand was now a torrent. Tumbling rather than swimming in it came that which she had called. Big—the biggest she had seen.

It passed the ledge on which she stood, reached, with the flowing of sand, the small level space between the last step and the beginning of the vegetation. And either through some motion of its own or because it had been carried by the sand and strove now to fight its way loose, it crawled forth on the ground, hunching its fat bag of a body together, sending forth reaching arms.

The wuul moved at last, a slow, relentless descent of its head, the mouth extending open to the farthest extent, ready to engulf the sand-thing. Tentacles tossed, slapped across and around the pulpy gray body. There was no sound aloud, but the wuul projected a fury, a pain. The wuul was gone!

On the flattened vegetation the sand creature sprawled. Simsa could also sense its vast surprise and rage. There were the trees downed by its opponent. On the air still lingered the reek of the wuul—only it was gone as one might snuff out the flame of a lamp!

Then she knew!

Trick—someone in that hovering flyer had worked this trick, one as intricate in its way as the false memory she had so carefully built for Thorn. Something (she still believed in the expertise of these makers of machines) had been in her head!

Simsa snarled as might any cornered animal. In *her* head! Someone had learned the first fear of the Forerunners and had turned that thread of memory against her—to hunt her into the open where she would be easy prey. They must have tested her in turn—for the wuul had waited, they had waited to see what she could command against their threat. And easily had she supplied them with that answer. She should have been aware that she was being fought with weapons close to her own, laughed at their wuul and kept in hiding.

A tentacle caught the edge below her. She doubted if she could send back this threat of her own, for it was real and its hunger was not a set part of any trap. As the wuul had seemed to do, it must have sensed or smelled her, for it was showing a surprising burst of speed, using its tentacles to draw itself up toward her, having reversed or perhaps never started the charge toward the wuul.

Raising the rod, Simsa felt more sure of herself. At least she had met this terror before and won past it. But as she strove to empower the rod, she realized that, once again, there was an end to the force she could summon to activate it. Her course of action since she had entered the ruins might have made the past clearer, but it also showed that the Forerunners—the Elder Ones—had not been invincible.

First, with all the force she could bring to bear, and then with mounting fear, the girl tried to confront the sand creature. There was no crackling lash of fire from the twin crescents—only a small glow. When she attempted to use her will, the thing seemed impervious to any mental contact. Although it had come to her call, it was too alien or perhaps even too far down in the scale of fire—or on another wave of contact—for her to reach it.

The puzzle of that she had no time to solve. She retreated to another ledge up as the thing drew itself along the rock surfaces below. Then, bursting into her mind like a thrust of spacer energy, came her name!

That sudden hailing unnerved her for an instant, almost too long, for a tentacle aimed to the farthest extent the creature could reach scraped just before her toes, and she scrambled back.

"Simsa—up—quick—"

Thorn? No, that had not been the spaceman. There was no clear picture in her mind, and still the communication was sharper, stronger than the young off-worlder had ever used.

This was someone who trained in the same methods she had so painfully learned from the Elder One at the beginning.

So forceful was that order that she turned and took the last two of the ledge steps, returning to the forefront of the ruins, at the swiftest pace she could muster. As she wheeled, for she had no intention of being driven back into the maze of the ruin's corridors with a sand dweller at her heels, there struck straight down from that reddish spot in the sky, which marked the flitter, a spear of light such as she had seen enough of in the spacers' records to recognize.

It was a weapon much like her rod, yet not powered by will and concentration of personal energy but by units of captive force upon which the people of the star fleets depend.

It struck full upon the sand-thing, which writhed as smoke, black and evil-smelling, rose from it. The thing lost its hold on the ledge to which it had just pulled and fell back, its tentacles waving vainly, striving to bring its fall to an end. It crashed at last into the sand flow which had formed a shallow pool, puddling just at the foot of the ledges. There it lay, still heaving a little, only half within the flood.

Now! Simsa had no desire to stay for Thorn or this other and more forceful personage to land, if landing was what they intended. The ruins offered her a way out. The wuul—

She stopped within the overhang of the doorway. That brain— that stranger—had driven her, as a man drives fleexe does out of the pasture, out of the trees. What was to prevent him or her from driving again? Wuul in the open was one thing, but wuul underground—or in narrow hallways—hallucinatory or not, was something she could not bring herself to face.

🔲 16 🔲

Simsa placed her back against the stone wall of a square-cut pillar that sided the entrance to the ruins. She forced her breathing to slow, brought under uneasy control fear and anger. There had been too much heaped upon her. The experience in the initiation hall, her flight from the flitter overhead, and the supreme effort she had made to produce the sand dweller had weakened her. She need only look at the barely lit points of her moon rod to tell her how little she had in her to withstand whatever was coming.

Not Thorn—that last message had never come from the off-worlder. Then who? Certainly not that officer who had seen in her talents—or supposed talents—a chance to renew his fortunes. And Greeta was dead. Who?

Not to know the enemy was one of the worst things she faced. For if one knew, at least there was time for some preparation. She had none except her own stubborn wariness and realization that she must not yield to any off-worlder.

The flitter was going to land. That blot in the haze resolved into a definite shape of the exploratory machine as it was descending to the lowest of the ledges. She tried to see who was on board, but the bubble of the cockpit cover had been tinted so that it was like facing a blind thing which depended on other than human sense to attack.

As it touched down, the whir of the antigrav was stilled and the world about her lay in deep silence. There was no sound of bird or insect such as she might have expected from the growth spreading out from the foot of the staircase—and Zass had disappeared!

The bubble split in two and the first of the flitter passengers came out.

Thorn! But who else? That had been no talent of the spaceman which had produced a creature perhaps a thousand years dead to drive once more into the open. He did not even look at her after one quick glance, but rather stood to one side as if he played only servant or guard to his companion.

The body that clambered out and put a scaled and webbed hand with thin fingers on Thorn's shoulder in a gesture of comradeship was humanoid in shape but manifestly not as human as the young man with him, or even Simsa. The clothing it wore was far more abbreviated than Thorn's—short breeches that came just a fraction down green-gray scaled thighs, a sleeveless shirt over which were numerous straps supporting a number of things which could be either tools or weapons. Around the head with the goggle eyes was a ruff of frilled flesh which stood erect, over which rippled flashes of vivid coloring as the alien stepped forward. A Zacathan!

This was one of the pacific nonwarriors of the galaxy, whose struggle was not against men or worlds, but rather to unravel and record the past—and whose long lives were dedicated to the belief that one scrap of knowledge added to their store was worth all the discoverer had to give.

But a Zacathan! She had not been aware that there had been one on board the spacer before her escape. Why had Thorn not told her? Why had she not sensed such a brain when she had been able to pick up the dangerous musings of the officer and Greeta?

And what could they do? Build hallucinations—the wuul had been proof of that—and perhaps break such a memory block as she had put on Thorn. What else?

She stared down the ledges, her eyes searching out those of the Zacathan and locking with them swiftly, so swiftly she had no time to deny it, mind to mind.

"What do you fear?" The evenly spaced words formed in her mind.

She answered with the truth before she could think clearly, his very presence had surprised her so. "You."

The saurian face was perhaps not constructed to easily form a smile, but she felt the gentle humor now in the other's mind touch.

"Am I then so formidable, gentle fern?"

"I think . . . yes—" Her eyes had narrowed. She had yet to marshal all that had come to her in this place, to truly make herself one with that other and those who had once stood behind her. "I think you are a very formidable person." She kept her voice low as she replied, not with mind touch (she wanted no more of that) but rather in the trade-lingo, aloud.

"As I think." Now he spoke and there was a hissing accent to his words. "It seems"—now his eyes released hers as he lifted his head a little to view the mass of ruin behind her—"that we have found something long sought."

"Chan-Moolan-plu." Out of the past she could no longer deny came that name, and immediately she knew what it stood for and why it was on this world.

"Chan-Moolan-plu," the Zacathan repeated. "Your home, gentle fern—once?"

She shook her head. "An outpost—a training place—before the Baalacki came." More and more the story awoke in her. No . . . home—home was—She shook her head again, not at any gesture or word from him, but because she knew that what she might say would mean nothing now. That planet which birthed the Elder One who was now a part of her was gone, vanished into a fog of time so great there was no reckoning it—in her own system of accounting years and seasons.

"And the Baalacki?" A little to her surprise, it was Thorn who raised the question.

"They made this world as you see it. They"—she shrugged—"are long since gone. Each people who rise, look to the stars, and roam the outer reaches have enemies, or acquire them along the way. And then a day comes where there is a final battle-locking. One may go down to the dust, but it is also true that the victor is left wounded, perhaps to death, and another empire falls apart." She made a gesture as if shifting some of that sand still bubbling below between her fingers. "What are left . . ."

"What are left," the Zacathan broke in as she hesitated, "are shards and pieces scattered here and there—which we strive to bring together so that we may understand—"

"Why?" Simsa interrupted him in turn. "To learn this or that trick of knowledge which will give *you* power so that again the wheel will spin and you and your ships and your alliances of planets be reduced in turn?"

"Some seek for that, yes. Others for knowledge which has nothing to do with that sort of power, gentle fern. We are many races, many species—surely it was so then, was it not?"

"The Sorkel, the Vazax, the Omer—" In her mind, she saw each she mentioned, scaled, winged, various-colored of flesh, different of brain patterns. "Yes, there were many of us and some who were always apart." Now she stared at the Zacathan in sudden enlightenment. "From whom, Lordly One, did you take your first memories?"

"Ah . . ." It was his turn to nod. "So you had your historians, also? As for our memories, those of my race are long and our archives go far back. We have our legends, also, gentle fern. That is why when I was informed of you, I came with what swiftness this time and space afford. I was on Kaltorn when Thorn"—she saw his fingers tighten on the young man's shoulder as if in affection—"sent a message by the mail launch. My dort-ship strove to match the flight pattern of the Star Climber, and your own actions pulled me thus to you."

Perhaps it was so, she could sense no evasion in his mind, whatever might be his speech. Yet different species . . . Yes, he could be weaving for her just such a pattern as she had purposefully set upon Thorn. Upon Thorn!

She spoke now to the spaceman. "You were never memory-changed!" Her words came out harshly, as if she accused him.

He shook his head and there was no curve to his mouth—that and his jaw were set grimly. "You succeeded," he told her in clipped words. "Only—"

"Only," the Zacathan broke in again, "there were certain signs of such tampering which are familiar to the initiated. It was not difficult to disperse the shadows once they were recognized."

She could have guessed that much. With all the knowledge that must be at his command, this burrower into the past could well have diagnosed what had happened to this follower and countered it.

Simsa raised the rod, pleased to see that there was a stronger beam at the tips of the two horns. "Then you know also that I am not one who can be caged so that which and what I am may be drained from me to increase another's power! Thorn . . ." Simsa hesitated, studying his set face, his eyes which held no warmth—he might be carved from some of the stone of this denuded planet. "He"—she spoke not to the man whose whole attitude was a defense against her, but again to the Zacathan—"Thorn was gone, apparently after he had delivered me into the hands of those who spied upon me, who strove to find ways to use what they thought I was. He was with one of those when I found him—they having traced me by some one of your machines upon which you depend so much. I had won free of what they had put or strove to put upon me. Why should he return to come ahunting again? If we wish to be simply truthful, I saved his life. He was going into the maw of one of those." She pointed the rod to the blob of the dead sand-thing, which still showed a little above the flood that had brought it here.

There was no change in Thorn's expression, and she told herself she did not expect any understanding from him now. Their partnership had always been an uneasy one even when they had struggled into the lost city on Kuxortal, fighting shoulder to shoulder there against the outlaws who had laired within that spawn of vegetation-devoured buildings. She owed him—Perhaps she did owe him! Had he never led her into the forgotten ways, she would not have met with the Elder One—never have been more than a child playing at useless things—one without kin or friends. Yes, she owed him much for that! And now she made restitution in words:

"I owe you, Thorn Chan-li." She used his formal name as one who lists debts. "There is no debt between us. I was wrong—the scales are even, or perhaps I owe you more for what I did in the valley. If so, demand your price of me now."

The Zacathan looked from the young man to Simsa and then back again, as one who stands aside and listens.

Thorn raised a hand in a repudiating gesture. "You owe me nothing," he said coldly. And Simsa believed that had the Zacathan's hand not still imprisoned his shoulder, he would have turned back to the flitter and left her.

"Good!" It was the alien who put force into that, as if he were genuinely pleased that something had been resolved between them, even though it was manifest that nothing had been done at all. "Gentle fern, far from a cage—all honor and ease await you. Thorn has told me that you had reason to mistrust certain ones on board the ship. Be sure that this was not our intention, nor could it have been carried out—not with Thorn's message already on its way to me. And it seems"—now he glanced from her to the pile of the ruins—"that our suggestion that fate often moves on the behalf of believers is also right. For without your flitting from the ship and landing here, we would never perhaps have found this—what did you call it?—Chan-Moolan-plu, a place of your own people, once."

"A place of power." Something in him quieted all the uneasiness, even the stiffness of her mistrust. "A place of initiation."

"And you have passed that?"

He was very quick to catch her up, she thought. "Yes." Never would she enlarge upon that. What she had done by that poisonous pool was hers alone—not to be shared.

"I will warn you," she said swiftly, "that there are matters here best left alone. Thrusting too deep into ancient secrets can bring—death!"

His lizard jaws spread apart in what could only be thought a smile, showing formidable teeth. "There is always peril in the unknown," he returned. "If one listens to the whisperings of dangers to come, one remains in the shadow of danger without profit. Be sure we do not go recklessly upon any trace of that which we search for all our days. And—"

What more he would have added she would never know. For beneath her feet the ledge swayed. That hole from which the sand gushed was growing large. As on another world released floods of water could undermine bands and cliffs, so here the moving sand was carving itself a greater runway.

Out of the sky flashed Zass—the zorsal giving tongue as she flew straight for Simsa. The flitter lurched nearer to the sand flood and there was a rumbling from out of the ruins. Without a word, Thorn sprang at her as she jumped in turn away from the forepart of the ruin. She had no time to defend herself against his grasp, to even move the rod, for he had her in a tight hold, the heating rod against her own body as he jerked her down the three ledges which were now tilting on the very brink of a raging flood, if one could so describe that wash of sand. And in it there moved more creatures, their sucker-grown and tentacled legs reaching out as they were borne along, some grasping the edge of the ledges for anchorage.

There came a crash that silenced even Zass's hoarse screams. Behind, some strained wall or floor had given way. But the Zacathan was waiting at the flitter and Thorn bundled her forward into the hands of the lizard man. Those closed upon her in the same tight hold as Thorn had used, and she was pulled into the outworld flyer, Zass streaking before her, Thorn pushing at her from behind, so she sprawled backward into the luggage space behind the two seats at the fore of the bubble. Thorn was in the pilot's seat and the bubble snapped down as he triggered a small lever on the board before him. The flitter arose so suddenly that Simsa, still unable to completely understand what had happened, flopped back again on the floor as the machine took to the air.

"Over it—on hold!" The Zacathan leaned far forward in the seat, his snouted nose pushed against the transparent covering of the cockpit. "No, not all of it—praise be to Zurl and Zack—a settling, but not all lost!"

Simsa edged up to a crouching position and endeavored to look below. She was in time to see the ledged stairway slip down to rise on the other side. And there had indeed been a toppling of some walls within.

"Cruise!" the Zacathan ordered again. "Let us see how bad it is."

Under Thorn's control the flitter began to circle about the spread of the ruins. From this perch aloft, the girl could see how extensive the structure had been. For it was no town, she knew that. This had been something of a temple, something of a school—and even more a legend. The Elder One had never been here. Her initiation had taken place on another world. But she had heard of this doorway to even greater knowledge all her past life.

There sounded another roar above the noise of the flitter. Simsa shrank in upon herself as she watched a full quarter of the structure below her tremble and slide in. There was a new gushing on the side of the mound. Where the sand still poured and puddled there came a green flood to cut into that thick mixture, in a spate of energy that carried it on and over the sand toward the vegetation beyond.

Simsa was not aware of her own small cry until she heard it. The water of the initiation pool was flooding out—sinking into the sand, vanishing forever from ruin or day. There would never be another to come and submit to its testing, to open thus the realm beyond the world.

"Sooo—" The Zacathan's voice was close to a hiss, yet when she glanced at him there was nothing in his eyes but a shadow of loss and of pity.

She resented that pity for an instant and then she knew what lay behind it. Not that there was lost to him and his kind another discovery, perhaps one of the greatest they might ever make, but rather that she had lost something that was worth much to her.

"It is gone." She voiced the only thing she might say. "The life is gone."

And she spoke the truth. It seemed to her that now lay only the broken or rapidly breaking stone, that what she had sensed in the walls bled from the past glories, as the water of dreams bled from whatever buried channel contained or refreshed the pool. She was as sure as if she had walked again within or could see through that maze of walls, that the great hall was no more—that those thrones which had once served the leaders of her kind had toppled and gone the way that the years prevailed.

"No," the Zacathan said slowly in trader's speech, as if at this moment he had no wish to invade her tangled and sorrowing thoughts. "You live. What was once here only waited to serve the last of those who had laid its first stones upon stones. Let it be, Yan—"

Simsa was about to ask who Yan was when she realized the Zacathan had been speaking to Thorn, using his friend name. He still did not acknowledge her presence and as the flitter wheeled outward and away from the ruin, she wondered if the choice the Zacathan had really made for her so forcibly back on the terraces was the right one.

As that exile of the valley had been before her—alone—so was she now. On Kuxortal, she had had ties, tenuous as those had been. But old Ferwar had been a part of her life. There were those of her own generation in the Burrows who knew her, even though she had no close relationship with any of those outcasts. The Elder One had had her friends, companions, her clan-kin—now she had nothing except this thing that had happened to her by chance.

By chance? Zass chirruped in her ear and she reached up her right hand to smooth the zorsal's small furred body. Was it chance that had brought the Life Boat to this forgotten world out of all the rest? She had always scoffed at the superstitions of the Burrowers and of those who followed the "gods" of the upper city—that anyone could be influenced by some unknown power about which they were largely ignorant was folly beyond folly.

Yet, she had met with Thorn merely by chance—had she been there at their meeting place a few breaths later, never would she have been drawn into the race across the haunted wilderness and therein met that which was the other part of her. And, had she not picked up the thoughts concerning her on the spacer and taken off . . .

It was indeed folly to think that this was all part of some greater plan, that she had been moved by another will as a gaming piece might be shaken and moved! She was Simsa, she made *her* own choices—went her own way. But why had that way, seemingly by chance again, become her path to this place of the past wherein those of the Forerunners had achieved adeptship and the greater knowledge?

What had in turn given her the power to summon the river of sand and in the end bring about the destruction of that which had endured so long? The Zacathan—She hunched herself into a small space, both the rod and Zass clutched to her—all that remained truly her own was in that grasp. She could sense no guile in him. He had not wanted her power—only her knowledge. And the two of those were not one and the same but separate. She was warned and she was armed—not only by what the Elder One had done with her, but by the place of initiation. She had very much to learn—whereas when she had first met that other Simsa she had felt ready to conquer the world itself, now she was humble and a little afraid. Though that was within her, outwardly she must wear the mask of the Elder One's own imperturbable self.

The feathery softness of the zorsal's antennae brushed the ebony skin of her cheek, and Zass nipped lightly, caressingly, at the hand holding her small body. Zass . . . she was thankful for Zass and—

Once more, she eyed the Zacathan measuringly. His head was turned a little away from her and he watched the last of the ruins slide by beneath them as they headed out over the barren rock that covered so much of this world. Yes, in him she could feel only some disappointment, a disappointment for the loss of that ancient seat of strange learning.

As if her very gaze upon him was like a touch on his shoulder or arm to summon his attention, his head swung around, the frill still erect and showing a faint shimmer of color over the scales there. He smiled.

"Not such a loss?" he asked strangely, as if he could read a thought that had not yet crossed her own mind. "A thing having served its purpose, can it not be discarded?"

Was that the truth? Had that invisible finger of fate pointed her straight to this place, in spite of all her belief in her own freedom, that she might be the last of her kind—

"Or the first, gentle fern?" Yes, he was reading her thoughts! For a moment, she felt the heat of temper flash and then she shrugged. She was without kin or country, or even world. If they found a place for her, why should she quarrel with that? She had never before put down roots—

"Why should you, if you wish it not?" the Zacathan continued. He read her thoughts but he spoke aloud, she was not certain why. "You are free to come or go, or stay—" He made a small gesture with his hand to indicate the country lying before them. "If that is your true wish?"

"No," she answered him also aloud this time. "I would . . ."

She hesitated. Would what? Go with these two and devote herself to their search for ancient knowledge? She studied the back of Thorn's dark head. He was the first off-worlder she had ever met—and she had once thought that they were all alike. Now she knew that they were different, different as an upper city lord from a Burrow-dweller. She had meddled—tried to fight him. Now, now she was glad that she had not been skillful enough to have accomplished her purpose. There was the officer and Greeta and there was Thorn and this lizard man—Doubtless there were many other gradations of thought and feeling out among the stars and on other worlds. Who was she to sit in judgment over what she did not know?

"I would go with you." It seemed to her that she took long to make that decision, but perhaps it was only the space of a breath or two. Now she added, not using thought speech but the tongue of the spacemen and speaking directly to the back of Thorn's head, "I would go with both of you."

"Well enough." That was the Zacathan. Thorn had said nothing; he might be a mindless, uncaring part of the machine he guided. She waited.

It was important that he say some word, make some gesture. But he did not and she began to question the wisdom of her own choice. After all, what did he have to judge her by? He had his own people, he was no exile.

The flitter hummed on across the fissured bareness of the rock plain, but they were lifting higher into the haze. Now she could make out only patches of the rock as mist began to draw around them, cutting off the solid planet beneath. Zass moved uneasily in her grasp. She loosed her hold on the zorsal and the creature gave a small leap, first to land on the forearm of the Zacathan, then into Thorn's lap.

The spaceman's hands were busied. Then he raised them from the board, but the flitter raced on. Apparently, no controls were needed for a set course. His head turned a little, but she could only see one eye and a part of his cheek, and the corner of his mouth that had been set in so stern a band.

"No more tricks?" He asked that slowly, with a measured interval between each word.

She stiffened. Tricks? There had been no trickery between them ever. What she had always done was what had seemed right and just to her. Then the humor that underlay his question reached her.

There had been little of that emotion in the Burrows. She was awkward about responding to it, as strange in its way as some of the thoughts of the Elder One. But now it was also the Elder One within her who knew what he would do—he was purposely belittling what she had done, making it a thing of little account so that it could be dismissed, perhaps forgotten except as an object lesson for her to live with for a while (though she did not believe that he meant that, either!).

"No more tricks." She smiled, and the movements of her lips then felt strange and new, but this was good, this strangeness. "There is one . . ." She spoke, now, in a language she had not known until the words rose from some place deep within her. "There was one and another—and another—"

She left the rod lying across her bent knees and, leaning, she did something that Simsa of the Burrows would have shrunk from, what the Elder One would not perhaps have countenanced in her own time. What did it matter concerning those two? She was herself— still herself and what she chose to be. Her fingers touched with the lightness of Zass's antennae those two shoulders nearest herself— the scaled and the suit-covered one—just for an instant. But it was enough.

THE END